KEITH THOMSON

SEVEN GRAMS OF LEAD

Keith Thomson played semipro baseball
in France and drew editorial cartoons
for *New York Newsday* before becoming a
writer. He lives in Alabama.

www.keiththomsonbooks.com

SEVEN GRAMS OF LEAD

SEVEN GRAMS
of LEAD

KEITH THOMSON

ANCHOR BOOKS

A DIVISION OF RANDOM HOUSE LLC

NEW YORK

ANCHOR BOOKS MASS-MARKET ORIGINAL,
FEBRUARY 2014

Library of Congress Cataloging in Publication Data
Thomson, Keith.
Seven grams of lead / by Keith Thomson.
pages cm
1. Fiction—Suspense. 2. Fiction—Espionage.
3. Fiction—Technological. I. Title.
PS3620.H745 S48 2014
2013025507

Anchor Mass Market ISBN: 978-0-307-94990-5
eBook ISBN 978-0-307-94991-2

www.anchorbooks.com

Printed in the United States of America
10   9   8   7   6   5   4   3   2   1

FOR MOM AND DAD

All know the way; few actually walk it.

—BODHIDHARMA

SEVEN GRAMS OF LEAD

Prologue

Mr. President, Flight 89 wasn't struck down by lightning."

"Don't tell me it was intentional."

"No, sir. It was an accident."

"The airline's fault?"

"Actually, scientists based in Wisconsin, Leonid and Bella Sokolov. Have you been briefed on them?"

"Maybe I ought to be."

"They won the Nobel Prize in Physics in 1985. We lured them from Russia two years ago, set them up in a hardened underground complex as part of the HPMD project."

"High Power Mass Destruction?"

"For all intents and purposes. Technically it's High Power *Microwave Device*."

"The E-bomb?"

"Yes, sir. The Sokolovs' part in the initiative has been to effectively weaponize a flux compression generator."

"Flux compression generator?"

"It generates an electromagnetic pulse on the order of terawatts—or about ten thousand times as powerful as a lightning bolt—and fries semiconductive material, meaning all electrical and electronic systems within its range cease to function. The problem with E-bombs has always been limited range, half a city block max. In theory, the Sokolov model is capable of reducing an entire city to the Stone Age. All computers, telecommunications, radar, power plants, power lines, lights, refrigerators, pacemakers—you name it—would be relegated to scrap. Machines would come to a stop. Planes would fall out of the sky . . ."

"In theory?"

"The Sokolovs generated a pulse lasting just a ten-thousandth of a nanosecond. Their objective was to blow out a lightbulb across their lab, and they did. Flight 89 was four miles away."

"So the two hundred and thirty people aboard were victims of friendly fire?"

"We're hoping to keep that to ourselves, for obvious reasons. The weapon itself is a watershed in national security."

"As long as no one else gets it."

"Yes, sir. Of course we'll make sure that that doesn't happen."

1

Midazolam, a short-acting sedative, is usually administered orally or by hypodermic needle. Canning liked to use a remote-controlled robotic housefly. On this mild August night, as Canning hid behind the hedges between Lake Michigan and the Sokolovs' heavily guarded house, his iPhone served as a remote control, sending the robofly darting through a partially open window and into a second floor bedroom. Canning had learned that when Leonid Sokolov was home alone, he favored the breeze off the lake to air-conditioning. All this week, Sokolov's wife, Bella, and their daughters were vacationing at the Blue Harbor Resort, fifty miles up the coast.

An infrared camera within one of the fly's bulbous eyes relayed real-time video to Canning's iPhone.

Sokolov lay beneath a quilt, eyes shut, mouth agape, his crown of white hair unmoving against a pillow. The fly would deliver enough midazolam to ensure that he remained asleep for ten minutes. In half that time Canning would climb to the second story and implant a subminiature device beneath the scientist's scalp.

Canning guided the robofly to a hover over Sokolov's upper lip. With a tap on the phone, the fly's abdominal cavity opened and released a midazolam mist, the bulk of which Sokolov inhaled without disruption of his sleep. Canning preferred midazolam to more conventional sedatives because its subjects awoke without any memory of their procedures. He knew the drug occasionally caused abnormally slow respiration, but the risk was remote.

Yet that's exactly what appeared to be happening now.

The iPhone showed Sokolov's rate plummeting from a normal twelve breaths per minute to just four. Then he ceased breathing altogether.

Forget implanting the eavesdropping device, Canning thought. Death was certain unless he resuscitated the Russian immediately and then turned him over to paramedics. But the American had gone to extreme lengths to avoid detection, from coming here in a stealth one-man submarine to dressing hood to boots in black neoprene whose surface was electronically cooled to prevent thermal sensors from registering his presence. Saving Sokolov was out of the question. The operational objective was now getting away with killing him.

Canning had learned long ago not just that anything that can go wrong on an op will, but that anything that cannot go wrong will too. It was now second nature for him to plan for contingency upon contingency. From the pouch hanging from his belt, he produced a coil of lightweight climbing rope tipped by a miniature titanium grapnel with retractable flukes. He tossed the grapnel onto the roof as a wave crashed into the shore, obscuring the patter of the four flukes against slate tiles. A tug at the rope and three of the flukes grabbed hold of the far side of a brick chimney. After making sure that the rope would bear his weight, Canning began climbing, his split-toed boots gripping the knots tied every sixteen inches.

Seconds later, he pushed the window open and hoisted himself into the bedroom. He unholstered a Makarov *pistolet besshumnyy*—silent pistol—and its companion suppressor, then snapped the two together. The pistol was loaded with nine-millimeter bullets he'd cast by hand from soft lead. From the foot of the bed, he fired once into Sokolov's forehead, the muted report no louder than the wind. Canning watched the Russian's central nervous system fail. No drama, just a quick fade. Dead within seconds.

Canning hoped the lead bullet would turn the

homicide investigation into a wild-goose chase. Toward the same end, on his way out, he drew a small envelope from his pouch and littered the floor with its contents, hairs and bits of skin belonging to other men, including two convicted felons. Over his neoprene gloves, he pulled on a latex pair whose fingertips would replicate a third felon's prints. He touched the footboard and nightstand, then climbed out the window, slid down the rope, and dislodged the grapnel.

Before returning to his sub, he planted a biodegradable battery-powered directional pin microphone in the grass.

Thus, the following morning, in a motel room 200 miles north, he overheard one of Sokolov's people knock on the bedroom door. No response, of course.

An FBI crime scene team arrived soon after, quickly concluding that an assassin had sprayed a sedative to subdue the burly scientist prior to shooting him.

Couldn't have been scripted any better, Canning thought.

Later in the day, *RealStory* broke the news of the Wisconsin murder story as well as the news that "the Wisconsin murder story isn't just any murder story." Russ Thornton, the site's authoritative blogger on current events, also wrote:

> *The lead bullet is odd. Outmoded as well as environmentally unfriendly, lead bullets haven't been*

*available commercially this century. The really odd
part is the bullet's weight, 108.0266 grains, according to the FBI. A grain is the smallest unit in the troy
system, equal to .065 grams. Nine-millimeter bullets usually weigh well north of 125 grains, or eight
grams. 108.0266 grains is seven grams on the nose.
7.00. As it happens, Joseph Stalin's solution to a
problem was "seven grams of lead to the head." Sokolov is believed to have been imported to the United
States to work for the Defense Advanced Research
Projects Agency—DARPA—a Pentagon division
whose successes include the global positioning system, the computer mouse, and ARPANET, which
evolved into the Internet. So conceivably this bullet
is a message to scientists still in Russia and thinking of leaving. A Kremlin spokesman insisted news
of Sokolov's death came as a shock. In any case, the
U.S. Marshals Service has relocated Sokolov's family
to a secret location.*

Not an entirely secret location, thought Canning,
sitting back from his monitor. The second part of
his contingency plan—hurrying to the Blue Harbor
Resort in Sheboygan and implanting Bella Sokolova
with the eavesdropping device originally intended
for her husband—had gone without a hitch. Canning
was able to hear the marshals whisk her and her two
daughters to a safe house in Cleveland.

He returned to Thornton's post. According to one

of the blogger's sources, the FBI was likening the Sokolov murder to the 2006 "neutralization" of Alexan-
der Litvinenko, another Russian émigré.

Perfect, Canning thought.

From a computer in his New York apartment,
Thornton managed to provide an inside view of
the law enforcement and intelligence communities
sharper than most insiders'. Canning's own sources
concurred with Thornton's account of the Bureau's
misdirection. And the director of DARPA, whose
post–Flight 89 accident conversation in the Oval Office Canning had listened to, was none the wiser.

Unfortunately, there was more to Thornton's
post. As Canning read on, his satisfaction turned to
concern.

> It's also worth considering that the seven-gram bul-
> let was a red herring. Murderers usually aren't big
> on leaving clues to their identities. It might be worth
> taking a look at American operators with service
> time in Russia or other means of acquiring this bit of
> Soviet-era arcana.

Canning had indeed learned of "Uncle Joe's remedy" while serving in Moscow.

The blogger was a loose end.

2

Two months later, the FBI closed the investigative
stage of the Sokolov case.

That's Public-Relations-ese for "hit a dead end,"
Thornton tapped onto his keyboard. The development was no surprise to him. The Bureau's success
rate in bringing killers to justice was just 62 percent,
a number inflated by cases in which the killers confessed from the get-go. He intended to add that to his
column when his phone rang, the caller ID flashing
JOHNSON, JANE. He knew no one by that name, but his
sources often used prepaid disposable cells, and when
entering the minimal user info required, they chose
ordinary names. Which made sense: If you're trying
to duck the National Security Agency, you don't input
LINCOLN, ABE.

Thornton answered, "Newsroom"—also known as his spare bedroom/office—and, for the first time in ten years, he heard Catherine Peretti's voice.

As if it had been only a day or two, she said, "Hey, I'm going to be in town today and I've been craving Grumpy. Any chance you can do dinner at eight?"

He leaned his desk chair back and gazed out the window. The dry cleaner downstairs was just opening, illuminating cobblestones on the still-dark West Village block. A call this early wasn't unusual—everyone knew Thornton always got to work before sunrise, catching up on the world events he'd missed during his four or five hours in bed. Callers from his past were also routine: media coverage was a commodity. It was Peretti's choice of venue that gave him pause.

Grumpy was her nickname for Gam Pei, a Chinatown restaurant usually filled with tourists. Anyone who lived in Manhattan knew that you could get good Chinese food just about anywhere in the city—except Chinatown. Gam Pei was especially bad, as Peretti had told him when he first took her there on a dinner date. At the time he was captivated by the Chinese mob, and Gam Pei's front windows offered a singular view of an overt triad hangout called the Goat Club.

The seventh time Thornton took Peretti to Gam Pei for dinner, he watched a taxi pull up to the opposite curb. As he had been anticipating, a Goat Club goon handed an envelope to the passenger, whom

Thornton recognized as the judge presiding over the trial of two triad members accused of gunning down a fruit-stand proprietor late with her protection payment. Thornton broke the resulting corruption story on his (then) tiny site. The same story reappeared the next day on the front page of every tristate paper.

Peretti applauded Thornton's professional success. *Grumpy* derived from her personal sentiments after a year of dating him. Before leaving his apartment that morning, she said, "I want a boyfriend who's interested in romantic bistros, or Burger Kings even, so long as I'm his focal point."

That was the last time he'd heard from her.

But not of her. She was a comer on Capitol Hill, having soared from intern to chief of staff to California senator Gordon Langlind, chairman of the Senate Intelligence Committee. She might have a tip now, and it would be a big one given the clandestine means of contact.

Thornton was curious. And, as usual, he had no evening plans—neither the invitation to the Cuban consulate cocktail party nor the Broadway opening had held as much appeal as staying home and fishing for stories online. But he usually ran the other way from stories involving people he knew outside his professional life. Ethics aside, best-case, your friend is pleased with her quotes along with your copy *and* your editor's "enhancements." Which would be a first in the history of journalism. The norm was blowback.

Still, he couldn't ignore the reason Peretti was

calling him. She knew the deal with journalists and their friends and family, let alone ex-lovers. And she interacted daily with legions of journalists who were none of the above, at media outlets compared to which *RealStory*, a quarter of a million readers notwithstanding, was a flyer left on a windshield.

She was in trouble.

"Love to," he told her.

3

At 7:39, Thornton climbed out of the Canal Street subway station, close enough to Chinatown that he could smell the salty fish—residents left it on the rooftops to dry in the sun, he'd read somewhere. He soon pushed through the heavy, ersatz bronze door and entered Gam Pei, a dark tunnel after neon-happy Mott Street. As his eyes acclimated, he made out the red and white harlequin floor tiles and the twelve-foot-high pressed-tin ceiling. While adding ambiance, the paucity of light helped hide the wear on the furniture as well as what appeared to be soy sauce splattered on the ceiling.

He had his pick of swivel stools at the bar. He sat facing the octogenarian bartender; *Billy* was stitched onto his cream-colored tuxedo shirt, its collar several sizes too large for his neck.

"What you have tonight, sir?" Billy asked in a thick Mandarin accent. Guangzhou, Thornton would have bet.

Thornton studied the beer list and ordered one he'd never heard of. "I was wondering how soy sauce could have gotten all the way up there," he added, indicating the ceiling panel above the corner booth.

Billy looked up, then shrugged—the way actors used to at the vaudeville theater on East 12th Street.

"I know about the shooting," Thornton ventured.

Billy's eyes widened. "How?"

You just told me, Thornton thought. "Blood dries black as a result of hemolysis."

Glancing around the bar, Billy muttered, "You cop?"

"No, but I write about them sometimes."

"Well, no story here, mister."

Thornton smiled. "Sometimes a stain is just a stain?"

"Right, stain just stain." Billy's forced laugh revealed four gaps where there ought to have been teeth. Not that bad, Thornton thought. When he wrote about CIA dentists pulling officers' molars and replacing them with cyanide-filled replicas for use in case of capture, he happened on the statistic that adults in the United States were missing 3.28 teeth on average.

While the old man searched the refrigerator, Thornton fixated on the black starburst on the ceiling, flipping through his mental Rolodex of triad sources until he inhaled a trace of lavender. He turned to find Catherine Peretti on the next stool.

"Just like old times," she said, pushing a tendril of dark brown hair back from her face and grinning.

He felt admonishment, but it quickly yielded to wonder. She was as beautiful as ever, her gray eyes blazing with whimsy to match full lips curved at the ends like a bow, poised to break into a laugh at the slightest provocation. Her snug jeans said she still ran daily, and that it was worth it. How in the hell had he ever taken his eyes off her for wannabe mafiosos?

"So how was your decade?" he asked.

"Eventful. I got married and had two kids, for starters."

Eight years ago, he'd read, with a sense of loss, the *Times* announcement of her wedding to a star at a white-hot hedge fund.

"Congrats," he said with manufactured enthusiasm.

"Girls Emily and Sabrina, six and eight, husband Richard, forty."

Peretti peeled off her suede jacket and knit cap, and Thornton processed the changes. There were shadows under her eyes, and she was no longer a blonde. Also, back in the day, if one of her hairs fell any way but ruler straight, you noticed, if only because she smoothed it at once.

"Outside of work," she continued, "my decade has consisted of helping with homework, watching ballet, watching gymnastics, watching swimming, and listening to attempts at piano. On occasion, I've had time to floss. How about you?"

"I had a second date recently."

"It's comforting to know there are some constants in the world."

He sat straighter and said, "One change worth noting is that now, given the choice, I would have taken you somewhere else for dinner."

"Is the Goat Club yesterday's news?"

"It was replaced by a dress shop, actually. Also the Kkangpae is the mob du jour. The reason I would have gone somewhere else is I know of about two hundred restaurants you might like."

She smiled. "Actually, I'm not here for the food, not that I'd ever come here for the food—" She cut herself off as the big entry door swung inward. Taking in the new arrivals, a senior couple who looked to have come straight from a bingo game in Peoria, she was clearly relieved, but nothing close to calm.

He stilled her hand with his, but the wedding band was a red light. He quickly let go, saying, "Let me know if I'm imagining any of this: You called me on a disposable cell, you used an alias, you came in disguise, and now you're worried you were tailed."

She took a deep breath. "Last night, I was running around the park in Potomac when one of your standard preppy neighborhood dads in a Gore-Tex jogging suit pulled even with me and said, very cordially, that my family and I would have 'major difficulties' unless I forgot what I'd just learned at work. And I have every intention of forgetting it, but first I need you on the story."

Thornton felt a familiar jolt. As well as anyone, journalists understand the fisherman's maxim: *The tug is the drug.* In this instance, the buzz was doused by his awareness that it would be in both of their best interests for him to hand off the story to someone else.

"Between the mobs and law enforcement, there are probably as many microphones in this place as in Nashville," he said. "We should go somewhere else after all."

Exiting the restaurant, Thornton pulled out his phone's battery so that his position couldn't be determined from cell tower data. So many of his sources insisted on this, it was practically a habit.

"Where's Jane Johnson's phone?" he asked.

Peretti walked alongside him, head lowered as if against a storm, though the night remained temperate. "Last seen in the trash in the ladies' room in the Bethesda Kmart."

"And your regular phone?"

"On a train headed for Florida."

"Lucky phone." Thornton led the way up Mott, passing the first two available taxis—just in case—before flagging a third heading west on Prince.

He directed the driver to the Lower East Side via a succession of left turns.

"The chance of anyone who's not a tail staying with us for three consecutive left turns is astronomical," he told Peretti.

"You've picked up some spook, haven't you?"

"What I've learned about tails can be summed up with *T-E-D-D*: Someone who's seen repeatedly over *time*, in different *environments*, and over *distance*, or who displays poor *demeanor*. Surveillants are easier to spot than you might think."

"How?"

"Sometimes they have no good reason for being where they are. Sometimes they even use hand signals to communicate with teammates. The hitch is the other times, when there's only imperceptible surveillant behavior, the sort I would sense rather than see—if I had that ability. So in answer to your question, I've picked up enough spook to get me in trouble."

"That's comforting." Peretti's laughter was interrupted by a screech of tires. A Verizon service van was rounding the corner behind them. Too sharply.

Feigning interest in a billboard, Thornton tried but couldn't see into the van through the brightly colored blur of lights reflected on its windows.

When the taxi took the next left, onto East Broadway, the van continued down the Bowery. Peretti regarded Thornton plaintively.

"It's eight-fifteen," he said. "It was probably just a Verizon service guy in a rush to get a customer who'd been told to be home between noon and eight."

But he couldn't discount the possibility that the Verizon guy was really someone other than a Verizon guy who had just handed the taxi off to a teammate in another vehicle. So he had the driver continue all the way down to Wall Street, which at eight-thirty was almost a ghost town by New York standards.

Thornton and Peretti got out at Water Street while the cab idled at a stoplight. He scanned the haze of exhaust for anyone else disembarking. There was no one. Or, rather, no one as far as he could tell.

He led her a block east to Pier 11, where the urban thrum dimmed. "Getting on a boat is another good way to tell if you're being followed," he said. "A tail probably couldn't get people to the other side of the river before we got there, so he'd be forced to stay with us." He indicated the esplanade, where a handful of late commuters were hurrying to one of the mammoth Staten Island ferries.

The sour smell of the East River was nearly overwhelming as he and Peretti ascended the gangway, which branched into three separate entrances. He directed her to the door on the left, then trailed her into the main cabin.

Just one passenger boarded after them, a thirty-ish Hispanic man, ironically unique in that none of his plain features stood out—a Yankees jacket was his only distinguishing trait. If you passed him on the street ten minutes from now and he'd changed into a Mets jacket, Thornton thought, you probably wouldn't recognize him.

The man opted for the door to the right, leading to the ship's upper level, but when Thornton and Peretti took two of the five hundred molded plastic seats on the main level, there he was, directly across the deck, on a bench beneath one of the ubiquitous Lucite-encased posters advertising bedbug extermination services.

Leaning close to Thornton, Peretti said, "I'm not sure, but I think he was on the subway I took from Penn Station."

Thornton felt a chill creep up the back of his neck. He snuck a look at the man's reflection in a window. Nose buried in a tabloid. A foghorn announced the ferry's departure, making it impossible for him to hear anything else, even if he had a directional mic concealed in the newspaper.

"Let's save our scheduled discussion for the Au Bon Pain in the St. George terminal," Thornton whispered to Peretti. The Staten Island side's morph of traditional French café and McDonald's did brisk business at mealtimes but transacted little more than the odd cup of decaf this late. Anyone following them there would be easy to spot.

Manhattan receded in the ferry's wake, the engines churning smoothly. Thornton and Peretti chatted about what had become of his former rugby team-mates. He used to play in the United Nations' recreational rugby league, primarily to develop sources; she enjoyed the games. The lavender scent of her hair vaulted him back to those days, which he now viewed through a golden filter.

He felt a twinge of disappointment when the Staten Island terminal came into view. An announcement instructed all passengers to prepare to disembark. The man in the Yankees jacket was among the first off, greeted by a Hispanic woman of about thirty carrying an excited little boy who wore a Yankees cap.

Peretti turned to Thornton, her cheeks reddening. "My imagination got the better of me, I guess."

"Better than the alternative," he said.

He steered her into the Au Bon Pain, deserted but for a pair of hollow-eyed young women behind the counter.

While Peretti was looking up at the menu board, a thickset man emerged from the men's room. He wore a black woolen overcoat, blocky glasses, and a tight orange ski cap. From inside the coat, he drew a sleek Ruger, pointed it at her, and pressed the trigger. The silenced barrel coughed twice. A plastic seat back flew end over end, cracking the glass fronting the café. Peretti dropped as though the floor tiles had been whisked from beneath her feet.

Thornton threw himself over her, to protect her from another shot. She lay facedown, her brown wig having fallen off. Blood seeped through her true blond locks. There was a second bullet hole in her suede jacket, between her shoulder blades.

The shooter knelt, inadvertently knocking a tented advertisement off a tabletop as he extended his gloved left hand to collect his bullet casings from the floor. The ad bounced off his face, then sailed away. Biting back a wince, he pocketed both casings. He shoved the Ruger into his waistband as he rose and strode out of the café.

Thornton clutched Peretti's shoulders and turned her face toward him. Seeing the dark hole between her eyebrows made his body temperature plummet. Blood burbled from the exit wound beneath her left collarbone. She'd lost consciousness but was still breathing.

"Call nine one one," he shouted to the two employees crouched behind the counter. Then he took off after the gunman.

A line of taxis idled at the curb just outside the terminal building, their exhaust blurring the dozens of people getting in and out. Thornton didn't see an orange ski cap but spotted the gunman anyway. He'd taken off the cap, but his leisurely pace gave him away: New Yorkers don't do leisurely.

Making a beeline for the guy, Thornton slowed to avoid a uniformed policeman, who sure as hell had not been paying attention.

The gunman waved toward the man in the Yankees jacket, now buckling the little boy into a booster seat in a Vanagon. A taxi suddenly darted into view from behind the Vanagon. The gunman opened the taxi's rear door.

Thornton turned to the cop for help, but a metallic thunk jerked his attention back to the taxi.

Leaning across the front passenger seat, the heavyset taxi driver balanced a black tube the size of a paper towel core atop the open passenger window. Aiming at Thornton, he tugged at a trigger. There was no click, no flash, but the air all around Thornton grew hot, searing away his consciousness.

4

When building his four-story Arlington Financial Center in the late 1980s, the developer hoped to lure boutique financial firms from downtown Washington. So many of the principals lived in Virginia; it made sense. Clad in mirrored glass, the structure was a perfect cube, except where the front half of the lower two stories should have been, there was nothing, or so it appeared. A closer look revealed a concrete pillar keeping the top two stories from collapsing. Critics lauded the bold architecture. At the same time, warehouses in downtown D.C. were replaced with decent-enough-looking buildings, transforming Foggy Bottom into Washington's answer to Wall Street and forcing the developer of the Arlington Financial Center to subdivide his sprawling suites for lower-rent entities, including a travel agency, an orthodontist, and a massage therapy collective. For the past two months, South Atlantic Resources, LLC—an engineering supplies distributor, if anyone asked— had been renting the three-office suite in the corner above the pillar, the building's least accessible area. Canning's reason for concocting South Atlantic Resources and signing a one-year lease—using an alias, of course—was to gather intelligence produced by the eavesdropping device he'd implanted in Bella Sokolova, his ultimate goal being the assembly of his own Sokolov E-bomb.

Every night, he came to the South Atlantic offices from his day job in the city and listened to the day's feed. Usually it began with Bella, back from the Cleveland safe house and home alone in Port Washington, Wisconsin, talking to her late husband Leonid as if he were lying in bed beside her. She didn't broach the topic of electronic weapons, or even science. Just memories, of walks together along the shore in Yevpatoriya, their daughters' births, family vacations—in short, nothing Canning wanted to hear.

When she finally got out of bed, Bella invariably switched on the TV in the den and watched whatever happened to be on, for hours on end, never changing the channel, getting up only to pad into the kitchen, dispense fresh ice cubes and pour more—Canning surmised—vodka. She spoke of work only when informing her DARPA handler, an excessively gung ho young case officer named Hank Hughes who called every couple of days, that she couldn't bear to go into the lab. Her daughters encouraged her to come visit them in Miami or Seattle, where they lived with their own families. When that failed, they encouraged her to at least get out of the house. She promised she would, but she didn't, not once in four weeks after the burial. The gate guard ran errands for her, leaving grocery bags and packages from the pharmacy outside the kitchen door.

The next week, Hank Hughes called to say DARPA could harden a laboratory for her in either Seattle or Miami. Bella felt it would dishonor Leonid to continue their work anywhere but their old lab, which DARPA had stealthily dismantled within hours of the Flight 89 accident.

A few days later, Hughes called again with news that the old lab had been restored. Too many estate issues still to settle here, Bella replied, before drinking away another week.

In their next talk, Hughes told Bella that DARPA had deployed two of its brightest scientists to Wisconsin to assist in the E-bomb effort. Would she at least bring them up to speed?

Leonid's fatal accident turned out to be a stroke of luck, thought Canning, listening to the call from the Arlington office and envisioning himself harvesting Bella's details of the E-bomb from soup to nuts.

She said she would think it over. If she indeed

thought about it during the next two weeks, it was while watching game shows and drinking.

This week, once again, the DARPA man called in hope of getting Bella to go to the lab. He tried several of the same exhortations that he had in the past, including repaying the country that had brought her and her family from Russia, contractual bonuses, the chance to perfect the "peacekeeping contraption" that would be her and Leonid's legacy, and a trip to Oslo to pick up another Nobel Prize. Once again, Bella said no.

This morning, however, soon after waking up, she called Hughes and said, *"Na miru i smert' krasna."*

Canning knew the old Russian expression to mean, "With company, even death loses its sting." But today he thought of it as "South Atlantic Resources is finally open for business."

Bella was finally going back to work.

5

Thornton awoke to a medley of electronic blips. He was lying on his back in a bed with metal side rails, his hospital gown drenched with perspiration. Five floral arrangements were packed onto the windowsill, the petals beginning to wilt. Raising his head from the pillow set off a network of fiery pain. An IV tube hung from a bag labeled FENTANYL 50MCG/ML. Fentanyl, he recalled, was a major-league painkiller, 100 times as powerful as morphine. Better not to think about how he'd feel without it. Around his left wrist was a plastic band identifying him as Staten Island University Hospital patient BALDWIN, MYERS, DOB 08/20/75. His actual date of birth was more than a year later, but Baldwin was his late mother's maiden name. He anticipated an explanation from the man slumped in the armchair to his right, FBI Special Agent Jim Musseridge, whom he'd met once or twice on the story circuit.

"How long?" Thornton croaked. It felt as if someone had lodged a sword in his throat.

"Good, you haven't lost your powers of observation." Musseridge's gruffness was almost as strong as his Brooklyn accent. "The flowers are from your Uncle Sam, part of the cover for your own protection. It's been four and a half days since you took a header on the sidewalk outside the ferry terminal."

Thornton felt an inclination to quarrel. His rusty faculties provided no backup.

The wrinkles in Musseridge's gray business suit indicated that he, too, had been in the hospital awhile. Or not. In contrast to the current generation of yoga-svelte G-men, the fortysomething Musseridge resembled an old school linebacker, the sort of guy on whom a fresh suit is rumpled in minutes.

"There was some bleeding inside your head," Musseridge went on. "They had to operate to relieve the pressure."

Thornton ran his fingertips over his scalp. He felt prickly stubble and a bandaged ridge of sutures.

"Luckily you've got yourself one thick noggin. But you swallowed some vomit, which led to pneumonia, so they had to put you on a ventilator for seventy-two hours. None of this probably sounds too good, but they say you should be out of here in a day or two."

A flashback broadsided Thornton: the man in the overcoat, materializing from the men's room, pointing a Ruger.

Finding the bed's lift control, Thornton started the backrest groaning toward an upright position. Too slow. Gritting his teeth against the pain, he used the side rails for leverage and sat up. The full events of the St. George terminal exploded back into his consciousness. "What about Catherine?" he asked.

Musseridge eyed his worn wing tips. "She didn't make it. I'm sorry."

Thornton hoped he'd misunderstood. "Is there a funeral?"

"There's a wake tonight down in Maryland."

"What time?" Thornton tried to get out of bed. The room seemed to tip.

The FBI man restrained him. "You're not gonna be able to get there, bud."

Reaching the same conclusion, Thornton lowered himself back to the mattress.

"So what was Ms. Peretti doing up here in the first place?" Musseridge asked.

"I was going to ask you the same thing." Thornton noticed a young man pacing the hall. The close-cropped white-blond hair and a more stylish model of Musseridge's suit proclaimed him an FBI agent. Where there was one Feeb, you could usually expect to find a second. Warren Lamont, if Thornton wasn't mistaken. Called "Corky" by his fellow agents, who teased him that he should have been a surfer.

"How about you tell me your story first?" said Musseridge.

Thornton provided the most accurate account he could, the only pertinent bit as far as he knew being the Potomac jogger who'd threatened Peretti. "I don't have any idea what she was planning to tell me," he concluded with regret.

Although Musseridge's tie required no adjustment, he tightened it. "The Bureau was hoping you'd provide a little more insight than that."

"It would help if I knew what she was working on at Senate Intel. A terrorist threat, maybe a Mexican cartel—"

"The answer could be in one of 1,854 classified documents she may have seen in the twenty-four hours prior to coming to New York. Or it could be somewhere else. Unfortunately, she didn't keep any kind of diary. We went through all of her calls and e-mails: nothing there. Based on our interviews with her colleagues, friends, and family, you'd think this was just a random act of violence."

"Except the shooter had a Ruger Mark III with a suppressor, and he used it like it was just another day at the office for him."

"Yeah, except that. We plucked the rounds out of the wall."

"Learn anything?"

"Twenty-two LRs, subsonic, hollow point—pretty much what you'd expect." Musseridge twisted his wedding ring. "Other than the victim, there was no evidence that a human had come in contact with the bullets since they left the Remington factory."

"So you have absolutely nothing on the guy." Thornton figured he was most likely to get information by putting Musseridge on the defensive.

The agent sighed. "We've got ferry terminal security video of the shooter described by the witnesses at the crime scene—the same guy you described—plus a shitty shot of him leaving in a cab."

"You couldn't find the cab?"

"NYPD found it, parked at a pub by the stadium." Musseridge meant the minor-league Staten Island Yankees' Richmond County Bank Ballpark, a fly ball away from the ferry terminal. "The cabbie'd been sitting at the bar for three hours as the incident went down. There were about fifty witnesses. Had his car keys on him the whole time."

"Still, there had to be some biological evidence, right?"

"We're talking about a New York City taxi, a ginormous ferry terminal, and a fast-food place. Hard to tell the shooter's hair and prints, if he left any, from the thousands of other—"

Thornton remembered. "He was wearing surgical gloves." Labs could lift prints from within the gloves.

"We didn't find them, and not for lack of dumpster diving. Which leaves us with this." Musseridge glanced at the notepad balanced on his lap. "A young woman holding an important position with the Senate Select Committee on Intelligence tells her husband and coworkers that she's going up to New York for a conference on commercial shipping security. Instead, she meets an old flame for dinner at a tourist restaurant where the two of them could go with a reasonable amount of confidence that they wouldn't run into anyone they knew. Later the same night, the same couple is seen on a ferry ride, awfully cozy." Musseridge looked up. "That's another reason you'd be ill-advised to go to the funeral. As far as the media knows, this *was* a random act of violence, and we've kept your name out of it, but not from Ms. Peretti's family. As far the Bureau's concerned, a fling isn't a federal offense. But you are gonna have to tell us how you happened to take her to the exact spot where an assassin was waiting."

The hospital bed suddenly felt like a witness stand. Thornton had been aware that Musseridge would fill out the FBI's requisite record-of-interview form—the infamous FD-302. Its categories included WITNESS, used when the interviewee may have seen the offense committed, INFORMATIONAL, for an interviewee lending assistance to the investigation, and SUBJECT, meaning the interviewee is believed to be involved in the offense. The abruptness with which Special Agent Lamont stopped pacing the hall and cocked an ear toward the hospital bed declared SUBJECT.

Thornton tried to tamp down his indignation, if only because the Feds took petulance as indicative of guilt. "We got on the ferry because she was afraid that she was being followed. We were close together to minimize the chance that the suspected tail would overhear us."

"Whose idea was it to go to the Au Bon Pain?" Musseridge pronounced the French word for "bread" like the English synonym for suffering.

"Mine, on the fly."

"And an assassin just happened to be waiting there?"

"Where are we going with this, Agent Musseridge? Jilted ex-flame?"

"Is that it?"

"There is no *it*."

"I want to believe you, bud. The thing the Bureau keeps stumbling over is, even if Peretti had a hundred tails on her, how could the shooter have known to wait in that one out-of-the-way men's room?"

"That's a good question. I wish I knew. Maybe he or his team had planted a mic on one of us?"

"We went over her handbag, the coffee shop, and pretty much everything in the vicinity with a fine-tooth comb. We also tore up your clothes and shoes looking for a tracking device."

"It could have been knocked off as I went down. When I came out of the terminal, the getaway driver shot me with some kind of heat ray."

"Heat ray, huh?" Musseridge wrote on his pad with unwarranted force.

Thornton said, "As in an active denial system, a directed energy weapon that—"

Musseridge cut him off. "I know what an active denial system is. You ever seen an ADS?

"On the Web."

"Well, I have seen one of them in real life. Used for crowd control. The thing was almost as big as the flatbed truck hauling it."

"I take it you didn't see one on the security camera footage."

"Nope." Musseridge rose, hefting the overcoat from the back of his chair.

Thornton was hit with déjà vu. "Wait."

Musseridge only slowed. "Yeah?"

"How about the placard from the table?"

"The what?"

"At Au Bon Pain, there were tented advertisements for a new soup on each of the tables. When the shooter bent over to pick up the bullet casings, he knocked the ad off the nearest table. It looked like it might have grazed his cheek."

Musseridge resumed his course for the door. "We'll look into it," he said with too little conviction.

6

Two hours after the FBI agents left his hospital room, Thornton braced himself against a cold metal handrail leading to Track 13 at Penn Station. The snorts and grunts from the engine of the Washington-bound train told him to hurry, but he could barely walk. He heaved one leaden leg ahead of the other. His ribs weren't broken, just bruised, they'd told him at the hospital. Yet once he was seated, every one of the train's lurches during the ensuing three-and-a-half-hour ride was a hot poker to his side. His head was worse. Still, all things considered, the painkiller's effectiveness bordered on magic. Otherwise he wouldn't have been able to leave the hospital. Or he would have collapsed halfway up the three flights of stairs to his apartment, where he'd stopped to change into something suitable for a wake.

An hour of stop-and-go traffic in a taxi from Union Station to Maryland didn't help matters. The good news, he thought, was that his injuries gave him a valid excuse to miss the black-tie society event he'd been obligated to attend next weekend.

The taxi left him at the corner of a quiet downtown street over which a moonless night had settled. Halfway down the block, he found the Potomac Memorial Chapel, which looked like a boutique hotel. Stately Federal architecture, impeccable furnishing, soft lighting, cherrywood polished to high gloss—all of it providing him with an ironic reminder of the difference between a hotel and a funeral home: You check out of a hotel.

He gazed through one of the tall leaded-glass windows. A set of French doors on the far side of the lobby allowed a partial view of a mahogany-paneled reception room. At least twenty mourners waited in line to view the casket. Thornton wanted to see it too. But it was only 6:36. He would wait for the crowd to reach its thickest. Just after seven, he reckoned. He wanted to mitigate the chance of being recognized.

He continued down the deserted block, digesting an assortment of pains with each step, bunching his lapels together to counter the nor'easter rattling bare branches all around. The five-buck woolen watch cap he'd bought at Penn Station was perfect for a night like this, even if he hadn't needed it to obscure his appearance. Steering clear of the streetlamps, he headed for a café at the end of the block.

The café door swung open. A prematurely gray man wearing a smart black pinstriped suit hurried out. He had the earnestness of a student body president to go with courtly looks, so the hollowness around his eyes and the slight stoop were jarring. This was the widower, Richard Hoagland, Thornton realized. Shuffling out of the café after Hoagland came a pair of downcast little girls in black dresses. They were younger versions of Catherine Peretti, especially the smaller one. Emily. Catherine's ghost would probably have shaken Thornton less.

Keeping his reaction hidden, he hunched so that his coat puffed out, making him appear stockier. A decade in which a slice of pizza on the run ranked among his more substantive meals had reduced his fullback's physique to that of a placekicker, and, he guessed, he'd dropped another ten pounds in the hospital. He slowed to avoid crossing paths with the family, pretending his attention was elsewhere, nodding reflexively in greeting only when they were within a few feet. Hoagland responded in kind, continuing up the block, toward the funeral home. "Go on ahead, find Aunt Bea," Thornton heard him tell the girls. Peretti had a sister, Beatrice. "I'll be there in a minute."

Then Thornton heard just two sets of footsteps on the brick sidewalk. He peered over his shoulder to find a pair of sharp eyes aimed at him.

"You shouldn't have come, Mr. Thornton," Hoagland said.

Thornton steeled himself. "Mr. Hoagland, I know it's natural to suspect the worst of a guy who used to go out with your wife, but—"

Hoagland thrust forth a palm to cut him short. "Let me start over. What I ought to have said was: You shouldn't have left your hospital room, given what I've heard of your injuries. But I'm positive that Catherine would appreciate your being here."

Hoagland appeared appreciative as well. But this was D.C, where genuine affection was conveyed by a deal memo. So Thornton remained on edge. Accepting Hoagland's hand, he said, "I wish we were meeting at a better time."

"Actually, the timing couldn't be better."

On that puzzling note, Hoagland turned to watch Emily follow her older sister into the funeral home. Thornton saw in Hoagland a softer version of himself. No surprise, Thornton thought. A woman who as a child enjoys a positive relationship with her father—Peretti had—is more likely than not to be attracted to men who remind her of him in some way.

Returning his attention to Thornton, Hoagland said, "I'm glad you're here now because I want to find out who killed Catherine."

They were alike in that too. Except one of them understood that it was out of his hands. "I told the FBI everything I know," Thornton said.

"Frankly, I'd have been happy if it had been you who arranged for the hit man to ambush her," Hoagland said, "because it would give me someone to blame. But there's too much mitigating evidence, not least of which is that Catherine always thought the world of you. She was a great fan of your work, too. As am I. In fact, I think Russ Thornton on the case is the best chance of the killer being caught. The FBI has nothing."

"I wish I had more than the FBI." Thornton was starting to like Hoagland and wished he could help him. He had no plans to investigate, though. His curiosity had already contributed to Peretti's death. Forgetting the impracticality of investigating a story that involves oneself, if he were to stick his nose further into the matter, the death toll stood to increase.

"I told Agent Musseridge and Agent Lamont everything I know, too," Hoagland said. "That took all of five minutes, I'm afraid. There was a time when Catherine and I talked shop every night, but then we had a baby, then a second, and then months would go by without our having time to discuss anything more substantive than the need for more diapers or a half gallon of milk. I don't have the faintest idea what type of damning information she could have found. Do you?"

Thornton felt like an AA member standing outside a pub. "It's hard to speculate."

"I'd be happy with even a half-decent for-instance."

"Could be anything," Thornton said, trying to shrug off the subject.

But Hoagland waved for him to go on.

"Well, as chief of staff of the Senate Intelligence Committee, as I'm sure you know, she read reams of classified material. It's possible that she happened on a report that wasn't supposed to be released to the committee, or she could have pieced together something that no one else did when she read reports from two different services who hadn't shared information."

Hoagland shook his head. "So far, based on what I've heard, the intelligence committee knows less than you."

"Or they're keeping it to themselves."

"Is there someone you suspect?"

"No, not at all. And you can be sure the Bureau will debrief everyone who might know anything, then polygraph anyone they suspect isn't being forthcoming."

"The 'box.' Do you believe those things work?"

"With a good examiner, they're effective enough of the time that they're more than worthwhile."

"But not nearly as effective as you, I'm betting, after all your experience with politicians and other professional liars."

"If only that were true. In any case, I don't have access to the classified material Catherine read that could offer clues. Also I don't do investigations; I only chronicle them. Most of the time, I'm just sitting around my apartment looking up stuff on the Internet."

Hoagland stared at the sidewalk. "So what do we do?"

Thornton had no good answer. Seeking to provide a dash of optimism, he said, "It would help to have an idea of what Catherine wanted to tell me."

"She told me she was going up to New York for a meeting on commercial shipping security. Obviously a cover story, right? That's what the FBI thinks."

Thornton shrugged. "You never know."

"You think it means something?" Hoagland asked.

"It might," Thornton said, but only because the guy's wife had just died.

The train doors were closing. Hobbling and stumbling, Thornton leaped into the last car and careened into a bulkhead seat. Without the energy to wriggle free of his coat, let alone stow it in the overhead rack, he sank into the cushions. Watching Union Station recede, he enjoyed the soothing rhythm of the wheels banging the rails. He loosened his tie, let his eyelids sag, and slid eagerly toward sleep.

But the image of Peretti's younger daughter, Emily, intruded. Her black dress had been much too loose. Was it because it had been a hand-me-down from her big sister? Or because she hadn't been able to eat for the past five days? Which again made Thornton wonder what the hell Peretti had died trying to tell him.

After a visit to the bar car, he succeeded in sleeping, in a position that would have been unattainable without the three bourbons: legs folded against his chest, the left side of his head against the window, his right hand wrapped around the back of his head.

He woke to a blindingly lit train already parked at Penn Station. He saw just a few passengers, all hurrying onto the platform or up the stairs to the terminal. His skull felt like it had been filled with cement. His limbs were too painful to be merely asleep; they were seemingly poked from within by barbs. In trying to rise, he found himself pitching forward. He grabbed the headrest on the seat in front of him. The only other passenger still aboard, an elderly woman at the other end of the aisle, shot him a disapproving look.

Propping himself into an upright position, he released the headrest. His right ring finger stung, and when he looked at it, he noticed a slight depression in the base of the fingertip. He wrapped the hand around the back of his head, placing the ring finger where it had spent the last couple of hours of the train ride. There was a small lump there, behind his left ear. Something beneath the skin. A sebaceous cyst, he guessed. Normal and utterly harmless. He'd had five or six of them over the years.

This one was unusually symmetrical, though. Like a Tic Tac. An absorbable suture? Probably not. It was nowhere near the incision.

He propelled himself to the end of the aisle and

jerked open the sticky sliding door to the small bathroom. A fluorescent cylinder above the mirror rattled on, revealing mustard yellow plastic walls imprinted with tiny fleurs-de-lis. He angled his head and folded his left ear forward to get a view of the lump. But even when he stretched the skin as far as he could, he saw no sign of the thing. Given the same treatment, a sebaceous cyst would be as plain as a rivet.

He detached a square of toilet tissue, moistened a corner with a drop of water, and adhered the soft paper to the area behind his left ear. Next he pulled at the corners of the square to conform it to his head. Then he squirted spearmint-green liquid soap from the dispenser and painted it onto the square, directly over the lump. He hoped to produce an impression of whatever was in his scalp.

When he held the paper up to the light, he saw a pale green image of a capsule with staplelike handles top and bottom and a perfect circle rising from the center of its face.

7

Beryl Mallery wanted Gordon Langlind's Senate seat.

"How do you explain the Dutchman?" Langlind asked her during their debate, three days before the election.

She didn't know who the Dutchman was, and she had a bad feeling that she should. No doubt Langlind was trying to shift the discussion from California's high rate of unemployment to his favorite topic, her personal life, which he had attacked viciously and explicitly throughout the campaign.

From the moment she entered the race, Mallery recognized that her "John Does"—Langlind's designation for the men she'd dated—posed a liability. She hadn't been lucky in love. Or, as the tabloids put it, she

"got around." Was that illegal? No. Immoral? According to the experts on the all-star campaign team she'd
assembled, hypocrisy was the only moral transgression voters couldn't abide. So at the announcement of
her candidacy, she acted preemptively, telling report-
ers, "As you may know, I'm thirty-six and I'm single.
My opponent will disregard the multibillion-dollar
online dating service I built from my dorm room
and try to position the fact that I'm one of my best
customers so that it disqualifies me from the Senate.
Here, in my view, are the real issues . . ."

Afterward, she opened her personal life to her
campaign team, urging them to claw through it as
if she were their opponent. They identified forty-
eight John Does she'd dated for longer than dinner
and eleven others who might be influenced by Langlind to declare her a deviant. Fortunately, none of
the men held a grudge, and her team gained their
endorsements.

But evidently the team had missed someone.

The Dutchman?

Had she ever met a Dutchman? Had she ever
known anyone from Holland for that matter? Business took her all over the globe, often, so she had
probably shaken hands with dozens of Dutchmen.
Just none she could recall.

Silence engulfed San Francisco's Hastings law
school auditorium as the 300 audience members hung
on her response to Langlind. A thousand times as

many people watched on TV. The camera lights made her pale skin look corpselike, she thought. And of course there was the urgency. The sum total was that different laws of physics applied in a live, televised debate. Time ticked faster than usual. Words had weight. The auditorium's sixty-eight degrees could bring water to a boil.

Langlind reined in his smirk, coming off as respectful. For fifty years he had been a gangly lummox. Then his overeating caught up to his metabolism, giving his features the look of the prototypical great man—inherited, like everything else to his credit. His florid complexion, attributable to liquor, played up his silver hair. The sharp white widow's peak gave prominence to a huge forehead, adding undeserved IQ points to his appearance.

"I'm referring to your gentleman friend in Montauk," he said, as if trying to be helpful.

Montauk. Yes, of course. The guy—what the hell was his name?—was married with kids. Or had been when Mallery met him. Had she wrecked his home? She wondered how much the Langlind team knew. And how in the hell had they found out about this?

She'd met him back in May, prior to declaring her candidacy. Having endured five straight twelve-hour days of contentious IPO negotiations at Morgan Stanley in New York City, she let the limo driver have the weekend off and took the train alone to East Hampton. Four weeks beforehand, anticipating the need to

clear her head following the IPO negotiations, she'd
had one of her assistants book her a suite at the Maid-
stone Inn. On entering the hotel's impeccable lobby,
Mallery saw three of the Morgan Stanley i-bankers
and their spouses. She turned and fled. Renting a car
at the mom-and-pop agency a block down Route 27,
she drove off in search of privacy. She ran out of road
at a charmingly ramshackle Montauk inn that, two
centuries earlier, had hosted wives awaiting returning
whalers. In the twenty-first century, its sunset happy
hour attracted locals and weekending yuppies. No
one recognized her. Back then, outside of Silicon Valley, people rarely did.

By the time the sun dissolved into the Atlantic,
she'd enjoyed enough Bloody Marys that she decided
it best to take a room rather than return to the road.
She signed in with a pseudonym, a habit resulting from
trips to LA where strangers would accost her with "investment opportunities" or slip business plans under
her hotel room door. Returning to the bar for a nightcap, she met a handsome thirtysomething American
lawyer on the tail end of a seven-week sojourn in Amsterdam where his firm had won a class-action suit
against a corporation that had been burying depleted
uranium on property that shared groundwater with
a primary school. In his free time, he built his own
wooden sailboats. He was racing one of them in Sag
Harbor the next morning.

Mallery imagined herself sending bottles of Dom

Pérignon to the i-bankers for enabling her to meet the man whom she had dreamed of since she first read "Cinderella." After four years of college, five years working in three big cities, and then three semesters of graduate school, she'd experienced such futility in finding a man who met her criteria that she parked herself at her computer for three consecutive days and nights in an effort to expand her pool of dating prospects to the entire world. At the time, online matchmaking services used algorithms that essentially gave equal weight to climbing Everest and replacing the toothpaste cap. Her product, modeled on software that matched kidney donors and recipients, hinged on a Male/Female Utility Quotient driven by individual idiosyncrasies. The formula evolved into a website on which 1 in 155 dates led to marriage, a seemingly poor rate, but better than her closest competitor by a factor of three. Mallery was 0 for 234 as her own customer when she met the Dutchman.

In the Hastings auditorium, there was a palpable feeling of expectation.

Mallery turned to Langlind. "Oh, you mean Sidney?"

Langlind raised his shoulders. That he didn't know the name reduced the likelihood that Sidney had been the Langlind campaign team's snitch. Probably it was somebody who'd seen her with Sidney at the bar and overheard the snippet about Amsterdam. Which was good, because if Langlind's people didn't know Sidney's name, or that he wasn't Dutch, they probably hadn't found out about the wife and kids.

"Interesting guy," Mallery said.

"Are you sure?" asked Langlind. "You'd only met him that night, and, with all due respect, you'd had a bit to drink."

The moderator nearly slipped off his chair in his rush to grasp the microphone. "Senator, is this necessary?"

Langlind shifted to choirboy mode. "I raise this incident with regret, and do so only because it speaks volumes with regard to my opponent's fitness for the United States Senate."

The moderator—a local anchorman—faltered, lost without his teleprompter. The only rule in the debate was decorum, but Mallery thought appealing to the moderator on those grounds would be tantamount to retreat.

Turning to Langlind, she said, "I am, to quote you, Senator, 'no poster girl for temperance.' Maybe someday I'll have a drink named after me, like you do." At Langlind's squash club, just two blocks down California Street, the members had named a mix of whiskey and schnapps the Passed Out Naked on the Locker Room Floor.

"You had, what, four or five Bloody Marys that night?" Langlind asked.

"Five, I think," she said. "Maybe they'll start calling it the Bloody Mallery."

The uncomfortable silence in the audience transformed to laughter.

Langlind didn't miss a beat. "Plus a bourbon, all in just two hours, leading to a trip upstairs to a hotel room for which, if I'm not mistaken, you paid cash and gave a fake name. Was it because the Dutchman was married with children?"

A roundhouse punch to the jaw would have left Mallery less dazed. She hadn't told a soul about Montauk. Not even Sidney could have known her bar tally. She'd paid cash, one drink at a time, to three or four different bartenders, each busy filling orders for the crowd of patrons. Could Langlind have had someone following her? Even if that level of surveillance were possible, why would anyone have ordered it? This was well before the party had asked her to run.

Gripping the lectern, she said, "What happened was, after the bourbons, Sidney and I were climbing the charmingly creaky wooden staircase together to my room. Then he took out his phone and texted someone, '*Hitting hay now, need to be up early for the regatta.*' He turned to me and explained, 'Don't want phonus-interruptus from the wife or kids.' Which was how I learned of them. And the affair ended right then and there."

The audience sat in stunned silence.

Pivot, Mallery exhorted herself. Shift the topic. Langlind's principal area of vulnerability was his poor record in the Senate; she often reiterated Ronald Reagan's killer question in the 1980 contest with Carter: *Are you better off?* Her campaign manager liked to say that the primary goal in a debate is convincing people you're honest; the secondary goal is to make them think your opponent's an asshole.

"As you may recall, Senator Langlind has brought up my 'John Does' before, once or twice," Mallery said to the audience, sparking a few laughs, in turn rekindling her confidence. "If it's important to voters, I'll dish on the night I painted Montauk red. But the question was how to create jobs in California. That's much more important to me. As I see it, the issue isn't my John Does, but the John Does out there who need work."

8

Thornton knew a National Security Agency analyst who might be able to help him. He'd first made Kevin O'Clair's acquaintance by e-mail while gathering background for an unmanned-aerial-system story eight years ago. Over the course of several more spy-tech pieces, their digital correspondence blossomed into analog friendship. But even if he'd never met O'Clair, Thornton would have felt comfortable in going to him for help today based on a single piece of biographical information. After earning a doctorate in electrophysiology at MIT, O'Clair passed up a fortune from Silicon Valley to work for the National Security Agency. In five years at NSA headquarters in Fort Meade, Maryland, O'Clair's diffidence and timidity proved impediments to career advancement. Still Wall Street recruiters contacted him every month with prospective jobs whose salaries were three or four times that of the highest government pay grade. His wife, pining for a lifestyle of country clubs and haute couture, threatened to leave him unless he cashed in. When they divorced, she moved with their then three-year-old son to Princeton, New Jersey. O'Clair obtained a transfer to the NSA's office in Manhattan, an hour from Princeton by train. Along with child support and alimony, the jacked-up cost of living left him in a cramped apartment on the outskirts of Jersey City. He'd once confided to Thornton that his bedroom, not much larger than its full-size bed, faced a FedEx depot where the beeping of delivery trucks backing up rarely ceased, and he continued to hear the noise even when it did. A hedge fund in nearby Greenwich, Connecticut, subsequently offered him an analyst position tailor-made for an introvert, at a base salary ten times what the NSA was paying him, as well as a bonus potentially in excess of the base salary. He needed no time to think about it. He declined the offer, resolute in his desire to serve his country.

But how to discreetly brief him, Thornton wondered on the cab ride home from Penn Station, trying his damndest all the while to keep his hands off the lump behind his ear. An eavesdropping device of some sort, he suspected. In which case it was a good bet that his phones and computers were being tapped too.

At his apartment, he texted O'Clair, "It's been too long since the last meeting of the Crossain'Wich Club." O'Clair would probably suspect something was up. There was no Crossain'Wich Club. The two of them had never gotten together for a Crossain'Wich. Or breakfast of any kind.

At ten o'clock the next morning, the friends sat across from each other in a booth at a now-quiet Burger King two blocks from the National Security Agency's offices in downtown Manhattan. O'Clair had been a cross-country runner at West Point fifteen years ago and never lost his string-bean physique. He attempted to counter his boyish face with a wide mustache. It made him a hard read. He had to be wondering why Thornton was now going on and on about the Knicks' defense, or lack thereof.

When the restaurant momentarily emptied, Thornton said, "Excuse me, I've got to hit the head."

Rising, he nudged across the table a small piece of water-soluble white paper that he'd purchased at a drugstore near his apartment. Hobbyists commonly use water-soluble paper as a dissolvable base for embroidery. Thornton had tossed a twelve-sheet package into his basket along with—for cover's sake—a bunch of other items. In preparation for his meeting with O'Clair, he jotted onto one of the sheets the details of the lump he'd found beneath his scalp and his related suspicions, including an explanation of how the assassin knew to wait in ambush at Au Bon

Pain. Thornton hoped that as soon as O'Clair read the message, he would drop it into his coffee. After all, it had been O'Clair who told Thornton the story of the young clandestine operations officer who made the mistake of trying to dissolve water-soluble paper in a martini.

Thornton walked to the men's room, pushed through the door, did three laps of the overly bright stalls, flushed a urinal, and walked out.

Biting back a grimace as he lowered himself back into his seat, he saw that his message was gone, in all likelihood responsible for the bubbles on the surface of O'Clair's coffee.

"So, dude, I was thinking it would be good for you to get in some fresh air, bag some endorphins," O'Clair said. "Princess Sarah's got Nathan this afternoon. What do you say to a hike?"

The thought of it caused a flare of pain in Thornton's rib cage.

"Sounds great," he said.

The overcast morning became a sunny and mild afternoon. After crunching for a mile through crisp blond and russet leaves alongside Riverside Park's jogging path, O'Clair turned sideways to fit into an opening in the three-story brick wall behind the West 103rd Street soccer field. Thornton traipsed after O'Clair into a space so dark he could see nothing beyond a rusty staircase, and he saw that much only because of O'Clair's powerful flashlight. Fifty degrees tops, the air reeked of mold and rodents. O'Clair explained that he had learned of this place while supervising an NSA-funded research project at nearby Columbia University.

At the muddy base of the stairs, he swung the flashlight to show the remnants of a pair of railroad tracks. Weeds as big as bushes hung from the three-story ceiling. Segments of the concrete retaining wall were scattered all over, like building blocks left behind by giant children. There were no signs of people—just rats, scampering away from the flashlight beam.

"My ex-brother-in-law still lets me have the family discount on weed," O'Clair said, setting the flashlight on a cement ledge twenty feet in, illuminating the close vicinity and throwing giant shadows of the two of them onto the far wall.

"Is it okay . . . ?" Thornton opened and closed a hand in imitation of the movement of a mouth.

O'Clair shook his head emphatically. "Oh yeah, totally. You're gonna love this shit."

He eased off his hiker's pack, produced an iPod connected to a small speaker, then balanced them atop the ledge. When he flipped a switch icon, reggae reverberated through the tunnel.

From his wallet, he drew a card-size magnifying glass with a built-in flashlight. "Okay, let's party."

Thornton bowed his head and submitted to an

examination of the lump behind his left ear. Again gesturing for Thornton to keep quiet, O'Clair tugged an appliance from his pack that resembled a compact personal fax machine. He used a rubber-coated coil to couple it with an instrument similar in configuration to a handheld hair dryer.

"Remind me to grab a quick shower later," he said, fitting the mouth of the blow-dryer over Thornton's lump. "If the princess smells the smoke when I pick up Nathan, she'll speed-dial the civil court."

Thornton was impressed by his friend's performance.

O'Clair pushed a button on the face of his fax machine. An LED panel glowed green and the image of a small capsule formed at its center. Data streamed along the base of the panel. "So is this good shit or what?" he asked, exhaling from an imaginary joint.

"Incredible." Thornton's incredulity required no acting.

O'Clair sang along with a recording of Bob Marley—"Buffalo Soldier"—while continuing to scan Thornton's body. The monitor yielded uniform green-gray surfaces that Thornton took for muscle and bone.

Setting the scanner down, O'Clair rifled once more through his pack and handed over a pair of headphones. Thornton slid the big foam cups over his ears, covering the area over the implanted device.

"Now we can talk," O'Clair said.

"Wasn't that the idea of coming to a subterranean cavern in the first place?"

"Actually, this is a New York Central Railroad tunnel, or it was until 1937. Theoretically it blocks transmission, but the capsule in your head has an on-board microphone that's still recording. On our way out of here, the instant it gets reception, it'll transmit all the audio it captured here, in a single burst. As far as I can tell, it captures every vibration of your left eardrum, meaning that whoever receives the transmission hears every word you hear or say."

"But not now?"

"Right. Thanks to the special headphones you're wearing, it's currently only capturing the words of Bob Marley."

Thornton tapped his head to indicate the implanted device. "I'm guessing this isn't something you can pick up at a Radio Shack."

"As you know, the NSA is the world champ of eavesdropping gizmos, or at least that's what I would have bet my life on until five minutes ago, but this capsule is a decade more advanced than any I've ever seen." O'Clair pointed from compartment to compartment on the image generated by the screen. "A capacitor powers a microcomputer, which runs the mic and the transmitter—standard stuff. The unique thing is what it's missing: There's no power source."

"No nine-volt battery?"

"Possibly the capacitor is charged by the movement of your head, the way a watch works. Or maybe it uses the temperature differential between your body and outside air, transforming the heat flow into

electricity. I didn't even know it was possible to min-
iaturize an energy harvester."

His suspicion of an eavesdropping device confirmed, Thornton had a flood of questions. "Any idea
how long it's been in there?"

"I'd say at least six weeks because there's no trace
of inflammation."

"From what?"

"A simple injection, probably, maybe while you
were asleep. Probably they hit you with ketamine first
to make sure you stayed asleep. Off the record, we use
ketamine. Hardly anyone has any reaction to it."

An odd thought struck Thornton. "Could they have
used midazolam?"

"Sure. Midazolam's just a stronger version of Val-
ium," O'Clair said. "The nice thing about ketamine is
it gives the targets incredibly vivid nightmares, which
makes for decent cover if you're in their bedroom
practicing dark arts."

"Could Leonid Sokolov's murder have actually
been a case of midazolam causing a reaction?"

"Oh." O'Clair's eyes bulged. "With seven grams of
lead to cover it up?"

"What if it had started out as an eavesdropping
op?"

"If Sokolov had been drinking an unusual amount,
yeah, there's a chance that the midazolam could have
triggered a respiratory depression. You think that's
somehow connected to you?"

"No, what are the odds?" Thornton said, despite a prickly sense that there was a connection. "Here's a better question: Why hasn't the thing in my head been picked up by metal detectors?"

"Actually, it appears to be constructed from processed collagen, like absorbable sutures, or maybe a comparable synthetic that the body can break down."

Thornton gripped the rocky wall to steady his nerves. "Tell me you can get it out."

"I can get it out. I brought a scalpel and some topical anesthetic. Wouldn't take a minute. Whoever installed it will know, though."

"Why can't we short it, making it seem like the device failed? Hardly a stretch, given I received a major blow to the head, right?"

"Yes. Evidently it was the swelling that jogged the thing out of its bed atop your temporal bone. If not for that and your pre-op haircut, you would have never detected it. The issue is, after we take it out, we can't reinsert it."

"Why the hell would we want to reinsert it?"

"To find out who put it there. Once the device is out, we can't reactivate it without them knowing it. Then we'll have no chance of tracking them."

His eyes having adjusted to the dark, Thornton saw that the underground train station was enormous, yet he was starting to feel claustrophobic. "And if we don't take it out?"

"We would need to find another person implanted

with the same kind of device, or, at the very least, we would need a second functioning device."

"Why?"

"The thing needs to transmit via cell phone stations. It sends your conversation as a data package."

"Can't you just track the data to the recipient?"

"Yes and no."

"What's the *yes* part?"

O'Clair sighed. "You need to understand the *no* part first. If you looked at it on a computer screen, the audio you're transmitting would be represented by a distinctive N-log wave, a signal sequence that looks like a seismograph readout. The problem is that you wouldn't have any way of knowing which signal is yours among the hundreds of thousands of other signals in the vicinity, generated by everyday cell phone conversations or radio-controlled toys or bar code scanners."

Thornton pointed to his head. "So the signal coming from me would look like a fish in an ocean full of indistinguishable fish?"

"Exactly. But if we had a second device in the same room as you, transmitting the same audio, then we would be generating two identical signals that a computer could pick out from the rest of the fish. From that point, a high school student could track the data."

"But we don't know if a second device even exists. We can't just somehow scan people for it, can we?"

"Yes, actually, with a radio-frequency detector

available at Radio Shack for about fifty bucks. The only problem is we'd get a false positive whenever a person had a cell phone on them."

"In other words, every time?" Thornton said.

Nodding, O'Clair aimed the flashlight down the tunnel. The steel drums emanating from the speaker could have concealed the approach of a marching band. There was no movement, no unusual shadows. "What we can do is run an old-fashioned counterintelligence op," he said.

He's spent too much time among spooks, Thornton thought. "Like what?"

"If you went to, say, a Metallica concert in Madison Square Garden, the recording device would still pick up everything you say."

"Filtration?"

"The energy harvester in this thing is a greater leap in technology than a car that runs on a couple double-A batteries. So I'm guessing that whoever developed it solved the issue of conflicting audio—like a foghorn on the Staten Island Ferry. But you could temporarily jam the recording device."

"With a radio jammer?"

"Right."

"How does that work?"

"It floods the eavesdropping device with a strong radio signal across a large part of the frequency spectrum so that the weaker signal from your conversation is essentially lost."

"If you're shooting a radio jammer at my head, wouldn't whoever's monitoring know what you're up to?"

"Not if you went someplace where transmissions are jammed all the time."

"Like at a radio station with a strong transmitter?"

"Yeah. Any significant source of electromagnetic interference could work. You would just need to be close to it."

"But if I went to a place like that, my personal Big Brother would know I'm onto him, and he'd send his associate with the Ruger."

"Not necessarily. If we play it right, Big Brother wouldn't know you're onto him, although he might suspect it—which would work for us. After we get out of here, simply tell me you have a meeting with someone from the agency. We'll pick a place next to a radio station."

"Which agency?"

"Doesn't matter."

"I guess the more ambiguous, the better," said Thornton.

"Now you're getting it." O'Clair smiled. "You tell me the person contacted you—just don't say how. To add verisimilitude, I'll send you an anonymous gobbledygook Hushmail beforehand that the eavesdroppers could interpret as an encrypted message."

Thornton was uneasy. "When I texted you this morning, I was hoping you would take me to your office—bring me in out of the cold, as it were—and let the professionals take over."

"Now you need to stay away," said O'Clair. "There's a chance NSA is behind this. Since the Patriot Act, the only rule has been *Don't get caught.* But even if we were as sure about trusting the NSA as we are about the sun coming up tomorrow, you know how it would play out—and this is true if you go to any of the agencies: You'd spend a day or two being polygraphed, then the brief would be cabled to heaven knows how many divisions, whose representatives would need to have an internal meeting and, after that, interagency meetings, and, finally, you'd get sent to someone in Tech who will know less than we do already."

"At least we'd have the chain of custody, my skull to their gloved hands and a petri dish, along with government scientists testifying that the defendant, Russell Thornton, had a crazy-sophisticated eavesdropping device in his head on the night of Catherine Peretti's murder. Maybe we can still extract audio that proves that my decision to go to Au Bon Pain was spontaneous."

"Maybe. But you'll lose the chance to find out who's responsible for her death. And possibly for Sokolov's death too, the repercussions of which I hate to even guess at—that guy was an electronic weapons pioneer in Russia; I doubt the Pentagon brought him here so he could teach physics."

Thornton decided that his friend was right. "The

thing is, I already know the killers are *killers*, and if that's not enough, they have unheard-of tech."

"But they're human."

"So?"

"So they'll make mistakes. They already have."

"Like what?"

"They bugged the wrong guy."

9

It's simple," Sokolova told the two DARPA scientists assigned to her. "So simple, in fact, that I'm afraid if I teach it to you, the Department of Defense will no longer have need for me."

"I very much doubt that," laughed one of the two new members of her team, a middle-aged electrophysicist named Daley.

"Dr. Sokolova is just being modest," said Hank Hughes, her DARPA handler. "Please proceed, Bella."

"Yes, please," added Canning, at the South Atlantic office 800 miles away, eating take-out pad thai while listening to the recording. He had a feeling that the 550-plus hours of Bella audio he'd endured was about to become worth every minute.

"You'll need to excuse my drawing skills," she said.

"Done," said Hughes.

Canning heard squeaks of a marker against a dry-erase board.

"This is a simple twelve-volt lead-acid battery," she began. "We place it at one end of our explosively pumped flux compression generator, which, basically, is a steel tube the size of a wastepaper basket that houses a copper cylinder packed with plastic explosive—we use a mix of Compositions C and PBX-9501. The solenoid coiled around the copper cylinder is made of Nomex-sleeved tinsel-copper wire, the same type used in aerospace conduits."

Although the audio was a recording and already backed up, Canning raced to write down everything Sokolova said. It felt like directions to a buried treasure.

"The current from the battery generates a magnetic field," she continued. "The solenoid then acts like a magnet. When we detonate the plastic explosive, the blast thrusts the inner cylinder against the outer tube, squashing the magnetic field between them, generating our ten thousand lightning bolts worth of electromagnetic energy."

"Where's the virtual cathode thing?" Hughes asked.

"That virtual cathode oscillator—or vircator—enters the equation after the energy produced by the flux compression generator goes through an inductor," Sokolova said over more squeaking of the marker. "The vircator is like a lens that magnifies the pulse, exponentially."

"Pardon me, Dr. Sokolova," asked twentysomething nuclear scientist Brooke Claiborne. "What is the relative size of the vircator here?"

"I'm drawing it to scale, dear," Sokolova told her. "It's about the same size as the flux compression generator; unscrew the antenna from the vircator and you can fit the whole system in the back of a car."

The younger woman gasped. "In all the time I was at Princeton, we weren't able to design—let alone assemble—a decent E-bomb that could even fit into this lab."

"Miniaturization was critical for the weapon to be deployable," said Sokolova. "Leonid reinvented the vircator as a tiny vacuum chamber. Within it, the high-current electrons pass through a polyester mesh anode, turning the other side into a virtual cathode, which causes oscillations that produce microwaves with peak power of one hundred milliwatts. A pulse of just one one-thousandth of a nanosecond and this system can take out everything within a fifty-mile radius."

The range was news to Canning. The best news, he reflected, that he'd ever heard.

10

Sitting back at his desk at the NYO—the FBI's New York City field office—Warren "Corky" Lamont reflected that, on big cases like this, the office is like your oxygen source. The next witness, the next phone call, the next classified document a courier shows up with: Any one of these could be the key. So any length of time away from your desk is an eternity, even as little as hitting the head, because you have this nagging sense that the case is going to take that crucial turn and that the information you had when you stepped out will be obsolete by the time you get back. The mentality in the office, meanwhile, is *bunker*. Pizzas are ordered, ties are loosened, sleep is rare. And it's not about pay or promotions. As the old saying goes, the FBI is a company of 10,000 agents all struggling to stay at the bottom. Just out of Quantico,

Lamont would tell friends that the buzz was comparable to the thrill of the hunt, but he came to realize that that trivialized it. What kind of hunt expended human capital, prevented the quarry from claiming additional victims, and concluded with justice done? And the best part of all came when the case was closed. He would go home at the end of that day, just like any other New Yorker piling into the subway, except—having kept the rest of them safe—he felt like a superhero.

He longed for just a drop of that feeling now. Seven days and twice as many pizzas into the Peretti case, the exhilaration had burned off. Lead after lead had led to dead ends. He spent yet another night hunched over his computer in the cube farm on 26 Federal Plaza's twenty-third floor, eyes glued to his monitor. He scrolled through the Au Bon Pain's security camera videos for maybe the hundredth time. The problem was that when positioning security cameras, fast-food managers were concerned with petty larceny, not homicide. As it happened, ten minutes prior to the Au Bon Pain shooting, one of the two cashiers whisked a dollar bill from her register drawer and into her blouse.

Lamont hoped to see the shooter arrive, Peretti and Thornton enter, or the crime itself. But all of that took place off camera. He slowed the video now in search of mere light fluctuations. What he wouldn't give for a shadow he hadn't already noticed.

His eye was drawn away from the computer by

the bank of fluorescents sputtering on. The cube farm transformed from a dawn-speckled gold to its true office-drab gray. At this time of day, the twenty-third floor could pass for the offices of any accounting firm or insurance agency. In a couple of hours, though, it would be more like the bleachers at Yankee Stadium, a microcosm of the city, packed with colorful characters such as his partner, Musseridge, who liked to share his opinions, often at the same time others were sharing theirs, making the place way, way more entertaining than the three field offices Lamont had rotated through during his rookie year. A cold, formal atmosphere was the norm.

He checked for e-mail, finding one from Musseridge, who had finally gone home late last night to have "a beer or six," as he put it, in hope of getting some shut-eye. Lamont clicked open the message, sent at 3:41 A.M.:

> corky, just remembering the journo thornton saying
> something about the shooter maybe getting a paper
> cut from one of the table ads at the frog place. i didn't
> put it in the 302 cause by then he was going on about
> a heat ray that sounded like his meds talking. but
> seeing how now we've got shinola . . .

Lamont hadn't seen a table ad or placard or anything of the kind listed on the FD-192, the crime scene unit's evidence list. That form had long since

been FedExed to the lab at Quantico along with all
pertinent items found at the Au Bon Pain. Nevertheless, the mere possibility that an exhausted investiga-
tor had bagged the ad and labeled it as something else
fired up Lamont like five cans of Monster Energy. An
error like that was a decent possibility, he thought.
To complete an FD-192, you had to detail every item
thoroughly, including an estimate of its dollar value,
and you had to do it by hand, meaning the form
wasn't available digitally. As Musseridge always said,
"Expect to see time travel before you see a paperless
Bureau."

Twenty minutes later, Lamont returned to his cube
with a copy of the FD-192, obtained from the rotor
clerk, the secretary who maintained pending case files
in a giant circular cabinet.

Lamont read the itemized list like it was a pot-
boiler, before reaching an unhappy ending: The closest thing to an advertisement from the restaurant was
a paper napkin.

On an off chance, he paid another visit to the rotor clerk, netting an FD-1004, the record of chain
of custody for additional evidence requiring special
handling.

It told the same story as the first form.

"Shinola," Lamont said to himself.

As he slumped in his desk chair, his gaze wandered to a printout of a photo, pinned to the side of
his cube, from his going-away party in Cleveland.

They'd taken him to a dingy pub off Market Avenue whose name he couldn't remember. It was the first and last time he and his colleagues had gone out after work—two pitchers of beer split between nine guys. He could just make out a dog-eared card on the grimy table, advertising the BRAT OF THE DAY.

Maybe the crime scene team had simply ignored a trampled placard lying on Au Bon Pain's floor, he thought. What if, once the restaurant reopened, someone just picked the thing up and stuck it back on a table?

He shot up in his chair, hammering his name and password onto his keyboard, then filling in the text boxes at the top of his screen and keying in a request for the Emergency Response Team's Au Bon Pain crime scene photos. A slug of Monster and a check of his in-box later, he saw that his security clearance had been verified by the Bureau's antiquated system. After a minute of churning, the monitor displayed a photo of a table with a tented advertisement for Au Bon Pain's new cheddar and corn chowder. Three more clicks showed almost identical ads on the three nearest tables. Thirteen more clicks revealed the same ad at each of the restaurant's twenty-six tables.

Except for one, the two-top closest to the men's room.

As if on cue came a raspy voice, grumbling that a large coffee used to be just fifty fucking cents. Peering over the workstation wall, Lamont spotted Musseridge shuffling from the elevator bank, balancing his usual cup of coffee—big enough to douse a fire.

Lamont bounded over, meeting Musseridge outside his office.

"Good morning," Lamont said.

"You're like my family," replied his official mentor.

"Thanks?"

"I get home and before I can take off my coat, they start in clamoring for me to fix this or pay for that." Musseridge elbowed his way into the office.

Lamont remained in the doorway, undaunted, while Musseridge took an excessive amount of time setting things down and carefully hanging up his overcoat. It was probably the first time in his life that Musseridge had put a coat someplace other than in a heap. Finally he said, "Okay, Corky, for the love of fucking Christ, tell me we got something."

"Tented ads were on all twenty-six tables—except the one nearest to the shooter."

"The ad got knocked onto the floor."

"It's not on the FD-192."

"Then it was so worthless, they left it on the floor."

"Suppose they didn't check it."

"They did."

"How do you know?"

"They expose every last square inch of the crime scene to blue light checking for blood spatter."

"I was thinking that the edges on the table plac-ards aren't that much thicker than a hair, so maybe the Emergency Response Team missed the blood," Lamont said.

"If the murder had taken place on a farm, I would bet on the ERT one-ninety-two-ing a needle in a haystack. And then they'd bag the whole fucking pile of hay." Musseridge slurped his coffee. He drank audibly only when he had an audience. "So what, you want to go there today?"

"Why not?"

"I'll tell you why not. Even if we find the magic flying placard, bringing it to a courtroom would be pointless. A piece of evidence that was left sitting for a week in a fast-food place is a defense attorney's wet dream."

"Still, if we find some DNA, we could narrow the list of suspects from three billion to one."

Musseridge switched on his computer and waited for it to come to life.

"And lunch is on me," Lamont added.

"I'll take that, but no way we're eating at Au Bon Pain."

"What's wrong with Au Bon Pain?"

"Nothing. But I thought you wanted to go there *today*."

"We need an EC for that?"

"What do you think?"

Lamont recited another Musseridge maxim: "You can't fart at the Bureau without first filling out a request form."

Musseridge nodded. "You're finally learning."

. . .

Returning to his cube, Lamont clicked the EC—electronic communication—macro in the keyboard's top row. The monitor gradually filled with a document template changed little since its WordPerfect inception in the early 1990s. He entered his name, his office location, and the eleven-character case ID, three times apiece. Before beginning his communication, he provided the requisite synopsis of it.

REQUEST TO RETURN TO LOCATION OF CASE 88A-NY-32478-7 SCENE FOR GENERAL INVESTIGATION

Finally he began the communication itself, referring to himself as THE WRITER per one of many Bureau directives whose purpose was lost to time.

THE WRITER SEEKS PERMISSION TO TRAVEL BY FBI VEHICLE TO

He paused to go online in order to collect the physical address of the Au Bon Pain as well as its telephone number.

By noon, he'd sent the completed EC to the division's supervisor, who, along with the Assistant Special Agent in Charge, had responded. The "mission" was a go. Just as soon as Lamont printed a hard copy of the EC, obtained the required signatures, photocopied the document three times, and, of course, filed the original.

At two fifteen, he and Musseridge stood in the parking garage. In Manhattan, the FBI needed to subcontract a valet service because, as Musseridge put it, "Finding a public parking spot around here takes longer than solving a case." Since the valets operated government vehicles, they had to undergo extensive vetting. Unlike in other parking garages, tipping wasn't permitted here, so turnover was high. New and inexperienced valets were the norm.

Following a wait of eight minutes—not bad— Musseridge hung a left out of the dark garage and into an explosion of daylight, making his way across Centre Street and onto the Brooklyn Bridge. Below the bridge, tugs and barges turned the East River into swirls of browns and grays, the view blurred by exhaust from stop-and-go traffic. Musseridge smiled, a rare occurrence. Lamont knew that after twenty-something years of driving the sort of American-made cars that ID'd you as a Fed sooner than your shield (Caprices and Crown Vics were known internally as G-cars), Musseridge savored the dealer-fresh white Cadillac Escalade SUV, part of his cover in an ongoing mob sting up at a Connecticut casino. Sitting in its leather sports seat was the only time he didn't complain about his back. Lamont attributed this to the thrill of the perk.

After another twenty minutes—possibly a record for the thirteen miles of I-278 and the Verrazano Bridge—Musseridge brought Uncle Sam's Caddy to a halt in the St. George Ferry Terminal parking lot on Staten Island. Before Lamont could set foot on the asphalt, he had to radio the NYO dispatcher with a street address, in case he and Musseridge were to require backup.

Entering the Au Bon Pain, it took Lamont a beat to get his bearings. He could have sketched its layout from memory. But the video hadn't encompassed much beyond the counter, and the photos had been stills. Now the place was full of the clamor and motion of the patrons and employees.

Because the store manager was cute or because there was free pastry in the offing, Musseridge assigned himself the task of apprising her of the FBI's presence and official operational objective, then obtaining her signed acknowledgment at the bottom of an FD-597, a form that yielded two carbon copies—using actual carbon paper.

Lamont found the table in question unoccupied, and replete with a tented advertisement for the restaurant's new cheddar and corn chowder. Sliding into one of the two chairs, he drew from his pocket a flashlight that to all appearances was a pen. He discreetly snapped a translucent orange disk the size of a dime over its bulb tip, then clicked on the 470-nanometer blue light, which would make bloodstains appear to darken, enhancing fourfold the contrast between the blood and the stained object. He aimed the beam at the triangular placard's three edges, and . . . nothing.

No surprise. The placards were replaced due to wear or, his hope now, shuffled between tabletops during cleanup.

He intended to scan every placard in the restaurant, but first he needed to come up with an explanation devoid of phrases like "blood spatter." While searching for the right words, he spun the placard before him. The photograph of the chowder made Lamont hollow with hunger; he'd eaten nothing since a cold slice yesterday afternoon. He would order something, he thought, until his blue beam ran across the placard's other side. Nothing on the left. But black spots on the right. Black spots that disappeared when he flicked off the blue light, meaning they were bloodstains.

He blinked to reboot an imagination that had possibly gotten the better of him. Again he saw the blood. This time it brought the euphoria of hitting a home run. Until he noticed a second substance within the blood. Probably the cleanser sprayed onto the tabletops. Cleansers typically contained ammonia or isopropanol, and the introduction of even water could kill DNA evidence. He could only pray that enough uncontaminated blood remained to make a match to an offender in the DNA database. Quantico was working on handheld devices that could profile such samples in seconds, determining the gender, ethnicity, and eye and hair color of the shooter, then search for matches in multiple DNA data banks around the world. Five years away, they said—which meant twenty-five, Musseridge said. For now Lamont opened a clear plastic evidence bag and dropped in the placard. He would collect the rest of the placards for good measure.

Although Quantico's evidence lab was the best in existence, it was far from the speediest. An expedited order could reduce the wait time only from weeks to days. All Lamont needed was a written request approved by his supervisor. And the Assistant Special Agent in Charge. And the Special Agent in Charge. And the Assistant Director in Charge. Still, the find was exciting enough that Musseridge forgot about getting the pastry in his rush to return to the office and launch into the paperwork.

11

Kevin O'Clair hadn't done fieldwork in his eleven years at the NSA. He'd never done fieldwork—period. This morning was a first. He drove his take from the divorce settlement—a ten-year-old beige Nissan Qwest minivan—along a desolate stretch of Queens Boulevard, passing discount stores, fast-food restaurants, and, mostly, abandoned office buildings. On a quiet side street between a run-down dry cleaner's and Bayside Putt-Putt—where the mini-golf course had been replaced by a go-kart track—he found Schechter's Home Appliances.

The store took up the first floor of a dilapidated split-level house. A worn banner announcing the business's fiftieth anniversary celebration sagged from the upper story. Who would ever guess that this location racked up $3 million in profits last year and stood to double that figure this year? Not even the proprietor, Irving Schechter, knew what a lucrative trade in electronic surveillance devices his son Leonard conducted from the basement.

O'Clair slowed as he drove past, on the lookout for any unusual motion.

"Then the Fire King said, 'I want the heads of all the Water Warriors,'" Nathan said from the booster seat in back, breaking O'Clair's concentration.

The seven-year-old retold television show episodes line by line. His facility was usually a source of wonder for O'Clair. Now it was throwing O'Clair off his game, and he needed to get back on it because of the black SUV that had been behind them since Queens Boulevard.

"Hang on just a sec, buddy," he said. "I really want to hear the rest of the story, but . . ."

Bypassing an open parking spot in front of Schechter's, he turned left onto a tree-lined residential block. The black SUV continued on, pulling into a Wendy's. O'Clair's shaky rearview showed a young woman yawning and stretching her arms as she slid from the driver's seat to the parking lot. Two boys flew out of the back. It was 9:42 on a Saturday. Probably a mom resorting to corn syrup to kill the eighteen minutes until the go-kart place opened, O'Clair thought.

Relieved, he doubled back to Schechter's while his son detailed the remainder of the plan for universal conquest. Bringing Nathan along this morning was a good cover, as long as he stayed in the minivan. Around strangers, there was a fair chance he would share the wrong information, like their names.

"Buddy, I'm going to need you to wait in here while Daddy runs into the store for a minute."

"But I'll get bored."

Just a few months ago, prior to reaching the age that he could be left alone however briefly, Nathan used to plead to be left in the car while O'Clair ran errands.

"I've got a question to keep you busy," O'Clair said.

Nathan perked up. "A puzzler?"

"Say you have building blocks that are each one foot long and one foot high. How many blocks would it take you to complete a wall ten feet long and five feet high?"

Nathan chewed it over while O'Clair parked in front of Schechter's.

"Got it," the boy exclaimed. "You need fifty blocks total, right?"

"Not quite. Again, how many to complete the wall?"

Nathan erupted into laughter. "Only one block to *complete* the wall."

Pride overrode O'Clair's disappointment in the longevity of the time killer. He reached around his headrest to his son's waiting palm for a resounding five.

"Okay, here's a tougher one: A Ping-Pong ball falls down a hole in a cement basement floor. The hole is one foot deep and only a tiny bit wider than the ball. How do you get the ball back out without damaging it if you can use only these three things: your Ping-Pong paddle, your shoelaces, and a plastic bottle of water?"

With Nathan lost in contemplation, O'Clair got out of the minivan and headed up a walkway of circular paving stones fragmented by wear and weeds. Ducking beneath the anniversary banner, he pushed open the door. An unseen bell tinkled as he entered an underheated showroom where off-brand toasters, blenders, irons, and vacuum cleaners packed worn shelves and glass display cases. Behind the counter, a doughy man of about seventy-five adjusted his bow tie. Thick eyeglasses magnified the hope in his watery eyes. "How may I help you, sir?" he asked.

"I'm here for the new iPod operating system."

The old man scowled. "Down the stairs." He shot a wrinkled hand at what appeared to be the door to a utility closet.

It led to a flight of warped stairs that groaned with each of O'Clair's steps. On a raised platform at the center of the basement room, Lenny Schechter sat puffing a clove cigarette in an ergonomic chair that faced a semicircle of six giant computer monitors. All four walls were lined with stacks of brown cardboard cartons stamped with Chinese characters, Lenny's inventory presumably—within days of an eavesdropping gadget hitting the market in the United States, manufacturers in Guangzhou started selling decent knockoffs at a fraction of the price.

Lenny resembled the man upstairs, minus forty years. He wore a pristine Mets hoody, vintage Adidas track pants, and a pair of fancy loafers. "How can I help, yo?" he asked, setting his cigarette in a chrome ashtray.

"I'm in the market for a nannycam," O'Clair said.

"This your 'client'?" Lenny tossed a glance at the upper left monitor.

Rounding the bank of monitors, O'Clair saw Nathan holding an imaginary Ping-Pong ball.

"My client, right," said O'Clair. "He's been learning French curse words from our *au pair*. Lord only knows what she's been doing to the poor kid while she's cursing."

Lenny shook his head in commiseration. "I hear this kinda thing way too much. The good news is that it translates into demand, then supply."

Like everyone at the NSA's New York office, O'Clair knew all about Lenny Schechter. Six years ago, his business consisted only of a URL and a conviction that search engines would bring him hordes of suspicious spouses and parents who didn't trust their nannies. Indeed, civilian eavesdropping exploded into a three-billion-dollar industry, but because the use of such products routinely violated electronic eavesdropping laws, placing the customer at risk of becoming another Linda Tripp and the seller being charged as an accessory, vendors preferred to operate in the shadows. Lenny was known at intelligence and law enforcement agencies not for any transgression but because agents did so much business with him. He provided the tools they needed at a fraction of the usual cost and without the government red tape. He even offered free overnight shipping.

This morning, O'Clair didn't have the luxury of time. The trap had been set. Thornton was due to meet someone "from the agency" at a Connecticut diner this afternoon. O'Clair had three hours to get the covert cameras in place.

"What do you have that's small and suitable for outdoor use?" he asked. Lenny's bestsellers, camcorders concealed in stuffed animals or potted plants, wouldn't work on the street.

Lenny tapped his keyboard. All six monitors combined to show a house key. "This little fella's the sweetest of the subminis on the market, if you're asking me. Captures audio within a twelve-foot radius and shoots up to eight hours of good-enough-to-incriminate-quality vid that you can download just by plugging it into a laptop or tablet. Same camcorder also comes in a ballpoint pen, a cigarette . . ."

The monitors flashed images of a Bic pen and what appeared to be an ordinary Lucky Strike, along with photos of cameras concealed in a pack of gum, a nickel, and an American Express card.

O'Clair paid $500 in cash for two sixty-four-megabyte cigarette-cams, the chargers and USB adaptors included.

Returning to the minivan, he was delighted when he opened the door to Nathan's exclamation of, "Pour the water into the hole and let the Ping-Pong ball float up."

12

Thornton sat at the wheel of his Inka orange 1973 BMW model 2002, a coupe that was at once boxy, sleek, art deco, and a rocket. His was also rusty and dinged and worth too little to interest car thieves—an ideal conveyance if your work took you to dicey places and you might need to get away in a hurry. Like most old cars, it was perpetually in need of one or two new parts at any time—a heater motor now—making it suitable for short drives in and around Manhattan, as opposed to the current eighty-mile journey on the Merritt Parkway through hard rain poised to become sleet and over slick autumn leaves. Normally Thornton would have used a rental car for a clandestine meeting, but this afternoon, he wanted a tail, so the conspicuous orange '02 was ideal.

It took an hour and a half to reach Torrington, Connecticut, a fading industrial town that remained gray even when the sun came out. He pulled into the gravel parking lot in front of Bill's, a vintage boxcar diner nestled against the radio station at the end of quiet Prospect Street. Taking a seat on a patched vinyl bench in the back booth, he ordered a late lunch and tried to block out the Muzak rendition of Barry Manilow's "Copacabana."

At three in the afternoon, the diner's population consisted of a stout Nicaraguan short-order cook with several gold teeth, an overweight middle-aged waitress, and a wan elderly woman nursing a cup of tea. None looked like surveillants, though that could have been the precise reason for their deployment.

Finishing his plate of spaghetti, Thornton paid, returned to his car, and drove halfway down the block before rolling into a gas station, an Exxon largely unchanged since its Esso days. He spotted no vehicles or pedestrians following him.

Leaving the tank set to fill with premium, he wandered into the minimart and chose an orange Gatorade from the refrigerated case. He paid with a fifty so that he would receive plenty of change, hidden among which, a surveillant might suspect, was a message. The young cashier had a pretty face and a set of curves that elevated her bland UConn sweatshirt to alluring. He asked her what she thought of the basketball team's chances come March. She made a compelling argument that the Huskies would once again reach the Final Four. He acted pleased, and in fact he was: If anyone were watching him, this conversation would raise a flag.

Three hours later, he arrived at O'Clair's Jersey City apartment building, which could have passed for a penal institution if not for the parking lot shared with the FedEx depot. Cobra-head streetlights burned so brightly that the night resembled dusk. O'Clair ushered Thornton into a ground-floor apartment that looked to have been decorated—carpets, furniture, even the four-by-six-foot oil painting of the Taj Mahal—with a brief trip to Sam's Club.

"You good with burritos for dinner?" asked O'Clair, leading the way into the kitchenette.

"That'd be great, thanks." Thornton set his overcoat on a barstool.

"Super." O'Clair set the microwave whirring. "Because I realized that microwave ovens have the same effect as radio jammers."

Thornton was grateful to be able to speak, rather than write notes by hand, which, since leaving the railroad tunnel, had been his only reliable method of communication with O'Clair.

"The hitch," O'Clair added, "is that keeping it on for more than eight minutes could arouse suspicion." Directing Thornton to a laptop computer at the ready on the adjacent counter, he brought up startlingly crisp images of Bill's Diner shot from across the street. "This starts at noon, about three hours before you got to Torrington," he said.

They watched time-lapse video of the lunchtime crowd leaving, one or two patrons at a time. Over the next hour, nobody entered the diner except a mail carrier who stayed for the time required to deliver a small stack of envelopes. After the mail truck shot back onto Prospect Street, the lot was lifeless until a comet slowed to Thornton's orange BMW. He was shown entering the diner and then, through a window, sitting down and ordering. After he left and drove off, no one entered for forty-two minutes, when four teenage boys pedaled up, dropped their bicycles, and piled into a booth.

"I didn't see anyone precede or follow you to the diner or to the gas station," O'Clair said. "You?"

"I didn't see a thing. But what if, at some point, a surveillant pulled up in a car across the street, offscreen?"

"That's what I figured. So I duct-taped a second cig-cam inside a trash basket at the end of Prospect Street, the lens aimed out through the perforated metal." O'Clair winced as he queued up the second video. "I'm afraid this makes the first tape look like an action flick."

The camera provided clear panoramic video of a beauty shop, a fast-food restaurant, a ninety-nine-cent shop, and several empty storefronts across Prospect Street from the diner. A painted Singer sewing machine ad had mostly flaked or chipped off the brick wall of the block's largest building, a vacant bank. The weekday traffic was sparse. The eatery and the Exxon station garnered all of the vehicles that stopped, save a van that parallel parked in front of the beauty parlor. The uniformed driver went into the beauty parlor; his features were mostly veiled by a baseball cap and sunglasses.

Stabbing at the van, whose logo matched the patches on the driver's uniform, Thornton exclaimed, "AT&T."

"What about it?"

"A Verizon van followed Catherine and me from Chinatown."

"Telephone services vans aren't exactly rare." O'Clair dropped onto a stool.

"What do you know about F6?"

"I take it you don't mean the function key on my computer."

"It's the code name for a CIA program, known by everyone involved as the Special Collection Service."

"How do you know about it?"

"I probably shouldn't, but a few years ago, I had a source who ran the New York bureau. The Special Collection Service's sole responsibility is bugging places that are almost impossible to access. My source used to use telephone and utility company service vans for cover all the time."

"So do other surveillants," O'Clair said. "And,

mostly, telephone and utility company employees. With respect to your source, nowadays those trucks are almost a cliché—anyone who's ever seen a cop show would be wary. Our people pose as cable TV or Internet providers. Cut the service, the residents beg you to come in. Sometimes they go as a tree-trimming company: gets them access to high floors. Or plumbers or exterminators, which gets them access anywhere—people want those sort of problems taken care of stat."

Thornton had figured as much. "The thing is, the same source invited me to a black-tie charity ball that's this weekend. I'd been looking forward to not going."

13

Traffic clogged the Jersey Turnpike. Hard rain and sleet hammered the Cadillac. As Musseridge drove, he grumbled about the latest round of nonessential home renovations that his wife considered vital. Next to him, Lamont couldn't have been happier. Just three days after receiving the ad from the Au Bon Pain, Quantico had a result: COLD HIT. The blood matched nine of the thirteen chromosome locations, or loci, on an FBI database specimen from a white forty-one-year-old named Ralph Brackman. In 1996, the failed academic had served a month for cocaine possession and distribution. The Bureau put the odds of unrelated people sharing so many genetic markers at approximately one in 113 billion.

An hour later, Musseridge parked the Escalade

across from Brackman's house, a run-down 1960s ranch, similar to half of the homes on the suburban block in Teaneck, New Jersey. The rest of the houses were undergoing major renovations or had already been expanded into residences that dwarfed their tenth-of-an-acre lots. Brackman's place sat between a three-story Tudor replete with turret and a sprawling yellow Mediterranean villa.

The backup team from the Newark field office radioed their readiness from a white cargo van parked at the far end of the block. Lamont received a similar message from one of the Teaneck PD patrol cars, the cops reporting that Brackman's wife had left home an hour ago, driving the couple's two young children to a local Catholic school, before proceeding to her secretarial job at a commercial construction company.

Getting out of the Cadillac, Lamont hoped the Teaneck PD also had eyes on Brackman, given the suspect's skill as a marksman. Alleged skill. The record offered nothing to suggest he was a hit man. Ralph Gerard Brackman was the only surviving child of Arthur and Penny Flaherty Brackman, who had been lifelong residents of Brooklyn. After graduating from City College in 1994, Ralph Brackman bounced around the tristate area in a series of career false starts and extensive stretches of unemployment. Now he worked out of his house as an "Internet consultant." There was no hint of criminal activity since the coke bust, no visits to pistol ranges, not even a parking ticket—though assassins took pains to avoid leaving such trails.

Lamont pressed the buzzer, and he and Musseridge waited on the stoop for twelve seconds, the average time span from ringing a bell to an open door. Converting his excitement into hyperawareness, Lamont noticed for the first time the cold drizzle, and, on the two neighboring houses, flames swaying in unison in lanterns suspended above the front doors. Then he heard hurried footfalls inside. Maybe the suspect had been in the can. Or readying a weapon. Lamont inched a hand closer to his holster.

Brackman cracked the front door. Unlike the shooter described by witnesses at the St. George Ferry Terminal, he was thin. Of course, he might have used padding as part of his disguise that night, or worn Kevlar. He also looked remarkably cheerful: His eyes sparkled, and his wide mouth seemed set in a smile, even as he peered out, circumspect, from beneath the bill of a Phillies cap. Rosy cheeks added to a youthfulness that made it easy to overlook the gray in his curly black hair. He wore only an undershirt, sweatpants, and socks. No sign of a concealed weapon.

"You guys from the FBI?" he asked.

If this surprised Musseridge, he didn't show it. "You expecting the FBI?"

"No, but the local detectives don't wear suits, and, all due respect, you guys look too old to be Mormon missionaries."

"So you were expecting detectives?"

"I'm the only person in the neighborhood who's been convicted of anything heavier than a DUI, so I get plenty of opportunities to 'assist' local law enforcement." Brackman pulled open the door. "Why don't you come in out of the rain? Tell me what I've done this time."

He was too cool, thought Lamont, joining Musseridge in the small foyer. The space opened to a living room lined with stain-them-yourself wooden shelves filled with books. The combination of a futon, a pair of worn Naugahyde recliners, and a large TV suggested the room was the hub of Brackman family life. A sleek MacBook sat on a coffee table alongside a chess game in progress. Although cramped, the room had the ordered quality of a ship.

Brackman waved at the computer. "Please, have a seat in my office." He sank onto the futon, the coffee table blocking the lower half of his body from the agents' view. Lamont wondered if the maneuver had been the calculated action of a veteran suspect. FBI researchers estimated that two-thirds of human communication is nonverbal. When a subject shifts uncomfortably in his seat, for instance, it's often an autonomic way of dissipating tension, indicative of deception. Ideally, your subject sits in a swivel chair that amplifies such behavior.

Musseridge smiled as he dropped into one of the recliners. "Phils fan, huh?" he asked Brackman.

It was a textbook opening to develop rapport. Musseridge could have gone straight for the jugular with, "Brackman, did you kill Catherine Peretti?" But casual conversation created a nonthreatening atmosphere. People tended to trust other people—law enforcement officers included—who were like them. And if you could get them going on neutral topics, like sports, kids, or yard care, it made it easier to tell when they began lying.

Lamont suspected Brackman knew how to game the system when he answered Musseridge by hesitating before asking, "Am I fan of the Phils?" Then he took off his cap and studied the logo. To buy time, a person bent on deception often repeats your question or pauses inordinately long before answering. People think ten times faster than they speak, so a pause of just five seconds can net nearly a minute's worth of material. Finally, Brackman said, "Two seasons ago, my son's little league team was called the Phillies. This past season, we were the Padres, which bummed the kids out—because of our proximity to Philadelphia, a lot of them are true Phillies fans. As a volunteer coach, I felt bad for the kids. I do enjoy the major leagues, but because I spend so much time with my family, I don't have time to follow the actual Phillies."

Overly specific answers also signaled deception. The subject inundates you with unrelated facts intended to influence your perception of his character. In this case, Brackman conveyed that he sympathized with the kids, volunteered to coach them, and sacrificed his enjoyment of major league baseball for family. When Musseridge veered to the topic of the murder, Lamont thought, Brackman could delay with impunity and provide all the superfluous details he wanted.

Musseridge sat forward. "Mr. Brackman, first of all, thank you for talking to us. We understand you're a busy guy, so I'll get right to the point. We're working the Catherine Peretti case."

Brackman squared a throw pillow beside him— tidying up surroundings was another classic means of dissipating anxiety. "The politician who was killed in the city?" he said. "Is *that* what this is about?"

"What do you know about the assassin?" Musseridge asked.

Nice play, Lamont thought, because the question carried the presumption that Brackman knew the killer was an assassin, a fact that hadn't been made public. If Brackman were innocent, he would say, simply, that all he knew was that Peretti had been killed.

Brackman cleared his throat. Another red flag— anxiety spikes can cause dryness in the throat. "It's news to me that it was an *assassination*," he said.

"Is there any reason you would have been at the ferry terminal in Staten Island at the time of the murder?" Musseridge countered, weighting his question with "bait," intended to deluge the suspect with new concerns: a witness who'd seen him leaving the terminal, security camera tape, or bio evidence the crime scene unit had recovered. If he were innocent, he wouldn't take the bait, but simply answer, *No*.

"It's been three, four years since the last time I was on Staten Island," Brackman said. "Some friends and I lucked into a box at a Staten Island Yankees game, but I had to leave after the fifth inning to pick up my kids. I swear to God, I haven't been to Staten Island since."

More points toward Dad of the Century. Plus he'd invoked God, at once asserting piety and calling on the best witness in the universe. In sum, textbook dressing up of a lie.

Musseridge leaned closer to Brackman, invading his personal space. "How do you explain your appearance on the surveillance video at the crime scene?"

Lamont questioned the bluff. Because their evidence was inadmissible in court, they needed cooperation from Brackman. At Quantico, Lamont had studied reams of cases in which murderers confessed. If Brackman thought Musseridge was lying, he would clam up.

Without swallowing hard, blushing, twitching, running his hand through his hair, or anything else on the list of mendacity telltales, Brackman replied, "I have two explanations for that. The first is, you've got it plumb wrong. The second is, the surveillance video was somehow altered, which would be fine by me because I would get rich suing whoever it was who did it. All things considered, though, I'd prefer to put this matter to rest, so let me show you—"

"Just hang on," Musseridge cut him off. Allowing a suspect to deny guilt increases his confidence. "We have one other problem, which is that you left some of your blood at the crime scene."

"Some of my blood was at the crime scene?" Brackman repeated the statement as a question.

Musseridge said nothing.

"When exactly was the crime?" Brackman asked.

"A week ago Tuesday."

Brackman appeared to mull it over. "Tuesdays my daughter has gymnastics, then my son has Boy Scouts." He shut his eyes, sometimes a subconscious reaction by a subject reluctant to see the reaction to the lie he'd just told. Opening his eyes, Brackman added, "After gymnastics last Tuesday, Scouts was a double feature— a den meeting followed by the monthly pack meeting. Then, at six o'clock, we had the annual Pinewood Derby. That's where you whittle blocks of wood into cars and race them down chutes. It's broadcast live on local cable. I'm not particularly proud of how our car did, but I'd be happy to show you the video if it means I can stop being a murder suspect and get back to work."

He snapped open his MacBook, clicked to a You-Tube page, and spun the monitor toward them, showing video of him with a boy who appeared delighted even when race cars that looked to have been assembled by NASA blew past his rolling doorstop.

"When did you get home?" Musseridge left unsaid that the Pinewood Derby timeline might still have permitted Brackman to drop his son and then drive to Staten Island by 9:13, when Peretti was shot.

"Let's see." Brackman hummed for a moment. "We left Scouts at around seven thirty or seven forty-five, then grabbed dinner at the Olive Garden in Secaucus. I guess we got back here around nine thirty. Pretty late for a school night."

Twenty minutes later, Lamont and Musseridge waited while the manager of the Secaucus Olive Garden cued up security camera video taken three minutes after the Peretti shooting. In it, Brackman appeared at the cash register desk, handed over his credit card, and helped himself to a mint.

"This fucking guy ever do anything that's not videotaped?" Musseridge said to Lamont on the way out of the restaurant.

Although the sky had cleared and the traffic was light, the return to New York seemed to take longer than the ride out. Even Musseridge was quiet. What was there to say? A DNA false-positive was a one-in-379 occurrence. The big game, the one for which Lamont had been jacked up all season, had been abruptly canceled.

Musseridge finally broke the silence at the Lincoln Tunnel. "Good news is it wouldn't have been admissible evidence anyway."

14

The Connecticut coast flew past the BMW 2002's passenger side, a sapphire Long Island Sound making appearances in Morse code bursts in and around clusters of trees at peak autumn splendor. Thornton paid the scenery no more than a passing glance. He was absorbed in trying to find a connection beyond telephone company service vans between the charity ball's host, onetime Special Collection Service agent Andrew Nolend, and Catherine Peretti. Three days of discreet digging—quiet use of public computers and print sources so as not to leave a digital trail—had provided no evidence that Nolend had known Peretti, had even been in the same city as her at the same time, or was in any way associated with her. More significantly, the Andy Nolend who

Thornton knew would never intentionally engage in impropriety, if only because it risked besmirching the "record," as he regarded not only his career but his life. Five years had passed, however, since Thornton had spent time with Nolend for anything more than an annual beer.

They first met eight years ago, when Nolend broke Thornton's nose. Having just arrived from Buenos Aires to serve as chief of the Special Collection Service's New York bureau, Nolend thrust a bony fist into the air in celebration after winning a United Nationals recreational rugby league game. Or, rather, Nolend intended to thrust his fist into the air. Thornton's face was in the way.

Despite the awkward beginning, they established a rapport bordering on friendship; Nolend liked to show off his near-encyclopedic knowledge of the foreign diplomats and industrial magnates among his subjects, and Thornton liked to listen. He realized that Nolend's expertise wasn't founded upon an interest in intelligence gathering or national security so much as an infatuation with his subjects' third homes and private jets—in short, a way of life attainable to a spy only if he sneaks in. It was no surprise a year later when Nolend left government service for the private sector, taking a job in a Los Angeles advertising agency that sought to win government billings. He did well there, garnering sufficient clientele from Silicon Valley to hang out his own shingle in San

Francisco's Mission District. Before long, his business filled two floors in the Transamerica Pyramid.

Thornton wondered why Nolend had issued him a free ticket to tonight's $10,000-a-plate event. *Real-Story* posted almost no society news. His best guess was that his old rugby teammate sought to flaunt his success, including his young second wife.

After parking at a long-term lot in Hyannis, Thornton boarded a hydrofoil that covered the twenty-two miles of a placid Nantucket Sound in an hour. Nantucket was a summer resort island that saw little tourism in November. Thornton had expected the high-speed ferry to be packed with people who looked like they could drop $10,000 on a plate. There were few passengers, though, all obviously townies.

At the wharf in Nantucket, Nolend was waiting in a silver mid-1950s Mercedes 300SL worth as much as Thornton's apartment. The onetime spook wore a royal blue linen blazer and a pair of Nantucket Reds, the salmon-pink chinos that had been fashionable on the island for a century. His polo shirt no longer hung off a cranelike physique, instead clinging fast to a build that told of hours in the weight room. His hair was sculpted too, layered with obvious precision. His infectious smile was the same as ever—though his teeth were whiter. "Great to see you, Russ," he said.

Thornton pulled the gull-wing door down with him as he sank into the leather passenger seat. He burned to say, *Nice to see you in something other than a phone company van for a change*, but opted for, "Same."

A delicate piano concerto drifted from at least eight speakers. The hot air from the vents felt good after the ferry ride.

"New station car?" Thornton asked.

"I've taken up collecting automobiles." Nolend's attempt to shift into gear resulted in a metallic grinding.

"For your kids?" Nolend's son and daughter from his first marriage would be about four and six, Thornton thought.

"For some reason, clients are more impressed by this thing than they were with my old Wagoneer." Nolend found first gear, sending the Mercedes banging across the wharf's wooden slats and up Main Street, a cobblestone block sided by high-end boutiques in the guise of quaint village shops. In two centuries, the village's primary external change had been the electrification of the streetlamps, and even that stirred a prolonged dispute between Nantucket's two factions, preservationists and fanatical preservationists. The most modern-leaning among the preservationists still maintained that the exterior walls of every structure be clad with the same unpainted, unvarnished, weather-grayed cedar shingles in which Herman Melville presented the island in *Moby-Dick*.

Nolend waved at the fork where Main branched off to Liberty Street. "Our new place has a guesthouse. How about you stay there instead of the hotel? The Seven Seas is quaint, but it always smells like low tide."

Thornton would have leaped at an invitation to stay in Nolend's outhouse for the proximity to clues. "As long as I don't have to share a bed with a savage harpooner, thanks."

Nolend continued onto Upper Main, which was lined with stately houses that originally belonged to whaleship captains. From there, the Mercedes zoomed west past vast cranberry bogs before the grass on the roadsides yielded to sand. Like most of his neighbors, Nolend had a driveway made of crushed clamshells, but his led to no house, just a boat slip, where a gleaming nineteenth-century paddle steamer rose and fell with the waves. A boatman emerged from the tiny wheelhouse as Nolend steered the car onto the deck.

"Good evening, sir," the man said.

Nolend cracked the driver's window. "How are things, Captain?"

Releasing the bowline, the captain said, "The bay's behaving herself this evening." He returned to the wheelhouse and fired the engine, starting the stern-mounted cylindrical wheel spinning, propelling the craft forward.

Thornton followed Nolend out of the car and onto a bench at the stern, behind the wheelhouse. As Nantucket drifted aft, the paddles accelerated, the slaps

against the water building to a steady and tranquil-
izing thrum.

Pointing to a nebulous landmass in the distance,
Nolend said, "The new place is on Muskeget."

"Doesn't the preservation trust prohibit building
on Muskeget?" asked Thornton.

"Well, there's been a *slight* modification of the
rules. A couple years ago, I heard about a seaman's
shack from the nineteenth century that was still
standing on the north shore of the island. I bought
it, suggested to the preservation trust's approvals
committee that it was a matter of civic duty for me
to restore and maintain the residence, providing we
added a few modern amenities, and maybe a few extra rooms. In essence, the code says that if you leave
one beam from the original structure standing and
shingle the exterior with cedar, you can do whatever
you'd like with the rest of the place. The day before
the approvals committee had to vote on our plan, by
the by, the chairman got an insanely good deal on my
Wagoneer."

As the boat drew closer, the hazy mass ahead
sharpened to dunes, atop which sat a block-long gray-
shingled house with a steeply pitched roof and cut-
stone chimneys. The more Thornton saw, the less he
believed that the AT&T van in Torrington and the
invitation here had been coincidental.

He tried an appeal to Nolend's vanity. "So I take it
your new bride isn't a government employee."

"Luisana was successful as a fashion model before she came to the States, but I would have married her regardless. Wait until you meet her. Gorgeous, and, thankfully, no interest whatsoever in little ones."

"But you have two little ones."

"Little enough to require diaper changes, I should say."

Thornton took a stab. "So I heard a rumor about another windfall of yours."

"Yeah?" Nolend regarded the paddle wheel. "Which one?"

"The one that got you your own island."

Nolend glanced back at the wheelhouse. The captain was absorbed in directing the vessel toward the dock.

"For your ears only?" Nolend asked Thornton.

Thornton started to say yes, amending it to, "Off the record, for background use only."

"Well, old chum, it turned out that the advertising game was short on spooks."

"Lucky for you, huh?"

"I learned that selling isn't as much about generating demand as understanding it, then telling people you have exactly what they want. Agencies and clients spend millions on focus groups, but most of the time come away with no idea of what influences purchases."

"So did you bring in the Stargaters?" Thornton was referring to the trio of psychics employed by the

CIA as part of an operation code named Stargate. They were eventually let go due to their complete inability to demonstrate psychic power.

Nolend laughed. "A couple years ago, after a brutally long and fruitless week of focus groups at a mall in Boise, one of our clients threw up his hands and said that he would pay any amount of money to be a fly on the wall in typical consumers' homes, to hear what they really thought as opposed to what they said in skewed focus groups. It gave me an idea. I had dinner with another old F-Sixer, a tech guy who was teaching electrophysics down at Stanford, and we ended up creating a device that actually allowed clients to be the fly on the wall and then some. To make a long story short, it bought me an island."

"So what's the 'it'?" Thornton asked as though merely interested.

Nolend seemed to deliberate, fighting back a smile before giving in. Thornton guessed that pride had won out. "You've seen a nanodrone before, right?"

"No, and I thought nobody can see one."

"You can—if you know where and when to look, and it catches the light. We reverse-engineered an F6 model, added audio, then flew the thing right into a prospective customer's kitchen."

"Probably Pollyannaish of me to ask, but isn't that illegal?"

"No, not if you get a signed release. For what the ad agency pays, the subjects never bother to read the fine print. Still, in case one of our rivals or some rabble-rouser gets a look at the release form, I'm checking into relocating our listening post from San Francisco to Barbados. When I played for the Sixers, I heard rumint about a domestic black op that put a listening post on Barbados because the island has virtually no electronic eavesdropping regulations. The audio goes to a transcription service, then the people at the service send the spooks in the U.S. *written* transcripts. It's a legal loophole."

Good old Barbados, Thornton thought. The Caribbean island was an offshore business paradise based on the minimal extent to which laws were enforced.

"As you can imagine, the intel we've gotten has been fantastic," Nolend went on. "Our proprietary research won the accounts I was able to found my agency on, and since then, business has been going so well it feels like cheating."

This was not the sort of admission made by someone complicit in a crime, Thornton thought. In any case, it provided the flimsiest of leads. If the domestic eavesdropping operation were black—the "black" meaning the elimination of any connection between what's being done and who's doing it—Nolend probably knew no more about it, and Thornton would find it near impossible to learn anything, even without the encumbrance of his eavesdropper. If and when such black ops appeared on government ledgers, they were veiled as "Transit Analysis Project" or "Currency

Classification Initiative" or something even blander.
Always best to keep Congress in the dark, the spooks
believed; oversight has a way of revealing the intelligence services' best-laid clandestine plans to their
targets.

Thornton still intended to extract all the information he could from Nolend. But before he could ask
another question, they reached the Madaket pier,
where a small crowd of event planners descended
upon the host.

While changing into his tux in a palatial room in the
"guesthouse"—essentially a twelve-bedroom luxury
hotel—Thornton reflected that his investigation had
yet to advance beyond square one: Some entity has
a superbug. The telephone company vans and Nolend's invitation—mailed to Thornton's apartment
two months ago and printed weeks before that—were
probably just coincidence after all. Thornton considered the familiar espionage refrain, *There are no
coincidences*. He countered it with the fact that John
Adams and Thomas Jefferson both died of natural
causes on July 4, 1826, the fiftieth anniversary of the
signing of the Declaration of Independence. And five
years later, July 4, 1831, president number five, James
Monroe, succumbed to mortality.

Thornton didn't see Nolend again until that evening, at a predinner speech in a room that evoked

a royal reception hall. Nolend was introducing the speaker, the director of the famine relief organization the event benefited, when Thornton found a seat in an audience of 400 people, many of whom he recognized from their positions in American government, business, and entertainment. His eyes were drawn to a strikingly beautiful woman in the last row. During the speech, he stole a look over his shoulder every chance he got. He'd seen her before on television, where she appeared pale. In the flesh, her paucity of cosmetics emphasized creamy skin, and silvery strands highlighted a chute of black hair. She wore a full-length, glittering amber gown that took to her lithe form like gold foil on fancy chocolate. Far and away her most compelling feature, though, was a detail Thornton had read about her recent run for political office: By revealing secrets from her personal life that she'd reportedly never shared, her opponent, Senator Gordon Langlind, had narrowly won reelection.

15

For security's sake, Tim Eppley had committed the directions to the safe house to memory. He was careful to keep his rental Kia below the speed limit. A fifty-buck ticket now could end up costing him a thousand times as much later tonight. Driving eastbound on the Chesapeake Bay Road, staying below forty miles per hour was no problem. The two-lane route was winding, slick, and dark—lined by so many trees that it was hard to believe there was a 64,000-square-mile body of water a few feet to his left. The still-leafy branches extended over the road, obscuring the moon and stars. The Kia's headlights reached into the darkness like luminous sleeves, revealing only the rutted pavement ahead and the occasional pine bough flying past.

Eppley tried to tone down his excitement in order to focus on driving. He'd been paid $25,000 in advance, and now, having finished assembling the E-bomb prototype, he stood to get another fifty K. Not bad for three weeks' work, especially for an unemployed twenty-year-old Cal-Tech dropout. Better, he stood to land a full-time gig at Blaise, arguably the most innovative advanced weapons development shop since the Skunk Works. The best part about the prospective gig was the chance to get to know his idol, Curtis Brockett, who, too, had wasted a year in school, at MIT, before founding Blaise and, five years later, making the *Forbes* list.

Three weeks ago, Brockett sent Eppley an e-mail beginning with a quotation from Sun-tzu's *The Art of War*: "Be extremely subtle, even to the point of formlessness. Be extremely mysterious, even to the point of soundlessness. Thereby you can be the director of the opponent's fate." The remainder of the message was just one sentence: "Opportunity's knocking, amigo." It was signed, "CB."

Eppley wasted no time in responding with another of the ancient Chinese general's maxims: "Opportunities multiply as they are seized."

A few hours later, Eppley's trial assignment commenced with a Hushmail from Steve Griffin, the VP of security based at Blaise's D.C. office. When deciphered, the message instructed Eppley to go to the Starbucks a mile from his Denver apartment, then check beneath the composting barrel left outside, full of coffee grounds for use by gardeners. The metal hoop around the bottom of the barrel extended below the base by an inch. Duct-taped into the hollow beneath the base, Eppley found a freezer bag with $45,000 in cash, his advance plus operating expenses.

Now Eppley turned right onto Griffin's street, Hill Road. After a mile, the beachy houses ended, as did the pavement, but Hill Road itself continued in dirt, ascending its namesake, terminating after another mile. He swung the Kia onto the dirt driveway, his headlights showing him a solitary saltbox cottage on a bluff with a commanding view of a bay, a matrix of purples, blacks, and grays intermittently flickering white in the starlight. There was one car in the driveway, another Kia. Although Hertz had given Eppley his Kia at random, he congratulated himself for driving the same car as Griffin, who was probably, like most tech-firm security guys, ex-CIA.

A few lights were on in the house. Getting out of his car, Eppley heard the ebb and flow of televised talk-show audience laughter. Anticipation offsetting his nerves, he hurried up a gravel path to the front door, on which, as instructed, he knocked four times.

The door opened inward, revealing a man in his mid- to late thirties with the erect bearing and boxy build indigenous to the military; his gray business suit conformed to muscles that looked like rocks. He wore his sandy hair cropped close. Not a crew cut; more like the cuts on actual oarsmen. His sturdy, chiseled face could have made him a soap-opera heartthrob if not for the cold eyes.

"Mr. Griffin?" Eppley asked, regretting the trade-craft breach as soon as the name was out of his mouth.

"Call me Steve, please," the man said in a voice that was surprisingly soft and cultured, rather than the bark presaged by his appearance. "Mr. Griffin was my father, and a deadbeat." He offered his hand.

"Great to meet you, Steve," said Eppley, struggling to keep from squirming as his right hand was nearly crushed.

"How about a drink?" Griffin asked.

What Eppley wouldn't have done for alcohol. But something told him the correct answer was no. "I'm good."

"Don't worry, it's not a test question. I could tolerate a vodka tonic myself."

"Well, I wouldn't want you to drink alone."

"Excellent." Griffin stepped into the kitchen, where the drink fixings waited on a granite counter. He waved Eppley ahead into the living room, which was painted sky blue and furnished sparsely in typical rental-house fashion, things the owner wouldn't give a damn about if they were broken or stained with red wine.

A few moments later, Griffin carried in a pair of translucent red plastic cups, the indestructible sort often found in such houses. Handing Eppley his, the

Blaise exec said, "Here's to being single, seeing double, and sleeping triple."

"Cheers," said Eppley, put at ease.

Griffin dropped into the adjacent wicker armchair, gesturing Eppley into the vinyl-covered sofa on the other side of the laminate coffee table.

"So tell me about your trip here," Griffin said.

This *was* a test question, Eppley knew. Secrecy was as much a part of Blaise as science. "That's a long story, starting with a severely mentally handicapped guy about my age who's been confined to a state-run home in northern Nevada for eight years."

Griffin sat back, propping black loafers beside the laptop case on the coffee table. "That's exactly the type of story I was hoping to hear."

"I took a back door into the state home's system and obtained a copy of the guy's birth certificate. I used it to get a driver's license and a credit card in his name, sent to an accommodation address. For the record, it was he who rented the Kia parked outside, and you're now talking to him. Then he—or, between us, *I*—drove cross-country in six days, stopping to buy our components at out-of-the-way academic supply stores, mom-and-pop electronics shops, places like that, paying in cash—thanks for that, by the way."

"I'd tell you you're welcome, but I get the feeling that I'm the one who ought to be thanking you," Griffin said.

With rising confidence, Eppley resumed his account. "When I got to your facility, I told the office manager that I was the representative from Exxon's engineering division, there to assemble the prototype of the portable petroleum hydrocarbon detector. Just like you'd said he would, he asked me how the drive from *New Orleans* was. So I said the line, 'Great, because I won a hundred bucks playing the slots at a Choctaw casino along the way.' Then he showed me into the back office, and that was about as much interaction as we had in the five days it took me to assemble the 'portable petroleum hydrocarbon detector.'"

Griffin gripped the arms of his chair, seemingly bridling his excitement. "So you did it?"

Eppley put on whiz-kid nonchalance. "It wasn't that much more complicated than following a recipe." He unzipped his jacket pocket, dug out the dedicated cell phone, and placed it on the coffee table. "And now it's good to go."

"*This* is the remote detonator?" Griffin asked.

Eppley worried that Griffin was disappointed. "I know, I know. You see it all the time in B-movies, but ordinary cell phones really are the state-of-the art remote detonators. All you need to do here is press down on the five key to speed-dial the number for Bob programmed into the contacts. Bob is the cell phone that's inside the weapon. When it gets the call, its vibrate wheel spins, triggering a low-amp wire fuse that detonates the half-pound brick of Comp C and PBX-9501."

"What if 'Bob' were to get a wrong number?"

"He can't. This is the only phone that can call his cell phone. I coupled the two phones into what amounts to their own Centrex network."

Griffin sat back, regarding Eppley with what appeared to be awe. "Mr. Eppley, Blaise Advanced Development Programs owes you a debt much greater than the fifty thousand dollars you're now due. I'd like to read you an e-mail that says exactly what Curtis Brockett has in mind."

Eppley tried to rein in his smile as Griffin reached into the laptop case on the coffee table. Griffin drew out a pistol. Eppley felt his scalp tighten with fear and—

Canning snapped the trigger, the loudest part of firing the integrally suppressed .22, sending a hand-cast thirty-eight-grain soft-lead bullet over the coffee table and into Eppley's forehead. The kid fell over backward, taking the cheap sofa with him. He bleated pathetically, but only for a few seconds. Then his central nervous system quit and he lay still. Canning liked the soft-lead rounds because they stayed in the head, which meant no gore on the safe house furniture. A little blood and brain matter oozed from the entry wound, sliding down Eppley's face, but that was the extent of it. Now all Canning needed to do was get rid of the corpse, and he would be in the "portable petroleum hydrocarbon detector" business.

16

The so-called barn on Madaket was almost as large as Nolend's house, with an interior of burnished cedar planks that would have been gleaming tonight even without the constellation of candles suspended from the rafters. If the place had any of the smells found in actual barns, like the musky scents of horses and hay, they were lost in warm air redolent of the exotic flowers representing every color in the spectrum, in mountainous centerpieces on fifty tables brimming with crystal and silver. Enjoying hors d'oeuvres and aperitifs, guests milled about a space that could be divided into dozens of stalls were the barn ever to accommodate livestock. Where a hayloft might go, there was a stage on which twenty-six Boston Pops musicians, all clad in tuxedo jackets and pairs of

Nantucket Reds, played an up-tempo waltz. Mallery sat alone at table eight, the fluttering candlelight underscoring the sharpness of her features in a way that reminded Thornton of Garbo.

He planned to wander over, introduce himself, then, at some juncture, ask her to dance. If she accepted, he would try to feel for a capsule underneath her scalp.

Before he could take a step in her direction, she was joined at table eight by a towering man whom Thornton had interviewed years ago. Back then, Clay Harken was the chief of the CIA's Special Activities Staff. Thornton didn't know what Harken had been doing professionally since retiring from the Agency, but in graying, he'd acquired the right look for a dramatic turn as King Arthur. Harken took the seat beside Mallery's, setting champagnes in front of both of their places. They clinked the flutes, her smile measurable in kilowatts. She was left-handed, for what that was worth. Nothing, thought Thornton, trying to conceive a new plan of approach.

He doubled back to the entrance, stopping at the table covered with tented white cards on the one-in-fifty shot that his read *Eight*.

Thirty-four.

The card gave him an idea, though.

A few minutes later, he returned from his room and headed for the nearest of the barn's five fully stocked bars. On receipt of a club soda, he weaved his way through the crowd and toward table eight, drawing inordinately long looks from strangers. His stitches had been removed, but the week and a half that had passed since his admission to the hospital was clearly not enough time to preclude guests from wondering what the hell a skinhead was doing here. It would have been smart, he thought, to buy a wig. And to get his tux taken in; it fit like a poncho. Then again, these things might work to his advantage right now.

Adding a stagger to his step, he jerked the chair next to Mallery's away from the table, the legs scraping varnish off the floor, drowning out Harken's attempt at a humorous impression of some sheikh.

Thornton said, "General Harken, I'm not sure that you'd remember me. I'm—" Casting out his right hand, he toppled Mallery's flute as well as Harken's, sending champagne streaming toward the ex-spy. Despite Harken's uncommon quickness in retreat, his lap was soaked. Thornton amended his introduction to, "I'm on the lookout for a rock to crawl under."

Beneath the table, Harken clenched a fist, which would have been lost on Thornton, as it appeared to be on Mallery. In keeping with his act, however, Thornton sat slumped forward in his seat and could see under the table.

Harken rose. "Actually, you've done me a favor, Thornton. I'm glad for an excuse to get out of this monkey suit." He turned to Mallery. "Beryl, will you be okay for a minute while I run to the house?"

"As long as you put something else on before you come back," she said.

With a laugh, Harken hurried to the exit, leaving her alone with Thornton.

She turned to him with the air of a child who had received a surprise gift. "You're Russ Thornton, aren't you?"

"Afraid so."

"I admire your work."

Good, he thought. When people didn't like it, they said, *I know your work.*

After she introduced herself, he said, "I thought I recognized you." He uprighted her flute. "Let me get you another drink."

"No need to bother. They're coming around." She turned, a simple string of pearls emphasizing a slender and graceful neck, and pointed to one of the servers. "Also you're probably best off remaining seated."

"Sorry. I took a header recently that landed me in the operating room. I'm starting to think there was a chart mix-up and they took out my cerebellum."

She nodded knowingly. "Skiing accident?"

"I wish it were something sexy like that. Truth is, I fell on a sidewalk. Luckily, what saved me, if you listen to phrenologists, is that I'm combative."

"So that sidewalk won't be messing with anybody else?" Her pleasant demeanor ebbed almost imperceptibly. Almost.

"I'm going to hazard a guess that you don't listen to phrenologists," he said.

"I've never had the occasion to, as far as I know."

"What do you know about phrenology?"

"Isn't it the theory that the shape of the skull is indicative of personality?" she asked. She'd paused, he noted, as though carefully choosing the word *theory*.

"That's almost it," he said. "In 1796, the German physician Franz Joseph Gall first put forth the notion that the shape and size of twenty-seven different areas of the cranium serve as indicators of character as well as mental abilities. Phrenology was relegated to pseudoscience not long afterward—in the mainstream. Tragically, if you ask me. I'll bet I can use phrenology to tell three things about your character."

She glanced at the server balancing a tray of canapés a table away. "You know, Russ, I'm absolutely famished."

"How about this? All the canapés you can eat, on me, if I'm wrong." Squaring his chair to face her, he raised his left hand. "May I?"

"Please." She smiled, amused. Or just a natural politician.

Veiling his discomfort with the sober air of a clinician, he waded his right forefinger into her soft hair, past her left ear, onto an area of scalp that seemed to conform to a smooth and rounded temporal bone, which told of confidence, according to one nineteenth-century phrenologist. Other practitioners maintained that the same space told of insecurity.

"Very interesting," he said, trying to buy time as

he probed further, pressing harder and delving deeper into her scalp, in search of an unnatural rise on the temporal bone. He felt only a smooth surface. Nothing else. Damn.

She laughed as though she were being tickled, really to mask her agitation in all likelihood. "Okay, Doc, okay." She held up a palm.

Her left palm. She was left-handed, he remembered. Maybe they placed the device on the side opposite the subject's dominant hand, making it that much further out of reach?

"One more cranial module, and the analysis will be complete," he said, extending his left hand, his index finger dipping into the hair behind her right ear and feeling for the temporal bone. He'd barely made contact with it when she pulled away. But the motion caused his fingertip to skip over a bump. A mogul, as her skull went. And rounded. Almost certainly the flank of an embedded capsule.

He sat back, dumbfounded. He managed to get out, "Beautiful, intelligent, and uncomfortable with phrenological examinations."

"You're one for three." Looking over his shoulder, she beamed. "More champagne!" Sliding to the edge of her seat, she aimed for the server dispensing flutes five tables away.

"Please allow me." Thornton said. Leaping to his feet and starting toward the server, he dropped onto Mallery's silver service plate a folded piece of paper resembling a seating-assignment card. On the face of it, he'd written in pencil:

PLEASE READ ASAP:

Inside, he'd added:

Our chat about phrenology (malarkey, btw) and every conversation you've had for months has been overheard. How Langlind knew about 'the Dutchman.' Meet me @2100 by pool for countermeasure. Fallback 2200. First, drop this note into my club soda; the paper will dissolve.

17

A dip in Nolend's pool, which was on the scale of a resort hotel's, would have meant hypothermia tonight. Still fifteen guests milled about the deck. Some sought refuge from the clamor in the barn, others a place to smoke without drawing murderous looks. Although the temperature had dropped into the thirties, the deck's forest of electric heat trees made Thornton's tuxedo jacket a layer too many. He took it off, folded it over the back of a chaise lounge, sank into the canvas-covered cushions, and gazed out at the moonlight bobbing on the Atlantic. He was glad for a chance to relax after the long drive up. But relaxation wasn't in the cards: Mallery appeared to be a no-show.

Possibly she'd been held up and would come at

ten o'clock, the fallback time. Although Thornton had glanced back and seen her reach for his card, he wondered if he'd done such a good job replicating the folded table assignments that she didn't realize it contained a message. Or maybe he'd overplayed Head Injury Guy and she'd just been brushing the card aside in her haste to get the hell away from the table before he returned.

He watched a young couple at the table across the pool engage in lively conversation. He heard only the rhythmic heaves and sighs of the waves, until, from directly behind him, came, "I have to tell you, Mr. Thornton, only once have I ever been on the receiving end of a lamer pickup attempt."

He turned to find Mallery, draped in a thick, black cashmere shawl. Hoping that she was playacting for their unseen audience, he sat up and said, "It's always nice not to be the lamest. Who gets the prize?"

She lowered herself onto the foot of the chaise lounge. "Guy sidles up to me at a bar in the Haight and says, 'Scotty's my favorite member of the Starship *Enterprise* crew. How about you?'"

"That's not so bad."

"Maybe not by your standards, but you're lucky. You can get away with any line because hunk and intrepid journalist are an unbeatable one-two punch."

"Thank you." He didn't flatter himself that her words contained any truth.

"So, if you'd like, expound upon the phrenological

significance of each of the twenty-seven subdivisions of the cranium?"

"How about a walk along the beach?"

"Wherever."

Apparently Mallery intuited the need to perpetuate their cover. As they wandered away from the pool, she looped an arm through Thornton's. She had to miss her shoes, cast aside when the heels hindered her progress through the cold sand, but she didn't show it.

"So does phrenology usually get the ladies onto the beach?" she asked.

"It's never once failed."

"Any reason I should know how you acquired your expertise? Skeletons buried in your backyard?"

"You can rest easy: I live in a third-floor apartment. Do you know who Margaretha Zelle was?"

"Your ex?"

"No, but she was the ex of a lot of other guys when she was known as Mata Hari. I learned about phrenology, like most everything else I know, while reporting. Margaretha Zelle made the news in 2000."

"Wasn't she killed during the First World War?"

"Executed by firing squad, after which her skull became part of the collection at the Museum of Anatomy in Paris."

"Funny that I've missed that museum."

"In 2000, the museum's archivists discovered that

the skull was missing. Eventually they concluded it had been stolen. My reaction was, *Why would anyone steal a skull? Or even want one?* Little did I know, skull collecting is a veritable subculture."

"Really?"

"Really, a function of the enduring popularity of . . ."

"Phrenology?"

"It drives devotees to skullduggery, literally."

"As in grave robbery?"

"Exactly. There's a long list of notable victims throughout history, including Mozart and Beethoven."

"Gives new meaning to the Chuck Berry lyrics, doesn't it?"

"*Roll over Beethoven . . . ?*"

" *. . . and tell Tchaikovsky the news.*"

Liking her no longer required any pretense on his part. She held up her end of the act, frequently making him laugh. When a wave broke too close to them, they skipped out of its way together. The only thing missing was mid-romantic-movie-montage music.

Ascending a dune brought their destination into view. "Hey, check that out!" he said.

The "restoration" of the nineteenth-century seaman's shack included a 4,000-foot airstrip. The lights lining the tarmac turned it into a white stripe through the night, the wash outlining the flock of private jets parked to the side. Releasing Mallery's arm, Thornton headed, as if intrigued, for the runway's inland end, the location of a radar system encased in a metal box the size of a refrigerator. Atop it rotated a dome-encased sensor with a cyclopean lens.

He walked to the metal rail fence surrounding the unit. "Looks like Robbie the Robot," he said.

Mallery stayed alongside him. "The Nolends know just everyone, don't they?"

He clutched the fence rails, pulling his body as close as possible to the radar unit, as if trying to attain the best vantage point. "Theoretically, the radar causes electromagnetic interference that prevents the device from recording."

Joining him, her playfulness vanished. "How did Langlind do it?"

"He, or, more likely, some organization sharing his interests, gave you a short-acting sedative, then implanted a subminiature, self-powered eavesdropping device behind your right ear. I'd tell you you're in good company, but the only other implantee I know of is me."

"Why you?"

"I've been wondering about that every waking moment since I learned about the bug last week. Do you know about Leonid Sokolov?"

Mallery nodded. "The physicist who was assassinated."

"The killer administered a sedative called midazolam first," Thornton said.

"Why?"

"The FBI thought it was to subdue him."

"Wouldn't shooting him in the head do that?"

"In rare circumstances, midazolam can be fatal. It's possible that the purpose of the shooting was to cover up an implantation that had gone wrong."

"Do you have any evidence of that?"

"None, and I don't want any; I hope there's no connection whatsoever to Sokolov—his secrets in the wrong hands could be disastrous. There is a connection to you, though: Catherine Peretti."

"The Langlind staffer who was murdered?"

"Actually, shot by a professional when she was seconds away from telling me some sort of secret."

Mallery gasped vapor into the cold air.

"So the obvious question is whether that murder had something to do with Langlind," Thornton said.

"If we'd had anything on him, we would have used it." Mallery rubbed behind her right ear.

"Try not to do that, in case anyone's watching, okay?"

Her hand moved through her hair, her fingers flipping wind-strewn strands from her eyes, as if that had been her intention all along. "Gordon Langlind could just be a stooge in this equation," she said.

"Why do you think so?"

"Since Great-Granddaddy Cloyd Langlind's first big oil strike in 1912, it's practically been a family tradition that the craftier offspring are sent to Wharton and then corporate headquarters; those who don't make the cut, like Gordon, are sent to law school and then are bought political offices on the chance they can be of use to the company. Langlind Petrochemical has a private espionage firm on a five-million-dollar-per-year retainer. The right nugget of intelligence on a prospective oilfield can mean the difference between a hundred-million-dollar loss and a hundred-billion-dollar profit. They would view an eavesdropping system of this nature as the wisest investment they could ever make. Also Cloyd Langlind's 1912 strike was in Kazakhstan, and the company's been in bed with the Russians ever since. Wasn't Sokolov assassinated by Russians?"

"That's never been determined. The case is essentially cold."

"Is it possible that someone else altogether dug up dirt on me, their goal being—for some reason—to keep Langlind in office?"

"Either way, it was election tampering." Thornton hoped that would be enough to secure her cooperation. "I have a friend in New York, an NSA electrophysiologist with access to a Faraday cage that blocks radio signals. Inside it, he can easily remove a device without the surveillants knowing; then he can track the signal to their listening post. The catch is he needs two devices to do that."

She said nothing. She just stared at the machine, her expression flickering between shock and horror.

"We should get going," Thornton said. "A radar

tower is only so fascinating, and it's the third source of electromagnetic interference I've had a conversation by this week. We need to decide on our next steps before anyone gets suspicious."

She looked away. "You've already done a nice job playing on my gets-around rep."

"Sorry, I didn't have much time to come up with a plan to get you alone, and that was before I realized Clay Harken was your date."

"Come on, Clay's older than my father. He's my security guard."

"Oh." Thornton hid his satisfaction that he'd been wrong. "So how about New York?"

She backed away. Then, no doubt remembering the inherent danger in distancing herself from the radar unit, she stopped. "Why wouldn't I just go to the local police station? That way the device can be entered into a chain of evidence and tested without our having to watch our backs."

"Because we can't find out who implanted the devices without two of them. Anyway, most cops hearing our story would tell us to take a place on line behind the folks with the tinfoil hats. And if our listeners realize we're onto them, they'll deactivate the devices."

"Okay, why not write up a statement of the case on your secret-agent dissolving paper and take it straight to the FBI?"

"The same risks in going to the police station apply to going to the Bureau—or to any other government agency."

Mallery focused on a wave rolling in, progressively larger until reaching the beach, at which point its top curled and turned silver in the moonlight. Her shivering, he suspected, had nothing to do with the cold. He extended a steadying hand.

She sidestepped it. "I know a good bar in New York," she said. "And I'm going to need it."

18

They devised a cover story, a romantic hookup tonight, to add credibility to a "spontaneous decision" to go to New York together tomorrow morning. Then they took their act to the Rose & Crown, a dark Nantucket tavern decorated with a colorful array of antique model ships. Save for the televisions broadcasting games, the establishment had changed so little since the eighteenth century that each time the front door groaned inward, Thornton half expected a man with a peg leg to clomp in.

Thornton liked the tavern because it removed them from any prying eyes on Muskeget. And the large, boisterous bar crowd precluded the conversation that a romantic hookup cover demanded. Conversation of any sort was problematic. As he had learned the past few days, it felt like trying to read with someone staring over your shoulder. Also Mallery seemed to be struggling to come to terms with the news that strangers had opened her head, implanted a machine, and been listening to her private conversations for months. Or maybe she blamed the messenger. Fortunately she had no trouble when the act called for drinking too much.

Ascending Main Street several rounds later, Thornton sensed that she would have clung to him even if it hadn't been in the script. The oceanside resorts had closed for the season, but the village still offered plenty of places to stay, principally two- and three-story townhouses from the eighteenth and nineteenth centuries that had been converted to bed-and-breakfasts. At Captain Orster's, constructed in 1743 according to the sign swinging above the door, a fittingly ancient innkeeper answered the buzzer. While lighting the way to the room with an oil lamp retrofitted with an LED bulb, he told them that "revelers"—evidently his euphemism for late-night drunks—sustained the inns during the off-season.

As soon as the innkeeper left them alone, Mallery said, "Sorry, Russ, I need to pass out." A line straight out of their script, alleviating the need to generate R-rated sound effects.

He knelt to steady the wooden stepladder to the antique four-poster bed. She started to unzip her gown before abruptly climbing the steps with it still on. He read her lopsided grin as a blithe decision to trash a $20,000 designer original rather than expose another inch of flesh.

During the night, if someone had planted a video camera in the room, he would have seen Thornton frequently shift positions, unable to sleep in spite of the comfortable bed. Mallery slept on her back on the side of the bed by the window, graceful even in the simple act of breathing. As compelling a woman, he thought, as he'd ever known—or known of. He felt like an interloper. He'd long since learned that a press credential was a golden ticket, able to gain a journalist access to almost anyplace in the world or anyone, but not as a part of the action, not as a doer like Beryl Mallery. Just as a chronicler. The thirty inches between them now might as well have been thirty miles.

He spent most of the night using his police scanner app, which ran transcripts of the radio communications between various New York metro dispatchers and patrolmen. Eventually the black sky dissolved to a slate gray; the dark shapes outside transformed into gables and chimneys and, with the first flecks of dawn, individual cedar shingles. At sunup, a ray landed on the leaded-glass window, which sprayed a checkerboard of light across the bed. Mallery's eyes opened.

"Well, I'll be damned," Thornton said. "Beryl Mallery in the flesh, as it were."

Apparently reminded of their audience, she gritted

her teeth before rolling across the bed and planting a loud kiss on his stubbly cheek. "Russ Thornton," she said enthusiastically, without a trace of corresponding emotion on her face. "I thought I'd dreamed it, but here we are in bed together, and with a nice long time until checkout."

"Unfortunately, I need to run."

"Hangover?"

"No, I need to get back to New York."

"For the usual reasons men need to skedaddle at seven on a Sunday morning?"

"For work, actually."

"*Work?* I would have expected something more creative from you."

"At around three thirty this morning, two men were seen trying to steal a two-hundred-foot-long section of eight-foot-high chain-link fence in White Plains."

"And there has been a dramatic surge in the value of fences?"

"If you're a couple of two-bit crooks with nothing but a used pickup truck, that much stainless steel is gold, practically. They could get twenty grand for it."

She yawned. "Stop the presses."

"That part of the story should put you off. Good cover does that. The real story is that the fence is part of Westchester County Airport's perimeter. Terrorists have been focusing on secondary targets, and Westchester Airport's high on the list. The police caught the thieves red-handed, but what if the theft was just a diversionary tactic? What if, sometime between when the two guys began cutting the wire and the arrival of the police, a third guy slipped into the grass alongside a runway and readied a surface-to-air missile?" Thornton didn't add that if there had been even a remote possibility that the thieves were anything more than bozos who, in the dark, failed to notice that the fence bordered a runway, Westchester Airport would have been locked down within seconds.

"Wow," Mallery said. "You need an assistant?"

"Depends on what the assistant brings to the party."

"A newfound lust for journalism. And a jet." As if nudged by humility, she added. "Fuel-efficient, as jets go."

"Is it a Sino Swearingen SJ-30-2?"

"How did you know?"

"I have a whole fleet of them. But I have to get my car out of the parking lot on the Cape; I'm going to need it in New York." Thornton would rather take Mallery's jet, but he was concerned about her people, at least one of whom had been protecting her while a subminiature electronic eavesdropping device was injected into her head. "For what it's worth, the drive down the coast is spectacular this time of year."

"The truth is, I want to be with you," she said, bringing their scene to a close, "even if we just circle a block all day."

. . .

The engineering supplies distributor South Atlantic Resources, LLC, was a front for an off-the-books joint enterprise of several government agencies, including the CIA and the National Reconnaissance Office. Or so the office manager, Lieutenant Mickey Rapada, had been told. Rapada knew for certain only that deception was the rule in the intelligence community and that he didn't need to know the full details in order to do his part for national security. He suspected the real operational objective was not, as he'd been told, the development of a "portable petroleum hydrocarbon detector prototype." A quick look online had taught him that such detectors were a fraction of the size of the machine the kid physicist had spent five days and nights banging together in the back office. Rapada had been told plenty, however, about the players who posed a threat to the op. Accordingly, at 0800 on a Sunday morning, he phoned the chief, who answered, "Goodwyn." It sounded like he'd been sleeping. Also his name was not really Goodwyn, but Canning— *Goodwyn* signified that Canning was under no duress and able to communicate freely.

"Sorry if I woke you, Norm," Rapada said. *Norm* meant a status of exactly that on this end.

"I'm already awake, getting some work done. What's up?"

"Action from subject one-forty-two."

Canning grumbled. "I don't have the scorecard on me, junior."

"Sorry, sir, I mean the blogger."

"What now?"

"He's on Muskeget Island at the same charity ball as the ex-candidate."

"I'm guessing they did some talking."

"Some sleeping together too."

"Not for the usual reasons, hence your call?"

"It was a little suspicious. Then, this morning, she got her things and, over the protest of her bodyguard, she left her jet and her pilot behind—and the bodyguard. She's planning to drive with one-forty-two to New York."

"How's his physical condition?"

"Not quite good enough yet for him to be island-hopping. In fact, earlier this week, he told the charity ball hosts he wouldn't be able to attend for that reason."

"Glad to hear it. It will be plausible for him to have another accident."

19

The ferry's engines beat Nantucket Bay into a lather, precluding conversation—fortunately. The playful morning-after banter had denigrated to a stilted discussion of current events. Mallery took advantage of the respite now to read e-mails. But soon, Thornton thought, to maintain the fiction of their affair, they would have to talk.

He thought of questions he might ask her. When you've excelled at everything from selling a record number of Girl Scout cookies to becoming one of the wealthiest women on the planet before your thirtieth birthday, can you sit back and enjoy life, or do you feel pressure to keep up the pace? Or is there no pressure at all because success comes as naturally to you as breathing? When you spend $10 million on a jet, do you find the expenditure easier than a person with a thousandth of your net worth does when parting with the funds for a car? How do you know whether new friendships are genuine or a function of the fact that you probably don't blink at parting with $10 million for a jet?

When Nantucket was reduced to a bump on the horizon, the engines dipped to a throaty hum. Questions ready, Thornton turned to Mallery, who continued to fire e-mails from her iPad. On Sunday at ten A.M.—seven A.M. in her colleagues' time zone—the tablet's incoming e-mail notification chimed like a slot machine.

"I take it you like e-mail," Thornton said.

She didn't look up. "What I get for skipping work yesterday."

Not everyone who takes Saturday off wakes up Sunday to 143 work-related e-mails, he thought. In trying to conceive a better tack, he recalled a CIA source once telling him that experience teaches spies to shun artifice whenever possible. *The closer to your base of experience you can play it, the less you need to fabricate,* the veteran spook had said. *The less you need to fabricate, the more convincing you can be. The more convincing you are, the greater the likelihood you don't get killed.*

Maybe all Thornton needed to do was let Mallery continue tending to her correspondence. Then the transcript from the ferry ride would read like that of any other Sunday morning for her.

He checked his own e-mail. The usual PR flak, and one message from his source at Homeland: *2 guys=just lousy fence thieves.*

Good, he thought. He and Mallery were no longer required to go through the motions of stopping at Westchester Airport. Instead he made a plan to take her to the Abbey Pub, the landmark tavern near the Columbia campus. He texted O'Clair, inviting him along. *Abbey Pub* was code for success in finding a second implantee. Thornton had no interest in actually going to the Abbey. *Sounds graet,* O'Clair replied, the intentional misspelling signifying all systems go on his end. He would set up the Faraday tent in a lab at Columbia. Once he'd extracted the devices and tracked the signals, he would alert the director of the NSA New York office of the development. If need be, the director could dispatch security officers to take Thornton and Mallery into protective custody.

Mallery was still volleying messages with Palo Alto when the ferry reached Hyannis Port. The engines died down, replaced by knocks of the pilings against the hull.

"I think we're here," Thornton said.

She took in the whitewashed pier with surprise. "Oh."

Although sunny, it was the sort of day that delineated winter from autumn. Passengers doubled their pace through the lot from the ferry to their cars, eager to get their heaters cranking. Chattering in spite of a parka fit for a Sherpa, Mallery was among the swift-est down the gangway. Thornton hastened to keep at her side. From the moment he stepped onto land, he had the odd sensation, whichever way he turned, that someone was sneaking up from behind him.

He crossed the parking lot to his car. Unpocketing his keys, he headed for the passenger door, where the red-orange was attributable to rust peeking through the paint. Mallery turned to the neighboring car, a late-model Lexus, apparently assuming that that was his ride. Hit with a wave of self-consciousness, he pried open the old '02's passenger door, the harsh squeak of the hinges scaring a seagull into flight. He hurried to sweep a pair of sweatpants from the pas-senger seat. Lucky thing, he thought, that the cold salty air had neutralized the interior's usual bouquet of motor oil and Doritos.

"Cool car," she said, sliding into the passenger seat.

Literally, he thought, recalling its heater-motor is-sue. "Thanks."

He rounded the car, unlocked the door, which merely squealed as he opened it, and dropped into the leather driver's seat.

"So how did you become a journalist?" she asked.

He'd often heard this question on the heels of talk of fancy cars or homes; usually the underlying ques-tion was *Why don't you have a job that allows you to buy such items?*

The engine turned over, to his relief. "Every season, my hometown paper used to hire a player on our high school football team to write up the away games," he said, driving out of the lot. "It saved them from having to send a reporter. And I stuck with it."

She shot him a sidelong glance. "That's just a cover story, right? Really you'd been in the CIA?"

"As a matter of fact, I was in the CIA." Intentionally leaving her hanging, he turned right at Ocean Street and followed the signs for Route 6. "On December 14, 2008, for a cocktail reception."

She laughed. Briefly. "So what's the reason you stuck with journalism?"

This was among his least favorite topics, but at least it was conversation. "My father was the president of the insurance agency his grandfather had founded, but effectively, he made a career of being taken advantage of. I have one brother who's thirteen years older than me. When I was in high school, he took over the insurance agency, and he got chiseled and duped to the extent that he made my father look like a Fortune 500 CEO. It didn't take long for him to run the agency aground."

Regarding him, she raised a hand to block the sun. "So you developed a thing against bullies?"

"I've never sent them Christmas cards." He turned onto Barnstable Road and accelerated past a crowd of seafood shacks and souvenir shops. "How about you? How did you become a Fortune 500 CEO?"

She sighed. "As it happens, my father's a journalist."

He smiled in spite of a bad feeling about where she was headed.

"Ever read *Love Bus Monthly*?" she asked.

"Somehow I've missed it."

"He published it out of our Love Bus, which was one of about fifty Volkswagen *Kombinationskraftwagens* in our hippie-come-lately colony in New Mexico."

"So you grew up in a Volkswagen Kombi?"

"Only until I was five and needed to be less than a hundred miles from a school. We rented a house in Phoenix, which was hard on Mom and Dad because they believed two hundred cubic feet was ample living space for a family of three, and that anything more was socially irresponsible. So, to answer your question, anything they'd done or hoped to do, I tried to do the opposite, and—"

Her phone beeped with a new text message.

"Excuse me for a second." With the speed and dexterity of a pianist, she keyed a response on her phone's minuscule keypad. Meanwhile the phone kept beeping.

The old BMW's heater chose to work, not that Mallery would have noticed if it hadn't: She parried messages for the better part of the next four hours, at which point Thornton began to wish they'd taken her

jet after all, because, he suspected, they were now being followed. A tall white Nissan van had stayed five
or six cars behind them since New Haven, eight miles
back.

On major commuting routes, if he recalled cor-
rectly, cars averaged 1.4 passengers, a figure that included the driver. Vans, used mainly for commercial
purposes, averaged 1.1. Two people sat in the front
seat of this van. Men or women, he couldn't tell; they
were too far back. By a two-to-one ratio over utility-
company vans, all-white were America's most common vans, making them the ideal hide-in-plain-sight
ride, or what a surveillant might rent—at the New
Haven Airport, perhaps. This was the height of leaf-
peeping season, though, making it difficult to rent
anything last-minute, particularly today, a Sunday.
If you were lucky enough to get a van, you might get
stuck with a deluxe model with eighteen extra inches
of headroom nobody but an NBA player needs, at
three times the price of an ordinary van. Then again,
the two people in the deluxe white van might just
be two tall people in a deluxe white van. Either way,
Thornton heeded the fundamental guiding principle
of countersurveillance—*See your pursuers but don't
let them know you see them*—and didn't try for a better look.

"You hungry?" he asked Mallery.

She remained focused on a spreadsheet. "Not
really."

"Mind if I stop at a McDonald's?"

She smiled. "Someone has to keep cardiologists in business."

He crossed over from the fast lane, resetting the blinker well in advance of the exit. The van remained in the fast lane. Then, a quarter of a mile before the exit, it signaled its intent to turn right.

Taking in the road signs lining the off-ramp, with listings of gas stations, hotels, and restaurants, Thornton said, "Crap, only Taco Bell." He turned off the blinker and sped up.

As did the van. He felt as if he'd just swallowed an icicle. Unless the bugs had somehow malfunctioned, whoever installed them had no reason to tail him or Mallery; the devices themselves could serve as tracking beacons. A good-case scenario, he thought, was that the two people in the van were FBI. But the Bureau would deploy a fleet of surveillance vehicles and maybe a helicopter, not just one van. A single van was too easily detected, as Thornton had just established.

His mind leaped to the worst-case scenario, which, unfortunately, fit the facts: The eavesdroppers were onto him and Mallery, and the van carried assassins, one to drive and the other to fire something like a compact active denial system, so that the killing would appear to be a traffic accident. Assassins liked highways because targets were especially vulnerable in speeding vehicles. Also mistakes were more likely and more perilous, and the incidents seldom yielded reliable witnesses. And what better highway to stage such an operation than the Connecticut Turnpike, commonly referred to by locals as the Highway of Death? Connecticut had designed its segment of I-95 to accommodate a maximum of 90,000 vehicles per day, but after five decades of explosive suburban growth along the corridor and the installation of two of the country's largest casinos, 200,000 vehicles was the daily norm, and the fatality rate of 2.7 per million vehicle-miles of travel nearly tripled the national average.

Thornton's car had retained the handling that made BMW's name, but it had a hard time topping ninety these days, so he doubted he could outrun the Nissan, the van's two tons notwithstanding. He might try anyway in hope of getting caught at a speed trap. But with vehicles so often limited to forty miles per hour by all the traffic, the Connecticut Turnpike offered such slim pickings that state troopers didn't bother.

A pair of yellow arches shone through the trees lining the road. A McDonald's in the food court at the next rest stop. Or, as Thornton thought of it, an escape route.

"Finally," he exclaimed, signaling right and accelerating toward the off-ramp.

The van followed.

Mallery didn't look up.

Thornton recalled a recent incident that he'd tracked online but never wrote about. Two men wearing ski masks and gloves entered a bank in nearby New Canaan, Connecticut. Brandishing guns, they ordered the customers and employees to lie on the floor. Encountering no resistance, one robber stood watch by the front door; the other jumped over the counter, heaped cash from the tellers' drawers into his duffel bag, then had the manager and assistant manager go to the cash vault and enter their combinations. The thieves made off with $103,400, in a Honda Accord reported stolen in New Haven an hour earlier. The car was recovered by police a half mile from the bank minus the bank robbers and any substantive clues. At the time, the story hadn't been *RealStory* material. But, Thornton thought, it might be useful today.

He planned to enter the food court, find a policeman, and, conveying with a finger to his lips that stealth was in order, hand off a note explaining that the two New Canaan bank robbers were about, having parked a tall white Nissan van outside. For the sake of credibility, he would write the note on his reporter's pad. Flashing the distinctive notebook—it was half the width of an ordinary page in order to fit in a back pocket—usually got him into crime scenes faster than an actual press credential. It was a good bet that the cop would read the note and investigate. Then, while the men in the van protested their innocence—maybe while being taken to a holding cell—Thornton and Mallery could get away.

The exit ramp sliced through a field of patchy brown grass before forking, one lane for cars, the other for trucks. Thornton took the car route, as did both a Saab and a station wagon behind him. The white van followed.

While the Saab and station wagon rounded the parking lot to get on the line for drive-through, the van accompanied Thornton to the food court.

"Want to come inside?" he asked Mallery, anticipating that she would. It had been six hours since she'd had anything to eat or drink or used a restroom.

She looked up. "I'm good, thanks." Then she was gone, back to her e-mail.

Going inside now meant leaving her out here, unaware and unprotected. He wasn't sure how to explain the situation—in the time he scrawled a note, the van might pull up and zap them with millimeter wave energy. He also didn't want to needlessly frighten her. Possibly he was just paranoid. He looked and spotted a New Haven PD cruiser. Empty—the cops no doubt inside the food court. But another option presented itself: an elephantine garbage truck was lumbering around the corner of the food court building.

Thornton wove through open spaces in the parking lot as if returning to the highway. The van shot after him, abandoning any pretense of stealth.

"Decided you wanted to live longer?" Mallery asked.

You got that right, Thornton thought. "Just save time," he said.

Taking an only-in-a-BMW ninety-degree left turn around the food court building, he found the garbage truck backing up to an enormous dumpster, completely blocking the right lane.

Perfect, he thought.

He jumped into the left lane, joining the moderate drive-through line just ahead of the Saab and the station wagon, drawing an angry honk from the former.

By the time the white van caught up, it couldn't get past the Saab, the station wagon, or the newly arrived Camry because of the garbage truck. Two more cars fell into place behind the van, preventing it from backing up.

Canning couldn't decide whether to drink the vodka. Russo-Baltique was by far the finest in the world. It couldn't be found in stores or bars. Its manufacturer wasn't even a liquor company, but a railway-car manufacturer. The golden flask was a small-scale replica of the 1912 Russo-Baltique automobile's signature radiator guard. This particular flask had been confiscated from Iranian smugglers on the Strait of Hormuz by a team from the U.S. Department of Commerce overseeing the embargo. The chief, aware of his old colleague's predilection for vodka, buried the unusual container in the paperwork as *one (1) bottle misc.* and shipped it to Canning. Would have never happened if the guy'd had an inkling that the going rate for a bottle of Russo-Baltique was $1.3 million. That is, if you could get your hands on one.

Canning could probably flip the bottle for as much as $2 million, or about five times the value of his Reston two-bedroom condo, in which he now sat after a long stretch at the safe house—a bathtub full of water, chlorine bleach, and sodium hydroxide did a good job of eliminating a body; it just took a long time. He longed to drink the vodka. Funny, because once upon a time, he couldn't tell the difference between Russo-Baltique and a four-buck bottle of Putinka. But over the course of his Russian tour, he developed quite the palate. And although he didn't realize it until now, he had wanted to drink the bottle of Russo-Baltique the way other men coveted Porsches or supermodels.

And why not indulge? The blogger, the lone remaining threat to his plan, was about to be flushed. Canning expected to make enough money on the sale of the E-bomb that he would be able to keep Russo-Baltique on hand at all times.

He pried off the yellow and white gold cap, topped with a Russian imperial double eagle. Setting a highball glass on the coffee table, he dispensed the liquor in a glistening chute. He thought of Mark Twain's adage, *The poetry is all in the anticipation, for there is none in reality.*

The wrong ringtone interrupted his thoughts. He fished the phone from his pocket, hit the green ANSWER button, and said, "Goodwyn."

"Good afternoon, Norm," said the South Atlantic Resources manager, Mickey Rapada, sounding so blithe that Canning surmised that something was very wrong.

"Is it really?"

"Well, we had no choice but to follow them onto a McDonald's drive-through lane. The clearance was nine feet, and even though the van's height is only one hundred and five inches, according to the specs, it set off the sensor."

"'Nothing is according to specs.'"

"Sir?"

"'Nothing is according to specs,' is the ninth of the General Laws of Augustus De Morgan, who's better known by his nom de plume, Murphy. Murphy's first law, of course, is 'Anything that can go wrong will.' His second is 'Anything that cannot go wrong will anyway.' He also wrote that 'If only two things can happen and one might lead to catastrophe, it does.' A buck says that's the case here, right?"

Rapada laughed. "The good news is you win a buck."

The onetime Green Beret was as tough as a badger, Canning thought, but his laughter failed to hide his unease at being the bearer of more bad news. "Tell me why, please."

"The manager of the food court came outside and told us we had to back out of the drive-through chute. A couple of New Haven cops, who happened to be at the McDonald's, helped direct traffic. Six vehicles in line behind the van had to be backed out."

"Murphy also wrote, 'The number of people watching you is directly proportional to the stupidity of your action,'" Canning said.

"I'm afraid Murphy's right again, chief," Rapada said. "By the time we got back onto the highway, the targets had a twenty-five-mile lead."

"You know where they're headed?"

"Yes, sir, I've been monitoring their feed the whole time. They're going to meet O'Clair at the Abbey Pub on upper Broadway."

"Double or nothing on the dollar that they made you, used the McDonald's drive-through lane as an escape route, and are really headed to see the supposed dope fiend from No Such Agency. How about you scramble another unit to get the lovebirds, and I'll take care of the dope fiend?"

"Sounds like a plan."

Canning liked Rapada. The kid believed "national security interests" justified any and all means, and he followed orders without question.

"Just remember this, junior," Canning said. "'In preparing for battle, plans are useless, but planning is indispensable.'"

"Murphy again?"

"Actually, Eisenhower."

A few *yessirs* later, Rapada rang off.

The Russo-Baltique was exquisite, but it might as well have been Putinka. Canning couldn't focus on anything except the blogger.

20

As planned, O'Clair texted Thornton: *instead of abbey, why not come as my guests 2 casa italiana?* The Columbia Italian academy's lavish *ristorante* was accessible only by university staffers.

Thornton replied: *love 2! grazie!*

Twenty minutes later, while he was parallel parking across campus from the Casa Italiana, on the west side of Broadway between 119th and 120th, O'Clair texted again: *u guys mind hanging for a few mins @ my office?—sorry, some work that won't go 2 bed . . .*

No problem, Thornton replied.

In theory, O'Clair's office at Columbia was more easily accessible than the scientist's regular office. To gain admittance to the National Security Agency downtown, visitors had to pass a full background check in advance of their visit. Upon arrival they faced a battery of additional security measures including a millimeter-wave scanner generations ahead of the imaging devices at airports. In contrast, Columbia University's fourteen-story interdisciplinary science building, home to as many as twenty classified military and intelligence service research projects at a given time, required visitors to simply pass beneath a ceremonial gate at Broadway and 116th Street, then stroll along a picturesque cherry tree–lined brick path through the quad.

Thornton and Mallery found two security guards sitting in lawn chairs by the gate, their police-model Segway electric personal transports—or, as he thought of them, $6,500 scooters—standing at the ready. The men nodded hospitably as Thornton and Mallery ambled past. The guards' primary functions, he guessed, were fending off panhandlers and dissuading freshmen from doing the things that freshmen do.

At the Science Building, an austere bluish gray steel tower, they pushed through a revolving door and entered a creamy marble lobby that offset the severity of the exterior. Probably typical for a Sunday, the vast space was empty, save for one more member of the campus security force, a bony, dark-skinned man in his sixties who sat at a small desk to the side of the entrance. He looked up from his magazine long enough to ascertain that Thornton wasn't carrying an assault rifle.

Then he fixated on Mallery. "I've seen you on TV, yes?" he asked with a musical Indian accent—Gujarati, Thornton guessed.

"It's possible," she said.

"Are you an actress?"

"Not by profession."

"Oh, well, so much for adding to my granddaughter's autograph collection." With a smile, the man returned to his reading.

And that, Thornton suspected, was the extent of the safeguarding of classified research here—a story for another day.

They rode an escalator up to an elevator bank across from floor-to-ceiling windows framing West 120th Street, a stretch of four- and five-story redbrick academic buildings. The elevator stopped at the fourth floor, the doors snapping open to reveal a corridor that evoked the Death Star. Lighting panels flush with the ceiling caused the metallic walls to shimmer a dull blue. Thornton led Mallery past a row of what appeared, through frosted glass portholes, to be laboratories.

A door to an office swung open and O'Clair wandered out. "Oh, hey, guys," he said, as if he hadn't been eagerly awaiting their arrival.

Thornton made introductions while O'Clair guided them down the hall.

"Russ has told me a lot of great things about you," Mallery said.

"That's only because he owes me money." O'Clair admitted them to a laboratory, in which they passed beneath a flap and into a glossy silver mesh fifteen-by-fifteen-foot tent. At its center stood a pair of stools and a cart that held surgical instruments and a lunchbox-size container made of the same silvery material as the tent.

With a wave at the surroundings, O'Clair said, "This is a Faraday tent, generally used for computer forensic tests. It's made of a highly conductive textile that redistributes electrical charges to cancel out external nonstatic electric fields. In other words, you can say whatever you want now and it won't be overheard or recorded."

"What else do we get to do here?" Mallery eyed the cart, on which a small scalpel blade gleamed in the light cast by the battery-powered lamp on the tent wall. Thornton thought he glimpsed squeamishness through her shell of poise.

"First, I'm going to remove the devices." O'Clair snapped on an opaque white surgical glove. "Then, to minimize the chance of anyone detecting their removal, I'll place the devices in this miniature Faraday tent." Pulling on a second glove, he tapped the lunchbox. "After that, I'll hustle them down the hall to my office; I've calculated that the capacitors store ten to twelve minutes of charge, meaning that once they're out of your bodies and operating autonomously, I'll have only that amount of time to track the signals."

Mallery sucked at her lower lip. "What happens if the signals' destination is the digital equivalent of a post office box?"

"We'll get actual physical coordinates regardless. If it turns out to literally be a post office box, or, say, a storage container in the middle of nowhere rented anonymously by someone paying cash, we can still get a fix on other devices transmitting to that location, meaning we'll be able to learn who else has eavesdropping devices implanted in their heads. From that we ought to be able to derive a single common denominator."

Mallery dug her hands into her coat pockets. "But there may be hundreds of people with these devices in their heads. You wouldn't have time to collect all of their coordinates."

"Hundreds of people with devices wouldn't be bad, for our purposes," O'Clair said. "The hardware necessary to handle that much data would be hard to conceal."

"What if the eavesdroppers get wind of what we're doing and empty the place?"

"I'll be monitoring cell phone tower data only. I can't think of any reason they'd be able to detect that. In the worst-case scenario, if they did catch me and rolled up their data-storage facility immediately, we'd still have collected a trove of intel. Even if I could safely get the two of you into NSA headquarters, we couldn't hope for better than that. And we could do a lot worse, because by going to the agency, we would alert the eavesdroppers to our intentions, in which case they flip a switch and the devices will cease to transmit, end of story."

"Reasonable," Mallery said. "By the way, is this going to hurt?"

O'Clair indicated a pair of small, preloaded hypodermic needles, as well as two bigger ones with red plungers. "I'm going to use a local anesthetic to numb the area of the scalp around the device, so it shouldn't hurt. But why don't we find out on Russ?"

O'Clair tapped the top of the nearest stool. Thornton draped his coat over the back and settled onto the seat.

"If for whatever unforeseen reason this does hurt, let me know," O'Clair said. "Just in case, I readied syringes with a minimal dose of instant-acting general anesthetic—you'd be out five minutes tops."

O'Clair stepped directly behind Thornton, who'd given no thought to pain until now. He resolved to smile throughout the procedure, for Mallery's sake. He felt a cold, damp swab pressed onto the skin behind his left ear. He recognized the tart scent of Betadine. The insertion of the needle didn't hurt so much as surprise him, but the anesthetic flowed in like fire.

"What are you waiting for?" he asked O'Clair.

Not buying the bravado, Mallery blanched.

O'Clair poked with the scalpel. "Feel anything?" he asked.

"Only the stool," Thornton said. True enough.

"Good, the local anesthetic has succeeded. Now I'm going to open the area."

Thornton felt only slight pressure, first from the incision and, again, from the insertion of another instrument.

"Tweezers," O'Clair told him.

With a faint clink, pincers clasped the device. O'Clair then extracted what looked like a grain of rice that had been steeped in marinade. He plunged it into a plastic cup full of a granular purple substance.

"Play sand," he explained, withdrawing the empty tweezers from the cup and snapping on a lid. "I experimented with a few things, but it turns out this is just right to replicate the pressure the device is accustomed to within the scalp—in the event it senses pressure at all, I should say."

"What if a change in pressure sends an alert that the devices have been removed?" Mallery asked.

"The only way to find out is to remove them." O'Clair waved her over.

21

With the devices in plastic cups in the ten-by-eight-by-four-inch Faraday container he'd cobbled together for the occasion, O'Clair hurried down the corridor to his office, leaving Thornton and Mallery in the lab. In the offices he passed, activity was minimal, here the odd unnatural fluctuation of shadows, there a faint click of a keyboard. Late on a nippy Sunday, even the most ardent workaholics—the science building had more than its share—could be found at home reading a book or cheering on the Giants.

O'Clair's cell phone vibrated. He fished it from his pocket, not bothering to check the caller ID, just powering the thing off to avoid further distraction. Every second he wasted was that much less power in

the devices' capacitors; one second might prove deci-
sive in whether he pinpointed the destination of their
transmissions.

He'd intentionally left the door to his office unlocked, which saved him nine or ten seconds now.
Inside the spartan workspace, he set the homemade
Faraday container onto his desk in front of his bulky
university-issued Dell computer, which was playing
a video of his son's second grade class production of
The Thanksgiving Story. O'Clair skipped his customary smile at the sight of Nathan in the role of Pilgrim
number 3, the boy struggling to keep the brim of the
Scotch-taped-together black poster-board hat from
falling over his eyes. Earlier, O'Clair had cued up the
Dell's video player so that an eavesdropper might
conclude that Thornton and Mallery were in the office along with their devices, and the captive audience
of an overly proud father. The idea was to explain
their silence.

"Beryl, why don't you and Russ have a seat and enjoy the show?" O'Clair said, as if they were here. "It
won't take me more than a couple minutes to finish
up." For effect, he leaned across his desk and sent each
of the guest chairs rasping over the carpet.

Dropping into his own chair, he unsnapped the
Faraday container's lid and removed the cups of purple play sand, placing each one onto its own coasterlike
docking station wired to an effectively anonymous
laptop computer he'd borrowed from a lab. Each

docking station contained a microprocessor-driven signal-isolation system.

Both bugs were transmitting. Good news. Their signals—the relationship between normalized power $\log_{10}N^2$ and frequency $\log_{10}$ Hz—were clearly depicted on the laptop's monitor as sound waves among a sea of similar waves. Unfortunately, it was a larger sea by half than O'Clair had estimated, meaning that identifying which two signals were generated by the bugs would require 50 percent more time than he'd allotted. He wished he'd contrived a visit to meet Thornton and Mallery in Nantucket—or anywhere other than Manhattan. A quiet Sunday afternoon notwithstanding, some 185,783 denizens of this part of the Upper West Side alone were talking on cell phones, texting, piloting radio-control helicopters, and so forth, with each electronic device generating a signal nearly identical to those of the listening devices.

Nevertheless the laptop might have enough time to find the right pair of signals. The frequency-detection and data-tracking software eliminated other waves in a fashion similar to a game of musical chairs. The wave-filled monitor faded to white, refreshing a moment later with 25,781 fewer waves; 160,002 remained. At this rate, O'Clair calculated, the program would isolate the twin signals generated here within—

The shrill ring of the desk telephone not only interrupted his thoughts, but raised the hairs on the back of his neck. He couldn't remember the last time anyone had called the landline. Certainly not on a Sunday. Between his cell and his landline at NSA, where he spent almost all of office hours, he had no reason to give out the Columbia number.

"Probably just a telemarketer," he said for the benefit of his audience. Also probably true, he thought.

Stabbing at the lever on the base of the phone, he muted the ring. As soon as the laptop found the matching pair of waves, he would need to spring into a Jerry Lee Lewis act on the keyboard in order to trace them.

The laptop refreshed again, minus another 21,494 waves. A minute or so and O'Clair would be down to the winning pair. He counted the seconds under his breath if only to negate his inner voice, which was saying that this process was interminable.

Fifteen more seconds and the system had whittled the total to 63,034 waves. The software was learning from experience, thus picking up speed. As its author, O'Clair might have felt pride, but he had no room for anything but apprehension. Nine minutes and fifteen seconds had elapsed since he extracted Thornton's device. Its capacitor couldn't last much longer without a human host.

A rap at the door shook him. Someone in the hall. The chatty guard from down in the lobby, Raj, maybe, bringing a Giants-Redskins game update. O'Clair sat quietly, focused on the monitor, hoping whoever it was would go away.

The handle turned.

Dammit. In his rush, O'Clair had forgotten to lock the door behind him.

The door opened a crack. Raj leaned his head in. He was panting, his face flushed. A big touchdown by the Giants, O'Clair figured—or nothing he had time to hear about. He kept his focus on the laptop.

Down to 5,629 waves.

"Doctor—"

"Can it wait, Raj?"

"Sarah's trying to get you on the phone. Says it's an emergency." Raj backed into the hall, allowing O'Clair privacy.

O'Clair eyed the desktop phone. Incoming calls flashed on both lines. He'd also racked up three voice-mail messages. His ex-wife would call only if something had happened to Nathan. He snatched up the handset.

"Is Nathan okay?" he cried into the mouthpiece.

"He's okay for now," came the voice of a woman— or possibly the electronically altered voice of a man— that could have fooled Sarah's friends. "And he will be as long as you give us the two devices."

O'Clair's breath froze in his chest. "Where is he?"

"The Madagascar building."

It meant nothing to O'Clair, until he recalled Nathan's mention of a soccer team trip to the Bronx Zoo.

"Apparently he wandered away from his pack, and he didn't pay attention to the Do Not Enter signs," the voice continued. "Open the e-mail we just sent to your personal account, and you can see him for yourself."

O'Clair swatted the space bar, freezing the video of the second-grade play on the university-issued computer. He clicked into his Gmail and opened the message titled HI, DAD! Activating the hyperlink in its text box opened streaming video of Nathan standing on a narrow concrete barrier that formed the border between two dark pools lit greenish yellow. Wearing his team's replica Manchester United soccer jersey, the boy was trembling. A dark form floated across the surface of the water in the foreground.

"That's a crocodile, eighteen feet from snout to tail," said the voice. "The Madagascar building is closed until April for renovation. There's no other human there now except my colleague with the stun baton that's keeping the crocs from little Nathan—for now, and, we hope, for good. Your boy has absolutely blown us away with his mathematical ability."

"How do I know this video is real-time?" O'Clair asked.

"Give me a word or phrase and we'll have Nathan repeat it."

"We're going to Disney World after this."

Over his computer's tinny speakers, O'Clair heard a man repeat the phrase, the words resounding against the habitat's damp walls. Nathan turned toward the camera. One of the overhead spotlights revealed his tears.

"We're going to Disney after this," he stammered. "Help me, Daddy!"

Agony clawed O'Clair's intestines.

The woman said, "Now, Dr. O'Clair, take the listening devices and bring them to the service elevator room down the hall. Give them to a man who'll answer to the name Mr. Kentucky? Got it?"

"Service elevator room, Mr. Kentucky, got it." O'Clair eyed the laptop. The data streams had dwindled to just 78. Remove the plastic cups from the docking stations now and the entire extraction would be for naught: The capacitors in the listening devices would run out of charge, and the data captured to that point would essentially be reduced to a screenshot of jagged lines, the recipient impossible to track.

The sound of a splash snapped O'Clair's attention back to the video feed from the zoo. Inches to Nathan's left, a snout pierced the surface of the murky water. The boy backpedaled, arms flailing in an effort to keep from falling off the slippery balance beam. A pole entered the video camera's frame, its tip producing a starburst and a blast of electrical static. With a growl, the crocodile submerged.

"Sixty seconds and our man walks out of the Madagascar building," the woman told O'Clair. "Starting now."

O'Clair's mind was a beehive of panic.

On the laptop, a mere seven data streams remained.

"Fifty-nine seconds, fifty-eight—"

Balancing the headset between jaw and shoulder, O'Clair pulled both cups containing the devices free of their docking stations.

"Good. Now, bring them to Mr. Kentucky, who's waiting in the service elevator room at the end of the corridor, to your right, and around the corner. You have forty-nine seconds."

O'Clair swiveled in his chair, rising swiftly, smashing a hip into the sharp edge of the steel-topped desk. He struggled to retain his grip on the two plastic cups, stacking them in one hand in order to yank open the door with the other.

He found the hallway deserted and silent. He burst into his practiced lope, needing just six or seven strides to reach the service elevator room, which was quiet but for the groans of the cables within the elevator shaft. Stacking the containers again, he plunged the lever handle, opened the door, then backed into the tiny concrete space that served as the service elevator landing. He nearly ran into its lone occupant, a stocky man with prematurely gray hair and a whisk broom of a mustache, both probably fake. The man wore a cigar-brown UPS jumpsuit and a pair of surgeon's glasses, the lenses extending into loupes.

"Mr. Kentucky?" O'Clair asked.

"Yes, sir," the man said. Deep, smoky voice. He reached for the plastic cups.

O'Clair handed them over. The man regarded the purple sand with a twisted smile.

O'Clair pleaded. "They're in there, you have to be-lieve me."

Mr. Kentucky's matter-of-fact nod offered some comfort. "They said you'd probably keep the things in something funky like this."

He poured the play sand into a sieve he had at the ready. The purple grains fell to the floor, some bounc-ing away, the rest coating his shoe tops. He studied the devices through the binocular lenses.

Nodding his satisfaction, he snapped up a cell phone and muttered into the mouthpiece. "Birds in hand, Alpha."

"Roger that," came the voice like Sarah's through the receiver.

"So my son's okay?" O'Clair begged.

"He will be." Mr. Kentucky handed him a clip-board with a sheaf of shipping forms. "I've just gotta get your signature first."

O'Clair took it reflexively. "Why?"

"Diversion." The man leveled a pistol that had been concealed by the clipboard.

Gaping at the silenced barrel, O'Clair backed to-ward the door. As he reached for the handle, the gun coughed. Pain flared in O'Clair's forehead and—

22

Thornton paced the sleek floor of the Faraday tent, his anticipation dissolving into misgiving in the fifteen minutes after O'Clair's departure. Five minutes more and a sticky trepidation coated him. Hearing men walking out in the corridor, louder as they drew closer, he stopped pacing. He recognized the Gujarati-accented voice of the lobby guard, saying, "What good can the paramedics do for him now?"

"We need to have official confirmation of death," said the guard's companion, a man with a gravelly voice lacking any distinct accent. His sturdy step was accompanied by a distinct medley of jangles and squeaks—a combination, Thornton suspected, of metal handcuffs, flashlight, thick gun belt, holstered standard-issue Glock 17, ammo pouches, a canister of pepper spray, and a baton: New York City cops were walking armories. "The more important thing now is securing the crime scene—physical evidence that could convict the murderer can be rendered useless if a single unauthorized person gets in."

"Poor Dr. O'Clair, he had a little boy, just seven years old."

Anguish speared Thornton. He needed to ignore it, he knew, and to entirely deactivate his emotions. Turning to Mallery, he shot a finger to his lips.

Unnecessarily. She'd heard the conversation too. Shock pinned her to her stool, it seemed, leaving her a shade paler than usual.

"The other thing is, it didn't happen very long ago, so the shooter may still be on the premises," said the policeman in the hall. He paused when his radio broadcasted a transmission from a dispatcher requesting that a unit in the vicinity of Broadway and 93rd respond to a 10-31. The policeman continued, "I'll want to talk to a Mr. Russell Thornton and a Ms. Beryl Mallery."

Thornton could think of no reason that a policeman would have their last names. No good reason. Mallery's arched brow said she was on the same wavelength.

"These people were the two visitors to Dr. O'Clair?" the guard asked, as he and the cop strode past the lab in the direction of the elevator.

The other man lowered his voice. "Caucasian male and female in their thirties?"

"Yes, yes, they arrived in the lobby perhaps an hour ago, but they seemed so . . . You do not suspect them in this, do you, Officer?"

"Not as yet. Do you know where I can find them?"

"Possibly Dr. O'Clair admitted them to a laboratory."

"Which laboratory?"

"Sorry, I do not know."

"You got a building passkey?"

"Not a passkey, but . . ." The security guard shuffled what sounded like a stack of plastic key cards.

"Thanks. Now, can you go back down to the lobby to admit the backup team?"

"Certainly, Officer Logan."

The elevator tolled its arrival. Thornton heard the guard board and the doors clap shut, leaving behind Logan, who obviously was not a police officer, Thornton thought. Thornton listened to the man unlock and open a door, then let it fall shut.

"Searching for us?" Mallery mouthed.

Thornton nodded. He drew his reporter's pad from his back pocket to jot down the plan he had in mind, until remembering he could speak freely. Or at least whisper. As he tiptoed to Mallery, another door opened, then closed. Any key card now and Logan—probably not really named Logan either—would find them.

Thornton whispered the first half of his plan to Mallery. Footsteps outside the laboratory door brought an untimely end to their plotting.

"Just follow my lead," Thornton said, as if everything would be fine. In fact, he'd yet to fully formulate the other half of the plan.

He pushed open the tent flap. She exited ahead of him, without a sound, turning right and then right again around the corner of the Faraday tent, into the two-foot-wide gap between it and the inner wall. Another right turn and she disappeared from his view into the space between the tent and the building wall that faced uptown.

Thornton was halfway down the gap between the tent and the inner wall when the door popped open; he froze in midstride next to a tall wooden bookcase. Logan clanked through the doorway, entering the tent. The heavy door thudded shut behind him.

When the echo dimmed, he called out, "Hello?"

Thornton said nothing. There was no sound of Mallery, in hiding behind the tent.

"Mr. Thornton? Ms. Mallery?"

Over the pounding pulse in his temples, Thornton heard only the buzz from the fluorescent tubes overhead and the whistling of air through the heat register.

"NYPD. Just need to ask you folks a couple quick questions is all."

Thornton struggled to remain still. In their haste to get out of the tent, he realized, they had left their coats on the backs of the stools.

"Please come out where I can see you," Logan said.

Thornton improvised, reaching across the bookcase for the pair of ring binders whose spines extended from the edge of the top shelf. A gentle nudge sent them toppling from the bookcase, dimpling the tent wall before thumping against the floor, one after the other, motion and sounds that might be mistaken for a man dropping to his knees.

Logan responded with gunshots that sounded like thunder in the confined chamber. Hands held tight over his ears, Thornton watched nine holes appear in rapid succession in the tent wall by the ring binders' landing spot. The laboratory wall became a haze of plaster dust. The two uppermost bullet holes in the tent combined to form a slit through which Thornton glimpsed Logan, a clean-cut, sinewy young man, kneeling in a practiced firing position. He wore a navy blue eight-point police cap with shiny black visor and a black nylon patrolman's jacket. His blue turtleneck collar was embroidered with gold letters, NYPD. A distinctive black SSE5000 radio—custom-made for the New York Police Department by Motorola—clung to his belt. Like his navy blue whipcord trousers and black oxford shoes, every element in the uniform looked authentic. Except it was brand-new, all of it. Meaning Logan could be a member of New York's Finest who'd recently been to the outfitters, or he was a killer in an NYPD costume procured in a haste that precluded a few washer and dryer cycles. Whoever he was, he exited the shot-up tent and, batting his way through a cloud of plaster dust, rounded the corner into the gap where Thornton stood.

Thornton backed up, flattening himself against
the wall on the side of the bookcase facing away from
Logan. He held his breath rather than risk inhaling
and coughing the plaster dust. When he sensed that
Logan was within reach, Thornton sprang, swinging
the syringe sidearm. He drove the needle through the
purported cop's pants and into his thigh, then hammered the red plunger, hopefully sending the drug
flowing into the femoral artery, the main supply line
of blood to the lower leg.

Surprised, Logan leaped backward. Seeing the
plastic tube stuck in his quadriceps, he smirked and
said, "Nice try."

O'Clair had said that the anesthetic acted instantly, but he was an electrophysiologist, not an an-
esthesiologist. And injecting the femoral artery had
been Thornton's idea. Maybe a shoulder or biceps
would have been better. Regardless, Logan was still
standing, leveling a stout Glock 17 still containing as
many as six bullets.

"You're dead," he said to Thornton.

"In point of fact, you are, or will be shortly," came
Mallery's voice from behind the tent. "Without the
antidote."

Keeping the gun locked on Thornton, Logan
looked in her direction. "Antidote?"

"If you want it, you need to tell us who sent you,"
she said.

As Logan looked in her direction, Thornton
inched a hand toward the shelves, planning to capi-

talize on her diversion by flinging a book at Logan's face, then rushing him to take him down.

Logan glanced back at him, his eyes narrowing. "Is this some kind of joke or—?" He fell to the floor like a sack of potatoes, out cold before his body landed.

"A stall tactic, actually," Thornton said. To Mallery, he added, "And a good one."

Peeking around the corner of the tent, she shook her head. "Beginner's luck."

Thornton stepped toward the fallen man with the intent of dislodging the Glock. But he heard two hurried sets of footsteps in the hallway, accompanied by now-familiar sets of squeaks and clanks. The backup unit. Thornton reversed course.

"We need to get out of here," he whispered, rounding the corner to the back of the tent. Stepping past Mallery, he unfastened the latch securing the lower window sash.

She looked at him as if he'd lost his mind. "This is the fourth floor."

"There's no other way out." Balancing expediency and stealth, he raised the heavy window. The influx of cold air numbed him. "Out alive, that is."

Something impacted the door to the lab with a crunch of splintered wood. A battering ram, Thornton guessed.

Climbing through the window, he looked over his shoulder to find Mallery directly behind him, her look of resignation hardening into one of resolve.

He stepped out onto a steel ledge extending from

the base of the window by just four or five inches. Clinging to the building's icy metal skin, he rotated his feet so that his toes pointed away from each other. Mallery lowered herself onto the ledge beside him, tentatively, until confident it would support both of them.

Thornton pressed the window shut, hoping to add a few seconds before the backup team considered that he and Mallery had resorted to such a foolish escape route. Through the glass he heard the door to the lab fly inward. The illuminated Exit sign in the hallway cast shadows of the men hurrying into the lab.

Ducking out of their sight, Thornton told Mallery, "Two of them."

"Better than eight."

The bitter air caused her to tremble but added a healthy pink to her face. Until she looked down. "Shit," she said.

Thornton shared her assessment. "We can do this," he said, clasping her forearm. He led her toward the next window, inches at a time. Then he reconsidered. "I'm not so sure what the point is, actually. Smash through the next window so we can be sitting ducks in that lab instead?"

Mallery nodded. "But what choice is there?"

Frosty wind sliced through the gaps between the buttons on Thornton's shirtfront as he studied the two-lane 120th Street, the sidewalks populated by a dozen or so pedestrians, none appearing to notice the man and woman up on the ledge. A taxi sped down the mostly deserted street. Parked parallel to the sidewalk directly below was a brown UPS delivery truck. The boxy truck's translucent white roof, meant to admit light to the cargo area, looked to be constructed of plastic malleable enough to provide some give. But even if they could jump onto it and keep themselves from bouncing to the street, the initial impact would seriously damage them—best-case.

As if reading Thornton's mind, Mallery said, "Dropping forty feet means hitting the truck at thirty-four miles per hour."

"Yeah, let's not do that." A rank gust of wind shifted his focus to an open boxcar-size dumpster on the sidewalk below, brimming with black plastic bags full of garbage. Pointing, he said, "Smells like the other day's manicotti, which would be a lot better to land on than, say, bottles and cans."

Mallery indicated a trio of young women descending the steps from Columbia Teacher's College, directly across 120th Street. "How about we call to them, and they get the real police?"

The women turned toward Broadway. In seconds, they would be gone. Leaving no one else in sight.

Thornton said, "Sometime in the next month, if we're lucky, homicide detectives would determine that the lobby guard was duped by men impersonating cops who had long since shot us and gotten away."

From inside the lab came an assortment of crashes,

the Faraday tent being torn down. The members of the backup team made their way closer to the window. Mallery stared at the trash bags below, her reluctance appearing to yield to a grim acceptance.

Thornton pressed his palms against the building and tensed his knees in preparation to spring off, all the while hoping some turn of events would prevent the need to do it.

"It's important to try and land feet first, then roll so that you absorb the impact with your shoulder," he said.

"How do you know this?"

"News story." Best to keep the rest of the details to himself, he thought. The story's subject, an MTA electrical worker, had jumped a similar distance from an unstable scaffold to a patch of grass at the edge of Union Square. He didn't roll, consequently breaking both legs, his jaw, his nose, and an orbital socket. "I'll go first."

His reasoning, that he wanted to make sure the trash bags would give sufficiently, was curtailed by a hoarse male voice from within the lab: "They couldn't have gone out the window, could they?"

"They might've," said the other man. "Text the New York COS and get some more warm bodies up here."

Although the dumpster was almost as big as a box-car, the height made it look like a shoebox to Thornton. Not the time to become acrophobic, he thought.

Or to think.

He leaped, arcing outward so as not to strike the building on the way down. Freezing air rushed around him like jets. His stomach rose into his throat.

Feet first, he told himself.

Too late. His already sore rib cage and his left cheek smacked into swollen bags, which gave, swallowing him into blackness. From his vantage point at the bottom of the dumpster, the garbage blocked out the light altogether. Blocked out fresh air, too. Wedging himself between two bags, he groped and kicked his way upward, holding his breath lest the stench overwhelm him. He toed something big that squirmed.

Surfacing, he was ecstatic. A flash blinded him. Using a hand as a visor, he focused on the source. The laboratory window rising. He pointed for Mallery's benefit. She looked to the window, then gazed to the overcast sky as if seeking divine intervention.

"Now," Thornton mouthed.

She gazed in his general direction, but nothing more.

As he wondered how he might coax her without giving her presence away, she stepped off the ledge, plummeting feet first, arms gracefully tucked to her sides, yet, from his perspective, like an incoming missile.

He flung trash bags aside to get out of her trajectory. She landed feet first, disappearing into the sea of bags. He threw himself into a prone position, spreading his legs to maintain stability—this was straight out of his old Red Cross lifeguard manual. He stabbed an arm into the darkness.

"I've got you," he said.

No response.

He hoped she could still hear him.

"Up here," he tried.

Was she unconscious? Or worse, was she—?

Her hand clasped his wrist, electrifying him. Grabbing her elbow with his free hand, he hauled her to the surface. Her face glistened with what he took for blood, until catching a whiff. Marinara sauce.

A man appeared at the window, the dwindling sunlight relegating him to a silhouette. Pointing a gun.

Thornton instinctively froze. Mallery too.

With a shrug, the man retreated into the lab.

Mallery used a sleeve to wipe the sauce from her face, then started out of the dumpster. The squeaking of her limbs against the damp rubber bags was heard four stories up: the gunman reappeared at the window, silenced gun flashing.

A bullet dinged the far lip of the dumpster, inches from Thornton's head, pelting his face with bits of paint and stinging his eardrums. Mallery ducked beneath the surface of the bags.

"Lucky shot." Thornton spat out a rusty flake. "Still, this isn't such a good place to be."

Counting on the combination of distance, poor

lighting, and movement to hinder the next shot, he grabbed the dumpster's lip and swung himself over it, landing on all fours on the street. The giant metal container was now between him and the gunman.

Another flash and a round stung the street, sending asphalt into his shin. Mallery jumped to the street, touching down beside him, and slipping on something wet. He lunged, catching her by the waist. A bullet cleaved the air where his head had been, pinging a parking meter across 120th Street.

With Mallery in tow, Thornton launched himself toward the corner of 120th and Broadway so that the entire science building shielded them from the gunman. A bullet clanked the building's façade, creating a splash of shrapnel, a shard of which sliced the rubber sole of Thornton's shoe, slitting his heel. He knocked the shard loose as he jogged down the sidewalk, at the same time releasing his grip on Mallery. She ran with him and soon, with long, catlike strides, outpaced him. Category of desirable problems, he figured.

23

The bitter evening limited upper Broadway to a smattering of students and a vendor trying to sell roasted chestnuts. Most everyone else huddled in a bus shelter on the far sidewalk. Thornton and Mallery sprinted down the sidewalk on the other side of Broadway. Suddenly she stopped.

He pulled up beside her. "What is it?" he asked.

"Them." She indicated the pair of campus guards, on the sidewalk four blocks down, charging toward them on Segways.

"Top speed of eighteen miles per hour. Might be comical if they weren't after us."

"You think Officer Logan duped them, too?"

"I don't want to find out." Looking across Broadway to his car, Thornton took into account the time required to unlock both doors—BMW manufactured the model back when power locks were only the stuff of car shows—and start the engine. Or to sit and wait while it failed to crank. "Let's get a taxi." He scanned the sparse traffic. Just three cabs, the medallion numbers on the rooftop signs all dark, indicating they already had fares. "Next time," he added.

With Mallery following, he ran across Broadway as far as the grassy median. He unpocketed his key and scurried the rest of the way to the '02, whose driver's side faced him. He unlocked and dove into the car, reaching across and swatting the passenger door open. Mallery dropped into the seat.

"The good news is the guys in the lab weren't FBI, so we can safely go to the Bureau now," he said, spinning the key in the ignition, spurring a croak from the engine. "In light traffic like this, we'll be there in less time than it would take to get a human on the phone." He tried the ignition again. The engine shook into a splutter that sharpened to a roar. He thrust the gearshift from neutral into first. The '02 leaped down Broadway, throwing his stomach backward. He liked the feeling. The car blew past the guards on Segways. In the rearview mirror, Thornton saw the men's faces twist with rage.

"How do you know the guys in the lab weren't FBI?" Mallery asked.

"The thing one of them said about texting the New York COS for some more warm bodies." Thornton plunged the shifter from second to third. "COS is spook for 'chief of station.' The FBI doesn't have stations."

Streetlamps sputtering to life showed Broadway to be empty but for a few cabs. Home free now, Thornton thought, and he would have said so except for the UPS truck now in the rearview. Like the one that had been parked by the science building. Or maybe the same one. It sped around the corner of 114th and Broadway. The driver was hidden from sight by the windshield, red and orange and blue in the wash of neon bar and restaurant signs flying past. The passenger was visible in part: his right hand out his window, bracing a silenced pistol against his side mirror.

Mallery's eyes gleamed along with the muzzle flash shown in her side mirror. She threw herself forward, landing in a ball in the passenger foot well. The bullet sparked a street sign a lane over.

"Despite what you may have seen on TV, it's hard to fire a gun with accuracy," Thornton said. Every couple of months, he practiced with a Glock 19 or a Sig Sauer P226 at the police firing range in Queens, an effort both to better know his subject matter and to develop NYPD sources—usually over beers afterward at the Parkside Pub or McFadden's. In the range's entryway, the department posted the number of bullets expended each year by its 34,500 officers in the line of duty, an average of just 600 bullets, along with the number of misses. "Police officers are accurate with only thirty percent of their shots. And a ton less accurate from a moving vehicle, especially when the target's also moving." The front tire on his side dropped into a pothole, rattling every part of the car. "Especially in Manhattan."

One of the two taxis ahead of him swung left to pass the other so that both lanes were blocked, with the cab on the right a length in front of the one on the left. Thornton downshifted to second, allowing his car to draw an S around the cabs. They now shielded the '02 from the gunman. That wouldn't last long, though.

"If we can get to the West Side Highway, we'll lose them," he said. "It's thirty blocks."

He ignored everything but his car and the UPS truck. Broadway dropped into soft focus. At the 111th Street intersection, he wrenched the steering wheel counterclockwise. The '02 executed one of its signature ninety-degree turns. He accelerated down 111th, a block between Broadway and Amsterdam lined with stores and apartment buildings. His mirror showed the UPS truck trying to keep pace while rounding the corner. Its left front wheel caught the curb, sending the vehicle partly onto the sidewalk. The gargantuan grille struck a metal garbage can, causing an eruption of trash and shattering the headlamp. Pedestrians jumped out of the way. The driver tried to return to the street, but the rear of the truck fishtailed. The entire truck tipped to the driver's side, booming onto the sidewalk, sliding and hitting the base of a streetlamp with a clank that might have been mistaken throughout the West Side for a head-on collision of speeding trains.

Climbing back onto her seat and regarding the ruined truck, Mallery said, "Shame about that streetlamp."

Thornton smiled as he shot the '02 across Amsterdam, which ran uptown. A block later, he shifted into neutral, swinging the car downtown onto Morningside Drive, which, as usual, was quiet. There were no businesses or residences on this stretch, just the vast expanse of concrete forming the back side of the Cathedral of St. John the Divine to his right and, to the left, the stone wall protecting vehicles from a precipitous plunge into Morningside Park.

"From here, we can just hop down to 110th and get back—" Thornton cut himself short at the sight of a Big Apple Plumbing van speeding west on 110th. It jumped a red light before grinding to a stop so as to block their way.

"See that?" asked Mallery.

"Yeah," Thornton said. "I was worried we weren't going to run into any vans."

He U-turned, sending the car up a tunnel-like stretch of Morningside, with a canopy of trees extending over the street from the park and no turnoffs for three blocks. He intended to turn at 113th. Then he glimpsed the distinctive kidney-shaped grille of a BMW ahead, a brawny model X5 SUV, driving the wrong way on 116th before barreling down Morningside. The tall white van from the Connecticut Turnpike—or a van just like it—pulled even with the X5. If Thornton were to continue up Morningside, his car would be blocked, rammed, or worse. Turning back meant contending with the Big Apple Plumbing van.

"Now what?" Mallery asked.

"I have an idea." Thornton clocked the wheel, sending the car thumping over a curb and onto a patch of grass, heading toward what appeared, in the minimal lighting, to be a rocky ledge dropping straight down.

Builders in Manhattan had steered clear of the thirty acres that became Morningside Park because of the impossibility of laying streets through the rocky valley that resembled the Hindu Kush, to an extent that shocked out-of-towners. No exception, Mallery shouted, "You want to drive off a cliff?"

"There's a bike path."

He aimed for the aperture in the stone wall. The car zipped through, bouncing onto a crumbling asphalt bicycle path that wound into the park. At no point was the path as wide as the '02. Undergrowth raked the bottom of the car. Coarse bushes stabbed and grated its sides.

A throaty rev announced that the BMW X5 had also made it into the park. Thornton picked up the SUV in his rearview mirror, gliding around a hairpin curve, its headlights growing brighter and larger. In seconds it was just three car lengths behind.

The woods thickened, making the '02's headlights

almost useless, showing Thornton what he was about to hit too late for him to react. Although better suited to withstand the beating, the bigger BMW faced the same problem. To capitalize, Thornton figured he just needed to find the playground. Somewhere around here, he thought. Sure as hell would help to be able to see ahead.

In the rearview mirror, by the light of the X5's dash, he made out the form of a man in the passenger seat, his pistol extending from the window. A bullet tore into the top of the '02's backseat, filling the interior with a cloud of forty-year-old cushion particles—probably horsehair—before fragmenting the glass face of the instrument panel.

Thornton sent the '02 hurtling down a hill so steep that the front fender scraped the road, raising sparks. The X5 driver had to crunch his brakes. The SUV went into a shrieking slide. The '02 opened the gap to the length of a football field.

In her mirror, Mallery regarded the luminous dot that had been the SUV. "Was that your plan?"

"No, that's coming up." Thornton focused on the road ahead. A diamond-shaped yellow sign appeared in his headlights. Branches blocked the words on the sign, but not its figures of two children on a seesaw. He slowed down.

"What are you doing?" Mallery said in alarm.

Before Thornton could reply, a thick tree limb hanging like a bent elbow materialized in front of the windshield. He zigzagged around it. Then he tamped the brake again, slowing. Two more bullets bit into the '02's rear panel.

"They're just trying to shoot out our back tires," he said, continuing to slow the car.

She slipped beneath her seatbelt and back into a ball in the foot well, her hands covering the back of her head. "You okay?" she asked, as if suspecting he weren't.

A bullet ricocheted from the trunk into the rear-view mirror. She ducked out of the way of the explosion of glass. The X5 was within five car lengths.

"That's it." Thornton pointed ahead to what appeared to be an expanse of grass in the faint glow of the yellow dome lamps surrounding it.

Mallery peered over the dashboard. "The field?"

Thornton hit the brakes. The '02 skidded, turning counterclockwise, the tires squealing, coming to a stop ten feet shy of the green area and facing the X5.

The SUV braked, the driver probably suspecting Thornton was reversing course.

Thornton went nowhere. He watched the X5 slide off the bike path, stopping on what was actually not grass but a green algae film, cracking it, and raising hundreds of gallons of water.

"It's a pond," Mallery exclaimed as the SUV sank.

Putting the car into first, Thornton rounded the pond. An upsurge of bubbles was the only trace of the X5. A beautiful view, he thought, taking the bike path past the playground, exiting the park, and turning down residential Manhattan Avenue.

The battered '02 drew looks from pedestrians and other motorists, but no one was more astonished than Mallery, who returned to the passenger seat, a jumble of relief and mystification. "Did you at some point drive a getaway car?"

Thornton felt a measure of contentment. "I've seen the CIA's old evasive-driving instructional film—it's on YouTube."

"I've got to check that out before I have to drive in LA again." She sat back as they continued downtown.

A few blocks later, she asked, "So which spooks have a station in New York?"

"All of them," he said. "There's an old joke that UN is really short for United Network of Foreign Intelligence Agencies."

"So you think these guys are from a foreign intelligence agency?"

Thornton turned right onto a clear 107th Street. "American services don't usually whack Americans on American soil, if only because of the ever-increasing likelihood of getting caught."

"There's nothing *usual* about this business, though."

"I agree. And it wouldn't be the first time that someone or some organization, convinced that the ends justified the means, placed a higher value on a secret than on human lives. They could be from any

number of domestic services, maybe an entity operating off the books, afraid that we know enough to
incriminate them."

"Officer Logan seemed as American as apple pie,
though."

"He could have been born in the USA and gone
on to be an Eagle Scout, then got duped by a foreign
service into expunging law-abiding citizens." Thornton turned left at an uncrowded Columbus Avenue,
sending them downtown. "There are also Russian
and Swedish and even Chinese operatives trained to
pass as Americans to the point that they land jobs at
the CIA and FBI."

"I get that a foreign intelligence agency running
a sophisticated eavesdropping operation might want
to keep tabs on someone who might throw a wrench
in their plans. But why would they get mixed up in a
California Senate election?"

"Maybe to continue getting 'product' from Gordon Langlind. The chairman of the Senate Intelligence Committee has access to a lot of goodies.
Maybe he was coerced."

"If he's an ideal candidate for anything, it's black-
mail."

"Catherine Peretti could have learned about the
arrangement."

"And made the mistake of taking the story to a
journalist who happened to have one of the devices
in his head?"

Thornton shook his head. "That would be too co-incidental. Alternatively, the eavesdropping operation is massive."

He turned right at West 79th Street, which led to a ramp up to the West Side Highway. The bright glow from the top of the ramp gave him pause. He couldn't put a finger on why before it was too late to turn back, or turn anywhere except into the traffic clotting the highway's southbound lanes. He braked hard to avoid rear-ending a Volkswagen. His forward progress was so slow, the speedometer needle didn't budge from its cradle. Two more cars fell into place behind him.

"What is this?" Mallery asked.

"People coming home from the weekend." He planned to add that an accident ahead of them had probably brought the traffic to a standstill, but motion drew his attention to his rearview mirror.

Three men appeared, ascending the narrow sidewalk alongside the 79th Street on-ramp. They wore NYPD uniforms. Logan brought up the rear, apparently no worse for the anesthesia. The trio waded into the stalled traffic and split up, disappearing into the brake-light–tinted fog of exhaust fumes. They would find the bright orange 1973 BMW in another minute, Thornton thought. Or less.

"See them?" Mallery said.

"Yes. Time to get that cab."

She nodded. Sliding the dome light switch to off, he cracked his door. Inching forward in his seat until the top of his head dipped below the headrest, he pushed the door out just enough to slip onto the highway, then ducked beneath the window line. Wind off the river rattled the elevated stretch of road.

Mallery followed him, this time without hesitation. Staying low to the pavement, they left the bullet-riddled '02 and scurried past twenty or thirty vehicles.

Apparently unseen by the purported cops on the opposite side of the highway, they gained the 79th Street ramp. They ran down its sidewalk, until rounding a curve and nearly colliding with the two Columbia security guards on Segways.

Which Thornton and Mallery could outrun. "Come on," he said, springing toward the opposite sidewalk.

One of the campus security guards had fired a Taser, Thornton realized, after its projectiles caught him by the cheek. Their sharpened electrodes knifed into his flesh, deluging him with searing pain and body slamming him against the pavement.

The other man corralled Mallery, cuffing her wrists behind her. Logan ran up, followed by his two cohorts. One of them had a gun, the other a black tube the size of a paper towel core that he aimed at Thornton.

24

Lamont's world snapped from black and white to Technicolor as the details came over the phone. He clicked off the Knicks game, threw on a dress shirt, and jumped into a pair of suit pants. From the sounds of it, Musseridge was in the midst of the same process in Brooklyn while relaying the news of the guns-blazing high-speed chase, the overturned UPS truck containing the NSA guy's body, NYPD impersonators, and the disappearance of Thornton and a billionairess. Still buttoning his shirt, Lamont ran out of his apartment, his jacket and overcoat bunched under an arm. Reaching the elevator landing, he pounded the DOWN button.

Should have taken the stairs, he thought a long ten seconds later. He paced the dimly lit eleventh-floor

corridor, the Alphabet City building silent but for
wind howling in the elevator shaft. It started to feel
like Musseridge's call had been a dream.

After a fifteen-minute taxi ride, Lamont took in
what the handful of curious passersby on West 111th
Street believed to be the aftermath of a spectacular
traffic accident. Another five minutes and he was
hoofing it crosstown on 110th, deployed by a supervisor to the pond in Morningside Park. Odds were, like
the UPS truck, the submerged vehicle was recently
stolen. The Bureau hoped that, in their haste to avoid
drowning, the passengers left behind clues beyond
the muddy footprints leading away from the pond.

Lamont turned uptown on Manhattan Avenue,
then into the park, passing a metal swing set, ivory in
the spill of headlamps aimed at the adjacent pond by
four NYPD squad cars and a chunky mobile lab belonging to the Bureau's Emergency Response Team.
Two of the team members were debating whether to
wait until arc lights were strung before hauling out
the car—evidence in water degrades by the second.

After apologizing to Lamont that the paper cup in
her hand represented the last of the coffee, the Bureau
supervisor on the scene briefed him: Three hours had
passed since the orange, 1970-something BMW burst
out of the park. In the interim, fifteen members of the
ERT had sealed the area and sixteen cops fanned out
in search of perps whom not a single person had seen.
About what Lamont had anticipated. If you're a perp,

which escape route would you choose, a dark and deserted park or a well-lit New York City street full of eyewitnesses?

Sure enough, the supervisor tasked Lamont with finding better witnesses. A dead-horse beating, Musseridge termed this kind of gig. Judging caffeine an operational prerequisite, Lamont wandered up Manhattan Avenue in search of a bodega, a local term for the little grocery stores that averaged one per block. The darkness masked a century's worth of deterioration, restoring grandeur to the Italianate brownstones originally built as mansions, now subdivided into at least ten apartments apiece. On 112th, Lamont found bodegas at either end of the block, both fronted by thick transparent plastic sheets to protect walls of fresh fruit and cut flowers from the elements. Outside the nearer store, an elderly Asian man sat on an upturned plastic pail. He dipped a spoon into a thermos, steam billowing from the hot contents.

In front of the far bodega, there was just a steaming thermos set beside an identical upturned pail. The attendant must have gone inside to ring up a sale, Lamont thought, when a middle-aged white man stepped out of the shop, tearing the wrapper from a candy bar. Rather than dropping the wrapper in the trash can two feet away, he let it fall to the sidewalk. If he hadn't littered, Lamont probably wouldn't have given him another thought. But now, watching the guy shove chocolate into his mouth, Lamont thought he looked familiar. Someone from the Bureau maybe?

Curious, Lamont followed, doubling his pace. Old sodium streetlights tinged the next block orange and showed no one else around. The area was silent, or, rather, playing Manhattan's version of silence, the low murmur that's a sum of steam banging through heating ducts, subway cars racing underground, thousands of motor vehicles in traffic, and millions of people no good at staying still. As if in response to Lamont's rapid footfalls, the guy he was following glanced back. He appeared wary—understandably, this late on a near-deserted Harlem block. Lamont noticed that his mouth was permanently set in a grin.

It was Ralph Brackman, Lamont realized. The DNA false-positive.

Except his hair was longer and he appeared to have gained weight in the few days since the visit to his house in Jersey. And hair didn't grow that quickly. Muscles either. Were the changes an illusion, a function of his stiff woolen peacoat, or shadow play? In any event, it was definitely Brackman. Lamont would have recognized that grin through the most elaborate disguise.

Brackman kept walking; Lamont kept following. If Brackman recognized Lamont, he hadn't shown it. From half a block away, so far out of context, maybe he wouldn't.

"Mr. Brackman," Lamont called out.

Brackman either didn't hear or continued ahead for some other reason. Lamont could only guess why: The Central Harlem blocks between here and 125th represented the five boroughs' greatest concentrations of brothels and illicit gambling parlors—places you left keeping your head down as a matter of course. You would pretend not to notice a friend or, of all people, a Fed.

A moment later, though, Brackman turned back. He looked right past Lamont, tracking the spray of approaching headlights to a taxi. The medallion number on the roof was dark—the cabbie already had a fare.

Shoulders sagging, Brackman tramped on.

Which was greater, Lamont wondered, the odds of Brackman being here now or those of a DNA false-positive?

Jogging to catch up, Lamont shouted, "Mr. Brackman."

The man stopped in the center of a cone of streetlight. Turning, he said, "You got me mistaken for somebody else, man." The voice was different, too—deeper, and smoky.

The guy could be Brackman's cousin, Lamont thought, or brother even, if he had one. Then he remembered: Ralph Brackman was the only *surviving* child of lifelong New Yorkers Arthur and Penny Brackman. Lamont revised his odds, taking into account the likelihood of a mistake in government death records and a hit man faking his own death: Seeing this man here wasn't such a long shot after all. Because monozygotic twins had identical DNA sequences.

Reaching for his holster, Lamont got out, "Sir, I'm Special Agent Warren Lamont with the F—"

—before the guy bolted across Lenox Avenue, narrowly missing the cab barreling around the corner from 112th.

The cab driver pounded both his horn and his brakes. His tires shrieked. His passengers, two young men, both screamed. Lamont threw himself backward, landing on the curb, its rough cement tearing into his palms. The taxi missed his feet by inches, continuing uptown, leaving behind only faint echoes.

Shaking the lingering taillight glare out of his eyes, Lamont sprang up and sprinted across the street and tried to close the block-long gap between him and the Brackman look-alike. The guy needed three strides for every two by Lamont. Perhaps cognizant of his disadvantage, he took a sharp turn up into yet another bodega. Headed for a rear exit?

Trying to dodge him, the young attendant stumbled into the plastic sheet fronting the fruit. Lamont charged past her, drawing his Glock, entering the bodega in time to see the guy's boots as he dove behind the cash register counter, scattering a boxful of little energy drinks.

The store's three aisles were jammed floor to ceiling with most every household item that could fit in a grocery sack. Need for cover drove Lamont into the aisle farthest from the counter, just as the guy popped up, blasting a pump-action shotgun. Uncooked rice erupted from a sack beside Lamont, the grains nicking his face, as buckshot blew past him, shattering a glass freezer door. His hearing was replaced with a whine.

The store settled, the air filled with a haze of cocoa powder and something resembling cat litter. Lamont dropped to a prone position, reducing the target area he offered. He reached his Glock out from the aisle, burning the side of his left hand against the gritty steel belly of a giant soup kettle. Good luck, he thought. The kettle offered him a better chance than bullets at the man behind the counter.

He laid cover fire for himself, turning a few packs of cigarettes on a shelf behind the counter into confetti. The Brackman look-alike dropped to the floor. Lamont used a small sack of rice as a potholder for his left hand and his gun to protect his right. He gripped either side of the nearly full giant kettle, hefted it chest high, then shot-putted it.

The kettle left a trail of vapor as it hurtled across the bodega and boomed onto the countertop before skidding into the cash register and falling onto its side. Steaming soup gushed over the far side of the counter, resulting in a bestial scream.

Lamont started toward his victim. The man stood up, shotgun leveled. His face was purple, one eye swollen shut, the other eye about to be. He fired again. The shot turned a ceiling tile into a flurry of cheeseboard particles. The soupy forestock slid out of his grip before he could get off another shot.

25

Thornton found himself in the fetal position on a freezing floor mat, his hands flexicuffed in front of him, ankles bound, mouth gagged with a rag that tasted of petroleum. His head, in dire need of painkillers, had been stuffed into a tight hood. He had no sense of whether it was night or day, whether he'd been out for minutes or hours. When he inhaled, prickly fabric drifted into his nostrils. He heard only a light breeze—white noise, he realized, emitted by noise-canceling headphones. There was no negating the tug of gravity, though. He felt wheels turning over smooth road surface, and, when the road turned bumpy, the abrupt rises and drops of a vehicle in need of new shocks.

He worked himself into a seated position with-

out his head hitting anything—so he wasn't inside a
trunk. The vehicle took a sharp left. Centrifugal force
flung him to the right, into an unpadded metal wall.
A few more turns and he'd gathered that he was alone
in the back of a cargo van, separated from the cab by
a metal wall. Possibly Mallery rode up front in the
cab; he couldn't get a sense of who was up there—no
traces of cologne or perfume or perspiration, nothing
at least that penetrated the exhaust fumes or the hood
filled with his own sour breath.

The van took an extraordinary number of turns,
traversing every manner of road. If the driver's objective had been to utterly disorient Thornton, he had
succeeded ten turns ago.

Eventually the van slid to a halt. Front doors
opened and closed—or so it felt. Thornton suspected
the side cargo door opened too, when icy air hit him.
Hands clamped onto his shoulders, others onto his
ankles, and he was dragged from the vehicle, then
propped into a standing position on flat pavement.
The view inside the hood stayed as black as ever: It
was still nighttime—or an overcast day. A cold wind
buffeted him, the air carrying waxy fumes of aircraft
hydraulic fluid. Despite his headphones, he heard the
wheels tear into a runway, along with the whine of jet
engines, which grew closer.

His handlers plucked off his shoes, then unsnapped, unzipped, and yanked off his jeans, along
with his boxers. Before he could guess what degra-

dation was on the agenda, they stepped him, one leg
and then the other, into a pair of tight-fitting, foamy
shorts. To take the place of trips to the lavatory on a
long flight ahead, he figured. This was shaping into
a textbook rendition, a benign term for kidnapping
with the purpose of detention and interrogation.

Two handlers prodded him up shaky stairs,
pressed his head down—presumably to avoid a whack
from the fuselage on the way through the door—then
dropped him into a seat in the warm cabin. The door
thudded shut, shaking the whole plane. So not such
a big plane. The scream of the engines cut through
the white noise. The aircraft lurched forward, taxied,
then sped up. The cabin throbbed as the jet jumped
into the sky, thrusting him backward in his seat.

If his captors were following the general rendition
procedure he'd read in the Kubark Counterintelligence Interrogation manual—KUBARK was the CIA's
cryptonym for itself—they sought, at this stage, to psy-
chologically dislocate him, maximizing his feelings of
isolation and helplessness in order to destroy his will to
resist interrogation. Unfortunately, he thought, this bit
of knowledge was of no more use than a condemned
man's grasp of the workings of the guillotine. Unlike
Peretti and O'Clair, he was alive only because he remained of use to his captors. Before killing him, too,
he suspected, they wanted to know what he'd learned
of their operation and whom he'd told. Unfortunately,
his answers were *Not much* and *Mallery*. Little to work

with in order to prolong his life. And whether Mallery's life had been spared for the same reasons: He could only hope.

The Kubark manual recommended diminishing the subject's will to resist by use of techniques such as prolonged constraint, extremes of heat and cold, and, the ace in the deck, sleep deprivation. Thornton knew he ought to sleep now, while he had the chance.

He tried. But his mind burned with questions, chiefly, as Mallery had asked: Who are these people? They might be operatives for a foreign intelligence service, he thought, aiming to spirit him beyond detection by American law enforcement. In that case, they would likely have had a go at him in the van, or in a room at the first motel or abandoned building the van came to. It was more likely that they were with an American service, or at least accustomed to working with American services, which routinely netted out on rendition because they wanted to employ harsher interrogation techniques than United States law permitted—the Pakistani ISI's provision of "torture by proxy" was the glue in that service's kinship with the CIA.

Thornton mulled which U.S. service might have ordered this rendition. The FBI and the NSA no longer seemed like contenders. Probably not Defense either, since Leonid Sokolov was their own asset. But there was still the CIA, Homeland's ever-expanding and often erratic Office of Intelligence and

Analysis, the Commerce Department's massive but little-known—to its credit—Bureau of Industry and Security, the State Department's ubiquitous Bureau of Intelligence and Research . . . and at least ten others that could and would find use for a revolutionary eavesdropping device.

After hours of ruminating, Thornton was more puzzled than when he began. His stomach fell as the aircraft began its descent. He felt the vibration of the fuselage when the landing gear dropped. A minute later the wheels punched the runway.

When the plane stopped, he was pulled from his seat, then prodded from the cabin and down the steps. Sunlight warmed his hands. Daytime, he supposed. The air was hot, ninety easy, and humid. Through the pungent diesel fumes, a light breeze brought the scent of tropical verdure.

He was steered across rutted pavement, then onto a smooth surface with a bit more give, split at regular intervals. Wooden slats, he guessed. A pier? There was no crash of waves, no scent of ocean, no distant cry of seabirds—or there were, and his hood and a white-noise MP3 blocked them.

It felt as though he were boarding a boat, or something else that dipped as his handlers led him onto it. One of the handlers then maneuvered him out of the sun, down three steep steps, and into a stuffy space that stunk of brine. A cabin below deck? He was pushed into a seated position on what felt like a cushioned bench. Engines churned, the whole craft pulsated, and a brisk launch threw him sideways. Salty air rushed into the enclosure. So a boat. For all he knew, the cabin contained ten other captives. But effectively he sat alone in a dark closet, for four or five hours, until someone hoisted him to his feet.

Nudged up the steps and back onto an open-air deck, he felt the craft slowing. To his surprise, off came the hood and earphones, revealing him to be on a spacious stern deck of a grimy commercial fishing boat.

He blinked against the sunlight. It still stung his eyes. He took in fog so thick that the bow appeared to be cutting a channel through it. His handler was a barrel-chested man of about forty with black hair shaved to the skin on the sides, gradually thickening to a flattop. The precise military cut contrasted with a nose that looked to have been broken at least twice and a scruffy salt-and-pepper beard.

A tall black man of about the same age stood at the wheel, focused ahead, his round face and stovepipe arms glistening with sea spray. He looked happy. Taking in his gold earring, Thornton was reminded of a seventeenth-century portrait of Captain South, the regal Martinican pirate, at the helm of his brigantine, *Good Fortune*. This man had a similar bearing despite his grimy overalls, a soiled T-shirt, and an even filthier baseball cap, embroidered with an anchor. Flattop's attire was the same. They were going for the look of commercial fishermen, Thornton thought.

"Where are we?" he asked.

"Kansas," Flattop said in an indeterminate accent, the response a variation of the *no comment* Thornton had expected.

The latter-day Captain South stared ahead at what appeared to be a low-lying thunderhead. As the fishing boat drew closer, the dark cloud solidified into two neighboring mounds of black lava. They were islets, without a blade of vegetation between them, just a trio of big, rust-spotted Quonset huts. The two huts on the larger islet had windows; the one on the other islet only a door. A second commercial fishing boat—or prisoner transport—bobbed alongside a rotting pier that bridged the two islets. The surrounding water extended without obstruction before blending into a sky that was the same mucky gray; Thornton couldn't tell where one ended and the other began. He heard only the rhythmic thumps of the bow across the waves. This place was a maritime riff on hell, he thought—and probably was supposed to think. If not, why had they let him see it?

"What happened to the woman who was with me?" he asked, not expecting an honest answer. Sometimes, though, subjects unwittingly revealed useful information in their choice of misinformation.

"She went to the mall," Flattop said.

No meaning that Thornton could parse. Flattop had a distinctive mode of pronunciation, though, particularly the *th* as *d* in *the*. It could only be New York. Or, a few thousand percentage points less likely,

New Orleans' similar *Yat*—as in *Where y'at?*—a ves-
tige of boatmen from the New York area who settled
in Louisiana a century ago. Of course, the guy could
also be a talented Pakistani ISI agent.

Thornton manufactured a grin. To inquire further
about Mallery would betray his concern, which might
be used against him. "Don't suppose you can tell me
how the Knicks did last night?" he asked.

Flattop looked out at the waves as if Thornton
weren't blocking his view.

Soon they docked in the harbor, which reeked
of low tide even though the tide was in. Pointing a
rugged black Heckler & Koch HK45 pistol, Flattop flanked Thornton, guiding him along a rickety
wooden pier to the windowless Quonset hut. Captain South brought up the rear, with a gun of his own
as well as a cudgel of some sort that he used to prod
Thornton, who wondered why they bothered with
weapons. Still bound at the wrists and the ankles, at
best he would waddle away. And then what?

At the entrance to the Quonset hut, Flattop holstered his HK45, leaned over the incongruously futur-
istic keypad, and punched in eight or nine numbers.
A lock disengaged with a whirr. Flattop pushed open
the door and stepped through. The captain propelled
Thornton inside, then swung the door to a ringing
close behind them.

Thornton clenched his nose against the damp air,
ripe with feces and rotting God-knew-what. Without

Captain South's faint flashlight, he would have seen only blackness. As it was, he barely made out Flattop ahead of him.

When Thornton's ankle restraints caused him to lag behind, the captain hit him in the small of the back and he lost a stripe of skin from his forearm to the coarse cinder-block wall.

The corridor took a sharp right, then another, and, improbably, another. The place was a maze. Probably by design, Thornton thought. Emanating from somewhere nearby, a man's savage screams resounded throughout the metal structure. Thornton might have been rattled if not for his educated guess that the screaming was a recording they'd tripped, like the ghostly wail heard upon entering an amusement park haunted house.

After the tenth turn, Flattop stopped abruptly and told Thornton, "Turn around." When he did, Thornton's restraints were unlocked and whisked away by Flattop, who added, "Now, arms apart, hands on the wall."

Using his flashlight beam, Captain South indicated a cinder-block wall streaked with muck. At least Thornton hoped it was muck. Palms pressed against it, he waited as they patted him down.

"Turn around a hundred and eighty degrees, slowly take off everything you're wearing, and let it drop to the floor," Flattop said.

Thornton complied, suppressing natural humiliation—or trying to—by telling himself that it was these goons who ought to be embarrassed.

"Now, mouth wide open, say, 'Ah.'" Flattop stuck out his slab of a tongue by way of demonstration.

He probed Thornton's mouth and every other part of his body that might conceivably conceal contraband. Presumably passing the exam, Thornton received a canvas jumpsuit that looked gray in the low light but might have been red. It was a size too small and stunk of sweat.

"You look beautiful," Flattop said. "Time for your interview."

26

Rounding the corner, Thornton had the sensation of plunging into a black void. A moment later, Captain South caught up to him, the guard's flashlight revealing yet another filthy corridor. After about fifty feet, the captain's beam showed another numeric keypad and Flattop again entering a code. Bolts released with a hydraulic hiss. Flattop pulled open a door, took Thornton by the collar, and jerked him into the fifteen-by-ten-foot "interview room," in which an overhead fluorescent panel illuminated a traditional gritty concrete that was as devoid of color as it was of hope. Thornton suspected that the long mirror on the opposite wall was not a decorative element.

"Sit," Flattop said, pointing him to the nearer of two chairs at the center of the room.

"Thanks." Thornton lowered himself into the wobbly desk chair—wobbly by design, he suspected. The ideal was a swivel rocking chair, on wheels, with movable armrests. "Behavioral amplifier," such a piece of equipment was known as in interrogation circles, because it magnified movements of the parts anchoring the subject, for example, his feet to the floor or his elbows to the arms of the chair. Since people dissipate anxiety through this type of movement, interrogators are given an indicator of nonverbal deceptive behavior. Thornton had learned of a few such behaviors when interviewing with a CIA polygraph examiner. People unconsciously put their hands in front of their mouths and eyes, literally covering lies, the woman had told him. They also involuntarily shifted into fight-or-flight mode, rerouting blood from regions that can temporarily do without it—especially the face—to the major muscle groups. The resulting sensation of cold causes subjects to rub their faces.

Unfortunately, what knowledge Thornton had of detecting deception would be of little use in deceiving an interrogator. Even veterans at questioning admitted to being as susceptible to being caught in a lie as their subjects. In fact they were often more susceptible since there were so many involuntary cues they needed to take into consideration. "It would be like a golfer trying to keep in mind eighty different improvements to his swing while hitting the ball," the polygraph examiner had told him.

Captain South brought in a big Styrofoam container labeled SOUPER MEAL. He peeled off its lid to reveal noodles and vegetables in a broth. Steam rising from the top carried an aroma of chicken and spices, making Thornton's mouth water. The captain set the container on the floor beside his chair along with a two-liter bottle of water, ice-cold if the condensation were any indication. Thornton was parched to the point that speaking required first unsticking his tongue from the sides of his mouth, and after at least thirty hours without food, it felt as if gastric acid were dissolving his stomach lining. He hesitated to touch the Souper Meal or the water, however, for fear that they'd been spiked with "truth juice," a mixture of narcotics such as sodium amytal, thiopental, or secobarbital and methadrine. As a result of their training, most covert intelligence officers could withstand enemy interrogation while under narcosis. But a few spilled unadulterated truth, no matter what. Some told the truth, but their speech was so garbled—a side effect of narcosis—that their responses were unintelligible. Others retained their diction but lost their wits. A truth serum with better than a 34 percent success rate had yet to be invented despite a decade-long effort by Russian SVR scientists at prisons packed with Chechens used as guinea pigs. If Thornton's physiology placed him in the ungarbled-truth-spilling minority, however, he would become expendable.

He would have to eat and drink sooner or later, but

abstaining now might make the difference in whether there was a later. The longer he held out, he reckoned, the longer he lived.

"Thanks," he said, "but I'm good."

Captain South looked to Flattop, who shrugged. Then the captain scooped up the items and silently trailed the other guard out of the room.

Their place was taken by a tall man in a white lab coat, gray flannel slacks, and shiny black lace-up shoes. Pulling the door shut with more force than necessary, he proceeded to the chair six feet from Thornton's. He sat, folding one lean leg over the other, then turned to face Thornton. Fiftyish, he had a long face with wavy blond-going-white hair and close-set, clear blue eyes. At first glance, he was the sort who might be found selling real estate or giving tennis lessons at a country club. Finer details suggested a different story. His excessive pallor, particularly in light of a Nordic complexion, told of a predilection for the indoors. Perhaps for places like this. Black site personnel typically didn't bother to bring razors from home. This guy had not only shaved this morning; he'd dressed up. His lab coat was freshly starched and spotless. The creases down the front of his slacks were perfectly straight. He sported a sunny yellow bow tie and gleaming black leather shoes laced in perfectly symmetrical loops. An Army Intelligence officer had once told Thornton that, often, good men were assigned to black sites, and the blackness coated their souls; others assigned to black sites found their element.

"Before we commence today's questioning, Russell," the man with the bow tie said in a midwestern baritone, "I want you to know the reason that we plucked you off 79th Street and out of your life: We want information. To get that information, we can do anything we want. I can do anything I want. Do you understand me?"

"Yes." The gravity of the man's tone infused Thornton's tone with deference. He felt to his marrow that this guy meant what he'd said.

"No one knows what has happened to you, Russell. You have simply disappeared." Bow Tie snapped his fingers, as if performing a magic trick. "These two tiny islands are known only to a handful of cartography fanatics who believe them to be uninhabited and uninhabitable. This is your entire world now. If you are ever to leave here, you will answer all of my questions. If you are not entirely forthcoming, if you tell half-truths, or if you tell anything other than the full truth, I'll know it as surely as I would know if the lights were switched off. And I'll become angry, and my superiors will become extremely angry, and then things will get far worse for you. Do you understand me, Russell?"

"Yes." Thornton suspected that, if he were entirely cooperative, they would in fact allow him to leave here—but only in a shark's belly.

Bow Tie flicked a droplet of moisture from the corner of his mouth, then launched into a wide range of questions, beginning with Thornton's childhood. *What elementary school did you attend? What did your father do for a living?* Establishing a baseline, Thornton suspected.

He answered truthfully. Had to, he figured, because interrogators studied extensively for this initial questioning, memorizing everything they could about their subjects. In part this gave the impression that they were omniscient and that any lie would be easily uncovered. On a more pragmatic level, once they reached the important questions, they could ill afford to pause and ask subjects to repeat names and places. If a subject realizes he's revealing information, he stops.

Mindful of this, Thornton waited for the interrogator to start fishing. And waited, his throat increasingly raw as he contended with two hours' worth of the likes of *What was your grade point average at Concord Academy? What were your SAT scores? What was the name of your freshman football coach at UMass?*

Finally, Bow Tie asked, "Who tipped you off about the ballistics in the Sokolov investigation?"

If this were about Sokolov, Thornton thought, then the eavesdroppers' game could be obtaining electronic weaponry, meaning he was hardly the only one whose survival was at issue. "No one tipped me off," he said. "It was just old-fashioned information wheedling."

The interrogator looked down his nose. "Come on, Russell, we know about your agency connection."

To Thornton, it was as if dark clouds had suddenly parted, allowing sunlight to illuminate not only the objective of the rendition, but a means by which he might survive. O'Clair's counterintelligence play in Torrington had caused Bow Tie's people to fear that Thornton was working in cooperation with some agency, thereby jeopardizing their operation. Thornton could delay the release of the guillotine blade by maintaining the fiction that he really did have an agency connection.

"Ballistics had nothing to do with anything," he said. "If I had had a shred of substantiation, the story would have been about an administration of midazolam gone wrong."

"How could you have known that about the midazolam?"

Speculation, Thornton thought. Unconfirmed until now, thank you. On account of a morsel of Stalin trivia, he realized, he'd been on the money two months ago: The seven-gram lead bullet was a red herring. He must have struck a nerve at the time with his hypothesis that whoever killed Sokolov had known more Soviet history than your average hit man. Whoever had been attempting to stick a listening device in Sokolov's head went on to stick one in Thornton's as damage control. The bug's feed would have alleviated their concern: His investigation was headed toward the same dead end as the FBI's. But then came his "meeting with someone from the agency" in Torrington, Connecticut.

"How did you learn about the midazolam?" the interrogator asked again.

Like a successful seduction, Thornton reminded himself, a good lie is built upon truth. "O'Clair figured that your operator used ketamine, because hardly anyone has an allergic reaction to it. From there it was mostly deduction." True and true.

The interrogator plucked a chin whisker that must have escaped his razor. "We know that Kevin O'Clair was not your agency contact. He was a low-level analyst at NSA."

Thornton said nothing. Pointedly, he hoped.

"We also know that after you discovered your Littlebird device, you told O'Clair that you'd been contacted by 'someone at the agency' whom you planned to meet in Torrington, Connecticut, at Bill's Diner. Please don't tell me the diner's proximity to a forty-thousand-kilowatt radio tower was coincidental."

"No, of course not. The purpose was to jam the Littlebird." Thornton made a point of saying *Littlebird* as if he'd been tossing around the term for ages.

The interrogator glanced at the mirror. Thornton wondered who Bow Tie's superior was.

"Who met you in Bill's Diner, Russell?"

Easy to tell the truth here. "No one."

"No one showed up at Bill's Diner?"

"No one showed up to meet me."

"We know about the encrypted Hushmail you received beforehand, Russell. Surely you know who sent it."

"I hoped someone from the NSA was going to help me." True enough. And of the intelligence agencies who were candidates to conduct an operation on the scale of Littlebird, Thornton could rule out only the NSA with any confidence, albeit not much.

"Who, Russell?"

"I don't have a real name."

"Do you have a pseudonym?"

"That's often how it is. For instance, when calling me on a disposable cell phone, Catherine Peretti went by Jane Johnson. If you're trying to stay below the radar, you're not going to go by Jane Jingleheimer-schmidt, right?"

Bow Tie cleared his throat. "What was the pseudonym?"

"Meade." Untrue, and if the interrogator read it as dissembling, great.

"Is Meade a man or a woman, Russell?"

"I couldn't tell you." Thornton pretended to rub his chin involuntarily. "No one showed up at the diner, remember?"

"But you did meet someone at the Exxon station."

"No, I just went there to get gas."

"You went inside."

"Oh, yeah. I bought a Gatorade. The cashier was cute, but she wasn't Meade—as far as I know."

"So to your knowledge, you never met Meade?"

"Never."

"And you never received an explanation for that?"

"None. Maybe whoever it was saw the AT&T van parked a few stores down. I mean, if I can pick up a watcher, surely the pros can."

The interrogator shot another look at the mirror. Snapping his eyes back to Thornton, he asked, "Did you have any further contact with Meade?"

Thornton hesitated, as a subject might do if inventing. "No, no further contact."

"Why not?"

"I don't know. If they tracked the AT&T van, maybe they got what they needed?"

The interrogator uncrossed his legs and sat up. "Russell, you remember what I said about leaving here, about the necessity of you telling the full truth?"

"I remember."

"Who is Meade?"

Thornton shifted in his seat, causing it to squeak. "I would assume Meade is a reference to Fort Meade, Maryland, home to NSA headquarters. Then again the NSA often poses as the CIA and vice versa, so . . ."

"Do you expect anyone to believe that a skilled journalist with curiosity to a fault failed to dig deeper than that?"

"I understand why you wouldn't believe that. But, I swear to God, it's true. I'm usually working on five or six stories at a given time, plus I have another twenty or thirty on the back burner. By the time I saw the full scope of this story, I was being chased by hit men dressed as New York City cops."

Bow Tie clamped his thumb and forefinger over his mouth. Bridling emotion, Thornton suspected. An interrogator can't show frustration. It encourages the subject to hold out. And the interrogator can't foster the hope that he might give up.

"We'll take a break here," Bow Tie said, rising. He pivoted toward the door, which someone opened on his approach. Thornton couldn't see who.

The interrogator hurried into the corridor, fading into the darkness well before his footfalls subsided. Thornton bit back a smile. He would bet his apartment that he'd succeeded in planting concern in his captors that their operation faced an unknown and potent threat. Which was a hell of a lot better than their having ascertained the truth: that they had nothing whatsoever to worry about. Now, however, they would seek to extract from him the true nature of the threat. He didn't expect the process to be pleasant.

27

Thornton preceded Flattop and his flashlight through the dark corridors, the journey culminating in an unlit ten-by-eight-foot concrete cell coated in grime, the ceiling too low for an adult to stand without stooping. The furnishings consisted of a wooden pallet topped by a mattress not much thicker than a magazine and a pillow of similar proportions. The adjacent wall sprouted a stainless steel toilet bowl, its seatback rising into a tiny cold-water-only spigot and basin.

Flattop swept the flashlight beam over the floor, pausing when the light centered on a large brown scorpion in the corner opposite the toilet.

"Watch out for that guy," he said, backing out of the cell.

The door swung shut and a heavy bolt snapped into the steel jamb, leaving Thornton in a blackness that seemed solid. Eyes shut, eyes open, there was no difference. Once the echoes of the closing door faded, the silence was complete.

He hurried to get to the cot, away from the scorpion. His progress was limited to small increments, a hand extended to avoid smacking face-first into a wall. The sticky cement floor sent a chill from the soles of his feet all the way to his kneecaps. Finding the wall, he lowered himself to the slick, rubber-coated mattress, which compressed to the point that it felt like he was sitting directly on the wooden pallet. He placed his back against the wall, drawing his knees toward his chest both to keep warm and so that his feet were three or four inches above the floor. While following the Pentagon-funded cancer treatment initiative to use the chlorotoxin from the venom of the Deathstalker scorpion—*Leuiurus quinquestriatus*—he learned that of the 1,000 species of scorpion, just twenty-five posed a mortal threat. He doubted his cell mate was one of them, if only because his captors needed him alive. But he couldn't be certain. Also 1,000 of the 1,000 species of scorpions stung without provocation. If his captors sought to keep him up at night, this would do the trick.

He held the thin pillow as a shield, sweeping it from side to side to fend off the scorpion should his scent lure the nocturnal hunter to the cot. Unfortunately, he still couldn't see. Not even his hand in front of his face.

He heard the scorpion clicking toward him, or he imagined he heard it; then he felt a tickle on the back of his scalp. He jumped up to shake off the bug but found no trace of it.

And this was only the beginning. He thought it ironic that, before today, he'd considered it torture to be left alone for more than ten minutes with nothing to read.

The fifty-seat ExpressJet bound for Montgomery, Alabama, was too small to plug into the Jetways at any of LaGuardia's departure gates, so Musseridge and his fellow passengers had to go down two flights of service stairwell, exiting onto the tarmac. The FBI agent didn't bother standing on line to borrow an umbrella from the gate agents, deciding the walk to the plane would take less time. The umbrellas were almost useless anyway; the jet engines shot the freezing rain sideways.

During the flight, Musseridge forked over seven bucks for a can of Bud. Ridiculous, but worth it. When the hell else did he get a chance to sit down for more than twenty seconds without someone wanting something from him?

He immersed himself in figuring out what the fuck Thornton and the billionairess, Beryl Mallery, were

up to. Amtrak had had no record of either of them
purchasing tickets to Alabama—or to anywhere. But
they could have used cash. He'd seen Penn Station's
security video of a couple paying cash for tickets to
Mobile, Alabama—Mallery owned a beach house
nearby. Could have been Thornton and Mallery; the
video was shot from so far away that no one could really tell shit. But an agent from the Bureau's Mobile
field office interviewed a cabbie who said, yeah, he'd
had a fare who looked just like the lady in the photograph. He took her to the nearby beach town, Point
Clear, Alabama. And with her was a guy who looked
like Thornton. Meanwhile Mallery sent an e-mail to
her assistant saying she'd met someone and needed
some time alone with him. The only trace of Thornton since his disappearance was also an e-mail, to
RealStory's managing editor. He'd met someone, he
wrote, and was taking a vacation for the first time this
millennium. Love was blind and stupid, Musseridge
knew well, but that didn't explain Thornton shirk-
ing his duty to give a deposition, and in this case the
victim had been a close friend of his, Kevin O'Clair.
What's more, the seven-year-old who'd survived
O'Clair was Thornton's godson.

From Montgomery, Musseridge took a wobbly
eight-passenger puddle jumper to Mobile. The rental
place at the airport stuck him with a too-small car
that smelled of cigarette smoke and the flowery spray
meant to mask cigarette smoke. Thing rode like it

was put together from Legos. He took it around the horseshoe-shaped Mobile Bay to Point Clear, which surprised him. Who the hell knew Alabama had a picture-perfect waterside village catering to superrich people?

Mallery's sixty-two-foot catamaran, worth what Musseridge could earn in his career if the Bureau let him stay on past age 100, was gone from the marina. Left its slip sometime during the night, the harbor-master said. Mobile Bay led to the Gulf of Mexico, and the Gulf led to the rest of the world.

Alabama private vessel license decals were fitted with transponders, but the Coast Guard couldn't raise a signal from the catamaran. There were any number of legitimate explanations for transponder failure, Musseridge heard from a lieutenant at the Coast Guard's District Eight headquarters in downtown Mobile. But Musseridge had long since ruled out legitimate explanations.

He set to work on the paperwork for an Unlawful Flight to Avoid Prosecution warrant and a global BOLO—be on the lookout—with instructions to all Interpol members to capture Thornton and Mallery.

28

With a series of hisses and pings, the cell door opened. Flattop stepped in, his beam sweeping the floor until finding the scorpion, in the middle of the cell.

"Batter up," Flattop said to Thornton.

Using the wall, Thornton pulled himself up, one hand over the other. Heavy lifting for him, a function of undernourishment and an electrolyte balance at dangerously low levels. He managed to circumvent the scorpion on the way out.

Now, he believed, the worst was over. He could gorge on a Souper Meal and drink water until he burst. Nothing he might say under narcosis would dispel the doubt he'd planted in his captors; the drugs wouldn't be trusted. As for Bow Tie, going through the same questions over and over again was an interrogator's most effective tool to trip up a liar. All Thornton needed to do was stick to his story, which was true, other than the name Meade. Easy enough, he thought. As long his memory remained operational, he would survive.

He realized the error in his thinking as soon as he entered the interview room. The chairs had been replaced by a simple metal twin-bed frame, the kind you might see in a college dorm. Its support was six horizontal metal slats and the same number of thin coils stretched lengthwise. Beneath this grid was a red electrical cord, clamped onto of one of the metal slats and running along the floor to a retrofitted car battery.

The interrogator stood by the battery. He wore a fresh-pressed shirt, another crisp lab coat, and another brightly colored bow tie—and he seemed in spirits to match. He waved at the bed frame the way a game show hostess might at a fabulous prize. "This is a *parilla*." He rolled the *r* in the Spanish fashion and pronounced the *l*'s as *y*'s. "The term derives from the cooking grill of the same name used in South America. General Pinochet liked to call this version the Chilean Polygraph."

Thornton tried to steel himself with the football player's reminder that pain is temporary. It may last a minute or an hour or all day, but it subsides eventually. Quitting, however, lasts a lifetime. And that wouldn't be long here.

"Take off his clothes," the interrogator told Flattop.

Thornton reflexively took a step away from the guard.

Patting the baton hanging from his belt, Flattop said, "Don't make this tougher than it's gotta be."

Thornton offered no resistance as the guard pried off the tight prison jumpsuit.

"Now lie down on the *parilla*," Bow Tie said. "Flat on your back, legs spread apart, arms above your head."

Thornton complied, trying to desensitize himself. On contact with the metal slats, though, goose bumps rose over most of his skin. The narrow coils running lengthwise bit into his upper back, and their bite was an itch compared to the too-narrow metal cuffs the men used to clamp his wrists and ankles to the corners of the frame.

"Spectacular," said the interrogator once Thornton was secured.

From a coat pocket, the man withdrew a coiled black electrical cord labeled in red capital letters embossed on white tape: LINE NUMBER 2. Thornton pictured Bow Tie burning the midnight oil with his labeling machine.

The interrogator let the cord drop to the floor, then plugged its pronged end into the car battery. To Flattop he said, "*Agua, por favor.*"

Flattop unscrewed the cap from an ordinary plastic water bottle, then tossed a few ounces onto

Thornton's bare chest. Although the water was room temperature, it made Thornton shiver. He asked, "Anything I can tell you to save a bit of electricity here?"

Bow Tie knelt by Thornton's left shoulder. "Who's Meade?" His breath delivered a bitter whiff of coffee.

"I wish I could tell you."

"Well then, this should jog your memory." The interrogator raised the black cord gingerly. At its tip was a small electrode emitting a benign buzz. Sounded like an electric shaver. On contact with the bed frame, it had the effect of a lightning bolt. Searing current blistered Thornton everywhere he was exposed to the metal, the energy seemingly sufficient to thrust him up to the ceiling if not for the shackles slicing into and burning his wrists and ankles. Fiery pain tore up his spine and into his head and extremities, along the way rending his muscles and tendons from the bone and sending them into violent convulsions. At the same time, it felt as though his blood vessels were bursting. The pain was like the worst toothache he'd ever had, everywhere in his body at once.

Involuntarily moaning, he tried to roll to his left, away from the current. He succeeded, providing only an instant of relief before a different part of the grid dealt a jolt as potent as the first. A grin divided Flat-top's stubble.

Closing his eyes against the pain, Thornton flailed. There was no escape; anyplace he landed blasted him with fresh current. An incandescent white plume took hold of his consciousness and spread. If it swallowed him altogether and put an end to this agony, he thought, it might be for the best. Then his spine and the base of his skull cracked down onto the slats.

The interrogator was speaking. Thornton couldn't make out the words through the static in his head. The current had ceased, at least for the moment. Opening his eyes, he took a deep breath of air, which smelled like roasted meat. He retched. But he still could breathe. Surprisingly, he remained in one piece. The static dimmed to a dull buzz, through which he made out, "Who is Meade?" Bow Tie was kneeling by his left shoulder. "Your choice, Russell." He held the electrode an inch off the bed frame. "Tell me who Meade is, or another *parilla* ride."

Thornton let his head settle onto a slat, wary of a shock. To his relief, he felt only cool, smooth metal flatten his spikes of hair. He shut his eyes and sighed, as if in resignation.

"Andy Miller," he said.

The interrogator said nothing, but his eyes gleamed with triumph.

Andrew Miller had been a research analyst, at least nominally, for the NSA. Thornton had read about him on one of the natsec news aggregators *RealStory* subscribed to. Miller had died in a Beltway traffic accident last week. The NSA employed 90,000 people—on the books. Miller was the sixth most common name in the United States, after Smith, Johnson, Williams, Brown, and Jones and before Davis. Chances were the NSA had several legitimate Andy Millers, and maybe one or two more who'd used the name as an alias. Thornton suspected that his life now hinged on "agency contact Andy Miller" proving no more enlightening to his captors than "agency contact."

29

In 1966, the U.S. government got into the prostitution business, opening brothels in New York City, San Francisco, and Stinson Beach, California, in each case with the blessing and cooperation of the local police. The Federal Bureau of Narcotics took a piece of the action, too, in the role of drug dealer. The prostitutes, many of whom were placed on the government payroll, duped johns into taking acid. Researchers from the CIA's off-the-books MK-ULTRA unit sat on the other side of two-way mirrors in hope of learning to use LSD to induce subjects to reveal secrets or do the bidding of the U.S. government. The operation lasted just a few months before Congress got wind of it and played its customary role, from the Agency's perspective, of rain on a parade.

In 1998, a similar program was launched by another American service, the Bureau of Industry and Security, the clandestine operations division of the Department of Commerce. As his first order of business, the leader of the initiative, Peter Canning, sought to avoid repeating the CIA's mistake: He secured a confederate on Capitol Hill, then congressman Gordon Langlind, who vouched for the sanctity of the Department of Commerce's $25 million Currency Classification Initiative. With the funds, Canning used cutouts to open brothels in Washington, Moscow, and Geneva. The Geneva branch paid dividends within a week, when a video of the director of Azerbaijan's Ministry of Industry and Energy—in bed with a woman who was not his wife—netted an American cartel including Langlind Petrochemical the exclusive drilling rights to a vast oilfield beneath the Caspian Sea, in spite of the fact that British Petroleum's bid had exceeded the cartel's by $100 million.

Two years later, there was an accident at the then burgeoning honey trap chain's new Paris branch, which was located in a charming art nouveau apartment building in the eighth arrondissement, two blocks from the Arc de Triomphe. A client paid for rough play but took it too far, strangling his hostess. These things happened. The problem in this instance was that the client was a CIA officer.

The manager called Canning, who was based at

the time at the DOC's Moscow station. A few hours later, Canning hurried from a private jet at Charles de Gaulle to a car bound for the eighth arrondissement. On arrival at the brothel, he firmly tied, taped, and stuffed the girl's corpse into a suitcase weighted with a pair of forty-five-pound barbells. He then rolled the suitcase two blocks and dropped it into a dark, deep stretch of the Seine. The CIA officer—who had a wife and three children—Canning let walk. Save him for a rainy day, Canning thought.

The rainy day came eleven years later, when Canning got into the E-bomb business. He gave the CIA officer the choice of explaining the Paris video to his family and colleagues, or doing a little work on the side. The man agreed, believing the side work was for the Department of Commerce. Today, after a search of Thornton's New York apartment proved fruitless, Canning asked his Langley asset to scour the proprietary Intelink for Andy Millers.

Canning heard back while walking through Times Square to his hotel at ten thirty P.M., though he would never have guessed the time based upon the crowds and the neon conflagration. His buzzing phone, to anyone not in the know, signified the availability of an update for his stock market app.

He hurried to the hotel next door to his, parked himself at one of the public computer terminals in the busy lobby, and logged on to the Yahoo! account he'd created for this purpose. The in-box contained no e-mails. He would have been surprised if it had. His spam folder contained one, headed SUPER BUY VI-AGRA. He clicked it open and scanned the message: *Viagra 120mg x 650 pills = $95*. He noted the second digit of each value: 2-5-5.

He crossed Seventh Avenue to a sports bar that was to giant television screens what Times Square was to billboards. The place was ablaze with game telecasts, mostly West Coast NHL and college basketball. Canning couldn't hear any of it over the cheering crowd. He didn't care. His objective was wireless Internet access for the laptop he'd bought for $400 in cash this morning at a no-name electronics shop on Canal Street.

Procuring a seat in a dark corner, he logged onto JamOnAndOn, "a site where musicians can commune, collaborate and critique." Its 10,000 users, mostly aspiring musicians, found the critique hard to come by. Take this month's entry number 255, *Give it up, babe*. The song had attracted a total of just three listeners since its posting last week. Each listener had given it three stars of a possible five, none of them bothering to write in the Constructive Comments box. Canning ignored the song itself but activated software that extracted and decrypted the text that was randomly distributed among the pixels representing sound waves. He came away with a list compiled by his CIA asset.

The first person on the list, Andrew M. Miller Jr.,

twenty-seven years old, worked as a systems analyst in the NSA's Comprehensive National Cyber-Security Initiative Data Center at Camp Williams, Utah. He qualified for handicapped parking, probably disqualifying him from the fieldwork required on the Thornton case. Also he went not by Andy or even Andrew, but by his middle name, Mitchell.

Candidate number two was Stanford School of Engineering's former dean, Andrew C. Miller, sixty-one. He now supervised the NSA's Trailblazer program, a data-mining initiative in Milwaukee. A possibility, but not a good one given his lack of ops experience.

Langley had an operations officer at Moscow station née Andrea "Andi" Miller, a twenty-eight-year-old whose first job after college had been at Fort Meade. She had sent multiple cables from Moscow to CIA HQs each day for the past three weeks, signifying she was deep into a case there, in all likelihood eliminating her, too, as Thornton's agency contact.

Canning's eye fell to the eighth and final entry, a forty-six-year-old research analyst. This Andrew Miller's CV concluded with the account of his recent death posted by Global Security Newswire.

Canning checked the Internet histories he'd hacked into and then imported to his laptop from the personal computer in the spare bedroom Thornton used as an office. And there it was: The blogger had read the Global Security Newswire report on the Beltway traffic accident.

"The blogger is bluffing," Canning wrote in an encrypted text message to Dr. Simon Wade, the former Special Ops shrink who operated the interrogation and detention facility known as Black Islands.

Now—*finally*—Canning could traffic his E-bomb.

30

Lamont engaged a strong wind in a tug-of-war over a door before exiting 26 Federal Plaza. Hurrying into the night, he was belted by a cold sheet of rain. His lone defense, a *Daily News*, turned to pulp. He hadn't looked at the sports section yet, but he'd read enough of the rest of the paper to determine there was no mention of his activity in Harlem the night before last. Good. No sense sending millions of New Yorkers into a panic over an assassination ring.

His overcoat was soaked through before he reached the end of the block, a wind tunnel lined by monolithic office towers. He forded the traffic jam on Broadway in order to take the shortest route to Kennedy's. Tires spinning in both directions sprayed rainwater onto the parts of his suit that had somehow remained dry.

Entering the dark tavern, he was enveloped by toasty air and the pleasing aroma of steak and ale. If not for the neon brewery promotions tucked into the front window and a few modern conveniences behind the bar, James Joyce might well have entered and settled onto a barstool here without blinking. The usual postwork crush of Wall Streeters had dwindled to a smattering of patrons enjoying late dinners at elegant mahogany tables and drinks along the vast, copper-surfaced bar.

Gene Garrison, a member of the FBI's Joint Terrorism Task Force, waited in a high-backed booth offering privacy as well as a view of the entire establishment. "Joint" referred to agents, investigators, analysts, and various specialists from other law enforcement and intelligence agencies who worked alongside Bureau agents at 100 FBI field offices nationwide. Garrison had been the CIA station chief in Amsterdam before joining New York's JTTF office—the nation's first, established by the Bureau in 1980 in collaboration with the NYPD. He stood as Lamont approached, reaching out not just to shake hands but to clasp Lamont by the shoulders without regard to the dripping fabric.

"Corky, you're a hero," Garrison said. "You've earned any drink you'd like."

Indicating the tumbler already on the table, Lamont told the waitress, "Whatever he's having, please." Based on Garrison's reputation, it would be the finest single-malt scotch Lamont had ever had.

Lamont peeled off his overcoat, dropped it onto the sturdy brass hook branching from the booth's frame, and sank onto the leather bench, all the while studying the man across the table for a clue: Why would the star JTTF agent invite a rank-and-file rookie for drinks? FBI agents didn't drink on duty, and technically they were always on duty. Lamont had plans to return to the office tonight. Was this some kind of test?

In appearance Garrison was the prototypical middle-aged man. His height was average, his weight about right, and his dark brown hair had a moderate amount of gray. Other than the custom-tailored suit, there was nothing to mark him as either management or a member of the graveyard shift, no fierce look of determination, no aquiline nose, no Rolex.

They finished two rounds, mostly with Garrison asking about Lamont's college pitching career and brief dalliance with the Houston Astros. Unsure why they were talking baseball, Lamont answered self-consciously.

Finally, the spy said, "Your captive has to escape."

Lamont hoped he'd misunderstood. "Unless the marshals missed a jackhammer when they strip-searched him, I don't see how that's going to happen."

"We'll need to come up with something plausible, for the record." Garrison signaled the waitress for another round. "Really, we'll put him in WitSec."

The rock anthem that had been playing in La-

mont's head in the two days since Ronny Brackman's
capture: It jerked to a halt. Despite murdering Peretti
and O'Clair and nearly shooting Lamont's head off in
the bodega, Ralph Brackman's twin brother stood to
get a fresh identity, a house, and a new car—likely a
Lincoln Navigator, the runaway favorite of coopera-
tors entering witness protection. With a decent lawyer, he might also bag a numbered bank account with
a balance in the mid–six figures.

"I understand the pros of going after the bigger
fish, but putting this guy in WitSec is wrong," Lamont
said.

"You've got to realize that he's just a murder
weapon in the grand scheme of things," said Garrison.

"Except they don't come any worse." Lamont
fought to keep the vitriol out of his voice. "Putting
away guys like him is the reason I signed with the Bureau instead of the Astros."

As Garrison would have read in Lamont's FD-302,
the assassin, born Ronald Anthony Brackman, had
been a low-ranking Army specialist who was one in-
fraction away from dishonorable discharge when he
faked his own death after an Iraqi rocket turned the
rest of his Gulf War unit to ash. Deserting the Army,
as well as a wife and twin toddlers, he assumed a new
identity and signed on with a South African private
military company for five times what the United
States had paid him. "Sociopath with violent tenden-
cies" played better in the mercenary community than

in the Army. In three years, he built up enough of a reputation to strike out on his own as an assassin.

Garrison leaned forward, lowering his voice to little more than a whisper. "The beauty of a WitSec with a guy like this is that he'll quickly get sick of sitting in the sun and begin sniffing around for his next illicit action fix. Which is why we'll have the U.S. Marshals keep their eyes on them. It's just a matter of time until he'll be in the dark hole where he belongs."

"What if he likes the sun and his government windfall?" Lamont asked.

"Sometimes, despite the best efforts of the U.S. Marshals Service, the guy's former employers, knowing their secrets are at stake, learn of his whereabouts and send another assassin after him. Do you know the official term for that?"

"What?"

"Karma."

Lamont laughed. He was mollified but far from sold. "Who's the bigger fish?"

"That's the question." Garrison sipped his whiskey. "According to his attorney, the hit man will give us the details of the offshore bank account where eighty grand was wired within an hour of his job uptown the other night."

"His bank account info? That's it?"

"There's no reason to think there's anything more to be had. He's a cutout. Intelligence operatives—or even two-bit gangsters—would be foolish to entrust their identities, much less a shred of actionable intel, to a psychopath like Brackman. And I would've bet he was a psycho even if I hadn't read your excellent three-oh-two. The honorable assassin doesn't exist outside of the movies."

"What good is knowing where he banks if we don't know the bigger fish's BIC?" Lamont meant the business identifier code. The Society for Worldwide Interbank Financial Telecommunication assigned a unique BIC to each institution that transferred funds. For the offshore banker, divulging Brackman's employer's BIC would be career suicide, if not actual suicide.

"We need that BIC," Garrison said. "Without it, we won't see so much as a ripple from the bigger fish."

"So then what's the play? Can Justice put the squeeze on the bank?"

"In theory, yes, but secrecy is the lifeblood of offshore banks. So in practice, we don't waste our time trying to do this by the books."

By *we*, Lamont realized, Garrison didn't mean the Bureau. This explained why Garrison hadn't approached someone more senior, like Musseridge, or Phelps, the special agent in charge of the JTTF.

"What do you have in mind?" Lamont asked.

Garrison grinned. "Step one is for us to have a late-night meeting in a dark tavern. As you may have noticed, the Bureau is somewhat straitlaced when *the means* can't be justified in a courtroom. *The ends* don't matter under American jurisprudence. Tainted evidence would cause your entire case to be tossed out of court."

"Along with my career. What's step two?"

Garrison sat back. "You find out why the Joint Terrorism Task Force includes officers from intelligence agencies unencumbered by such restrictions."

31

Squeezed high into the eastern Pyrenees is Andorra, a country the size of New Orleans known for its skiing, shopping, and offshore banks. This evening, as he had after work almost every day for the past twenty-eight years, Óscar Lasuén hefted his considerable bulk onto a barstool at the Salvia d'Or, a restaurant in Andorra's capital city, Andorra la Vella. As usual, Lasuén ordered a Crema Catalana, no doubt the first of several, the regimen that made his return home bearable, although his interaction with his wife had dwindled to little more than her terse reporting of the leftovers he might microwave himself for dinner.

The Salvia d'Or, built from smoke-blackened stones held in place by dark wood beams and lit only by candles, looked much the same as when it first opened in 1701. In all the years since, the tavern had probably never been graced by a young woman as beautiful as the French tourist who happened onto the stool beside Lasuén's. Brushing snowflakes from her golden hair, she turned and asked him, in broken Catalan, if he knew anything about Andorra. Lasuén, who considered himself something of a raconteur as well as an amateur historian, told of the extraordinary soap opera that comprised the tiny nation's seven centuries of joint rule by France and Spain. The young woman, a language student, stumbled over words here and there. Lasuén happily translated into French.

When she inquired about the Salvia d'Or's *escudella,* a traditional Catalan soup known for its *pilota,* a giant meatball spiced with garlic, Lasuén invited her to join him for a bowl. She hesitated in accepting, agreeing only after extracting a promise from Lasuén that they not speak a word of French.

They dined at a cozy corner table, three courses and too many glasses of Crema Catalana to count. Afterward, she invited him for a nightcap at her hotel, which was just down the block. He said he would love to, but he couldn't. Perhaps, taking into account the prurient stares from the crowd of regulars who knew him, he feared repercussions. Whatever the case, it was a crying shame, thought Max Qualls, the CIA case officer feigning interest in a *trinxat* of bacon, cabbage, and potato at a table in the opposite corner. Óscar Lasuén was the chief private banking officer at the Banca Privada d'Andorra, and he aspired to succeed the bank's longtime chairman, his father-in-law. The woman he'd spurned was in fact French, but no tourist. She was a hooker named Dorothée, in town on business. Qualls had hired Dorothée with the objective of generating Lasuén's willingness to do anything to prevent his father-in-law from receiving the X-rated video covertly shot in her hotel room. Qualls wouldn't have asked Lasuén for much more than a BIC.

Now Qualls's colleague from Langley, Wendy Kammeyer, something of a wild card, would have to get the BIC the hard way.

Kammeyer took the train from Barcelona to Zaragoza, where she put on a platinum blond wig, extra layers of makeup, and the sort of parka and stretch pants worn only by Olympic skiers or amateurs who never leave the lodge. The most important part of her costume would be noticed by no one, a pair of contact lenses that transformed her gray irises to a dull blue. She'd heard that the lenses cost $250,000. Each.

In Zaragoza, using a Spanish passport and a Visa card with the name Penélope Piera, she bought a bus ticket to Andorra la Vella. During the four-hour as-cent, she tried to ignore the spectacle of snow-laden peaks in order to learn the part of Piera, mistress in need of a discreet bank account for her generous cash allowance. Kammeyer had been an actress before being drawn to clandestine service by the opportunity to lose herself in roles twenty-four hours a day. The summer after graduating from Vassar, she had played Minnie Mouse aboard a Disney cruise ship. She went on to receive a decent *Village Voice* review for her turn as the cold and calculating Martha in an off-Broadway production of Albee's *Who's Afraid of Virginia Woolf?* She created a character combining elements of the two for her role this evening in Andorra la Vella.

The six-story mirrored-glass Banca Privada d'Andorra was on the corner of a dense commercial block nestled into the base of a mountain. The building reminded Kammeyer of a D-cell battery. It shone with distended reflections of the trio of Gothic buildings across the street. She entered the lobby, fifteen minutes late for her five o'clock appointment with private banking officer Xavier Belmonte. She'd let the time lapse, in keeping with her character, deliberating on the purchase of a silk scarf in one of Andorra's incredible array of duty-free shops—the tiny country had 2,000 in total, one for every four of its citizens.

If not for the PC tower and chip-thin flat-screen monitor in Belmonte's office, Kammeyer might have believed she'd stepped through a wormhole in time to the House of Rothschild in its heyday. Dropping into the wing chair in front of the red-leather-topped Louis XV desk, she said, in the Catalan of a native Barcelonan, "I totally love your décor."

"*Gràcies, senyora*," Belmonte said, his reserve suggesting that he'd had nothing to do with it.

His charcoal business suit revealed a broad-boned athlete gone soft. He had a small chin, a slit for a mouth, and sunken cheeks offset by a bulbous nose. His smooth skin was either olive to begin with or had recently taken some sun. His prematurely gray hair and thick, steel-rimmed glasses would have made it hard for Kammeyer to guess his ethnicity if she hadn't read the standard cradle-to-today dossier on the Marseille native. He switched to his mother tongue, which Kammeyer also understood, to relay her request of a *café crème* over the intercom.

After inquiring about her trip up to the city and her shopping experience, Belmonte deftly segued to her banking needs, beginning by proposing she open what the bank termed an Advisory Account. "We make our skills available to any client who wishes us to actively participate in the management of her assets," he said. "Our top-rated team of advisers is at your service." The leading alternative was the so-called Custody Account, "for clients who prefer to manage their assets directly and make their own investment decisions."

"I wouldn't be too smart if I passed up the one

with the top-rated advisers," Kammeyer said—or, rather, Penélope Piera said. Wendy Kammeyer knew that 99 percent of Belmonte's clients were his clients because they wanted no noses but their own in their accounts.

Opening the account required the digital equivalent of paperwork, which Kammeyer filled out on a tablet computer provided by Belmonte. As soon as she finished, he looked it over along with her passport. Under European Union pressure, Andorran banks had recently agreed to inspect prospective clients' passports. A glance was the extent of their inspections, however. Belmonte only looked at Kammeyer's passport a second time so as to avoid staring when she plucked six stuffed letter-size envelopes from the pockets inside her parka.

She withdrew a total of €160,000 in €100 notes from the envelopes. She was stacking the bills on Belmonte's desk when his secretary hurriedly delivered coffee on a silver tray along with a selection of sweeteners and a perfunctory cookie, then bid him *bonne soirée*.

Excellent, thought Kammeyer. The late hour of the appointment was the key to her plan. She let the coffee sit until certain she and Belmonte were alone; then she took a sip and reacted as if it contained vinegar.

"I asked for skim milk," she said. "I beg your pardon, but dairy fat and my skin are archenemies."

"I am terribly sorry, *senyora*," Belmonte said, his

focus elsewhere, probably on trying to get a handle on how she could have misinterpreted *café crème*. "My assistant must have made an error. Would you allow me to run to the pantry?"

Kammeyer lit up. "You don't know what that would mean to me."

The moment he left, she shot a hand to her left eye and pinched out the contact lens. When his hasty steps faded down the marble corridor, she rounded his desk and placed the lens over the uppermost USB drive on his computer tower. The lens launched a six-legged spiderlike robot one-fiftieth the size of the head of a pin. Originally intended for the targeted delivery of medication, the nanobot had been adapted by Langley's "toy makers" to deploy spyware. The nanobot might now invisibly penetrate the Banca Privada d'Andorra system, capturing the BIC of the institution that had wired funds to the account of gun-for-hire Ronny Brackman. The spyware would infiltrate the system at that institution when Penélope Piera decided to wire €10,000 there tomorrow.

The nanobot needed about thirty seconds to do its job. Success and the blue iris overlay on the lens would temporarily turn green. Kammeyer watched from a squat behind the desk, lest any passersby see her from the hall. Failure was a 1-in-25 proposition, a function of the inability of the lens to gain recognition by the USB port.

After twenty-five seconds, the inner circle of the

lens was red like a bull's-eye. Make that 1 in 25 *in ideal conditions at a Langley lab*, Kammeyer thought.

She wasted no time replacing the dud with the contact lens from her right eye. Twenty seconds later, she extracted the lens from the USB port. This time the inner circle glowed a green as lovely as any she'd ever seen, just as Belmonte returned, a fresh mug of coffee in one hand, a plastic container of *llet desnatada*— skim milk—in the other, and understandable circumspection in his eyes.

"I lost a contact lens," Kammeyer said. Rising, she opened her hand to display the lens. "But don't worry, I found it."

The next day at noon, Lamont met Garrison at Giorgio's on Chambers Street. The place had the look of a run-down cafeteria, but busy FBI agents came here and stood on line for fifteen minutes because the pizza was the best in the city. The CIA man had called Lamont and said he had good news and that, to celebrate, he was going to take a holiday from his low-cholesterol diet. Enjoying a pepperoni slice now, Garrison talked sports, leaving Lamont to wonder whether the "Eagles' shitty offense" was code for troubles encountered in penetrating the Andorran bank.

As soon as they were back on the sidewalk, wading into the thick lunch-hour pedestrian traffic on

Chambers, Garrison said, "Good news and bad news. The good is the eighty grand to the liquidator came out of a numbered account at the Bank of Reykjavik, where, according to our 'research,' the account holder is a corporation called Windward Actuarial." Garrison halted as the sign on the far side of Broadway turned to the red hand—DON'T WALK. "The bad news is, we have no idea who Windward Actuarial is."

"Doesn't incorporation require listing a verifiable human owner?" Lamont asked.

"It did, past tense. Now you can get anonymous bearer share corporations in three places—Belize, Nevis, and Guatemala. Because those governments are eager for the business, they don't ask for any ownership information and don't keep any kind of public registry or database, except for a list of the physical mailing addresses they send the certificate to."

The street sign clicked to an icon of a man walking. Pedestrians shot across Broadway, but disappointment held Lamont in place. "So after all that, the Bank of Reykjavik is of no use to us, even if it wanted to be?" he asked.

"Not necessarily." Garrison clapped a hand on Lamont's shoulder, starting them both onto the crosswalk. "We did get one thing. The Bank of Reykjavik, unknown to any of its employees, gave us the physical address that Windward Actuarial's incorporation certificate was mailed to. Dollars to doughnuts it's

an accommodation address; there's no phone, fax, or
anything else listed. It is a space of some sort, though,
in a small office building in Bridgetown, Barbados,
which might be something. At worst, Corky, you'll
have had a trip to the tropics courtesy of Uncle Sam."

32

Paris is a good town to spot a tail. Capitalize on the plethora of channels—the quiet one-way streets, the narrow bridges, the maze of Métro corridors—and your surveillant has little choice but to fall in step behind you. So Canning told himself as he slid on eyeglasses designed specifically for the occasion. His light disguise also included an absurdly expensive charcoal virgin-wool business suit just like those worn by the bankers comprising much of the male population in Paris's affluent and old-line sixteenth arrondissement. He smiled at the notion that, if this morning's meeting went as he expected, he would never again need to give consideration to the price of a suit—or the price of anything.

Heaving open a wrought-iron door, he stepped

out of the century-old apartment building whose fourth floor served as a safe house. A buttery dawn made the rue de Passy evoke an Impressionist painting, although the rumbling of early traffic could be heard. The street itself was quiet and still; a fluttering moth would have stood out against the contiguous limestone façades. Canning didn't put it past surveillants to deploy drones smaller than a gnat, for which reason he'd placed sensors among the lilies in the fourth-floor window box. Should the devices pick up transmissions in the 900 MHz to 2.52 GHz range, his cell phone would vibrate three times.

The phone remained still. Effectively a green light.

To be on the safe side, he planned to duck into several buildings and underground passages en route to the meeting. Also he would change clothes, twice. Turning onto rue Notre-Dame-des-Champs, he sensed nothing amiss. No one else was out. As he rounded the corner onto boulevard Raspail, the delicious aroma of *pains aux raisins* surrounded him. Within the little *boulangerie*, preparations were under way as usual.

He hurried down a stairwell, then toward the Métro station via a humid ceramic tunnel that amplified his footfalls. With a pair of midpoint exits and a three-pronged fork at the far end, the tunnel was a textbook surveillance detection route. It, too, was deserted. Until two men followed Canning down the stairs, one about five seconds before the other, both in charcoal suits just like his. Probably both early-bird bankers. At least one could be a spook, though. It was difficult to tell, but not impossible; even the best surveillants could be manipulated into revealing their cards.

At the end of the tunnel, Canning turned onto a sparsely populated platform just as a Porte de Clignancourt–bound 4 train hissed to a stop. No one disembarked. As both banker types followed him aboard the third of five cars, the doors snapped shut and the metro launched into a dark tunnel. There were three other passengers: another suit, a nurse, and a party girl for whom it was still last night. Canning took mental pictures of each; he would recognize them if they reappeared along his route this morning. The Direction Centrale du Renseignement Intérieur— France's FBI—would put multiple tails on him, as many as fifty, if they had any idea what he was up to. And CIA surveillance would have no "reruns." Langley would think nothing of dispatching a team of 100.

A few minutes later, the metro rolled into the Saint-Germain-des-Prés station. Canning rose slowly, giving a surveillant ample time to get up too. Stepping out of the car and onto the platform, he regarded the mirrored film glued inside his tortoiseshell frames, providing a rear view. He searched for as little as a passenger muttering to himself—i.e., into a hidden microphone. No lips moved. No fingers tapped at keys or dug in their pockets for phones. No one, for all intents and purposes, did anything.

He transferred to the line terminating at Gare

d'Austerlitz, one of the city's six major railroad stations. There he climbed up to the street, walking against traffic on the pedestrian lane of the pont d'Austerlitz, a bridge over the Seine supported by a series of five stone arches. Halfway across, he halted abruptly, as if taken with the view, the river transformed to a mosaic by the early morning sun. This was a timing stop, to see if anyone's pace altered along with his. Again, he saw nothing—or, as he thought of nothing in this case: an idyllic view.

It was a five-minute walk to the meeting place, the Gare de Lyon, northern terminus of the Marseille railway. Canning spent an hour, taking turns at random, observing who reacted and who didn't, finding nothing out of the ordinary. Finally a one-way street brought the Gare de Lyon's celebrated clock tower into view. Canning chose not to enter the train station through the front doors where the crush of early commuters might obscure a dozen tails. Instead he clambered down the stairs to the adjoining Métro stop before riding an escalator up and into the station's palatial beaux arts lobby. Any remotely competent team would post someone at a secondary entrance like this. Canning's countersurveillance was impeded for a moment by shafts of sunlight from the latticed ceiling. He was forced to squint. Bad luck.

But he'd taken bad luck into his planning. He climbed aboard a TGV. The high-speed train thrummed its readiness to cover the 250 miles to

Lyon in less than two hours. Canning strolled down the narrow aisle, passing thirty-three seated teenage girls, all in kelly green tracksuits. Nine heads turned. Another time he'd be glad he still had it. Now he was just glad no one was in the aisle behind him.

At the other end of the car, he took the stairs back down to the platform and made his way to a brasserie at the back of the lobby. His eye went past the crowd to a high-backed booth in the far corner that offered the advantage of a view of the entire place. A heavyset middle-aged man in a three-piece camel hair suit sat there, dissecting a big breakfast. His chin was a small island in a sea of tan flesh, but he had kind blue eyes and a pleasant smile. In the latest French fashion, his dark hair, short on the sides, rose on top—with the help of a lot of mousse—into a peak. *La Gazzetta dello Sport*, the popular daily printed on distinctive pink paper, was spread across the table, signifying that his own countersurveillance jibed with Canning's.

Canning proceeded to the counter, ordering a *café au lait* and a croissant from one of the four workers, all of whom had appeared in recent recon photos. With his *petit déjeuner* in hand, he passed two occupied tables, stopping at one of several that were empty. He and the man in the booth struck up a prescripted conversation, in French, about last night's rugby match.

Cheerfully introducing himself as Laurent, the man said, "Why don't you join me?"

Canning took inventory of the crowd. The nearest patron, a businessman three tables away, was out of earshot given the general clamor of the station.

Soon after Canning lowered himself onto the bench opposite Laurent, their conversation shifted from sports to current events. Then Laurent said, "So what's too good to be true?"

Like his hair and blue irises, the name Laurent was fake. Canning knew his tablemate was in fact Izzat Ibrahim al-Hawrani, once a high-ranking officer in Iraq's Republican Guard. By way of response, Canning asked, "What if someone offered to sell you an E-bomb capable of frying Washington and the vicinity?"

"I suppose I would be curious if he really had such a device." Al-Hawrani nibbled at a brioche. Canning had anticipated an expression of elation from the man who now led the National Council of Resistance of Iraq, an assembly of deposed Ba'athist Party members exiled to France in 2003. With the billions of dollars smuggled out of Baghdad, the council underwrote al-Qaeda spin-off Tanzim Qaidat al-Jihad fi Bilad al-Rafidayn—the Organization of the Jihadi Base in Mesopotamia—which waged an Iraqi insurgent brand of jihad. The organization's relentless attacks on security forces in Iraq attracted a steady flow of volunteers, yet in Sisyphean fashion, failed to advance the cause.

"Say the guy used some office supplies from his

day job for his own purposes," Canning said. "Over the course of a few months, he collected all the pertinent details and had the device assembled by a physicist—a cutout who subsequently took a long vacation. Then he left the weapon for you—plug and play—close to the heart of Washington."

"That's a good story." The Iraqi's features didn't budge. "I would have to take it with a few grains of salt."

"The guy would expect that. So the ante would be low, just to cover his operating expenses. The ante gets you a remote detonator. If the device doesn't work to your satisfaction, you go home having lost nothing."

"Except the ante."

"That's how it is with games of chance, right?"

"What's the ante?"

"Eight million."

"And if the device works?"

"You wire the guy another two-ninety-two million. Then he supplies you with enough technical details that the e-mail you send taking credit to *The Washington Post* is the e-mail they publish. But it would be better to e-mail *The New York Times* because the *Post* won't regain the ability to publish anything for weeks."

Clouds dimmed the light through the latticework, shadows magnifying the reservations that creased the Iraqi's brow. "How would I alleviate my concern that my friend's service is gaming us?"

"To what end? To pick up a few million bucks by selling defective fireworks? To screw over an old pal from Moscow?"

"But he's always been such a devoted servant of his country."

"Of course. If he hadn't, he wouldn't have gotten the promotions to be in position to pull off an operation on the scale we're discussing. Keep in mind his stepfather."

"I know, he was Mukhabarat from Umm Qasr."

"Not his father—may he rest in peace. His stepfather."

"Ah, yes, the American Air Force colonel."

"May he rest in peace." Canning sipped his coffee. "Within the week."

Canning's resentment of the United States began the day his mother became one of the colonel's personal spoils from the First Gulf War. The man soon uprooted mother and son from a village outside of Basra that wasn't just idyllic; it was believed to have been the location of the Garden of Eden. In the States, he moved from one bleak military housing compound to another—that he provided a roof was the best that could be said for the guy. In a sense, Canning had been looking forward to this breakfast for twenty years.

Al-Hawrani set down his brioche and leaned closer. "The council would be concerned that the price reflects impure ideology."

"You can assure the council they're getting a hometown discount," Canning said. "I have no doubt that, off the top of your head, you can name a dozen players who would happily pony up ten figures for this system."

The Iraqi ceded the point with a grunt. "The Chinese have spent more just trying to steal the technology. But if your guy is flying the Son of Islam flag . . ."

"Sometime after this op, maybe immediately, he's going to need to fly the coop. Why shouldn't he have a golden parachute—not unlike the members of the National Council of Resistance of Iraq?"

Turning toward the window, al-Hawrani watched the Lyon train grind away from the station. He was deliberating, Canning suspected. The time passed slowly.

Finally, the Iraqi raised his orange juice and said, "To *al-Ba'ath*."

Al-Ba'ath translated loosely as *the resurrection*, Canning knew, but in this context it meant, specifically, retribution. Laboring to maintain an appropriately sober mien, he clinked the juice glass with his coffee cup.

33

There were two new scorpions—that is, two that Thornton had seen during the few moments there had been light in the cell. So maybe more than two. He continued to play goalie from the cot, swishing the pillow, now in tatters, to ward the things off. The routine was interrupted only when a Souper Meal and water bottle dropped through the flap in the door. Each time he raced to the door and back along the safe path revealed by Flattop's flashlight. These meals seemed to come on a random schedule, except that Thornton wasn't hungry. Still the provisions were never enough and always repulsive. Days had passed since he'd slept. That is, it seemed days had passed. Maybe it had been a week. He could no longer delineate one day from the next. It didn't help that the temperature fluctuated between freezing and roasting. Then there were the runs. He'd had to heave the cot as if it were a sled, himself aboard, so that his ass was positioned inches above the toilet rim—not on it—so he wouldn't sit on one of the damned bugs. The toilet didn't flush. Or maybe it did, weakly, and he didn't hear it over the men's screams from the surrounding cells. Also a baby cried for hours on end. Thornton recalled that Iraqi interrogators, believing that no sound induced greater psychological stress, piped recordings of wailing infants into subjects' cells. Or was that Russian interrogators? His mind wasn't firing. Once, a gunshot in close vicinity left his eardrums throbbing. He felt hot blood leaking down his face, but it turned out to be a hallucination. A delusion, technically; he still couldn't see anything. The point was, the new scorpions in his cell were more adventurous than the first, frequently tapping close to him. The other sounds he could tune out. But the bugs forced him to stay awake to maintain his perimeter. Since the Dark Ages, sleep deprivation had been recognized as an effective means of coercion. Or maybe it was the Middle Ages. Anyhow, in most modern democratic countries, depriving a detainee of sleep for more than forty-eight hours—or was it seventy-two?—was an illegal form of torture. After seventy-two hours, Thornton had read, your electrolyte balance drops to the point that your brain goes haywire. By now it had been forty or fifty hours since the *parilla*. Plus thirty or forty hours awake before the *parilla*. And, Jesus Christ, the *parilla*. A minute on that thing probably equated to another 100 hours of sleep dep. The next ride could be worse. Electroshock torture often results in cardiac arrest. Thoughts of the next "interview" expanded in his head like toxic gas, further filling him with a nightmarish sense of foreboding.

Finally Flattop came to fetch him, then prodded him into the interview room. At the sight of the *parilla*, and Bow Tie kneeling beside it, tweaking a control knob on the retrofitted car battery, Thornton couldn't get the words out fast enough: "I made up Meade. I made it up to stall you. I have some suspicions about Sokolov's death, but, really, I don't know shit."

The interrogator rose, regarding him with sympathy. "We figured as much, Russell," he said.

Flattop drew his HK45, pressed its cold barrel against Thornton's right temple, and snapped the trigger.

Another delusion.

Thornton was still in the cell.

Don't do that, he urged himself. Don't do that again.

He felt a scorpion shimmying up his back. He swatted until his back was raw, and . . .

He must have imagined the bug.

But they did put a wolf in the cell. No, really. Thornton could smell its damp fur, hear its panting, feel the damned thing padding closer. *Dreams and reality are blurring*, said an educated voice in his head. *Don't let your mind get the better of you.*

"Easy for you to say, buddy," Thornton replied.

Hot, sticky perspiration coated him. A moment later he was shivering uncontrollably. And he itched all over, ached all over, especially his spine. His skin was cracked with rash or infection. He coughed; his lungs felt like they were clogged with dust. He couldn't remember his survival plan anymore. Just that he'd had one at some point. In his entire life, he'd never panicked. Now, as if the natural order of things had been reversed, or gone out the window, he felt nothing but panic. It cost him the ability to feel anything. He—his life—was eroding like a flooded riverbank.

He heard snakes and gongs and gunfire.

It was the door unlocking.

Maybe.

He shook cobwebs from his head.

The door opened outward, bringing the shape of Captain South, the other guard, slowly into the gray gap. Must be Flattop's day off. Or night off. Thornton caught a whiff of musk and salt. No dream, unfortunately. It was *parilla* time.

His panic intensified, his heart beating harder and harder, hard enough to explode. Which might be better than the *parilla*, he thought, when a slender woman in a prison jumpsuit like his stepped in front of the captain.

Mallery.

"Russ, are you okay?" she asked.

"Glad to see you," he said, though he wasn't entirely sure that he was seeing her.

"I got us a ride out of here." She inclined her head toward the captain. "We need to hurry."

34

Thornton said, "Glad to see you," but it appeared to Mallery that he no longer had glad in his repertoire.

"I got us a ride out of here," she said, cocking her head toward Albert, the boat captain. Since ferrying Mallery here—hours after bringing Thornton, he said—he had served as her guard. "We need to hurry."

Thornton remained cross-legged on his cot, swinging a big wad of filth—originally a small pillow?—from side to side. His skin was gray, even in the pink wash of Albert's flashlight. He'd lost more weight in a week than Mallery would have thought possible, and he would have probably looked gaunter still if all the caked-on grime and matted blood were hosed off. A ghost of the man she remembered.

"Albert has a boat," she tried. "He's packed clothes for you, first aid, and food."

"And cold beer, man," added the boat captain.

Thornton squinted against the light; otherwise his expression remained blank. He kept up whatever he was doing with the pillow. Mallery found the scene heartrending.

"Russ, we're getting off Torture Island," she said. "You with me?"

He focused on her. "I hope they're treating you okay."

It had been nothing close to okay. "Four-star compared to this," she said. "How about we go anyway?"

"Hang on." He shook his head. "Are you actually here?"

"For now." Exigency tugged at her. The longer they lingered, the greater the likelihood that their escape would turn into an extended tour of the basement.

"How is this possible?" Thornton asked.

"The pen is mightier than the sword, especially when you use the pen on a checkbook." Mallery doubled the pace of her words to stress the need for haste. "Albert's now a fairly wealthy man, and he stands to get even wealthier."

A grin shone through the captain's anxious countenance.

Thornton seemed stuck in a daze. "You wrote him a check?" he asked.

"Wire transfer, actually," Mallery said. "But if he's going to spend any of it, we need to leave."

Thornton's eyes darted around the cell. With what Mallery read as an understanding nod, Albert probed the floor with his beam. A large bug of some sort skittered away from the light. Thornton set down the pillowy thing, propelled himself to the edge of his cot, then stopped.

"What about the other guards?" he asked.

"There was only Soriano in this building," Albert said.

"The guy with the flattop?" asked Thornton.

"Right." Mallery inched toward the door. "Let's talk more on the boat, okay?"

"There *was* only Soriano?" Thornton seemed to be getting up to speed.

"Improvisation on Albert's part," Mallery said, biting back her anger. The original plan had been to lock up the other guard. In the process of locking him up, deciding that it would be "better he tells no tales," Albert suffocated him.

Thornton fixed lucid eyes on Mallery. "How it is with the best-laid plans," he said, pulling himself up by the wall—or trying to. He couldn't grip the slick cinder blocks.

She hurried over, catching him by the elbows and helping him to his feet.

"That bar you wanted to go to in New York: I've got your tab there," he said, staggering toward the door. "For life."

With a smile, she helped him into the hall. Pulling his arm around her back, she acted as a crutch. And not much of one; she had her share of dings. They barely kept pace with Albert, who lit the way through the dark corridors.

At the exit, Albert stooped, bringing his right eye level with a panel on the side of the door. Bolts within the wall whistled free of sockets. He threw a hip into the crash bar, opening the door to an inky darkness. Fresh air rushed in, briny but still delicious to Mallery after a week essentially underground. Outside, particles of fog twinkled in the floodlights.

She tended to Thornton as Albert hurried ahead, his soft footfalls against the wood-slatted pier accentuating the silence. The fishing boats bobbing beside the dock were both around fifty feet long, with dented hulls and small wheelhouses near bows surrounded by forests of masts, poles, and torn netting. Disguise, Albert had told Mallery. Each craft had been retrofitted with a pair of monstrous ten-cylinder diesels, allowing for cruising speeds of twenty-one knots, or about twenty-five miles per hour.

Albert stepped aboard the farther of the two boats, causing it to dip, then opened the sea cocks so water would flow in. After untying the lines, he leaped back onto the pier. The current immediately sucked the boat to sea.

"Now they got no boat, we got one," he said, hurrying back to the presumptive escape craft; *Mermaid III* was painted across her transom, above *Barbados, W.I.*

He unfastened the *Mermaid III*'s lines, hurdled

her starboard rail, and landed at the helm. With a twist of the ignition key, he brought the surrounding seawater to a boil.

Mallery took Thornton by the wrist and led him down the steep, muddy slope to the boat. As they reached the pier, a tall man appeared from the darkness at the other end. Mallery recognized the bow-tied interrogator for whom she had recounted, eleven times including twice backward, every last detail she could recall from the moment her jet landed at Muskeget until her capture in New York. Doc Wade, Albert had called him once, when he thought she was out of earshot, causing Wade to shush him. Shock froze her, causing Thornton to pitch forward.

"How in the devil did you get out?" the interrogator asked, aiming a pistol at Thornton.

"Put that thing down on the pier, man," said Albert, emerging from the wheelhouse, leveling his own gun.

The interrogator dropped his weapon but not his bombast. "Go now and you're a dead man," he said. "Wherever in the world you are, we'll get you." Turning to Mallery and Thornton, he added, "You two as well."

"You're working for the CIA, aren't you?" Thornton asked.

The interrogator laughed. "Eliciting, are we, Russell?"

Albert advanced to the transom, sharpening his aim. "Tell them, Doc."

"Russell, consider this your last wish," the man said. "Yes, CIA."

Albert nodded, as if his own suspicion had been confirmed.

Thornton laughed. "I guess it's true what they say about interrogators making the worst liars."

"What was the tell?" asked the interrogator.

"When you asked, *What was the tell?*" Thornton said.

Not bad for a guy who was a zombie five minutes ago, Mallery thought. But even at the height of his powers, to obtain the secrets of this place, Thornton would need to do the entire job of an interrogator in seconds—or less, based on Albert's jittery glances at the other islet.

"I have a proposal for you," Mallery said to the interrogator. "Tell us who you in fact work for and I'll wire ten million dollars to your account, too."

The interrogator whistled amazement. "Is that what you told Albert you'd pay him?"

"He's already been paid one million," she said. "He gets the other nine once we're safely away."

"I would love ten million dollars, Beryl. But I have to decline if only because my employer would find out and have me imprisoned before I could spend a cent."

It was what she'd expected to hear. And it was what she wanted. "I have a better deal for you, then," she said.

"It won't matter if you offer me the moon and the stars."

"The offer is nothing. Zero dollars and zero cents. Unless you accept, I will wire you ten million dollars, Dr. Wade, then good luck convincing your employer that you *weren't* paid to stand by while we took off."

The blood drained from his face. "Okay, okay," he grumbled.

A light turned on in the farther of the two Quonset huts.

With Thornton in tow, Mallery launched herself down the pier, slowed because he remained intent on Wade.

"Who runs Littlebird?" he asked.

The interrogator's response was lost beneath a gunshot. From Albert. The bullet raised bits of mud and small stones on the far side of the pier. The interrogator grabbed for his gun, whirled at Albert, and fell to the pier like a spent top. His body twitched twice; then he lay still.

The killing infuriated Mallery. "Jesus, Albert," she groaned.

At least he had some reason this time: Lights were popping on all over the bigger islet.

Jumping to the helm, Albert turned up the throttle, bringing the engines to a roar. "Hurry!" he called to Mallery.

She and Thornton ran, managing to reach the boat in seconds.

Inexplicably, he released her hand and continued to run, passing the fishing boat.

She started after him. "What are you doing?"

"You'd be amazed what valuable information people carry around in their wallets."

He stopped halfway down the pier, where Wade lay. He rifled through the dead man's clothing. The knot in Mallery's stomach tightened with each passing instant.

"Come on, come on," Albert urged Thornton, who appeared to come up empty-handed.

With a sheepish look, he hurried back to the fishing boat, wobbling to the extent that Mallery waited for him to collapse. Sure enough, as he stepped over the stern rail, he fell face-first onto the cushioned bench and lay there, unmoving. Mallery swung herself aboard, landing beside the bench. She noted with relief the steady rise and fall of his chest.

Albert threw the throttle, blasting the bulky craft to sea, the bow knifing through fog. Mallery dropped to the deck, bracing for bullets. She heard none. The detention complex receded into dark shapes against a dingy sky, and then, gloriously, to nothing.

Keeping her jubilation in check, Mallery rose to see how Thornton was doing. He remained prone on the bench but still breathing. They had about 200 nautical miles to their destination, the Marshall Islands, in the northwestern Pacific, nine or ten hours along the route Albert favored, outside normal shipping lanes.

Rest was probably the best medicine for Thornton now, Mallery thought.

Motion behind her drew her attention. She turned to a view up the barrel of Albert's gun. Shock knocked the wind out of her. She croaked, "What do you want?"

"*Nobody* telling tales. If the CIA or whoever finds out it was me who shot their Dr. Wade, ain't nowhere in the world I'll be safe."

Mallery fought the inclination to sink into a supplicant position, fearing the movement might spur him into a precipitous use of his trigger. "I have no reason to tell anyone. You have my word on it. I'm only grateful to you."

Impassive, he added his left hand to the grip, steadying the gun. The boat continued chugging forward.

"How about we up it to nineteen million on arrival?" she tried.

He squinted through the gun sights.

"Or . . ." She scrambled to think of something he might want.

Saying nothing, he tweaked his aim.

Crushed by awareness that she was going to die, Mallery closed her eyes. Gunshots cracked, the last sounds she would ever hear, she thought. Hot droplets peppered her face.

She opened her eyes to see blood erupting from Albert's chest as bullets picked him up and flung him against the starboard gunwale. He bounced off, landed face-first on the deck, and lay still as his life's blood streamed from his back.

"I'm sorry I had to do that," Thornton said from the bench. His face had a green tint, matching Mallery's queasiness. He'd rolled onto his side in order to extend his right arm and aim the gun that he must have taken from the slain interrogator. "I'm also sorry I didn't do it sooner."

Gratitude propelled her to him. She wanted to tell him that he no longer owed her anything, that they were square now. It was all she could do to keep from sobbing. He opened his arms and she burrowed her face into his chest, letting his warmth and closeness—something she'd previously thought of only as a measure of distance—melt her horror.

She'd drifted off, she realized. She was alone on the bench. Her eyes felt cried dry. The fog was gone. Stars glinted in an amber sky. There was nothing else in sight save an expanse of sea so vast that she could see the curvature of the earth.

Thornton stood like a statue at the helm, scrubbed clean, and seemingly rejuvenated, like he'd knocked back a pint of adrenaline. He'd changed into clean khaki shorts and a royal blue soccer jersey, no doubt belongings of the late Albert, the lone trace of whom was a purple streak on the deck leading to the gunwale between the portside davits. The only significant effect of detention Thornton exhibited was his weight loss. It had chiseled the thick, corded muscles in his arms and legs.

Rattling against the captain's chair beside him was a stack of empty Miller High Life cans, duct-taped together.

Mallery asked, "Did you drink all that?"

He turned around. "Good morning."

"It doesn't look like morning."

"It's a quarter past midnight, Atlantic time.

"*Atlantic* time?"

"We're just east of the Caribbean."

She sat up. "That's nowhere near the Marshall Islands."

"Albert probably wasn't telling the truth—what are the odds?" Checking the big compass ball atop the instrument panel, he adjusted the wheel.

She interlaced her fingers, palms up, and raised her arms above her head, trying to stretch some of the soreness out of her body. To undo the past week, particularly the hour-long sessions in the box the size of a foot locker—to "help you focus," as Dr. Wade put it—she'd figured she would need months in an ashram. But simply having survived acted as an elixir. She let her lungs fill with ocean air and asked, "So where to?"

"I was thinking Trinidad and Tobago, west of here by about a hundred nautical miles, which we can do in five hours. As soon as we land, we contact the U.S. embassy. The FBI can bring us in from the cold, or the tropical equivalent."

"Any idea what Dr. Wade would have told us?"

"Probably another lie. Which wouldn't have been bad because it would be one more service that we could have ruled out."

"Who have you eliminated so far?"

"NSA, CIA, FBI, maybe the military. Which still leaves fifteen American intelligence services—that I know of—none of whom would even confess to employing a black site interrogator. Still, Wade could be a decent clue."

"What makes you think we're dealing with Americans?"

"They've been playing by our rules, or at least our unwritten rules, taking us offshore in order to use interrogation techniques that are illegal back home."

Compassion welled in her. "What did they do to you?"

He glanced at the instruments. "Nothing worse than I've had at the periodontist's."

"What's keeping them from trumping up charges, so that as soon as we show our faces, they can take us right back?"

"They may well try, but whoever they are, we'll be better off with U.S. embassy officials and marines around."

The five-hour delay troubled her. "Why not call for help right now?"

"I imagine the Torture Island team is already searching for us. Using the ship's radio would be the same thing as transmitting our location."

"Wouldn't a boat like this have a transponder?"

"Yeah. First thing I did after you fell asleep was tie the thing to a life vest and set it adrift. In hindsight, my first order of business should have been radioing the FBI."

Mallery was confused. "But if you had used the radio—?"

She stopped short when the noise she'd initially taken for wind grew into propeller chops. Starlight delineated the helicopter, swooping out of the night like a bat.

"I figured this was coming when they didn't do anything to stop us from escaping," Thornton said, taking up the beer cans. "So I worked up a plan."

35

Despite the three Red Bulls he'd found in the galley, exhaustion blunted Thornton's senses. Crouched on the deck, he judged the helicopter to be 1,000 feet off the stern. Could be 500, though. Hard to gauge. Either way, too high to make out much more than the general shape, an all-purpose craft with main and tail rotors, like a Bell JetRanger 206. Maybe a 206A. Equipped with a thirty-millimeter chain gun that could turn the fishing boat to splinters at 850 rounds per minute. The good news was that such a helicopter was better for their sake than a craft with coaxial rotors—one above the other, eliminating the need for a tail rotor. Much better.

His search of the boat had netted two safety flares, each in its own disposable launcher. He held one of the launchers away from his body now, aiming the flare at the dark patch of sky where he anticipated the helicopter would momentarily slow to a hover.

"Is that a flare?" asked Mallery from the cabin. Safer below deck, he'd thought, because the copter surely had night vision.

"Yes."

"But if they're not here to rescue us . . . ?"

"This thing burns with thirty thousand candle-power. Ought to severely screw up their night vision."

"I like it."

"Got the beer cans ready?"

"Just about."

"Great." He pulled the cord at the base of the launcher. With a hiss like a just-opened Coke, the round shot into the sky but didn't ignite.

"Dud?" Mallery asked.

"It doesn't ignite until it reaches maximum al-titude." He clambered down the steps into the dark cabin. "I think."

Just as he hit bottom, the bunks, tiny galley, and various compartments lit red in reflection of the flare, now a luminous ball, turning the sky around it pur-ple. A parachute popped up, reducing the flare's rate of descent to that of a feather.

As Thornton had hoped, Mallery was spraying the deodorant can into the dime-size hole he'd gouged in the side of the lowest of the eight cans forming the tube. The chalky aerosol fumes rose through gaps he'd created by cutting off the lids and punching three tiny holes in the bases of all but the bottom can. Into the open mouth of the top can, he'd wedged the plastic compass ball from the control panel.

Over the splutter of spray against aluminum, Mallery said, "Miller time." Her nonchalance belied her apprehension.

"Cheers," Thornton said as he took the cans.

Snatching the box of matches from the galley, he lay prone against the staircase, the coarse all-weather carpeting nicking his elbows and knees. Now he just needed to light a match and stick it into the hole in the lowest can. The flame would ignite the de facto propellant gas in the tube, firing the compass ball.

The helicopter slowed to a hover at about thirty feet above the waterline and 150 feet off the starboard side, or almost exactly where Thornton had anticipated, figuring the pilot would choose to stay just outside the effective range of a handgun. The heavy *fwump-fwump-fwump* of the main rotor dwarfed all other sounds.

Thornton drew a match. The rotor blades' wash sucked up seawater, raining it onto the stern deck and splashing the cabin. He hadn't planned on contending with any water, and this was a deluge. Spinning away from the open cabin door, he flattened himself against the wall in an effort to keep the match dry.

Mallery was shouting something. He couldn't make out what over the noise of the helicopter. Following her stare through the starboard porthole, he saw the helicopter obscured by a burst of golden smoke. He couldn't fully process the accompanying scream, like a steam whistle, until the rocket smashed into the fishing boat above deck.

The boat heaved to port, about to capsize, it seemed. Shattered glass and shrapnel rained from the wheelhouse into the cabin, cutting Thornton's arms and neck. Mallery dropped to the floor, using a cushion to shield herself. Everything not tied down or bolted in place slid, fell, or flew sideways, including Thornton, the match that had been in his hand, and the matchbox.

Stretching like a first baseman, he snared the matchbox, then was flung back to starboard as the boat righted itself. The hull boomed back onto the waves, raising a two-story wall of water. Through the open cabin door, Thornton saw the wheelhouse roof splash down 100 yards to port. Seawater sprayed into the cabin.

All in all, he told himself, this was good. If it hadn't been for the flare, the helicopter would have delivered more than what amounted to a glancing blow.

He plucked a fresh match from the box, threw himself up the stairs, aligned the mouth of the beer-can tube with the helicopter, and lit the match. Cupping his free hand to shield the flame, he dipped it into the hole in the side of the lowest can. The gas in the tube sizzled, igniting. With a bang and a streak of fire, the compass ball shot toward the tail of the helicopter before disappearing into darkness.

The target was the helicopter's tail rotor, which combatted the twisting force produced by the main rotor. With a malfunctioning tail rotor, forward speed could keep a helicopter flying straight. A helicopter with a malfunctioning tail rotor would lose control in a hover, however. And if the fragile tail rotor, which spun at 2,000 revolutions per minute—or about 400 miles per hour at the tips—were impacted by a ball traveling 100-plus miles per hour, the results could be catastrophic.

"Please," Thornton said to no one in particular.

He heard no impact and saw no further evidence of the compass ball.

Then the helicopter pitched forward, somersaulted, and plummeted into the waves, all in about three seconds, before transforming into a yellow fireball, parts flying every which way.

Not trusting his senses, Thornton rose from the deck boards for a better view.

Mallery appeared behind him, her eyes wide with wonder.

"Look out!" he shouted, but she didn't see the incoming projectile in time.

Diving, he wrapped his arms around her, sending them both splashing onto the deck. The spearlike projectile slashed the air millimeters above them, striking the portside gunwale and lodging there. It was half of a rotor blade. Other debris splashed down aft of the fishing boat, which continued ahead at twenty knots.

Thornton found himself lying on top of Mallery, trying to regain his wind, her breath hot against his face.

"And there I was worried that all that beer had gone to waste," she said.

Another time, he thought, he might have enjoyed the feel of her body—firm in the right places, soft in the right places—but the prospect of more flying wreckage prompted him to disentangle his limbs from hers and spring to his feet.

Deciding all was clear, he extended a hand to her. "You okay?" he asked.

"Better than them," she said with a glance at the wrecked helicopter.

Together they watched the ribbons of smoke dissipating into the starlit sky. He felt the same nausea that he had after shooting Albert. This time, he also felt a measure of exhilaration. As a journalist, the ideal was to write an explosive story exposing bad guys—then hope their lawyers didn't get them off. Using actual explosives, he thought, was relatively utilitarian.

"Are we safe now?" Mallery asked.

"We're eighty or ninety miles from anywhere, and off the radar grid," he said. "So we might have a minute or two."

Turning to face him, she shook a wet tangle of hair

back from her eyes. Getting fired on and soaked gave her an alluring wildness, he thought, especially in the prison jumpsuit. Waterlogged, it left little to the imagination.

She cupped a hand over his left shoulder. "Russ, thank you," she said.

"Anytime." He burned to draw her toward him, but she took a step away.

"That wasn't right," she said with an edge of rebuke, leaving him chastened. "What I meant was . . ."

She stood on her toes and kissed him on the mouth.

Only when he felt her arms circle his waist too did he consider that this was more than a thank-you gesture. After another moment, though, she pulled free.

"Probably not the best time for this," she said.

"Right," he said, to let her off the hook.

She didn't move.

"I don't know that we'll get a better time, though," he said, reaching for her.

They picked up where they'd left off, her pent-up emotion apparently as strong as his own, the combined sentiments flaring to the sort of ardor he'd always thought of as the stuff of fiction. His hand gravitated to her jumpsuit's top button, which popped open. The suit fell to the deck. Making even shorter work of his clothes, they raced down to the cabin and the intact bunk. They made love at a sprint, as though both mindful that another aircraft was liable to swoop down with guns blazing at any moment.

.   .   .

Getting out of the taxi at Orly Airport in Paris, the charter flight passenger listed as Brett Proctor almost didn't hear the trill of his satphone over the whine of jets. "Goodwyn."

"How are you, Norm?" came Rapada's voice.

"I'm guessing not quite as well as I'd thought I was prior to the phone ringing."

"Well, the two guests at the vacation house—"

Canning grumbled. "In English, please?" In the event that the multimillion-dollar secure communications system had been breached, Rapada's secret-speak could be cracked by schoolchildren. "Where are they?"

"All we know right now is that the helicopter experienced catastrophic failure, survivors doubtful."

"What about the fishing boat?"

"We don't know. What do you think about scrambling a Hornet?" Rapada meant an Israeli-made drone armed with a pair of Mini-Spike electro-optic guided missiles, each sufficient to turn a fifty-foot fishing boat to flotsam if the helicopter hadn't already.

"How long to deploy a submersible?" Canning asked.

"Two, three hours."

"Do that, too. Search for the fishing boat and debris near the crash site. If we don't find anything, in the *four* hours that will have passed, the distance the boat will have covered"—Canning estimated eighty miles, squared it, then multiplied by 3.14—"means a search area twice the size of Maryland. A swarm of Hornets wouldn't be able to find that."

"We can have the fishing boat reported stolen."

"Good. Say drug runners did it. Throw in that they murdered an honorable fisherman and his schoolteacher-daughter who was helping him out for the day, some bullshit like that, to get the local cops' sympathies. And speaking of locals, rouse whoever you can on Trinidad and Tobago. Stands to reason that's where our 'guests' will be checking in next."

36

The fishing boat chopped toward Scarborough, the nearest island in the archipelagic Republic of Trinidad and Tobago. Through the portholes, Thornton saw nothing but water and sky in gradations of black. Mallery lay asleep in his arms—or he lay in hers, depending on the perspective—with the top of her head snug in the curve of his neck. Her breasts, nestled against his sore rib cage, should have hurt him but had the opposite effect. Although this day was only sixty-two minutes old, thanks to her it was already the best day of his life. Or it should have been. After all, they would soon be at the U.S. embassy in Port-of-Spain, handing off to the FBI the raw material to avenge Catherine Peretti and Kevin O'Clair as well as Leonid Sokolov—and to make sure Sokolov's

DARPA project stayed at DARPA. In the process, Mallery stood to acquire Langlind's Senate seat, and Thornton would report the biggest story of his career. For some reason, though, the benefits of reaching Port-of-Spain didn't stir him. Which was odd. Just a function of his fatigue? Or was it that he had overlooked something? He had a sense of having missed a critical piece of the puzzle.

Mallery's eyes opened. "Everything okay?" she asked.

"Just wondering how it could be any better," he said

Evidently he failed to manufacture sufficient conviction: "What's wrong?" she asked. "Could they have sicced satellites on us?"

"No, probably not. Even if the Joint Chiefs decided that they wanted a satellite redirect right after the helicopter went down, they still would have to wait another hour for imagery."

"How about drones?"

"It's possible, but even a squadron of Global Hawks couldn't cover the square mileage we'll have put between us and the spot where the helicopter—" Feeling as though he'd stumbled onto what had been eluding him, he stopped himself.

"The spot where the helicopter *what*?" she asked.

"Where it went down." He propelled himself off the bunk. "We need to go back there. I have an idea."

"What about the idea where we survive?"

He dug in Albert's bag for clothes, finding himself a pair of khaki shorts. "It would be better if it appeared we didn't—if we want to find out who's after us, that is, and why."

She bristled. "What do you have in mind?"

"Sinking this boat—making it look like the helicopter sank it, actually." He tossed her a sweatshirt. "Leave the engines running, slash the fuel lines, then toss a flare onto the deck: That ought to do it."

"And then what? We'll be in the middle of the ocean in a life raft?"

"This boat is equipped with Zodiacs, actually, which are pretty rugged and have ten-horsepower engines. More than good enough to reach Barbados, a hundred miles or so north. That's where the Littlebird listening post is, I think."

Pulling on the sweatshirt, she grinned. "Because it says *Barbados* on the back of this boat?"

"Among other reasons."

Pointedly, she raised an eyebrow. "Would people from a secret operation paint their secret location in big letters on the back of their boat?"

"If they needed the boat to blend in, sure. By the way, I don't think they planned on either of us seeing the letters on the back of the boat, or at least living to tell anyone about it. But even if we did, what more would we make of it than there's a black site near Barbados and a local fishing boat used for prisoner transport?"

"So then why have we made more of it than that?"

He pulled a T-shirt over his head. "If you're going to run an offshore business and hide in plain sight, Barbados is your island. It's a haven for human trafficking. Offshore banks—which, as you know, aren't the sort where Grandma keeps her Christmas club account—have been going up on Barbados as fast as the plaster can dry. Also, Andy Nolend told me he'd heard of an American black op with a listening post there. The key is the island has virtually no electronic eavesdropping regulations, creating a loophole for American intelligence operators who are prohibited by law from wiretapping Americans: They can transmit the audio directly to people on Barbados, who send back written transcripts. If the Littlebird operators believe we're in Davy Jones's locker, they won't be expecting us in Barbados. If we can get a place for you to lay low, I might be able to find Littlebird Central."

"How would you do it?" she asked. "Barbados isn't exactly a one-horse island."

He put on a baseball cap embroidered with an anchor. "All of the towns there are one-horse compared to Bridgetown, the capital. I'm thinking Littlebird Central would have a lot of computer hardware, power usage, maybe a mess of antennas. Outside the city, people would sure as hell notice that. In the city, probably not. Maybe I can access utility-company data, or land a source at the utility company and find out who has the highest power bills. On account of the computers, Littlebird Central's bill should be up there."

"Wouldn't nosing around like that raise red flags?"

"Good question. If it's shaping up that way, Bridge-town's still small enough that I could canvas it on foot in half a day. Instead of a storefront, they're probably using an office that's on an upper floor or tucked away, with an innocuous name designed to dissuade people, like Acme Sewage Consultants."

"But even if they're fronted by a candy store that you can waltz right into, their systems will have electronic security, right? You would at least need pass codes and, probably, an electronic evidence retrieval team."

"That was my thinking in going to Trinidad and Tobago. I figured we would turn over what we'd come up with to the FBI, let them hit Barbados and bag the evidence. In retrospect, the problem with that plan is the gauntlet of red tape between an electronic evidence retrieval team and Littlebird Central. On top of that, the Bureau is almost certainly searching for us now for the wrong reasons, so we'd need to take a leap of faith that our contacts there could keep our reappearance on the QT. Also, to take action on Barbados, they would need internal approval, then have to bring in the CIA—probably State, too. By the time an electronic evidence retrieval team made it to Barbados, Littlebird Central will have been long since cleaned out. But if we play dead, the Littlebird operators will think they're in the clear."

Mallery gazed through a porthole. "Suppose I could get you an electronic evidence retrieval team?" she asked.

Even with her extraordinary wherewithal, this didn't sound possible. "How?" he asked.

"Take me with you."

37

Goodwyn."

"Sorry if I woke you, Norm."

On a jet that appeared to be racing the sun across the Atlantic, Canning sighed. "If only you had." That would mean he'd been able to sleep on the flight; Thornton and Mallery's continued existence jeopardized his entire operation.

Rapada said, "The latest is the fishing boat's lying on her side on the bottom of the sea, about a quarter mile from the wreck of the helicopter."

"But there's no sign of the lifeboat."

"How did you know?"

"Murphy's twenty-fourth codicil: *When a slice of toast falls on your white carpet, the probability it will land jam side down is directly proportional to the cost of the carpet.* But this isn't bad news."

"Why not?"

"In a lifeboat, they'll be easy prey for a drone."

The fourteen-foot Zodiac lifeboat sliced through waves at twelve knots, or about fourteen miles per hour. Sitting by the tiller, Thornton saw no other crafts of any sort, just the still-dark sea and the tip of the sun spraying violet into a cold gray eastern horizon. For the eighth time in the four hours since scuttling the fishing boat, he took up his crude astrolabe—he'd made it by cutting a paper plate in half, adhering one end of a shoelace to the half plate's center point, and weighting the other end of the lace with a hexagonal nut. As he aimed the flat edge of the half plate at the fading North Star, the shoelace fell on a line between the seventy-five- and eighty-degree notches on the round edge of the plate, slightly closer to seventy-five, meaning the North Star was seventy-seven degrees above the horizon. Accordingly, the Zodiac was traveling along a latitude of thirteen degrees north, or right on course for Barbados. Thank you, Cub Scouts.

He and Mallery took turns sleeping beneath the red waterproof boat cover that transformed the bow into a low-slung cabin, giving the Zodiac the appearance of carrying only one passenger.

Toward the end of his next shift at the tiller, Thornton squinted through a noon haze at what appeared to be a blue whale on the horizon. Given the distance, he ruled out anything smaller than a cruise ship. As the

Zodiac drew closer, the blue mass grew, and browns and greens emerged, along with inequities on its surface. It was Barbados, he realized. Soon he made out high cliffs of sandstone and jagged coral, with towering waterfalls pounding the bay and raising a mist that blurred a forest of every conceivable shade of green. There was no maritime activity on this side of the island; the sheer cliffs precluded landing. Closer still and the vapor subsided to reveal trees dotted with oranges, lemons, and limes. Hundreds of varieties of flowers covered the hillsides and meadows.

For some reason, Thornton had an edgy sense but dismissed it. In the absence of scientific evidence to the contrary, he believed premonition to be purely psychological. And, in this case, perhaps, a function of too much Red Bull.

They say that after twenty years of service, a Special Forces veteran will have a topaz ring, a Harley, an ex-wife, and a job as a Walmart greeter. Carlton Busby thought he was way ahead of the game. Just a year out, and he already had a hot second wife, Ryota—he met her at the bar she was tending on Koh Samui—plus a gig with Macedon, the private military company, at fifty grand more than what old Uncle Sam had been paying him, plus a complimentary three-bedroom condo in a sweet gated community in Boca de Río, Venezuela, just a few clicks from the base.

Most of Macedon's business was assisting the

Venezuelan Army and the Fuerza Aérea in Operación Centinela, the fight against drug smugglers from Brazil and Guyana. But sometimes the private military company's clients were American services with operational objectives identical to the Venezuelans': deploy a drone and turn a cigarette boat into ash. Today the client was the DEA. Or so they said. Someone pays you a million bucks to play a video game, the right question is, *Who do you want shot?* Today the answer was a Brazilian couple with a boatload of meth they'd cooked out on one of the uncharted rocks east of the Caribbean. What's more, the meth heads had raped and murdered a kindergarten teacher.

Busby was eager to pull the trigger—actually a red button atop a joystick. But first, he had to find the couple's Zodiac boat.

He piloted the Hornet unmanned aerial vehicle, or UAV—what civilians call a drone—from a ground control station, though it sounded like he was in an actual cockpit, because the speakers played the buzz of the props and the chopping air. The place was a combat vet's dream: big dark room with the thick kind of carpeting that makes you want to walk around with your shoes off, arctic AC, and, best of all, the base chief's cook, Señora García. The old lady brought in fresh coffee or anything else you wanted, and she was one badass baker.

In the middle of the room were two consoles, one for the person serving as the UAV's sensor operator and a second for the pilot. Each console was furnished with a supercomfortable leather chair, a desk with a computer keyboard, and a cluster of monitors that showed real-time video from the aircraft's nose camera, feed from the variable-aperture infrared camera— for nighttime or low-light viewing—and synthetic aperture radar that could provide a picture through clouds or smoke.

An hour into the sortie, the sensor operator told Busby that she'd picked up a craft whose peripherals matched the specs. Using a standard flight stick that transmitted commands over a C-band line-of-sight data link, Busby lowered the bird to 3,000 feet above sea level, high enough that the targets wouldn't be able to see or hear a thing. From that height, the Hornet could let you read the brand name on a pint of whiskey. The big capital letters stenciled onto the side of the fourteen-foot Zodiac might as well have been the Hollywood sign.

MERMAID III.

The Zodiac rounded the southern tip of Barbados, sugarcane fields for the most part, bringing into view a line of contemporary resorts and glitzy condos. Thornton used binoculars salvaged from the *Mermaid III* to search for threats. If he and Mallery were intercepted by a patrol craft, they would be calling lawyers from the inside of a detention center—if they were lucky. The closest thing he saw was a couple of kids fishing from a dinghy.

Mallery raised the boat cover a few inches. She had changed into a T-shirt and a pair of shorts, both of which hung off her like drapes, which was good. Albert's clothing, along with effects of the wind and salt air on her hair, had transformed her from a re-fined cosmopolitan woman to a party chick returning to a hostel after a day at the beach.

Stretching her arms, she yawned. "So back in Nantucket, using my site's metrics, I calculated that as a couple, we would score only about fifty out of a possible hundred and ten."

Thornton feared she was about to write off last night to post-traumatic stress. "That high?"

"When I get back to the office, I'm going to have to alter the algorithm to give more weight to escaping a black site together and saving each other's lives."

She kissed his knee. A gentle peck, but it sent a frisson of excitement throughout his body.

"Getting back to navigating ..." She pointed to one of the maps from the fishing boat. He ducked his head under the boat cover to get a better look. "There's a small fishing harbor just outside Bridgetown. Good place for us to hide in plain sight?"

"Maybe," he said. "Also where we'd be expected to go, if there's a welcome committee for us. Anything else near the city?"

"There are docks along the Careenage, which is

an inlet running right into downtown. Very crowded, though."

"Crowded is good."

"I'm not so sure about this place. The map says, 'Warning! Theft is endemic here. Lock your boat tight if you must leave it unattended.'"

"A thief would be doing us a favor. Remind me to leave the motor running."

"Designate the Zodiac as target." The velvety French-accented voice of the sensor operator, Nathalie Léglise, wafted into Busby's headphones. Nathalie was a redhead whose sexiest feature—and she had no shortage of them—was a black eye patch.

"Pilot copies," Busby said into his pipe-cleaner mic.

"Suspect One confirmed, Suspect Two likely concealed by camo," came the nasal voice of the mission's sentinel, Nick Aardsma, from the front office. Aardsma was also Macedon's cofounder, having gotten into the private military business after a dishonorable discharge from the Air Force a couple of years ago. Already he'd gotten himself a fifteen-bedroom villa in Boca de Río with his own cook, maid, and a genuine limey butler.

"Pilot copies," Busby said. A tap of his F1 key and an image of crosshairs snapped onto the shaky high-angle video of the Zodiac.

In the stern, by the motor, the head of a guy in a baseball cap—designated SUSPECT 1—stuck partway out from beneath a red tarp of some sort, under which SUSPECT 2 was probably guarding her fortune in meth. The tarp, heated by the sun to ninety-eight degrees, fucked the drone's infrared. A good effort at concealment by the targets. But not good enough. The intel packet said SUSPECT 1 had an extreme buzz cut. It stood to reason he would hide it. Also the crewmen's uniform on the *Mermaid III* had included baseball caps with embroidered anchors. Busby zoomed in on the cap. Sure enough: anchor.

Into his mic, Busby said, "Sentinel, please seek permission for tail one-oh-four"—his Hornet's tail number was 104—"to come south thirty degrees."

"Sentinel copies," said Aardsma.

Getting permission for Busby to change the flight plan was a simple matter of Aardsma radioing one of his contacts over at the Fuerza Aérea—the Venezuelan Air Force—and getting a *sí*.

Busby dropped the Hornet to well within the three-quarter-mile range of the Mini-Spike rockets. To Nathalie, he said, "Sensor, while he's doing that, you can lock up the target."

"Roger," said the Frenchwoman.

"Pilot, Sensor, one-oh-four is cleared hot on the Zodiac," came Aardsma's voice. "Engage at your discretion."

"Pilot copies," Busby said. "Spin up a weapon, Nat."

"Sensor wilco."

She ran through the prelaunch and launch check-
lists with him, everything a go. She selected and
armed her lasers. He concluded the sequence with,
"Three, two, one, rifle," and punched the red button.

It only clicked. Any old stock rocket-launch MP3
would have been a lot more gratifying. Three seconds
ticked off. Long-ass seconds, because there was no audio of the actual Mini-Spike firing. Just the splutter
of the drone's engine and props, same as ever. There
was nothing to see, either; the rockets were too fast to
track with the human eye, and there was no computer
iconography, not even the basic straight line for a
missile, like the missiles in the first-generation *Space
Invaders*.

Impact did come, however. The Zodiac disappeared in a mass of orange fire and black smoke. It
looked real enough, but on the monitor the mass was
the size of a nickel. The effect was like the rudimentary animated explosions from an early version of
Medal of Honor. In just two seconds, the flames and
smoke completely dissipated into the air. The raft
reappeared—that is, what was left of it: charred flecks
floating atop the waves.

"Excellent job," came Aardsma's voice. "Come on
out and get some of Señora García's *empanadas*."

38

Bridgetown was the urban planning equivalent of a ransom note composed of letters cut and pasted from wildly different publications. Many of the buildings were three- and four-story Georgians or Palladians that would have held their own in any European capital. In and around them were comely pastel Victorians. Here and there was a charismatic wooden chattel house, built on blocks of coral and trimmed with gingerbread fretwork. Then there were the "offshore" financial institutions, bank after bank, some of them sleek constructions of steel and glass that seemingly defied physics, others imitations of the Georgians and the Palladians wedged into tiny spaces that undermined the intended majesty. The rest of the city was filled with the same three-story building, duplicated again and again, the architectural objective apparently having simply been something that would remain standing for a decent number of years. All were painted in too-bright colors and trimmed with too much chrome. They housed boutiques and storefronts on the street level, apartments or offices on the upper floors. Everywhere Day-Glo signs proclaimed the likes of 50% OFF! or GRAND OPENING! Crowds swarmed in and out.

"What do you say we go shopping?" Thornton asked.

"How could we live if we passed this up?" replied Mallery.

He joined about twenty customers in Mo's, a lemon-yellow discount clothing store advertising SHOES, 2 FOR 1. He patted his pocket, feeling the seven $100 bills he'd taken from Albert's wallet before covering the dead boat captain with a tarp and setting him adrift in the *Mermaid III*'s portside Zodiac lifeboat in hope of decoying any searchers. While packing the *Mermaid III*'s other Zodiac, Mallery found $1,500 more in Albert's duffel bag. The total of $2,200 ought to go a long way toward the purchase of disguises now.

To minimize the chance of their being seen together, Mallery waited a minute before entering Mo's, then plucked a blouse off a rack and headed to the dressing rooms. Thornton remained behind, choosing a floral-print shirt for himself in XXL—bulky clothing veiled stature. For the same reason he also picked out a pair of stoplight-red board shorts with more square inches of material than any pair of long pants he'd ever owned. Next, in defiance of conventional spook wisdom that wearing hats aroused surveillants' suspicions, he fished an Atlanta Braves cap from a bargain bin. It would keep him from being the only male tourist on the island without a baseball cap. The Braves cap would also serve to hide his unique haircut, with the bill draping his features in shadows. These measures would throw off human searchers.

Cameras were tougher. Baseball caps made no difference to facial recognition software. Even bushy mustaches and beards were useless. In order to fool the machines, Thornton had read, you had to think the way they did. For instance, you could compress or distend a photo and a human would instantly recognize the subject, but a computer couldn't. Computerized facial recognition applications took into account relative positioning, sizes, and shapes of the eyes, nose, cheekbones, and jaw. Accordingly Thornton selected a tube of zinc oxide. When applied, the white sun-protection cream was capable of widening the bridge of a nose so that it boggled a system running principal component analysis or even the latest three-dimensional recognition software. The wraparound sunglasses Thornton chose would accomplish more of the same. He completed his outfit with a pair of Nike knockoffs, leaving part of the balled-up tissue paper in the toe of one of the shoes in order to alter his stride.

For Mallery, he picked out an extra-long T-shirt, the sort commonly worn over a bathing suit, this one with a silk-screened image of Peter Tosh, designed to divert attention from her face, though he suspected that if the surveillants were male, her bare legs would provide ample diversion. He chose a pair of sunglasses for her too, with frames big enough to negate the pronounced contour of her cheekbones. He also got thick glam-rock-style makeup, which could thwart skin-texture analytics, and a can of mousse to keep tendrils of hair pasted to her face—a monkey wrench to systems running linear discriminate analysis. Finally, he selected something called Dreamscape Instant Blonde.

At the counter, he added a box of on-sale Chiclets. Properly wadded in the mouth, the gum wouldn't draw a second glance from other humans but could utterly discombobulate elastic bunch graph measurement-based software.

Ten minutes later, he met an almost unrecognizable Mallery around the corner. They proceeded onto Broad Street, one of the city's main drags, thick with people and vehicular traffic, all of the cars in need of new carburetors. Steel bands competed from either end of the block.

Over the commotion, she asked, "So where to?"

"Good question," he admitted. "I'm hoping that

the answer leaps out at us while we're walking around, and if it doesn't, that we'll at least have some candidates."

The signs they passed offered no help. BC. LOWE & CO. DOLLARWISE. UNITED SERVICES. Any of these names might uniquely resonate with locals or in fact front Littlebird Central. A narrow gap between the three-story Dollarwise building and its four-story neighbor revealed a stripe of tropical sky, the first bit of sky Thornton had seen in a while. He glumly realized that he'd underestimated the scale of the city. He turned to Mallery, whose bright expression lacked only the proverbial lightbulb.

"In my experience, voice recognition software is problematic at best," she said. "Which has me thinking: So many organizations now get their podcasts converted into transcripts by offshore services staffed by human transcribers. Maybe this is as easy as looking up transcription companies."

Could be, Thornton thought. "The thing is, our gang wouldn't need or want new business other than their own. A big CIA listening post in Berlin was fronted for years by a generic College of Religious Studies. Other operations don't even bother with a sign."

"Those would just whet our transcribers' curiosity—in which case, maybe the cover is a generic tech company."

"Good thinking." Thornton kept to himself that,

unfortunately, of the last four businesses—BC, Lowe & Co., Dollarwise, and United Services—she had eliminated only Dollarwise. The best field officers, he reminded himself, had a knack for adapting a plan when things went wrong. The problem was, those were the best field officers. He didn't know what to do in order to adapt.

But he could try something different. That notion alone sparked a new idea. "They might want to be on a busy thoroughfare like this," he said, "but there are lots of reasons a quieter street would make sense."

They turned onto Pine Street. Still crowded, but smaller, narrower, and cheaper. On the sliver of a sidewalk, a man rushed past them shoving a squeaky shopping cart full of fish, some still quivering, the stench so strong Thornton half expected to be able to see a shimmer in the air.

"I like this block," he said.

But by the end of it, he had counted another fifteen signs for businesses that could front the listening post, and at least that many offices without signs.

"How about we stop in there?" Mallery waved at a café on the far corner. "Get ourselves a cold drink, then look on the Web or at the local yellow pages, make a list, and work our way down it?"

"Or we could just ask him." Thornton pointed to a FedEx truck down the block. A sweat-soaked deliveryman sat smoking a cigarette on the steel ramp extending to the street.

. . .

Mallery walked down the street, trying to neaten hair that the dye and sea air had nearly turned to plastic. She succeeded only in clearing her eyes. Thornton had her back from the café. Still she felt naked. Her checkbook was useless now. Without a support staff at her beck and call, or even a smartphone, she was on her own, reduced to old-fashioned smarts. Well, that and her smile.

As she approached the FedEx man, she faked a genuine smile to the utmost of her election-campaign-honed ability, the one that reached all the way from the mouth to the eyes and wrinkled the skin on the outer corners of the eyes. The man was overweight, in his thirties, with no hair other than thick eyebrows turned down toward a don't-mess-with-me coun-tenance. He smiled back, his eyebrows relaxing to a straight line. He tapped his cigarette ash on the dolly ramp, stood, and took a step toward her.

She had to play a role now: island-hopping party girl. A bartender in Woodside she knew was a good case study. Or, rather, inspiration. A guy, but his qualities might translate: He lived for the day and was overly trusting, flirty, and naïve. Slipping into char-acter, she felt a refreshing measure of release from her other worries.

"Hi," she said, "I'm hoping you can help me out." She added a self-conscious giggle.

"That makes two of us," he said with a thick Bajan accent.

She laughed as though he'd said something funny. "I made friends in Montego Bay with this girl, Mary, who said I could crash at her place when I made it to Barbados. Now, here I am, and I'm supposed to meet her at her office, but I forget the name of it. And there are *so* many offices . . ." Another giggle.

Prompting one from him. "What kind of office?"

"They do stuff with computers."

He whistled. "That's a lot of places, honey."

"Right, right, I knew that. She's in some kind of data entry. They probably have huge computers, lots of high-tech stuff. She said she has a couple friends there who do the same job she does."

This was enough for the FedEx man to rattle off the names and addresses of two transcription companies, three translation services, an accounting firm, and four other businesses. Mallery memorized them.

"You know what, I'm pretty sure it's Stillman," she said of the accounting firm. She actually had a strong hunch it was Bridgetown Data Entry.

He tapped the cell phone clipped to his belt. "How about we find out if they've got a Mary working there?"

"Nah," she said as casually as she could manage. "I want to surprise her."

"I'd for sure give you a ride, but Stillman's on Swan Street. No cars and trucks allowed."

Thank God, Mallery thought. "You're so sweet," she said.

He gave her directions, then dug a curled business card from a shorts pocket. "Use this in case you can't find Mary, or if you do find her and you girls want to know about some cool clubs or whatnot," he said, scrawling his name and number on the back of the card.

"Goodwyn."

"How are you, Norm?"

"You tell me."

"Unfortunately, sir, SOLAS, the Safety of Life at Sea organization, requires lifeboats on both sides of a boat—"

"In case the boat is, say, turned onto her starboard side on the sea bottom, blocking our submersible system's view of the empty lifeboat davits on that side? So I guess you're calling to say that we spent a million taxpayer dollars to blow up the wrong Zodiac."

"I imagine Murphy has a law that predicts this?"

"Murphy wrote a list of lucky breaks compared to the chain of events up to now. But this development isn't that bad, because we're getting to know our enemy: They're sharper than we thought, with greater operational know-how and better ability to execute. They scuttled the fishing boat, right?"

"The second pass of the submersible suggests that, sir."

"So they're hunting for us. Which means we now have a very good idea of where they're headed."

39

While Mallery went to look at Bridgetown Data Entry, Thornton set off for their other leading contender, EB Data Storage, two blocks away. As he walked, the cafés and boutiques gave way to simpler stores now closed for the night, low-end hotels and the sort of bars no one bothers to name. He turned onto a stretch of Pine Street that was a collection of office buildings put up on the cheap, including the pink concrete box at number 122 whose third-floor tenants theoretically included EB Data Storage.

EB's listing in the Barbados telephone directory had seemed to be the extent of their marketing efforts. The top floor had no company signs, but the streetlamps allowed Thornton to read a handwritten *EB* in a plastic slot on the buzzer panel. He continued past the building, his motion causing the security camera mounted above the door to pivot, its red bulb flashing on. Widely available online at around ten bucks apiece, fake cameras with realistic motion-sensitive lights were becoming a main line of defense for small-business owners the world over. Even if the camera were real, he thought, it was unlikely that anyone at EB Data Storage was monitoring its feed right now, at six P.M. Unless EB was the Littlebird front. In that case, it was possible that another camera, concealed among the buzzers perhaps, was currently transmitting real-time video of him.

He kept going, trying not to look back. But 122 Pine Street's front door jerked open, loosing a shaft of cool air onto the street. He turned and looked because it would have been unnatural not to. The man exiting the building in turn looked at him. Would have been odd if he hadn't. He was a serious-looking big guy, maybe 225, most of it muscle, topped by a shaved head so large that in the glare of passing headlights, it looked like he was wearing a football helmet. He clambered down the steps and made a beeline toward Thornton. Thornton's fight-or-flight synapses exploded.

Needlessly. The man turned away, opening the driver's door of a fifteen-passenger van with a fiery Emery Brothers logo painted onto its side, prompting delighted hoots and shouts from the fifteen or so boys inside, all wearing orange soccer jerseys with *EB* on the fronts.

The big man—their coach, Thornton guessed—

turned on the van and zoomed off, allowing Thornton to see another young man stepping out of a lime green office triplex two down from EB Data Storage's building. This guy was tall, white, with short white-blond hair. He wore standard tourist garb—polo shirt, Bermuda shorts, flip-flops, a baseball cap. Despite a fake mustache, Thornton recognized FBI Special Agent Warren "Corky" Lamont.

Resisting the urge to hide, Thornton maintained a steady pace, crossing Pine Street at the next corner. He watched Lamont's reflection in the broad storefront windows. Following the agent out of the small office building was a man whose brawn and upright bearing defied his sixty-some years. He wore a custodian's uniform, but he had the flinty face of a cop. Ex-military maybe, Thornton thought. Serving as building security now, perhaps. Which would be odd in a part of town where none of the businesses had security beyond fake cameras.

Holding the door open, the man said to Lamont, "You might try Islander Actuarial over on Swan Street instead, sir. They are usually not as busy as we are." The lines sounded stilted, Thornton thought. Delivered before many times.

"Thank you, sir," Lamont said, walking off, head down.

The guard watched him go, then darted back inside the building, whipping a phone from his overalls and speed-dialing before the door closed, blocking Thornton's view.

This was the place, Thornton thought. Had to be.

He made out WINDWARD ACTUARIAL engraved on a brass placard by the door, between similar signs for LM INSURANCE and SOFTEC. SofTec had been on the list the FedEx guy gave Mallery.

Thornton returned his attention to Lamont, who yanked open the passenger door of a car idling at the corner, a dark blue, late-model Lincoln that screamed *U.S. Embassy.*

Lamont grumbled to the driver, "Looks like we'll need to get together with our liaison agency after all. It's going to take a warrant to get in there."

Exactly why, Thornton reflected, he'd been averse to going to the Bureau. Any warrant request would serve as a tripwire, causing Littlebird to close shop post-haste. Thornton considered chasing down Lamont, making an appeal to his reason. But that would bring his driver—CIA, possibly—into the game. Even if the driver were another FBI agent, the Bureau always slowed things down with red tape. Better, Thornton decided, to go to Windward Actuarial himself.

40

Catering to the big resorts, Margarita Island was a bamboo-faced restaurant with a faux-straw roof. Surfboards, life rings, and beach toys hung from the inside walls, along with starfish or blowfish filling the gaps. Seated at the bar, which was constructed from a cross section of a dune buggy, Thornton watched a tiny, dilapidated Peugeot ascend the sandy driveway. The Peugeot's dashboard lights showed him its driver, the FedEx deliveryman—Ferdinand, he'd scrawled on the back of the card he'd given Mallery. The Peugeot was a problem. Thornton and Mallery had been hoping for the FedEx truck, so that he could make a delivery to Windward Actuarial.

The back bar mirror revealed another problem. Ferdinand, now extracting himself from the Peugeot, wasn't wearing the FedEx uniform Thornton also needed. The FedEx man had opted for a satiny collared shirt in spite of Mallery's bubbly mention over the phone of her affinity for men in uniform.

"Okay, slight change of plans," Thornton said.

"What do you have in mind?" asked Mallery, perched on the next barstool.

"We add a second round of drinks."

"I'll need that anyway. What else?"

"During the first round, find out where the truck is, where the keys are, and where his uniform is."

"That should naturally work into small talk."

"Do your best. Other than that, same plan as before. Either I, from here, or you, from your table, will take care of his second drink." They each had a cigarette whose filter he'd replaced with four capsules' worth of powdered chloral hydrate. In countries like Barbados, you didn't need an appointment with a psychopharmacologist—or even a prescription—to get the potent sedative. You just walked into a drugstore and bought Benaxona, the Mexican-made insomnia remedy. Thornton had calculated that four doses ought to put Ferdinand out for ten to twelve hours.

As Ferdinand bounded into the restaurant, Mallery sprang from the bar, embraced him, and exclaimed, "You came!"

The hostess, in bikini top and grass skirt, sat them in a booth. Watching via the back bar mirror, Thornton found it hard to hear their conversation over the music, but he made out *FedEx* and *truck*. Good.

After about thirty minutes, Ferdinand drained

the last of whatever had been in his ceramic coconut, rose, and lumbered toward the CABANA BOYS room.

Mallery shot to the bar. "Good news is he has the keys on him, the truck is parked at his house, and his uniforms are in his dresser," she said. "Bad news is he wants to get out of here now—it's too pricey."

"Did you try a free drink?"

"I offered to buy another round, of course."

"You paying probably doesn't count as 'free' to him. I'll try and get the bartender to bring you over two more drinks 'on the house.' People often have a hard time letting anything go to waste that they've gotten for free."

"Worth a try." Mallery hurried back to the booth, sitting just in time to light up at Ferdinand's return.

Thornton ordered another daiquiri for Ferdinand and a second bottle of beer for Mallery. He deployed the rapidly dissolving chloral hydrate into the ceramic coconut while the young woman tending bar turned around to change his $100 bill.

She delivered the drinks to the booth along with the news—which cost Thornton an extra twenty—that Margarita Island was having a buy-one-get-one-free special tonight. Ferdinand pumped a fist in response.

Toward the end of the round, he began to teeter. Mallery suggested she drive him home, pantomiming the operation of steering a wheel. Ferdinand appeared to protest but fell from his bench in midexplanation.

Playing the Good Samaritan, Thornton hurried

to assist the young woman in getting her date off the floor and outside for some fresh air.

The parking lot had no resuscitative effect. "So far, so good?" Thornton asked.

"Not exactly." Mallery helped him shoulder the deliveryman's weight. "The last thing he said was he wanted to go to a hotel."

"Let me guess. A wife and kids at home?"

"Just one kid, a newborn."

"What a guy. Time for Plan C."

"What's Plan C?" she asked.

"We need to work on that."

They dragged Ferdinand to the Peugeot. Thornton fished through the FedEx man's pockets until he found a wallet with a driver's license. He stabbed a finger at Ferdinand Ring's home address. "Plan C."

After a twenty-minute drive to 1032 Palm Forest Road, he left Mallery and the dozing Ferdinand in the Peugeot on a dark roadside, then hiked fifty yards up a rocky driveway. This sparsely populated part of the island was illuminated only by the starlight trickling through the dense canopy of leaves and branches. At the top of the driveway, he came to an old chattel house, the rot in its frame evident in silhouette. A faint light and a flickering television screen shone through a window, beside which the FedEx truck was parked. Thornton was tempted to simply drive it off, but if whoever was watching TV reported the theft to the police, the jig was up.

There was no doorbell, no light above the stoop. Thornton climbed the steps and knocked on the door, which was eventually thrown open by a small, dark-skinned young woman with delicate features. The dim light made it hard to peg her age, but there was no doubt about her emotion: fury. But apparently intended for someone other than Thornton. Taking him in, her face softened to wariness. Withdrawing a step, she looked poised to slam the door and lock it.

"Who are you?" she asked.

"Hi, Mrs. Ring. I'm Gartland Fredericksen, Fed-Ex's regional vice president for operations." He flashed Ferdinand's business card, which only listed, in mouse type, the address, phone number, and e-mail address of the Bridgetown FedEx depot. "First, let me assure you that Ferdinand is fine."

The woman put a hand to her heart, without sincerity.

"I should add, ma'am, that it's my pleasure to meet you." He extended a hand.

She accepted, shaking limply, apparently bewildered.

"FedEx won a last-minute contract to service the Realtors' convention here on the island tomorrow," Thornton went on. "We need Ferdinand along with every other warm body we've got to sort packages through the night. That's the bad news. The good news is the shift pays double overtime."

The woman smiled. A forced smile, Thornton

thought. Was she buying the act? Because if she were, she ought to have asked him in. Or maybe she simply didn't want to wake the baby.

"I just need to pick up a uniform for Ferdinand," Thornton said. "And take the truck back to Bridgetown."

41

The narrow Pine Street building consisted of three stories of cement painted a faded tangerine, with three rows of hurricane shutters. Painted over the old name on the sign was DELUX INN, along with five stars. Thornton and Mallery maneuvered their drugged 250-pound captive into the diminutive white-tiled lobby, which smelled vaguely of a locker room. Draping Ferdinand's arms around their shoulders, they gave him the appearance of staggering.

The sallow night clerk avoided eye contact. He'd seen stranger, Thornton guessed. Probably he knew that no good could come of getting involved. The question of passports was never raised. Paying cash, Thornton had a room key in hand in sixty seconds. Then he and Mallery hauled Ferdinand up the stairs, the drinking song warbling from a second-floor room drowning out their clatter.

The third-floor room was just large enough to contain a dresser missing one of its five drawers and a concave queen bed, onto which they lowered Ferdinand.

"This room is perfect," Thornton said.

"What exactly are your criteria?" asked Mallery.

He steered her two steps toward the window and pointed through the louvers at Windward Actuarial, on the other side of Pine Street.

Pleased, Mallery set about making a bed on the floor from the sheet and blankets Ferdinand wouldn't need because the only air-conditioning was a creaky ceiling fan that barely stirred the muggy air.

Thornton sat against the wall by the window. Propping the *Mermaid III* binoculars on the sill, he began his surveillance. For five and a half hours, he saw no sign of life. Then, at eight thirty, a sleepy-eyed young woman got off a municipal bus and climbed the steps to the Windward Actuarial building. An employee, he guessed, based on the utter lack of joy with which she punched five buttons of the numeric keypad above the door handle: 5-1-9-4-7, he saw through the binoculars.

An hour later, he drove the FedEx truck up Pine Street. He wore a FedEx uniform shirt that was too big by a couple of *X*'s but terrific in terms of hiding his physique. His disguise also included the FedEx ball cap, wraparound sunglasses, and a wad of chewing gum swelling his cheek. The pièce de résistance was a shaving cut on his chin, bleeding through the small square of toilet paper. Someone seeing such a unique feature, according to spook wisdom, would fixate on it rather than him.

Pulling the truck parallel to the curb in front of Windward Actuarial, he opened his door and started to jump to the street. Remembering that such a move could wreak havoc on the safety-pin rigging taking in Ferdinand's purple uniform shorts by eight inches, he carefully lowered himself from the driver's seat to the curb. Pushing the door shut behind him, he hurried around the truck, lifted the rear gate, extended the ramp to the street, and wheeled down a dolly with a crate addressed to Windward Actuarial.

He climbed the stoop and pressed the buzzer. In response, evidently, someone hurried downstairs. Opening the door, the flinty security guard didn't appear at all surprised by the sight of the new FedEx man. But he should have been. For one thing, Thornton was white, unlike the islanders who constituted the entirety of Bridgetown's workforce. Thornton hoped the guard's familiarity resulted from a security camera preview before opening the door, as opposed to a brief sent by a Littlebird operative.

"How are you this morning, sir?" Thornton asked.

"You people finally get rid of Ferdinand?"

So that was it. "No, sir, he should be back tomorrow."

"What happened to him?"

"Nothing a little rest won't take care of." As soon as Thornton finished here, Mallery would wake Ferdinand, thank him for an unforgettable night, and send him on his way.

Looking over the guard's shoulder and into the small vestibule, Thornton asked, "Do you have a service entrance or an elevator, sir?" He already knew the building had one other entrance, in the back, leading in from a onetime delivery area now reduced to a narrow alley by a new construction opposite it.

The guard turned toward the stairs. "Ain't no elevators in none of these buildings."

While the man's head was turned, Thornton looked for the alarm control box. Mounted on the wall just inside the front door was a Chamberlain model A200, a high-end unit typically found in businesses at much higher risk of break-in, like jewelry stores.

The guard looked back to Thornton, who shifted his gaze and pretended to admire the foyer's diminutive crystal chandelier.

"You can just leave this right here," the man said, tapping the box, his eyes lingering on the shipping label, which specified Dell Computer in Austin, Texas, as the sender. Thornton had filled the label out himself, having taken it from the stack of blanks in the truck. He put the new label on the heaviest carton he could find, which contained a window air-conditioning unit bound for a bank.

Thornton scowled. "Please don't tell me Ferdinand doesn't carry up your deliveries for you."

The guard shrugged. "The boxes have to go up two flights."

"Relax, it's FedEx," Thornton said, quoting the motto painted on the sides of the truck. "Also we can't ask our customers to do our jobs. I will personally make sure that Ferdinand brings up your boxes from now on, no matter how heavy they are."

Even if the guard didn't mind carrying the box himself, Thornton hoped, he would be averse to any external inquiry.

"If you just set it on the third-floor landing," the man said, "that'd be great." He started up the stairs.

Thornton handed him a pen with a form to sign. The pen was out of ink in order to delay the guard. Straining beneath the weight of the carton, Thornton jogged past him, aiming to put enough distance between them so that he could "mistakenly" enter Windward Actuarial.

He reached the third-floor landing well ahead of the guard. But the windowless doors on either side of the landing—one labeled SOFTEC, the other labeled WINDWARD ACTUARIAL—were both shut. A key card was required to work the levered handles.

Hoisting himself up to the landing, the guard handed over the form he'd managed to sign. "Just set the box right here, man," he said by way of farewell.

On his way down the stairs, Thornton took in motion detectors fronted by wall sconces and, in some cases, mirrors. He also noticed an active infrared system, the sort that picked up the discrepancy between the body temperature of an intruder and the temperature of the room. The stairwell was also armed with passive infrareds, optical systems that detected *any* changes in ambient infrared radiation. Approaching the second floor, he spotted another mirror, which, when he looked at its side, revealed the reflective glass to be a façade for a continuous-wave radar motion detector, a device that used microwaves to detect changes in anything's position. On the way out, he saw what he believed to be an ultrasonic motion detector, which emitted sound energy in waves from quartz crystal transducers—any disruption in these waves caused the alarm to sound.

He'd read that to thwart an active infrared system, you cranked the heat in the building to the nineties, 98.6 ideally, and the human body essentially became invisible to the sensor. But like most buildings in the tropics, this one had no heat. As for the other systems, he hadn't a clue.

He had some serious planning to do before breaking in.

42

Lamont loved the beach, and this one was beautiful beyond belief. If he'd seen it in a movie, he would have thought the effects people had gone over the top in boosting the greens and blues and whitening the sand. From a chaise, he admired the model— she had to be one—gliding into one of the infinity pools. It had been his good luck that, until tourist season hit full stride, the resort cut the embassies amazing deals. The problem was, he didn't want to be here. He burned to get back to the noisy diesel-reeking city down the coast and find out what the actuarial firm was hiding.

He went back to his room for the fifth time that morning to check for a reply to the EC he'd sent last night. To his surprise, he found what amounted to an approval. The Bureau would permit him to ask Mitchell Firstbrook, the CIA's Barbados chief of base, to broach a joint operation with Colonel Marston of the Barbados Defense Force.

Lamont squeezed into his tiny rental car and sped down a magnificent coastal road to which he paid little attention. Eventually he pulled up to a modern three-story office building painted mustard yellow.

Firstbrook didn't keep him waiting, which Lamont took as promising. The position of base chief on such islands was often bestowed upon veteran desk jockeys as a reward for a couple of decades of toeing the line, meaning they could barely get dressed in the morning without using red tape. Although forty-nine years old and just sixteen months shy of eligibility to retire with full benefits, Firstbrook approached the job with the zeal of a rookie. He wore a crisp, tropical-weight khaki suit. His gray hair was closely cropped above a ruddy, pleasant face. Lamont liked him on sight.

"I lobbied for this posting," Firstbrook said, leading Lamont back to his office. "Barbados has eighteen billionaires and many more aspiring to that position with plans that hinge on getting away with something. It's not Moscow or Geneva, but it's a place where one man can make a real difference."

Lamont asked how, and Firstbrook modestly substantiated his claim with his reply: In just over a year on the job, he had single-handedly caught two men who were laundering money for Hezbollah, he'd brought down a bank whose management had just embezzled $270 million from pension funds, and, for good measure, he'd saved a local girl from drowning at the municipal pool where he swam laps every morning. He might have worked out at the posh private club available to embassy staffers, but he preferred public pools because they enabled him to befriend locals, and thus collect intelligence.

Lamont also learned that when Firstbrook's budget precluded a Sensitive Compartmented Information Facility—SCIF—the base chief assembled one himself. An SCIF was essentially a windowless steel room that blocked electromagnetic eavesdropping and prohibited signals from escaping, allowing for the most sensitive conversations inside. Firstbrook even devised a way to filter the electrical current.

Seated across the homemade SCIF's conference table, Firstbrook sighed. "Unfortunately, Colonel Marston is deep-sea fishing on his yacht, unreachable. He likes to go with his sons, usually for a day or two. Without him, there's not much we can do."

Lamont's disappointment gave way to curiosity. "The colonel has a yacht?"

Firstbrook rolled his eyes. "A thirty-seven-foot cabin cruiser that normally would have cost three hundred eighty grand, but the broker gave him the standard government discount, a hundred percent off. That's Barbados. But all in all, Willie Marston's one of the good guys. He'll help us. We just need to sit tight for a day or so."

Lamont asked, "How about any judge? All we need is a basic search warrant."

"Yes, and there is a judge we can call. And you should see *his* yacht. Which is the problem. It may well have been paid for by another company that we think is fronting a massive Eastern European money-laundering operation, so bringing the court in on your case is a risk the Agency can't afford to take. In the meantime, I've set the wheels in motion. Marston should be back tonight or tomorrow morning. Windward Actuarial isn't going anywhere. There are worse things than spending a day at one of the world's most beautiful beaches, right?"

43

Entering a business during off-hours, a man wearing a service or technician's uniform—Verizon, for example—is 30 percent less likely to arouse neighbors' suspicions than a man in plain clothes. And a man in such a uniform entering a business accompanied by a female colleague is a full two-thirds less likely to arouse suspicion. Thornton and Mallery incorporated both of these National Crime Database statistics into their plan to access Windward Actuarial.

At ten that night Bridgetown was packed with diners and clubbers, none of whom looked twice at the royal blue jumpsuits he and Mallery wore, along with matching Raytheon ball caps. Probably the company's name was both sufficiently recognizable and nebulous. Thornton would have preferred a telco but felt lucky to have come across these at the same secondhand store where he bought the nineteen-inch color TV that had also been on the shopping list for tonight.

Mallery's cap concealed most of her hair. Her severe, black-rimmed, prescriptionless eyeglasses along with pasty makeup went a long way to blunt her looks. No masking her nerves, however. As the two of them turned onto Pine Street, Thornton broke cover, placing a hand on her arm to steady her. He was strangely calm. Not a single butterfly. Probably because he had to juggle so many elements of the break-in, he thought.

Challenge number one came now, as they climbed the steps to the Windward building's entrance: the external security camera—or cameras. If a facial recognition system saw through their disguises, Thornton and Mallery were in big trouble. Provided they were fortunate enough to break in.

He tapped the numeric keys on the pad above the front door handle. 5-1-9-4-7. The deadbolt disengaged with a thunk, giving them thirty seconds to enter the vestibule and disengage the alarm system.

While Mallery stood guard on the stoop—to all appearances filling out a form on her clipboard—he stepped into the cool vestibule and turned right, finding a red alarm bell icon flashing under the heading ZONE 1 on the control box. This symbol indicated a breach in the security zone that encompassed the vestibule and the front door. In twenty-seven or twenty-eight seconds, the symbol would be given voice in the form of a klaxon. He could turn the entire security system off, a simple matter of entering a second code. Three digits, four digits, five. He didn't know. He didn't know the code.

What he did know was that, throughout history, every time someone invented a security system, someone else found a means of vanquishing it. Take the near-indestructible U-shaped metal Kryptonite lock, a staple of bicycle rack security for fifty years. One day in 2004, a guy figured out that by wedging in the somewhat malleable plastic barrel of a Bic pen, anybody could pop the lock. The next day his discovery was all over the news. More recently, a home security expert took to the Internet and boasted that he could thwart most burglar alarm systems by finding remote controls from other types of systems, a video game that operated on the same radio frequency, for instance. Earlier today, in a few seconds of surfing the Web on a grimy laptop at the secondhand store under the pretext of giving the computer a test drive, Thornton learned that the Windward Actuarial building's Chamberlain A200 security system was susceptible to jamming by the remote control to most Panasonic TVs.

He unpocketed his Panasonic remote now. The count in his head reached twelve-Mississippi. Eigh-

teen seconds to klaxon. He aimed the remote at the
security system control box. The conic tip of the remote flashed a wan red. Using the channel selection,
he punched in 1-0-1, then moused down. The display
on the control box reflected neither maneuver, though
he'd followed each step to the letter. So what now?

Eight seconds to go. Seven.

He thought of one more thing he might try. The
cure-all ENTER button. He clicked it. The alarm bell
icon was replaced by a message. DISENGAGED.

Exhaling in relief, he opened the door. "We're
good," he told Mallery. Unless it's a silent alarm, he
thought.

She entered, shutting the door behind her. "Let's
go to work," she said.

Aiming the TV remote at the control box, he entered the numbers 102 through 117, disengaging the
remaining sixteen alarm zones.

By the pink light of motion detectors, they charged
up the stairs to the third floor. No alarms sounded.

Someone from the Bic pen school had also virally
spread the word on opening lever-handled doors
equipped with key card locks. Consequently today's
shopping had also included eight-gauge steel wire,
about an eighth of an inch in diameter. Thornton un-
coiled and straightened ten feet of it. He knelt on the
carpet in front of Windward's door, stood the wire
parallel to the door, then folded it about five inches
above the handle. He shaped those five inches into a

hook, which he forced through the gap between the base of the door and the jamb. He aimed the hook straight up, until it clicked the inside levered handle. Getting a firm grip on it, he yanked down, at the same time throwing his shoulder against the door. The door fell open, taking him with it.

"How about that?" he exclaimed.

"Fantastic, except . . ." Mallery stared into Windward Actuarial.

Thornton looked around the office—carpet, bare walls, and nothing else. It made no sense. It was impossible that the Littlebird team had emptied the place during the brief periods when he or Mallery wasn't watching from the hotel. The back alleyway was too narrow to allow a desk through. "Maybe they put everything somewhere else in the building," he said.

"You overheard the security guard tell Lamont to try an actuarial firm that wasn't as busy," said Mallery. "Maybe Lamont had been using Windward as cover, really trying to access another business in this building, or maybe he'd just gotten it wrong. If you're a transcriber, you would probably wonder what you were doing in an actuarial firm. But you wouldn't think twice if the name of the place were SofTec, right?"

Ten seconds later, they were across the hall, at SofTec's door, identical in appearance and size to Windward's, meaning there was no need for Thornton to adjust the hook or the wire.

In less than a minute, he and Mallery were inside

SofTec, mouths agape at the contents of the thirty-by-thirty-foot windowless space: three rows of three cubicles, each row bridged at head level by a steel rack crammed with hard drives, some as small as cell phones, others the size of briefcases. Perhaps 1,000 drives in all, they emitted a medley of processing sputters, fan-blade whirs, and all manner of electronic clicks and grunts and beeps. Several thousand tiny bulbs—orange, yellow, and red—and green LED panels combined to project an aura like that above Manhattan at nighttime. The office's organizing principle seemed to be piling on hard drives into the overhead racks as needed. The racks sprouted a multicolored jungle of cables and cords that all but encased the three cubicle rows.

"It's what we expected," Mallery said as she wandered around. "The audio from the bugs is collected on the hard drives, then transcribed by people in each of the cubes. See the headphones?"

"Yes." Dodging one of the bulky posts supporting the nearest rack, Thornton stepped over a series of power cords and entered a cubicle. He recognized the pair of foot pedals from his newspaper reporting days. They were used in transcription to keep the hands free to type—one pedal for pause and play, the other for rewind. He picked up one of the lightweight headsets. Plenty of padding on the headband. Holding one of its thick cups to his ear, he heard a voice. "This terminal is picking up a woman speaking a foreign language. Romanian, or maybe Hungarian," he told Mallery.

"Could be a live transmission," she said.

Setting the earphones back on the desk, he followed the cable from the terminal to the drive in the rack directly overhead, to which someone had taped a strip that read:

The hard drives on either side had labels with similar characters.

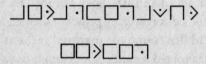

The same thing was on all the hard drives. "I should have figured they wouldn't just spell out for us whose audio is whose," said Thornton.

"We can read the labels," Mallery said from the far side.

He stared at her. "What am I missing?"

"Ten years in computer labs with bad lighting and worse ventilation, during which time you would have had more than your fill of encryption." She pointed from label to label.

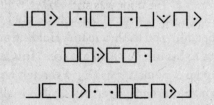

"These all have between six and twelve characters, no spaces. Last names, right?"

"Probably." Thornton didn't see what difference it made.

"The longer ones, Eastern European, Spanish, maybe end in *A* or *V*, a lot with *VA* or *OV*. Plus *A*s and *O*s and *E*s are mile markers. I think you were listening to someone named Cavanova. Davonova? Gavanova?"

Feeling like he'd witnessed a magic trick, Thornton exclaimed, "Galina Ivanova is Hungary's new minister of finance."

"You know what's in her head and you can place some pretty good bets on the Budapest Stock Exchange domestic equity indices."

"Interesting. Any idea how it fits into the puzzle?"

"It tells us they're going with first initial and last name here, and now we have eight letters." Mallery looked at the labels to either side of Galina Ivanova's. "Also the drives are in alphabetical order." She chuckled. "I don't know why they even bothered with code."

Thornton shook his head in wonder. He started to speak but was interrupted by an odd creak. He whirled around. The door was still closed.

Mallery looked at him, her shoulders raised.

"Building settling," he said. And hoped. He cursed himself for neglecting to set up even a rudimentary tripwire to notify them of the arrival of another person.

On her clipboard, Mallery jotted out the alphabet on two grids.

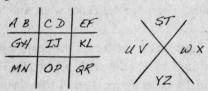

"Each letter's represented by the part of the grid surrounding it," she said. "If it's the second letter in the slot, then it gets a dot in the middle. For example, here's *A* and *B* and . . ."

She wrote:

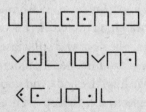

She tapped the three drives perched on the rack just above her head. "These three drives are for subjects named Johnson, the one before is Jemison—why is that name familiar?"

"There's a Stanley Jemison on the board of ExxonMobil."

She continued perusing the labels.

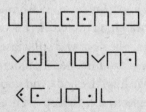

"A. Kellogg, S. Kirkendall," she said. "Scott Kirkendall, secretary of defense?"

"Could be."

"And X. Laibe," she read. "Has to be Xavier Laibe, right?"

"How many X. Laibes can there be?" Thornton wandered toward the *T*s, wondering if he'd see a hard drive labeled with his own name. "Who is he?"

"He heads up mergers and acquisitions at Morgan Stanley, which took my company public. To be a fly on his office wall is to potentially have billions of dollars' worth of insider information."

"Maybe that's the reason you initially were bugged." Thornton took in a smaller, newer hard drive:

$$\lrcorner\lor\sqcap\sqsubset\sqcap\cdot\sqcap\rangle\lrcorner$$

Something Sokolova. He recognized it as the female variant of the surname Sokolov. Leonid Sokolov's wife—Bella? There was no shortage of Eastern Europeans represented here, and Sokolov was the fifth most common Russian surname, following Smirnov, Ivanov, Popov, and one that Thornton couldn't immediately recall—but what were the odds? He hurried back to Mallery to double-check the symbol for *B* she'd written down.

"G-gee," she stammered. "G. Langlind."

Thornton couldn't get the question out soon enough. "Can we find out what he's been saying?"

"We would need to do heavy-duty hacking to get audio, but we should be able to bring up the transcriptions right now." Without waiting for a reply, she pulled the USB cable down from the hard drive, climbed over a cluster of wires, slid into a chair in front of the computer, and plugged in the cable. A tap at the keyboard and she awoke the monitor. Nothing but white pixels and a trash can icon in the lower right corner.

She hit RETURN. Type flooded the screen. She read aloud from the top. *"And can I get a half and half with that, please?"* She moused up. "Apparently, this is him at 3:04 this afternoon, in the Senate Dining Room with someone named Selena."

"Probably Seldridge," Thornton said. "Selena Seldridge."

"Sounds familiar. Senate staffer?"

"Rumor has it, his mistress."

She groaned. "And he beat me on family values."

"He beat you by getting into bed with the wrong people, Selena Seldridge aside. Can you search by date?"

"Maybe. There's a search box."

"Try the day before Catherine Peretti was killed. October twenty-third."

"Got it."

"Any mention of her? One *R* and two *T*s."

Mallery quickly filled in the search box, resulting in: "Nothing on October twenty-third. But three days later, we have Langlind saying, *Unfortunately I can't go to Cathy Peretti's wake. Will you send the family some flowers and a nice note from me?*"

"She hated being called Cathy," Thornton said. "I guess she wouldn't have told the boss that, though."

"He wouldn't have listened anyway," said Mallery. "Swell guy. Let's try searching under 'Cathy.'"

Mallery typed, then scanned the results. "Check this out, from October twenty-third."

Thornton ducked beneath the rack and swept cables aside in order to read:

{TELEPHONE DIALING, TELEPHONE RINGING, TELEPHONE ANSWERED}

MAN: YES?

LANGLIND: HI, SORRY TO HAVE TO CALL YOU ON THIS LINE.

MAN: I THINK YOU GOT THE WRONG NUMBER, BUDDY.

LANGLIND: RIGHT. I MEANT TO SAY, "HELLO, I'M CALLING ABOUT YOUR AD IN THE ALUMNI MAGAZINE."

MAN: THAT PROPERTY IS NO LONGER AVAILABLE.

LANGLIND: I'M INTERESTED IN BOOKING FOR NEXT YEAR.

MAN: WHAT'S THE MATTER, MR. ROBERTSON?

LANGLIND: CATHY SAW A SATELLITE PICTURE OF HIM ON A YACHT THAT NIGHT, THEN SHE DID SOME DIGGING . . . AND NOW SHE KNOWS.

MAN: OKAY, IT'LL BE TAKEN CARE OF.

LANGLIND: HOW?

MAN: IF YOU NEED TO KNOW, YOU WILL.

{TELEPHONE HUNG UP BY MAN}

LANGLIND: SHIT.

{TELEPHONE HUNG UP BY LANGLIND}

Thornton felt an urge to punch the monitor. "It would seem Langlind is more than just a stooge."

Mallery continued to study the transcription. "What's the significance of a satellite picture of someone on a yacht?"

"Catherine could have seen satellite imagery of a man on a yacht on Lake Michigan the night of Sokolov's murder. The assassin supposedly used a miniature submarine to get to and from Sokolov's property. The FBI, the Coast Guard, and Homeland all failed to find any trace of the sub. Maybe it was deployed from a yacht, then returned to the yacht after Sokolov was killed. Whatever Catherine pieced together, it was damning enough to cost her her life. Speaking of which, did the interrogator ask you anything about Sokolov?"

"He asked me all I knew about *both* Sokolovs. But I didn't have much to tell him, other than about the murder story. I wouldn't have known anything about them, except one of my old computer science professors happened to be an electronic warfare junkie."

Thornton had the sense of finding a way out of a maze. "I think the seven-gram lead bullet really was just a diversion. Leonid died while they were trying to stick a Littlebird in him, so they stuck one in his lab partner instead. There's a B. Sokolova here."

Mallery paled. "So then this is about what the Sokolovs were working on."

"Any way to tell who Langlind was talking to?"

"I don't think the transcriber would have known unless he or she went back to the original audio and listened to the dialing tones, assuming there were any. Whoever reads the transcript could request additional analysis—that would be a reason they keep a junkyard's worth of audio around after they've already transcribed it."

"How about searching under 'Sokolov'?"

Mallery returned her hands to the keyboard, but before she could type the name, the lobby door groaned open. Then came heavy footsteps, at least two sets, flying up the stairs.

Thornton flashed back to the guns he saw for sale

at the secondhand store, the less powerful of which fired two-and-a-half-inch nails at 1,400 feet per second, his for the taking. He'd failed to consider the need for a weapon until now.

"Hide," he said. Not much of an idea, but his only idea.

44

The key-card snick resonated throughout the SofTec office. Thornton crouched behind the row of cubicles farthest from the door. At the other end, Mallery sat with her back to the wall, eyeing him plaintively. He *had* planned an escape route: the back alley. The problem was, using it required getting out of SofTec, a windowless room with only one door— now swinging inward.

A tall man appeared in silhouette in the corridor to the left of the open doorway, gun in hand, flame darting from the mouth of its sound suppressor. A bullet pinged the steel hard-drive rack above Thornton's head, ricocheting harmlessly away, but the impact caused the entire structure to teeter. He was surprised that none of the equipment fell off.

When no one returned fire, the gunman dove to the carpet, bouncing up into a kneeling position, placing cubicles between him and Thornton and Mallery. A muted report came from a second shooter, in the doorway behind the tall man, the bullet stinging the floor near Thornton and raising a cloud of carpet fibers. The shooter, a squat and powerfully built man, scrabbled in and slid into a kneel at the opposite side of the front cubicle row from the tall man.

Thornton wondered if the gunmen had been instructed to minimize damage to the equipment. Or maybe they knew they required little in the way of cover fire.

The tall man called out, "Ma'am, sir, come out with your hands on your heads."

His accent was midwestern. He probably wasn't a SofTec transcriber, but he definitely knew where Thornton and Mallery were hiding. Thornton guessed that there were video cameras in the room, not only for security but to monitor the transcribers. The gunmen might be watching the feed now, in real time, on their phones. Still they couldn't be certain that Thornton and Mallery were unarmed. Otherwise they would have just strolled into the office and hauled them out. Or shot them.

Thornton hit the Panasonic TV remote, reactivating the building's alarm sensors. The local police force might be bought off, but it was unlikely that the officers would permit a cold-blooded execution in front of a crowd of witnesses drawn by the blare of the klaxons.

"You've just reactivated the alarm system," said the shorter gunman, his wide face illuminated by his cell phone. "All that does is notify *us* that you're here."

Nodding, the tall man fired, the bullet sparking the second of the three overhead storage racks. Both men advanced to the middle cubicle row.

"Help me," Mallery begged.

Fearing she'd been struck by the ricocheting bullet, Thornton whirled to find her driving her shoulder into the post supporting her end of the rack bridging the rear cubicle row. Getting the idea, he threw his full weight into the post on his side.

The wobbly rack fell forward, crashing into the middle rack, which in turn dominoed the front rack, all in a second, followed by a rain of hard drives and computer monitors, the shattering of glass, the crunching of bones, and the men's screams. Enveloped by a cloud of kicked-up dust and sparks, the room reverted to its usual medley of beeps and clicks.

Thornton saw a right arm protruding from beneath the toppled middle rack at a grotesque angle. The squat gunman lay dead like a mouse in a trap. The tall man was slicked in blood. His left fibula poked through his pant leg. But he remained standing, his Beretta pointed at Thornton's face.

The heat fled Thornton's body. This, he knew, was it.

"Wait," he shouted.

The gunman added a second hand to the grip, steadying the Beretta.

With a muted report, he fell, like a tree, dead before hitting the carpet. Mallery stood behind him, her face ashen even in the monitors' green glow. Her trembling hands clutched the other gunman's Beretta.

Thornton seized the tall man's Beretta and waved her out. She was still shaking when he met her at the door.

"Thank you," he whispered, pulling her toward him and planting a soft kiss on top of her head, as much as he could do for now. No reason to think there weren't more gunmen waiting in the hall.

Pointing his just-acquired Beretta ahead as though it were a flashlight, he pulled the door open. Fortunately the hallway was empty. The *hee-haw* sirens of police cars rose from the streets, growing louder. The gunmen either had been lying about the alarm system or had simply been wrong.

"Great. *Now* the police come," Mallery whispered.

Thornton was glad her head was back in the game. He led her down the stairs to the second-floor corridor. Finding it clear, he proceeded to the next flight. If they could make it to the ground floor before the police arrived, it would be simple to escape via the back alley.

Mallery stopped suddenly.

Thornton looked back, mouthing, *What?*

She said nothing. Just pointed through the darkness at one of the mirrors on the wall. Thornton made out the reflection of the security guard, creeping from the rear corridor, wearing a bulky pair of goggles. Night vision, probably. He reached around the bannister, firing a pistol.

On the second-floor landing, a chunk of wall inches from Mallery's head exploded into powder, the blast reverberating throughout the building. Thornton tugged her back into the corridor, out of the line of fire.

To keep the guard at bay, Thornton fired the Beretta through the banister. Although minimal, the muzzle flash set the chandelier aglow, revealing the guard in a crouch at the base of the stairs. The man raised both hands to shield his eyes. The flash, through infrared lenses, must look like a fireball, Thornton thought.

He hoped to temporarily blind the guard by turning on the recessed lights above the stairs. But the light-switch panel was in the guard's direct line of fire. And even if he or Mallery could switch on the lights, how the hell would they get down the stairs and past the guard?

There was another option. "I don't want to have to shoot you," Thornton called down to the man. "But I will if you don't set your gun on the floor."

"Kiss my—" Whatever else the guard said was swallowed by a deafening report from his gun. The bullet drilled into the wall about a foot above the light-switch panel.

Two, maybe three police cars screeched to a stop

outside, their roof lights outlining the front door in red, then blue, then red again.

"Any way they're here to help us?" Mallery asked.

"If we use them as a diversion, possibly," Thornton said.

Someone pounded the door and barked, "Bridgetown Police, open up."

Thornton lunged for the landing, swatting the switches on the wall panel into the upward position. Though the bulbs illuminated little more than the stairs, the guard reeled, flinging off his goggles as though they were burning him.

Thornton fired, sending a bullet ricocheting off the chain suspending the chandelier. The cluster of crystal and metal swung up to the ceiling, bulbs shattering. He fired three more rounds in a row, the third splitting the chain's midpoint. The chandelier itself dropped onto the guard, knocking him to the floor and costing him his grip on his gun.

"Now!" Thornton said.

Mallery sprinted down the stairs after him. Ahead, the guard was on hands and knees feeling around the dark vestibule for his gun.

As they passed him, Thornton heard a crash ax hit the door. Another crash and the door tumbled inward, ringing the marble floor.

Thornton and Mallery flew into the dark rear corridor an instant before the policemen entered the vestibule. He carefully opened the back door, pointing her down the trash-filled alley. Swan Street shone before them, as bright as noon, the crowd of revelers unaffected by the police sirens a block away.

The alley stunk of garbage. Rats scurried away as Thornton and Mallery ripped off their Raytheon uniforms and tossed them into one of the dumpsters on their way to Swan Street.

Glancing over his shoulder, he made out four policemen bursting into the alley. He and Mallery melted into the crowd on Swan Street, where the many clubs and bars were at their peak, with patrons spilling onto the street and turning the pedestrians-only thoroughfare into a party. Perhaps 100 tourists danced to a steel band fronted by a guitarist whose electrified chords muffled the police sirens.

Hoping he and Mallery would pass for two more tourists—for which reason they'd worn tourist garb under the Raytheon suits—Thornton danced, or attempted to move in time to the music unlike a man with an injured rib cage. Mallery moved in sync, reaching up and tilting his mouth to hers. The cops weaved past without noticing them.

Hallelujah, Thornton thought. Until considering that it was just a matter of time before the police blockaded the area, sealing them in. The plan was to get off Barbados as soon as possible, catching a cab or a bus to Grantley Adams International Airport. At an ATM, Mallery would withdraw the maximum $2,500 from the numbered account she'd opened for Albert, who no longer needed the funds. Then they would walk the half mile from the main terminal to Barbados General Aviation, the area for private jets as well as local charter pilots who offered wealthy enough tourists an aerial view of Barbados and the surrounding islands. Thornton and Mallery would assume the role of such tourists. Once in flight, they would pay the pilot extra to make an "unscheduled landing" at the general aviation field on the nearby island of St. Lucia. No passports were required for intra-Caribbean flights. As Thornton had had the misfortune of reporting, passengers arriving at general aviation fields seldom faced more stringent security measures than a friendly, regionally accented welcome.

Now, releasing Mallery's waist, Thornton said, "Shall we hit the sky?"

"Can I have a rain check on the dance?" she asked.

Before he could reply, someone poked his back with what felt like a gun. Thornton didn't need to turn; he could see the reflection of the gunman in a storefront window. Peeling up Thornton's shirttail, the man plucked his Beretta from his waistband.

"Beryl Mallery, meet Special Agent Lamont," Thornton said, the shock taking a backseat to the feeling of letdown.

"Pleased to meet you," she said, her cordiality ebbing at the sight of his pistol.

Lamont discreetly patted down Mallery, taking her Beretta. "The Bureau has issued a warrant for the two of you for unlawful flight to avoid prosecution," he said, "and I'm guessing that'll be a parking ticket compared to what you'll face for the B and E at Windward Actuarial."

"Not that we admit to having any idea what you're talking about," Thornton said, "but what if that building were chock-full of clues to the identity of the organization responsible for the deaths of Catherine Peretti, Kevin O'Clair, and Leonid Sokolov?"

"What proof do you have?" Lamont asked.

"To see it, all you have to do is go to the SofTec office, across the hall from Windward," Thornton said. "Unfortunately, by the time your EC is approved by your ASAC, your SAC, and your ADIC, the whole building will likely be cleaned out, and Beryl and I will be just two more names on the victims list."

"I'm not going to argue with you," Lamont said. It wasn't clear whether he meant he was unwilling to debate Thornton on the topic of FBI bureaucracy, or that he had no patience for anything but bringing them to justice.

Thornton found Lamont hard to read: For some reason, the agent lacked his usual conviction and alacrity. Perhaps he was deliberating.

After a moment, he smiled and said, "How about this? How about we skip the paperwork, get the CIA chief of base and some marines, then get the hell back into that building?"

45

Although the metal walls were bare and painted the traditional federal dove gray like those of bigger-ticket sensitive compartmented information facilities Thornton had seen, Firstbrook's SCIF was impressive, and not just because the base chief had done the work himself. Unlike in most SCIFs, the ventilation was fantastic. Enjoying the cool air blowing across the room, Thornton sat at a small conference table, his back to the door. In the chair across from him, Mallery shifted with the excitement and apprehension of a player whose side has just seized the lead in a tight game. At the end of the table, Lamont jotted notes on the top sheet of his stationery—the four places at the table had been set with sheets of thick linen Department of State eagle stationery and the classic Parker stainless steel ballpoint pens standard to U.S. embassies.

Firstbrook made his way through the entrance and to the empty chair at the head of the table. He carried a tray with four eagle-embossed cups of hot coffee, a small pitcher of cream, and a container of sugar. In the open doorway, one of the pair of marine guards said, "I can serve that for you, Mr. Firstbrook." Hardly characteristic of the usual relationship between soldiers and bureaucrats, Thornton thought; it spoke well of Firstbrook.

"I would take you up on that, Cap," the base chief told the marine, a baby-faced southerner who looked like he could bench-press a tractor, "but I'm worried this tray's too heavy for you."

Laughing, "Yes, sir," the captain stepped out, closing the heavy door behind him.

To get back to SofTec that much faster, Thornton raced through an account of what he and Mallery had seen there. As he touched on the implications of an eavesdropping device implanted in Bella Sokolova, Lamont's head sagged, as though he were on the verge of nodding off. The strong gusts of air-conditioning alone should make it impossible for anyone to fall asleep here, Thornton thought.

Lamont backed away from the table, as though preparing to stand. He teetered, the motion fanning his stationery across the table. A moment later he collapsed to the floor and lay motionless.

Mallery raced toward him. Thornton suspected the worst even before she pressed her fingers against the side of the agent's neck and said, "His heart's stopped." She looked to Firstbrook. "Do you have a defibrillator?"

"No point," the base chief said. "He's gone."

His apathy, in combination with Lamont's emptied holster, led Thornton to a sickening conclusion. Turning to Firstbrook, he asked, "Did you poison him?"

"No, you did, using chloral hydrate." The base chief sat back. "Your disguise was good—good enough to defeat principal component analysis software in the Pine Street Pharmacy's security system, but not good enough to fool Langley's facial recognition system. In the video we have, you're shown purchasing Benaxona, an insomnia remedy packed with chloral hydrate. The autopsy will show that's what killed Agent Lamont."

Mallery glared at Firstbrook. "You really think you can pin this on us?"

"I do, but the collateral damage from your defense would be too great." Firstbrook drew a pistol Thornton recognized as a Sig Sauer P229. "The marines won't be able to hear you shout, but they will hear the shots when I prevent you from fleeing."

"Now we know why you're so gung ho about your Barbados posting," Thornton said, trying to buy time.

Firstbrook snapped. "You think I had a choice?"

"You're choosing to break the law," Thornton said, thinking over a possible plan.

"Fortunately, the record will say otherwise." Firstbrook turned the gun on Mallery.

"The issue," Thornton said, "is that this is a crime scene." He waved a hand at Lamont.

Firstbrook glanced at the body—as Thornton had hoped he would. In that fraction of a second, Thornton snatched the top sheet of Lamont's stationery and dropped it to the floor, where the air-conditioning current sent the paper hydroplaning. The paper-thin gap between the door and jamb stopped it, but a corner poked through to the other side. With some luck, the marines would notice it.

"What was that?" Firstbrook asked.

"Evidence." Thornton directed a righteous stare at the base chief. "Lamont's warning to me that you'd poisoned the coffee."

Firstbrook turned to the door and snapped up the piece of paper. It just noted the purpose of the meeting along with the place, time, and attendees.

Scanning it, Firstbrook scoffed, but Thornton used this distraction to grip the thick steel Parker pen like a dagger and spring from his chair, intent on Firstbrook's atlantoaxial joint, the fibrous sheet between the top two cervical vertebrae. When Thornton wrote the post-9/11 story titled "What to Do If You Find Yourself on a Plane with an Armed Hijacker," it hadn't crossed his mind that he would ever try this himself.

Firstbrook whirled around, leading with his gun, as the stout ballpoint pierced the nape of his neck. Thornton kept up the pressure, driving the pen through the base chief's rigid atlantoaxial interspace and into the rubbery medulla oblongata, the lower half of the brain stem. Firstbrook spun away, aimed his gun, and pulled the trigger. Then he seized up like he'd been struck by a freeze ray. The gun still fired, the steel compartment around them amplifying the report into the level of a bomb blast. The bullet hit the ceiling over Thornton's head, ricocheted, and burrowed into the conference table. Unable to breathe, Firstbrook keeled face-first into the top rail of his chair. The impact cracked the wood or his jaw or both, causing his gun to jump from his hand and skate across the table to Mallery, who snared it. Firstbrook looked up at her from the floor as he died—evidently.

Taking no chances, Thornton pressed his fingers against the base chief's carotid artery. Finding no pulse, he struggled to keep from throwing up.

"I wish it hadn't come to that," he said.

Although she too looked sick, Mallery shook her head. "It was better than the other choice," she said.

"What other choice?"

"That's my point."

The door wrenched outward. Two M16 barrels preceded the marines into the SCIF. This wouldn't look good, Thornton thought. Lamont and Firstbrook both dead on the floor with he and Mallery standing over them, a gun in her hand.

The captain ordered Mallery to drop the weapon and instructed her and Thornton to turn and face the wall. As he and the other marine patted them down, the captain added, "I'll be volunteering to be on y'all's firing squad."

Thornton doubted that a firing squad would come into play, based on his knowledge that Utah was the only state still practicing that form of execution. That knowledge offered him no consolation.

46

Rapada was worried.

"The kid put the cell phone in nearly two weeks ago," explained Canning, hunched over the petroleum hydrocarbon detector—as he'd been calling the device Eppley had assembled here in South Atlantic's back office, and which Rapada suspected was actually some sort of illicit weapon. "The problem is, a cell battery doesn't last that long, especially on crap disposable phones like the ones he used."

Canning flipped open a hatch in the middle of the device, which looked like a giant spark plug. He unscrewed and extracted a small plywood panel adhered to which was a cell phone minus its faceplate. Setting the panel on the desk, he studied the phone's LED. "Yep, this baby needs charging."

He drew a six-foot-long white cable from his tool-box and clicked the USB connector at one end into a slot in the phone's base.

Kneeling to insert the two-pronged plug at the other end into a wall socket, he asked Rapada, "Do you have any idea how many improvised explosive devices are recovered intact by bomb squads because the bomb makers fail to take into account a problem known to any child with a rechargeable electronic toy?"

"So this is actually a bomb?" Rapada said, as if only curious.

Canning chuckled. "I didn't think that'd get past you."

Rapada's worst fears had been confirmed. Play it cool, he told himself. Get to the bottom of this and stop the bastard.

"Is it for al-Qaeda?" he asked. A guess, but wrong guesses prompted corrections from arrogant types like Canning.

"I'm glad you don't know." Canning stood up. "With the blogger and his girlfriend on the sidelines now, you were the only loose end." He drew a long, integrally sound-suppressed pistol from his toolbox.

But not before Rapada freed the CIA-issued Sig Sauer P229 from his waistband. He'd taken the gun from the office safe earlier for exactly this contingency, finding ten .40 S&W rounds in the magazine, another in the chamber. He pointed it at Canning and pulled the trigger. The result was a tinny click. But nothing more.

What the hell?

Rapada reflexively racked the slide—ejecting a round—and fired again.

Another click.

Had the firing pin been filed down so it couldn't reach the primer?

"It wasn't really the CIA who issued that gun," Canning said, aiming one of his own.

47

Two Deputy U.S. Marshals prodded Thornton to the back row of a DC-9, one of the "Con Air" fleet. He was dropped into the middle seat, aggravating his back, which stung from "accidental" elbows. Kidney shots, as the marines at the embassy surely knew, leave no marks. He was now one of the 1,000 passengers the Justice Prisoner and Alien Transportation System transferred every day between judicial districts, correctional facilities, and foreign countries. His hands were held in front of him by signature U.S. Marshals Service cuffs, custom-forged from high-strength stainless steel and overmolded with ordnance-grade black polymer. His ankles sported a matching pair, with the two sets connected by high-tensile chain strong enough for use in towing a semi.

As the marshals took seats to either side of him, Thornton saw that each man carried a U.S. Marshals Service standard Glock 23 and a Taser X26, which delivered nineteen 100-microcoulomb pulses per second of incentive for prisoners to cooperate.

Another pair of marshals deposited Mallery into the flying paddy wagon's front row. Thornton saw little more than that she was wearing an overly starched orange jumpsuit, like his own. This was his first glimpse of her since the marines placed him in the musty subterranean chamber labeled BREAK ROOM on a door that locked from the outside—U.S. embassies and consulates were officially prohibited from having designated detention facilities since neither the State Department nor the CIA had the legal authority to detain anyone. He could only hope that she hadn't been harmed.

The DC-9 soon jumped from the Grantley Adams International Airport runway and into the night sky. Thornton watched Bridgetown's lights grow smaller and smaller. He wouldn't have guessed he'd be sorry to see Barbados go, but without so much as a mouse pad of evidence from SofTec, he had only his version of the story, and no more proof of the existence of Littlebird than of Bigfoot. What he did have: two charges of first-degree homicide at the U.S. embassy and a bevy of additional criminal charges in Bridgetown. To face them, he had put in a call to the ideal lawyer for this case. Mallery certainly had potent legal representation—the two of them had been separated immediately after the SCIF incident, so they hadn't been able to coordinate strategies. Unfortunately Thornton's call had yet to be returned, and it was doubtful prisoners had in-flight telephone privileges.

He might as well sleep, he decided, while he had the chance.

He was out in a second. Two thousand sixty-five miles later, he woke to the landing gear punching a Reagan Airport runway that was delineated from darkness by the first hint of sunrise.

Within seconds of arrival at the terminal, Mallery was led off the plane. There was no sign of her when Thornton reached the tarmac. He was stuffed into the backseat of a black Lincoln Navigator that was parked by the tail of the jet.

A short drive ended at the loading dock of the towering U.S. Marshals Service headquarters in Crystal City. Across the Potomac, Washington shimmered in a glossy dawn that intensified the cold darkness of the underground corridor into which he was propelled, his cuffs slicing his shins as he struggled to keep pace with his handlers, each gripping one of his elbows.

He was locked in a room that was underlit despite a quartet of fluorescent rings on the ceiling. The walls were paneled with dingy powder blue fiberglass. Musseridge sat behind a plain wooden desk, his right hand on his holster.

"Please take a seat," he said with a cordiality

Thornton attributed to the presence of a recording device.

Thornton clanked over and lowered himself onto the bridge chair facing the desk.

"Why did you poison Special Agent Lamont?" Musseridge asked.

Thornton still hadn't heard from his lawyer, and he knew it was foolish to say anything without an attorney present. On the other hand, if the Littlebird operation's reach included a CIA base chief, he might sorely need Musseridge on his side.

"I have a question for you," Thornton said.

Musseridge folded his arms. "That's not how this works."

"If I had had any intention of harming Agent Lamont, why would I have waited until we were locked into an SCIF with a CIA officer at the table and two armed marine guards standing outside?"

Musseridge waved a hand in dismissal. "Same answer I give every other perp who asks, *Why would I have done that?* You thought you could get away with it."

Regretting the wasted ten seconds, Thornton changed tack. "Lamont was killed for the same reason Peretti and O'Clair were. All three got in the way of an operation whose objective has been to eavesdrop on the Sokolovs. Firstbrook was in on it. You'll want to get into the SofTec office in Bridgetown before it's rolled up. That's what Agent Lamont was trying to do."

"I know about the operation at SofTec," Mus-seridge said. "It's why you and Miss Mallery broke in and planted the bomb."

Thornton hoped this was a bluff. "Bomb?"

"A brick of Semtex 10 you evidently took from a locked safe at the Bank of Barbados construction site. Didn't you once write a story on safecrackers?"

"I also once wrote a story about a civilian who solved an FBI cold case."

"Well, the blast demolished whatever Mallery was bankrolling there."

"Suppose I told you SofTec fronts a U.S. intelligence service?"

"I'd ask if you had any evidence."

"You'd call it hearsay. The evidence was at SofTec. Maybe still is. There's a good chance the security guard knows something."

"In that case, it's unfortunate you blew him to bits."

Thornton cursed to himself. Why the hell, he wondered, was he bothering with Musseridge? It was increasingly obvious that he would have to obtain evidence by himself. He regarded his two sets of cuffs, each set with its own lock. The person with a Bic pen-type method of unlocking them probably hadn't been born yet.

The door swung open, forestalling Musseridge's next question. Thornton made out four men clustered in the dark corridor. A fifth, a U.S. Marshal, stepped past them and into the doorway, his gray crew cut catching the faint light. Thornton recognized him as the leader of the Con Air detachment. The marshal beckoned Musseridge, who lugged himself over with all the enthusiasm of someone going out into a rainstorm.

The marshal muttered a few sentences, to which Musseridge protested, apparently to no avail: Head lowered, he stepped aside, admitting the four men. The weight-room builds on each were evident despite their billowy navy blue DOJ windbreakers— Department of Justice. They whisked Thornton into the corridor, then back the way he'd come, lifting him off the floor to negate the delay posed by his ankle chain.

"What's this about?" he asked.

If any of them heard, they gave no sign, possibly due to reluctance to have their responses recorded by the U.S. Marshals Service mics.

Thornton had an inkling that things had taken a positive turn. After being Mirandized at the U.S. embassy in Barbados, he'd telephoned Gordon Langlind's spokesperson, who was a onetime *RealStory* source. He asked her to forward a message to the senator, who, according to Mallery, had gone to law school. The message was, *Serve as my legal representation in Washington; otherwise I use Mr. Robertson.* Mr. Robertson had been the code name Langlind used on the phone call he placed at 9:02 P.M. on October 23, the transcription of which Thornton and Mallery read at SofTec.

Langlind had apparently taken the bait, and, accordingly, was now extricating Thornton from Musseridge's custody by remanding him to the Department of Justice. A claim of a national security matter superseding the Bureau's case would do the trick. Such transfers took place frequently. The DOJ agents might now facilitate a private conversation with Langlind in which Thornton could obtain the truth about the Littlebird operation, not to mention testimony that would exonerate him. Thornton also considered several much less rosy scenarios.

48

The unmarked Durango navigated sluggish Beltway traffic out to Alexandria. Thornton sat in back, bookended by Department of Justice men. He took in the Virginia suburbs through side windows whose nonreflective tinting couldn't possibly meet the legal requirement of allowing in at least 35 percent of outside light. Despite it, on this brilliant autumn morning, the prim colonial brick homes and their tidy yards and sparkling picket fences looked pretty enough for use in an advertisement for America.

Gradually the houses grew farther apart and the woods thickened. The Durango turned up a long, steep driveway, passing through a tunnel of tall trees, hedges, and overhanging boughs. The driver parked by a detached garage across from a house that predated horseless carriages, a majestic two-story colonial.

Pushing open his door, the DOJ man to Thornton's right jumped down to the gravel. The man on Thornton's other side nudged him to follow before getting out himself and circling the Durango's hood. The two then removed Thornton's restraints.

"You're free," the first said to him, "for now."

"There's a knocker on the front door." The second man cocked his head toward the flagstone path leading to the front of the house. "Tap it six times in a row, slowly. You'll be asked, 'Is that you, darling?' You reply, 'I'm here to read the water meter.' Got it?"

"All except one thing," Thornton said. "Where's Mallery?"

The men swapped blank looks before responding to the driver's exhortation to hustle, climbing back into the Durango. The driver executed a lightning three-point turn and blasted back down the hill. Thornton was left in total silence, save the rustle of branches and the calls of the few birds yet to head south. There was no hint of civilization other than the house. This was either a fantastic refuge, he thought, or a great place to whack someone.

He proceeded to the front door, passing window after window with the kind of shutters that could actually shut. Four steps brought him onto a slate stoop as big as most patios. Gingerly he pulled back the large knocker ring from the claws of the pewter eagle on the door. Before he could follow the DOJ agent's instructions, the door swung inward, revealing none other than Senator Gordon Langlind, in shirtsleeves, gabardine suit pants, and a rep tie. He held a tumbler of scotch in his free hand, perhaps explaining why he seemed happy to see Thornton.

"How're you doing, Russell?"

"That depends on what's happened to Beryl."

Langlind turned out of the foyer and headed toward the living room. "She was released on the recognizance of her own attorney. It's my hope to bring this business to a mutually agreeable conclusion, and, toward that end, I think we'll get further without her."

Thornton followed Langlind into a vast living room, decorated like Mount Vernon but with the odd contemporary splash, including recessed lights, heat and air-conditioning registers discreetly cut into the tall baseboards, and a bevy of abstract paintings and sculptures.

"I got this place for Selena," Langlind said.

"It's nice." Thornton reflected that he should have figured that this was the mistress's place. Langlind could pull in and out of the driveway here in his limo—or in a Sherman tank—without fear of anyone hearing or seeing.

"Drink?" asked Langlind.

"I'm okay, thanks," Thornton said.

The senator waved him to the closest of two facing wing chairs in front of an immense stone hearth. Taking the other seat, Langlind said, "So we're off the record, yes?"

Whatever it took, Thornton thought. "Every syllable."

"No tape recorder?"

Thornton plucked at the sides of his jumpsuit, where pockets would be. "I don't even have a pen."

Langlind slid forward in his seat, his expression serious. "Littlebird is one of the national security stories you need to keep to yourself."

"That's a lot of them."

"You've earned a reputation for discretion."

Langlind was being too nice. He'd been drinking, yes, Thornton thought, but still, the geniality was a notch too high, even by the standards of elected officials. What if Langlind's game, like Thornton's own, was to obtain information pertaining to the Littlebird operation? Once Langlind ascertained that his role had yet to be discovered by the authorities, what would stop him from giving a signal summoning men from the woodwork, their weapons drawn, game over?

"Why is discretion in order with this case?" Thornton asked.

"Two reasons. The first is, quid pro quo, our good friend Beryl Mallery's criminal charges will be dropped. And yours too, of course. Reason number two is national security. Littlebird supplies more than a trillion dollars' worth of intelligence per annum to American corporations, bolstering our interests more than any ten weapons systems. Yes, in order to keep the secret, they may have gotten a little carried away. Everyone knows the spooks get carried away sometimes."

"What's the TFI going to do about it?" Thornton tried.

"The Office of Terrorism and Financial Intelligence? Littlebird isn't a Treasury operation. Why would you think that?"

Thornton took another stab. "So it's Homeland?"

With a smile, Langlind cut him off. "You know all that you need to."

"I do know that this isn't just a national security matter. If that's all it was, the path of least resistance would have been for the Littlebird operators, whoever they are, to appeal to my discretion from the get-go. As you know, I hardly ever refuse to hold a story that would jeopardize national security. But instead of coming to me, they went on a killing spree, which would have included me, too, if not for a couple of lucky breaks."

"No one's excusing their actions. Rest assured, there will be repercussions."

"I'll rest assured when I know which spooks exactly got carried away and what the repercussions are. Until then I'm an accessory in the murders of innocent Americans like Catherine Peretti."

The senator shifted uncomfortably. "She got mixed up with the wrong people."

"Yeah." Thornton sat upright with—calculated— indignation. "You."

Langlind looked at a painting. "I don't know what you're talking about."

Thornton countered with a bluff of his own. "I uploaded the recording of the phone call where you say Cathy knows too much and your buddy tells you that she'll be *taken care of.*"

Langlind paled. "You have a recording of that?"

"Why do you think I broke into SofTec?"

"What's SofTec?"

"The listening post."

"Is that the place where the Littlebird audio goes?"

Thornton realized that the chairman of the Senate Intelligence Committee was no more than a glorified cutout in the operation. The recipient of Langlind's "Mr. Robertson" call about the supposed ad in the alumni magazine, however, was responsible for killing Peretti, for starters. Who had Langlind called?

"I take it you didn't know there was a Littlebird in your head," Thornton said.

Alarmed, Langlind, who wore his watch on his left wrist, shot his right index finger to his right sideburn and rubbed, probing for the device.

"If you're right-handed, it's behind your left ear," Thornton said. "But it's pretty difficult to feel it."

Langlind tried.

"Anyway, it's disabled now, on account of SofTec blowing up," Thornton added, though it was probable that the Littlebird operation had a redundancy system, maybe even in Bridgetown. He wanted Langlind to keep talking.

The senator clutched his forehead, as though trying to staunch pain. "You have to believe me, I had no idea whatsoever that they were going to kill Cathy."

"What did you think they were going to do? Send her a strongly worded e-mail?"

Langlind took the remaining half of his scotch in a single slug. He got up, poured another from the crystal decanter on the mantelpiece, and dropped back into the seat with the weariness of having just climbed a mountain. "How can we keep my name out of this?" he asked.

"Right now, your name's conjoined to the operation, and it's only going to get worse," Thornton said. "If, however, you were to implicate the true guilty party . . ."

"There's no way I can do that."

"No one has to hear that call recording." Thornton put on an air of sympathy. "You were used. If you tell me who had Catherine Peretti killed, you can walk away."

Langlind winced. "To face charges of election fraud."

"That's something we can work—"

"Also you're assuming they would let me walk away."

"They'll be in Allenwood."

"They'll take me to Allenwood with them, given what they've got on me. And that's at best."

Thornton recalled Mallery's speculation that Langlind Petrochemical might have made hay with the Littlebird intel.

Langlind thrust himself into an upright position. Still he appeared to be crumbling. He continued to feel for the Littlebird, muttering, as if to whoever implanted the bug, "So that's how you knew . . ."

Election fraud and passing along inside information probably ranked among the more benign of Langlind's transgressions, Thornton suspected. "Senator, this is your chance to make amends," he said. "If nothing else, you'll be acting patriotically, potentially saving lives."

Langlind rose abruptly, inadvertently elbowing his tumbler from its perch on the arm of the chair. The glass shattered against the stone fireplace. He didn't seem to notice. Fixing moist eyes on Thornton, he said, "No matter what, I'm a complete goddamned disgrace."

He punched the wainscoting to the side of the mantel. A hidden panel sprang open, revealing a pistol of heirloom variety, a Colt model 1911, it looked like, with a hand-detailed steel barrel, ivory-inlaid grip, and, more pertinently, .45 ACP bullets sufficient to take Thornton's head off. Hands slippery with scotch or perspiration, Langlind struggled to get a firm grip on the weapon.

Thornton threw himself over the side of his wing chair, then dove for the floor behind the seat. The leather and stuffing would reduce the speed of a lethal shot by only a few negligible miles per hour, but if Langlind couldn't see him, he would have greater difficulty hitting him.

Thornton landed sharply, the sounds lost beneath the roar of the gun.

In the reflection on a ceramic sculpture, Thornton saw Langlind topple before the fireplace apron knocked the gun free of his mouth and he lay stockstill, a crater where his left eye and cheekbone had been. Brain tissue and blood streaked the white wainscoting like spilled paint. Suicide, Thornton realized, with a mix of shock, relief, and revulsion. His hands and forearms were dappled with more blood. He pried what he took for the ricocheted bullet from his forearm. A skull fragment, he realized.

What the hell were you thinking in coming here? he asked himself.

Followed by the more pressing question: Now what?

Call the police? He'd gathered no evidence, only left it: His fingerprints were everywhere, including in blood on the wing chair. Which was the least of it. Another brick of Semtex would be required to erase his biological presence from this scene. And still he would be damned by testimonies of four witnesses from the DOJ. Calling the authorities now would only add another lifetime to his sentence.

The pool of blood beneath the body was spreading along the floorboards toward Thornton. An odd idea struck him: What if Langlind has his cell phone on him now?

Thornton could scroll through the list of outgoing calls and find out whom Langlind called the day before Peretti was killed.

Why the hell not?

Rising from behind the wing chair, he averted his focus from the gruesome remainder of Langlind's face. Kneeling by the body, which lay on its left side, he dipped his fingers into the right suit pants pocket and hit something metal and boxy. He withdrew the keyless remote for a Ford. Nothing else in the pocket.

That the cell phone would be in the gabardine suit coat draped over the sofa was too much to hope for. He got up and looked anyway. Nope, no sign of it.

Stomach clenched, he returned to the corpse, took hold of the slick shoulders, and rolled over the torso. Heavier than he looked, Langlind fell onto his belly with a splash, the blood peppering Thornton's face. Grimacing, he shot a hand into Langlind's left pants pocket. He found a BlackBerry.

He backed away and began scrolling through the recent calls.

And there it was: OCTOBER 23, 9:02 P.M.

Same as on the transcript.

The recipient's number was in the 305 area code: northern Virginia. Thornton tapped open the Web browser and accessed the potent reverse phone directory to which *RealStory* subscribed.

Nothing for this 305 number. Could be that the phone was a prepaid; often, even long-held cell numbers didn't appear in directories.

He wished he had reason to believe the FBI could get any further with the number. But if and when Musseridge and company got around to it, the phone would long since have been disposed of.

For a time, though, Thornton realized he had capital that might net him the identity of the killers. For as long as no one else knew Langlind was dead, he could pose as the senator and call the 305 number . . .

But then what? It was unlikely the person on the other end would answer by name. And, although Thornton once wrote an in-depth feature about a versatile theater actor, he couldn't pass for Langlind to save his life.

He noticed, however, that Langlind had texted frequently. None of the accessible texts had been sent to the 305 number. But what was there to lose in texting it now?

Thornton chose TEXT, then entered *"need 2 meet u asap someplc crowded,"* and hit SEND, blipping the message into the ether.

Awaiting a response, he took in a colorful Gustav Klimt lithograph and a distorted face painted by Dalí. The silence from the corpse was unnerving.

A whole minute passed.

What the hell was he expecting?

Time for a different plan. He pocketed the phone, thinking about finding himself some clothing that wasn't covered in gore and then—

The phone vibrated, shocking him.

Mr. X had texted back:

1130 bm

Eleven thirty, one hour from now. Unless 1130 were code for, say, twelve thirty. Encrypting a meeting time by the addition or subtraction of a certain number of hours or minutes was typical in clandestine circles. But "Langlind" had asked to meet *asap.* Also the real Langlind was clumsy with tradecraft, as exhibited in his transcribed attempt to call Mr. X, as well as in answering the door here. X probably would be wise to steer clear of encryption. It was likely 1130 indeed meant eleven thirty.

So what was *bm*? Basement? If so, why not just *b*? Thornton suspected *bm* was a location in and of itself. Closest the search engines got him was a public relations firm, Burson-Marsteller, on Vermont Avenue. Doubtful. He could text back and ask, but if *bm* were a previous meeting spot, Mr. X's suspicions would be aroused.

Thornton keyed in *BM* as a search term for Lang-lind's thousands of texts, netting jut one result, *submission*, used in regard to a *Post* op-ed ghostwritten for him by one of his staffers.

Thornton tried a colon, used almost uniquely in reference to times in texts. He netted forty-seven. Two offered a lead. Both at eleven forty-five one September morning and at eleven forty-eight on another, Selena Seldridge had proposed that she and Langlind meet "@ the big man." Could Langlind have been so deficient in tradecraft that he rendezvoused with his mistress for lunch at the same place he conducted clandestine meetings? No-brainer.

So where was *the big man*? The Lincoln Memorial fit the bill for a public meeting spot, but it seemed *too* public. Tour group leaders and politics junkies would recognize Langlind. Thornton returned to the BlackBerry's search engine and entered *big man washington dc*, generating the moniker for an untitled sculpture by artist Ron Mueck. This *Big Man* could be found at the Hirshhorn Museum and Sculpture Garden, which "showcased modern and contemporary art and sculpture." Looking around this house, one would conclude that Langlind—or at least the homeowner, Selena Seldridge—had an affinity for modern and contemporary art and sculpture. Also the Hirshhorn was on the National Mall, seemingly public enough, but not too public, as opposed to its neighbors, the Smithsonian and the

National Air and Space Museum. It was more easily accessible, too, with less security and fewer cameras. In short, a decent location for a clandestine get-together, and just a fifteen-minute walk from Langlind's office.

49

John Doe number four met the Department of Justice SUV by the side door to the Mandarin Oriental hotel. He whisked a cashmere overcoat from a Saks shopping bag and held it out for Mallery. Considerate of him, she thought: she wouldn't have to suffer the indignity of being seen in the orange jumpsuit. She backed into the coat, the high collar nicely countering the knifelike gusts off the Potomac.

He nodded to the driver, the SUV pulled away, and he pulled her into a warm embrace. "You okay?" he asked.

As she'd told her campaign staff, this John Doe, whose real name was Lloyd David, looked as good as Michelangelo's *David*, dressed in an Armani suit. She realized, with some surprise, that she no longer thought of him as more than a friend and a lawyer.

"For the first time in a long time, it feels like I'm not behind enemy lines," she said, adding, for the fourth time since arriving in D.C., "Where's Russ Thornton?"

"Theoretically, with his attorney," David said. "I was hoping you knew, actually."

She shook her head. "Last time I talked to him, the marine guard was dragging me off to a holding room."

"Well, you'll know as soon as we do." He held the door and trailed her into a palatial corridor.

It was nice for a change to be someplace that wasn't a deathtrap.

"The partners who'll handle your defense can meet you here or at the office," he told her. "After all you've been through, if you want to rest first, they'll understand."

"I'm ready to get on the witness stand right now."

"I figured you'd say that. There are a few more clothing-shop bags in the room. Pick out what you want, and as soon as you're ready, we'll be ready."

He pushed the elevator button. The brass doors parted, revealing a cavernous mahogany elevator. She leaned against the stout brass handrail, deriving a measure of contentment from its solidity. David inserted a key card and selected the top floor. The car rose quietly, as though drawn by a hot-air balloon.

He regarded the mirrored ceiling. "You look great as a blonde."

"I had *too much* fun as a blonde," she said.

The car coasted to a stop, the doors hissing open. He ushered her to a corner room, where he held his key to the handle. When the lock disengaged, he pushed the door inward, waving her ahead. Stepping across the threshold, she gazed into his eyes, which were as beguiling as ever. Yet she thought of Thornton, which made her wonder why David had been hoping she knew where Thornton was.

"How did they get to you?" she asked.

He whitened. "How did you know?"

"I didn't." She was probably the more surprised of the two. "I've learned that sometimes it pays to ask."

"I had no choice." He eyed the ceiling. "But there may be a solution."

Mallery heard what sounded like a quarter dropping into a vending machine's coin return tray. A crimson dot appeared between David's eyebrows, and he crumpled to the carpet, revealing a matching crimson starburst on the wallpaper where his head had been. Shock belted her.

"As Pasteur said, 'Fortune favors the prepared,'" came a soft voice behind her.

A brawny military type in a porter's uniform, pushing a luggage trolley. He held a pistol with a long barrel—a silencer, she guessed.

"Don't go anywhere," he added.

For a moment she remained in place. Then she leaped into the hotel room, landing in a marble foyer and immediately whirling around, slamming the door shut, snapping the deadbolt, and slapping the security latch into place. Another coin-return sound and a projectile of some sort flew at her face, missing by a fraction of an inch and shattering the mirror behind her. It left a circular gap in the door. The deadbolt cylinder, she realized, plucking it from the glass shards piled beneath the remains of the mirror.

The man opened the regular lock with a key card, then rammed the security latch to pieces with the heavy luggage trolley.

"Don't do more stupid things and there's a chance you won't die," he said, "at least of unnatural causes."

Keeping the gun pointed at her, he used his free arm to lift David from the carpet as though he were no heavier than a golf bag.

"What will it take for you to let me go?" she asked.

The man flopped David onto the trolley. "You mean how much money?"

"Is that what you want?"

"You don't have enough."

Good, she thought. They were negotiating. "How much is enough?" she asked.

He ran a hand over his sandy crew cut. "Not to be immodest, but I can't put a price on my life."

If, like Firstbrook, he had been coerced or just following orders, perhaps they could reach another type of deal. *There may be a solution* were David's last words.

"Who would kill you?" she ventured.

"Glad you asked," he said.

"Why?"

"It tells me you don't know, which is more than ample compensation for having to give up this suite. Thanks to your late attorney, we need to relocate." He pointed at one of the two large duffel bags on the trolley. "I need you to curl up in here and be as quiet as its current contents."

He leaned over and unzipped the duffel bag, stuffed with white hotel towels—to make the bag appear full on the way up to the room, she surmised. And now he'd replace the towels with bodies.

"I won't do it," she said.

"What makes you think you have a choice?" He kneeled to remove the towels, not a simple job.

This was her chance.

She reached back with the hand that had been cupping the deadbolt cylinder, then threw a fastball. It struck him in the temple with a clonk that must have been heard all the way down in the lobby. Eyes going white, he toppled toward the trolley, landing in a seated position, his spine cracking against one of the thick brass stanchions. Still he was able to raise his pistol and snap the trigger. Something pierced her right thigh. A rocket, it felt like, boring through bone and tissue before bursting into flames. She hadn't imagined that a bullet could be so painful. Or that anything could be.

50

Thornton turned Langlind's Ford Expedition onto Independence Avenue. The ultramodern Hirshhorn Museum loomed ahead like a spacecraft touching down on the National Mall. If the basis for choosing the art museum were smaller crowds, it was a poor choice, he thought, taking in the line snaking from the entrance. His mind played a feverish montage of other "big man" candidates—the twenty-foot-tall statue of Jefferson, its neighbor the thirty-foot Martin Luther King, the bronze FDR.

If worse came to worst, he thought, he could use Langlind's phone to text Mr. X requesting a new location *2 b on safe side.*

He checked the phone. As he'd feared, the local police scanner site's live audio feed now included an

Alexandria PD dispatcher's request for units to respond to a 911 call at the address he'd just left. A code
36: murder.

Further complicating matters, he had just ten
minutes until the meeting time. Still he drove another
five blocks before pulling into a parking spot across
from a McDonald's on 4th Street Southwest. The police dispatched to the Alexandria house would almost
certainly figure out that Langlind's Expedition was
missing. Thornton had to assume that the SUV was
equipped with a LoJack or comparable system. The
precise location of a stolen-vehicle recovery system
within a vehicle was known only to the company that
installed it. Parking too close to the Hirshhorn could
electronically clue the authorities to his whereabouts.
As would his safety net, Langlind's cell phone. He exited the Expedition, crossed 4th Street, and tossed the
phone into an open side of the truck delivering Coca-
Cola to the McDonald's.

As he continued toward the Mall, he spotted a
Capitol PD cruiser in an intersection two blocks up
Independence. He was thankful he'd worn a disguise
to keep Mr. X from recognizing him. It would help
with police, too. He hoped. From the cedar-lined
his-and-hers closets in the master bedroom in Selena
Seldridge's house in Alexandria, he'd taken one of
Langlind's custom-made business suits. Several sizes
too big, the suit made him look bulkier, an effect
augmented by two of Langlind's cashmere sweaters,
which he wore underneath. Hair extensions from Sel-

dridge's closet hung down the back of his neck, like a mullet. He'd topped them with a traditional Stetson. Incredibly misguided, all of this, an inner voice warned.

Just as he stepped onto Independence, the Capitol PD cruiser slid to a stop fifty feet ahead. Two policemen bounded onto the curb in front of him, causing his stomach to plummet. The cops blew past him, weaving through the crowd of pedestrians before turning down 4th Street. Toward Langlind's SUV? Thornton suspected that a seasoned operator would abort the meeting rather than risk capture, or risk that Mr. X had gotten wind of Langlind's demise. But taking these risks was Thornton's only option.

Approaching the museum entrance, he added a swagger befitting his appearance, which he thought of as "oilman with a rockabilly side." He joined the line for the metal detector. None of the fifty seniors descending the tour bus gave him a second look.

Inside, a security guard beckoned him through the metal detection portal. He hoped that the clips holding the hair extensions in place were plastic. His four layers of clothing, two too many for the mild afternoon, caused him to sweat enough as it was. While passing through the portal, he mopped his brow with the outermost of his four left sleeves. The guard waved him ahead. Thornton tipped his cap, intending to appear polite; his true intent was concealment. Why give the security camera a free shot?

The building was shaped like a doughnut, the

exhibits within a ring that surrounded an outdoor sculpture garden. Other than exchanging a smile with a young woman strolling a happy toddler, Thornton had no interaction with any of the patrons. At the sign for the Mueck installation, he turned down a long corridor that ended at the untitled sculpture, a photorealistic portrayal of a middle-aged bald man sitting in a corner, naked, head in hands, the agony in his eyes unmistakable even thirty yards away. Three times the size of life, Thornton judged, based on the man in a trench coat standing beside the sculpture. Mr. X? If so, alone, unless he had associates elsewhere—Thornton took note of the men's and women's rooms at the corridor's midpoint. No one else was in the corridor, whose bare white walls emphasized the sculpture.

Apparently sensing Thornton's arrival, the man in the trench coat glanced over his shoulder. Taking in Thornton without recognition, he turned back to the sculpture. Which gave Thornton a fairly good idea of why and on whose orders Catherine Peretti had been murdered. The man in front of him was her husband, Richard Hoagland.

51

Thornton said, "I want to help," by which he meant he wanted to learn why Peretti had been killed, so he could help the prosecution in the coming murder trial.

Hoagland's blank stare flickered to recognition, then to shock. "Russ, what are you doing here?"

"Exactly what you encouraged me to do: investigating." It now seemed likely to Thornton that by making the suggestion, Hoagland had really meant to discourage him. "And I have a question for you: Is the secret to your hedge fund's success the information that you collect using eavesdropping devices implanted in people's heads?"

Hoagland chuckled. "Have you been talking to one of our competitors?"

"Look, I get it. In your business, the only crime is being on the wrong side of a deal. Littlebird wasn't just the chance of a lifetime, but one for which you would risk the wrath of God. If someone threatened to expose the operation, even a family member, your bosses wouldn't hesitate—"

"Russ?"

Thornton waited.

"I actually have to run to a meeting." Hoagland turned to go. "Call next time you're in town, and let's get together."

"Hang on." On the chance that Hoagland was afraid to talk, rather than just unwilling, Thornton grabbed him by the elbow. This drew strange looks from the young couple wandering down the corridor. Thornton released Hoagland with a laugh, as if the move had been horseplay, but added under his breath, "My Littlebird was removed. If there's one in your head, it's out of commission."

"How could that be?" Hoagland was transfixed. Or a hell of an actor.

"Haven't you heard that the listening post in Bridgetown is a pile of rubble?"

"No. What happened?"

"According to the authorities, I blew it up."

"Why would you do that?" Hoagland asked.

An odd question if he had any inkling of the truth, thought Thornton. "I didn't," he said. "Actually, the last thing I would have wanted was to destroy the evidence. Whoever you're covering for was responsible, and took out a security guard and a local cop in the process. If you give me names, maybe we can get you enough brownie points to avoid doing time."

Hoagland paused, as though reflecting. "I can't help you," he said finally.

"Think of it as helping Emily and Sabrina."

"That's exactly what I'm doing. Catherine was told what would happen if she talked, and obviously it wasn't an idle threat. Afterward, it was made very clear to me that if I said anything, the next funeral wouldn't be mine; it would be one of the girls'. Not both. Just one."

"Incremental incentive?"

Hoagland exhaled. "Now you have some idea of what I'm up against."

"I'm glad to know you're not responsible for Catherine's death. But what happens when whoever they are decide they'll sleep better if you're no longer around? Tell me the real story; I'll post the details to my site. I won't mention your name, but you'll no longer be a liability for the bad guys because a quarter of a million readers will know the truth. Also the bad guys will have their hands full with law enforcement agencies."

Hoagland hesitated and then said, "Catherine promised me she wasn't going to tell anyone, so I don't know this for sure, but I believe that in going to see you, she was planning to expose the 'bad guys.' And how did that work out?"

"Unfortunately, they were already onto her. But

they're not onto you—for now. The thing is, that window won't be open long. Whoever they are, they won't worry about murders. They've actually pinned a couple on me. In fact, the police are looking for me."

Four of the seniors from the tour bus joined the young couple already admiring the sculpture.

Hoagland stepped closer to Thornton, opened his mouth as though about to speak, then, apparently thinking better of it, sighed.

Hearing police chatter reverberate from a radio around the corner, Thornton's stomach tightened. "Look, I know it's a DOC operation," he said—a guess, but not entirely a blind one.

Hoagland looked on in bewilderment. "How did you find out?"

"Process of elimination, plus something somebody said." Thornton wondered why he hadn't figured it out sooner. The Bureau of Industry and Security, the Department of Commerce's clandestine operations division, was one of just a handful of services with the budget to stage a show on the scale of Littlebird, and that sort of intel was their bailiwick.

He heard, or imagined, the voice of Musseridge over the radio. "In a fucking cowboy hat."

"Listen, I may have to split any second," he told Hoagland.

Hoagland moved behind the *Big Man*, acting more interested in the sculpture than in Thornton. Thornton followed, bringing them out of earshot of the other patrons.

Hoagland said, "Even though I knew they could have been eavesdropping when you and I spoke in Potomac, I hoped that you could help. The fact is, my firm is a DOC off-the-books operation. I signed on because I wanted to be of service to my country. And, bluntly, it helped that I stood to make twice what I was earning at Goldman. As the company grew, management brought in more analysts and traders, all legit. Most of them don't know about the DOC—they're what we call 'cutouts.' All are compensated well enough not to ask too many questions. Those of us who do know wonder whether we made a Faustian bargain. This morning, for instance, I had to go 'service a dead drop'—is that the right phrase for hiding something in plain sight?"

"It depends," Thornton said. Dead drops once were a staple of clandestine exchanges, but in modern times were a rarity due to the ease of covertly sharing information online. "What did you do?"

"I went to the Willard Hotel and stuck an envelope to the back of a radiator in a corner of the lobby. That's when I got the text I thought was from Langlind. I figured his wanting to meet me was related to the envelope."

Thornton thought better of explaining how he came to text Hoagland. "What was in the envelope?"

"I didn't open it—I've learned it's better not to know."

"What was it that Catherine found out?"

"She happened to see satellite imagery of one of

our Commerce Department liaisons taken the night
Leonid Sokolov was killed—the exact same imagery
the FBI used two months earlier when looking for
their 'Russian.' They either didn't notice or didn't
think twice about a Commerce official in a yacht on
Lake Michigan five miles away from the crime scene.
But Catherine noticed. She also knew that the guy was
a spook. And, most importantly, she hadn't forgotten
your theory that Sokolov's killer had operated in Russia. She did some digging and found out that the guy
had served in Moscow for a couple years. From there
it was connect-the-dots."

Patrons came and went, but no law enforcement.

"So who's the guy?" Thornton asked casually.

"Peter Canning."

No bells. "Is he the one who sent you to the Willard Hotel?"

"Yes. Why?"

An unnaturally quick motion registered in Thornton's peripheral vision. He peered over his shoulder in
time to see a uniformed man dart across the opening
of the corridor. The uniform was similar to the security guards', but a darker blue. And Thornton heard
the jangle of cuffs.

"I think I can help after all," he said.

52

THE CAPITOL POLICE SECURITY CAM FACIAL RECOGNITION SOFTWARE REGISTERED A COLD HIT AT THE HIRSHHORN ART MUSEUM . . . While leading two D.C. plainclothes FBI agents and fourteen uniformed policemen and women to the Mueck corridor, Musseridge mentally composed the FD-302 he would type up later. *IN THE COURSE OF APPREHENDING THE SUSPECT, THE WRITER HAD NO ALTERNATIVE BUT TO DISCHARGE HIS WEAPON.*

And there he was, in the cowboy hat, one of six patrons checking out a sculpture of a huge naked guy. Ideally, in this situation, Musseridge got as close as possible to a suspect without his knowing. But the long corridor here precluded sneaking up. He signaled for the D.C. Metro cops to handle the crowd. Then he gestured for a Capitol cop to hand over his megaphone.

Flicking it on, Musseridge said into it, "Mr. Thornton, this is the FBI. Please put your hands in the air and turn around nice and slow." The order resounded against the bare walls.

The guy who turned around looked a little like Thornton, but he was leaner, with sharper features and more polish. He resembled Peretti's husband, the hedge fund guy, Musseridge thought. Of course that guy didn't wear a cowboy hat or have a fucking mullet.

Turning to the Capitol cop, Musseridge said, "That facial recognition software of yours needs to be shit-canned."

Thornton climbed from the top of the radiator in the empty men's room, hoisting himself through the window. When the tour group in the courtyard sculpture garden shifted its attention to a Calder, he gathered up the tails of Hoagland's trench coat and let go, a ten-foot drop. He landed on mercifully soft grass.

Fighting the urge to sprint, he ambled out of the courtyard and back into the building, in time to see the phalanx of law enforcement officers streaming down the Mueck corridor.

He passed through the main exit, turning onto Independence. The Willard Hotel was a little more than a mile away, and it seemed likely to him that the package in the lobby there had something to do with Sokolov's E-bomb. It would be odd if it didn't. A connection to one Sokolov or the other had cropped up at every stage of what had amounted to his investigation. Beating the intended recipient to the envelope offered a singular chance not only to obtain tangible evidence, but also to prevent thousands—maybe hundreds of thousands—of additional deaths.

He found Hoagland's Volvo station wagon two blocks from the Hirshhorn. As he clicked Hoagland's remote and opened the doors, a police cruiser rolled up the block. Fighting the instinct to hurry, Thornton lowered himself onto the driver's seat.

He drove the Volvo up 9th to Pennsylvania, where he turned left at the boxy concrete Hoover Building, the headquarters of the FBI. Of all places. He continued driving, right beneath the Bureau's nose.

A few blocks later, he found a parking spot in front of Pershing Park, just across from the Willard Hotel. The twelve-story beaux arts palace had been a hive of activity for well over a century—its lobby largely responsible for the term *lobbyist*—making it a textbook dead drop location.

Walking across Pennsylvania Avenue, Thornton felt exposed. Other than Hoagland's trench coat, his disguise now consisted only of a pair of tortoiseshell glasses he'd found in the Volvo. The lenses distorted his vision to the extent that he couldn't be sure whether it was his imagination or not that the doorman was staring at him.

He entered the soaring lobby, the ornate ceiling and its plethora of crystal chandeliers supported by six massive Ionic columns. Guests wandered in and out of shops and restaurants.

Two of the giant room's four corners had radiators, waist-high units with clawed feet, every last cast-iron pipe adorned with as many flourishes as could fit. Behind the second radiator he checked, Thornton found where the envelope had been: Now there was just a torn corner of a manila envelope held against the back of a pipe by a magnet the size of a silver dollar. He suspected the magnet was made from an alloy of iron, boron, and rare-earth neodymium, explaining why the scrap of paper remained. Such magnets were popular for dead drops because the document couldn't be loosed by a gale-force wind.

Thornton used both hands and all his strength to pry the magnet free, absorbing a lightning bolt of pain to his bruised rib cage. To avoid drawing the attention of the pair of men in kaftans and kaffiyehs who were chatting on the sofa six feet away, he looked away, pretending to be captivated by something outside the window. Then, in fact, he was truly captivated. A swarthy young man was hurrying up the sidewalk, sliding on a pair of sunglasses although the hotel's shadow made the block nearly dark. He wore a black overcoat and held a manila envelope under his arm.

53

"Excuse me, sir," said the doorman with a smile suggesting that he held Thornton in high esteem, or, more likely, he'd recognized him from a photograph e-blasted around town by the FBI.

Before the man could say any more, Thornton, pretending not to have heard him, took several strides toward the side exit.

"Sir?"

Thornton kept on toward the door. Perhaps not the best play, he thought. Sidestepping a luggage cart, he shoved his way through the revolving door and onto the sidewalk. Spotting the man in the black overcoat near the intersection, Thornton accelerated.

The man took a hasty left onto F Street. By the time Thornton turned the corner, the guy was gone, too quickly to have been picked up or to have gotten into a parked car. Into a store? No, down the ramp to the Willard's underground parking garage: Thornton caught sight of his overcoat.

Adrenaline acted like rocket fuel. Thornton flew past an office furniture store and onto the ramp leading down to the garage. It was so dark that he failed to discern the black overcoat, not until the man appeared in front of him, pointing a polymer Beretta Storm with steel inserts. It was a lightweight gun, yet capable of blowing sizable holes in someone.

Thornton held up his hands and said, "It's okay. I'm with Canning. You forgot this." He turned his left hand to reveal the neodymium magnet. The disk flashed pink in the wash of the illuminated exit sign.

"Bullshit, you the journalist," said the man, his accent Middle Eastern, heavy on the vowels. Maybe Iraqi or Kuwaiti—Thornton couldn't tell.

The guy shot a quick look at the entrance, then another to the base of the ramp. No one was coming. He raised the Beretta to within inches of Thornton's chest.

"Wait, there's something else you need to know," Thornton said, inching his hand toward the Beretta.

The magnet rose out of his palm, clicked against the steel barrel, and stuck there—just as he'd hoped. If the guy pulled the trigger now, Thornton thought, he risked a KB—shooter shorthand for *kaboom*: A bullet traveling near the speed of sound with nowhere to go could cause the barrel to explode.

The gunman seemed aware of the danger. He backed away, trying to pry the disk off the muzzle. Thornton lunged, hammering his right shoulder into the man's stomach, knocking him backward, yanking his legs from beneath him. The rugby coach who'd taught Thornton the "dump tackle" would have been proud. The back of the gunman's head struck the sidewalk. Thornton landed on top of him, then rolled left, snaring the gun with no resistance from its owner.

Thornton sprang to his knees, then banged the gun against the curb, knocking off the magnet. Then he plunged the muzzle into the guy's belly. "Who are you?" he asked.

"Mossad," the guy said, too quickly.

"Okay, so we can rule out Mossad. One more wrong answer and I'm going to find out if it's true that a bullet can pass through the spleen—" Thornton stopped short, noting the manila envelope lying on the cement.

As he plucked it up, a cell phone protruded from the hole at the corner. He suspected it was a remote detonator. In which case, was an E-bomb close by?

"Where's the bomb?" he asked.

The guy shook his head. "Fuck you."

"He had to have gone this way," came a familiar voice.

Thornton glanced over his shoulder and, through the glare from F Street, made out the Willard doorman leading two policemen along the sidewalk.

Turning back to the man lying beside him, Thorn-

ton whispered, "There's a key difference between me
and them: After you tell me where the E-bomb is, I'll
let you go."

The man groaned. "How would I know where it
is?"

Which suggested that there was indeed an E-
bomb. But a foot soldier servicing a dead drop probably wouldn't be told the weapon's whereabouts.

Glancing at the angled mirror atop the ramp,
Thornton saw the doorman and policemen hurrying
past. As he turned back to his captive, a black Mercedes sedan sped down the ramp. He saw a gun pok-
ing out from the driver's window.

Thornton dove for the pavement, placing his captive between himself and the gun. The gun flashed
and a blast shook the tunnel. The bullet snapped the
foot soldier's head sideways, apparently for good.

The Mercedes braked a few feet from Thornton.
The driver leaned out the window for another shot,
revealing a bull neck and bald head. Thornton aimed
the slain foot soldier's Beretta and fired three times,
pausing only when the Mercedes began to roll forward. It picked up speed, heading straight ahead
when the ramp turned, the hood impacting the wall
with an ominous thud. The horn went off, resounding
in the tunnel. Thornton recognized the rear license
plate's distinctive red, white, and blue stripes—
diplomatic tag issued to a foreign mission or embassy by the State Department. The two-letter prefix,

which indicated the country, was DM—Israel. As if a
Mossad operative would be foolish enough to show
up in an embassy car, Thornton thought.

Figuring that he would learn the impostors' true
identities soon enough, he gathered up the manila
envelope and sprinted for F Street. Finding it clear,
he jogged toward 14th before ducking into the office
supply store. Reflected in the glass door, he saw the
doorman and two policemen doubling back from the
far corner.

"Can I help you?" asked a saleswoman.

Over her shoulder, Thornton took in a row of ergonomic desk chairs lining the back wall. He asked,
"Do you have the kind of desk chair that's good for
your back?"

She smiled. "Right this way." She turned toward
the back of the store.

He went the opposite way, exiting onto F Street as
the doorman and cops turned into the parking garage. He ran to the corner and peered around, spotting a smattering of cars and pedestrians on 14th
Street, but no cops. He joined the pedestrian traffic
to Pennsylvania Avenue. When no one tried to stop
him there, he stepped onto the crosswalk and, within
seconds, was in Hoagland's station wagon, sliding
forward in the driver's seat so that his head was below the window. He tore open the manila envelope to
study the cell phone.

It was a high-end disposable, the sort he some-

times picked up for use with dicey sources. Its call
log showed four calls placed to the lone contact listed,
Bob, number 5 on the speed dial. Possibly a phone
dedicated to the bomb, the calls having been made
to test the connection. This information ought to be
enough for the FBI to locate the weapon.

Finally, it was time to call the authorities for
help. Thornton weighed the pros and cons of dialing
Musseridge—the devil he knew—when the phone
rang. Best not to answer it, he thought, until the caller
ID appeared: MALLERY, BERYL.

He punched ANSWER. "Hello?"

"Hey, Russ," she said.

"Where are you?"

"Listen, I finally found the guy I've been looking
for, and I want you to leave the two of us alone here—"

What sounded like a robust slap was followed by
the upending of furniture. Thornton's blood froze.

A man's voice came on the line. "Ask her a proof-
of-life question." Soft and gentle, not the rasp Thornton had imagined for Canning. But this was Canning.
Mallery had said as much.

Thornton scrambled to think of a question only
she could answer. He came up with *What was your
first home?* The answer, a Volkswagen Kombi. But he
recalled that that conversation had been recorded
by Littlebird. Canning might well have techs at the
ready with a searchable Littlebird database. Thornton
needed something he'd learned after the devices had
been removed. One came to mind, not his favorite,

but it would do. "According to your site's metrics, how do we score as a couple?" he asked.

"Initially, in Nantucket, I calculated fifty," she said. "Now, one hundred and ten."

Although at this juncture Thornton had no business deriving satisfaction from her answer, he did.

Canning returned to the line. "Acceptable?"

"Couldn't have been better," Thornton said.

"Then I want the phone you're now speaking on. In exchange you get her, alive."

"Good," Thornton said. Understatement. "Meet someplace public?"

Canning scoffed. "Like the Hirshhorn Museum?"

It was what Thornton had been thinking. He took it as a mandate to think faster. "What do you have in mind?"

"Unfortunately, since Hoagland is busy stonewalling the police, he won't be able to die in a traffic accident. The flip side is you have his car, so you can come to us. I'll text you directions. As you've surmised, I'll know where you are at all times because I'm tracking the phone, which is also hot-miked." Thornton understood this to mean that the mic within the cell phone's mouthpiece transmitted constantly, whether or not a call was in process. It was a means of electronic eavesdropping almost as old as telephones.

"That's how—one way how—I will know if you apprise anyone of what we've discussed," Canning added. "In fact, if I even suspect anything . . ."

Thornton heard more rustling followed by Mallery's piercing scream, nearly costing him his grip on the phone. The blare of a car horn brought him to his senses. He returned the receiver to his ear to catch Canning saying, "Any hijinks, she gets two and a half grams of lead in her lovely head. Now, get moving, beginning with a right onto Independence."

As Thornton cranked the Volvo, he noticed a police car pulling up at the Willard's main entrance. He considered transmitting some kind of SOS to the policemen but decided he didn't dare. Probably they were looking to arrest him.

Unfortunately, he thought, the disposable cell phone constituted his only means of stopping Canning. Assuming Canning killed him. And Canning would try—that was a given. He almost certainly planned to kill Mallery too, as well as E-bombing thousands of others.

54

On a phone call designed to appear as if it originated at a sporting goods store in Kansas City, a man whose voice sounded very different from Canning's conversed with a middle-aged woman at a customer support call center in Mumbai. In fact, while pacing the backyard of the safe house overlooking Chesapeake Bay, Canning spoke on a satphone, attempting to convince Izzat Ibrahim al-Hawrani to continue with the E-bomb operation. Although both of the Iraqi's operatives in Washington had gone down, Canning maintained, success was imminent.

The problem, Canning knew, was that he himself had made several critical mistakes. In his rush this morning to traffic the remote detonator and capture Mallery, he'd left Mickey Rapada's body in the

South Atlantic Resources office. The corpse could be erased once the E-bomb detonated, but without Rapada to service the dead drop, Canning had leaned on Hoagland—who was a cutout in the E-bomb op. *Was*, until Thornton filled him in. The banker wouldn't dare talk to the FBI, but the Bureau might elicit actionable intel without his realizing it. Or one of his colleagues would say too much. And God only knew what Langlind had blabbed after Bridgetown went down. Meanwhile the mess in the Caribbean would bring in DOC Internal Affairs officers, with CIA and ODNI breathing down their necks. All the loose ends added up to a net about to ensnare him, Canning thought.

He glanced at the tall mast bobbing in and out of sight. He'd acquired the sailboat—rather than a motor-powered yacht that the E-bomb pulse would cripple—as part of his escape plan. He could still sail away now, but as a defeated and penniless fugitive. The most grievous error, he reflected, had been his failure to anticipate the need for a backup remote detonator, a simple matter of adding another ten-buck cell phone to the Centrex loop.

He admitted none of his mistakes to al-Hawrani. After all, things going wrong was to be expected, and Canning had planned accordingly. In a matter of minutes, his biggest loose end was about to hand deliver the remote detonator. The blogger was about to become a Ba'athist martyr.

55

There was little late-afternoon traffic, a rarity in D.C. Thornton wondered if Canning was monitoring the grid and guiding the Volvo clear of congestion. Canning's texts directed him onto Capitol Street, past the Nationals' stadium, and across the Frederick Douglass Bridge. As an increasingly suburban Maryland flashed past, Thornton thought it curious that Canning hadn't simply pulled a van into a parking space on 9th Street to make the "swap." Possibly he preferred to meet at a location where he would be in complete control or, at least, minimize his chances of exposure. Or maybe this was just more misdirection. Maybe the text messages would loop Thornton back to 9th Street. Canning seemed to like deception. To a fault, Thornton reflected. If

Canning had shot Sokolov with an ordinary nine-millimeter round, as opposed to one cast from seven grams of lead on the nose, Thornton would have had no insight whatsoever into the incident. Peretti, in turn, wouldn't have thought twice about the satellite image of Canning on a yacht. And Thornton would be spending this evening Web crawling in his apartment.

Another text sent him *EAST ON 260*. He'd never been to this area and didn't know much about it, except that Route 260 was also known as Chesapeake Bay Road. Chesapeake Bay, the Atlantic inlet extending through Virginia and Maryland for 200 miles, couldn't be far away. Because of its proximity, a forty-minute drive from downtown, many of Thornton's Washington sources had weekend places here. It was likely, he thought, that he was headed to a safe house, bolstering his suspicion that Canning was alone with Mallery—as she'd said, *I want you to leave the two of us alone here.* Good, because Thornton's plan depended on that.

The phone rattled in the center console with a new text. *RIGHT ON BAYSIDE RD IN .2 MI.*

On Bayside, Thornton could see the water. The road more or less clung to the shore.

RIGHT ON HILL IN .3, came another text.

Hill lived up to its name, rising gradually to a broad view of the bay. The street appeared to be split between weekend places and full-time residences, half of the houses lifeless, the other half with raked yards and cars in the driveways.

.8 MORE MILES, according to Canning. As the houses ended, the yards reverted to woods, and the paved road to one of dirt. A bumpy half mile further and a solitary saltbox cottage came into sight.

YES, texted Canning.

Thornton's fears were overtaken by a sense of mission. First he pressed the VOLUME DOWN button on the phone until the ringtone was muted. Next he used a thumbnail to pry open the air vent on the station wagon's center console. Then he slid the phone into the duct, a compartment spacious enough to hold several phones. Finally he replaced the register. He'd learned this means of concealment from heroin smugglers—in reporting on the DEA's attempts to thwart them.

He turned the Volvo up the dirt driveway. At the top, he parked with the driver's side facing away from the cottage. The front door swung open, revealing Canning in a sleek black jogging suit, holding a fourteen-inch-long pistol. Thornton recognized it as an integrally sound-suppressed AWC .22LR, the Navy SEALs' weapon of choice. Not only could the semiautomatic pistol fire with water in its barrel; water enhanced its sound suppression. SEALs had dubbed the gun "the Amphibian." Hardly the garden-variety .22 Thornton had planned on. He would have to adapt.

"Good to see you, amigo." Canning ushered him into the cottage. "Come on in and grab yourself a brewski."

Thornton stepped into the living room. The minimal furnishing was meant to withstand sand and wet swimsuits.

"Where's Beryl?" he asked.

Canning tapped the front door shut, his tight tracksuit revealing the dramatic expanse and cut of his muscles. "First things first: turn around, hands against the wall."

Thornton submitted to a thorough pat down, which netted Canning the keys to Langlind's Ford—Hoagland's keys were still in the Volvo's ignition, improving the slight chances of getting Mallery away from here.

"You're supposed to have a good memory, Russ. What about the one thing you were supposed to bring?"

"Show me Beryl," Thornton said.

With an eye roll, Canning produced his own phone, pressed REDIAL, and cocked an ear to the driveway. No ring was heard. Which was why Thornton had muted the disposable phone. Using a simple app on his own phone, Canning could still triangulate the disposable's signal to bring him to within twenty-five feet of it. But unless he had a radio-frequency detector too, that meant a search area of 2,000 square feet. The car alone had myriad hiding places, which was why customs officials relied on dogs. And Canning couldn't be sure that the phone was in the car.

"I want to see her," Thornton said.

"No problem." Canning jerked Thornton around. "This way."

Canning crossed the living room and opened the narrow broom closet door, revealing Mallery. She'd had to contort herself to fit in there—or Canning had contorted her. Probably the latter, as she was hog-tied, still in the orange jumpsuit, which emphasized a pallor unrelated to her terror. Blood soaked her right side and shimmered on the closet floor. A quart of it at least, maybe two.

"What happened?" Thornton asked, acting merely concerned, as though the sight weren't horrific. A 120-pound woman had just four quarts of blood.

She said, "Nothing worse than I've had at the hair salon."

"Let her go now," Thornton told Canning. "I'll go get the phone. That was my plan."

"Don't take this personally, Russ, but what if I let her go now, then you don't get me the phone?"

Thornton had no immediate reply. He'd bet everything that Canning wouldn't risk having to search for the detonator.

"I propose the following," Canning said. "You get the phone. Then I untie and release Beryl. And then we do the basic Checkpoint Charlie exchange."

Thornton almost believed him. "Let's do it," he

said, stepping toward the door. "Pick you up in a minute," he added to Mallery.

Her reaction was lost as Canning tapped the closet door shut before following Thornton out of the house.

Outside, there wasn't another soul in sight. Thornton hurried around the hood of the Volvo, opened the driver's door, and slid into the seat so that his trench coat billowed out, concealing his actions from Canning.

Canning watched him from the tail of the seventeen-foot-long station wagon. Twenty-one feet away, Thornton estimated, as he flicked off the air vent register, withdrew the disposable cell phone with his left hand and, with his right, the Beretta Storm he'd acquired in the Willard Hotel parking garage. He backed out, using his body to keep the gun hidden from Canning. Then he whirled away from the car and, in the same motion, slung the phone as hard as he could at Canning's head.

Thornton knew that if you throw an object at a man's head, he has to sense the motion and process the information before he can move. His reaction will be either to catch the object, to duck, or to blink while turning his head away. Any of these reactions would create enough time for Thornton to aim and fire the Beretta, but not enough time for Canning to get safely out of harm's way. Canning might reflexively return fire, but Thornton would already be in motion. In combat training, police fire at moving targets twenty-one feet away, with only one in five shots hitting. Thornton took it for granted that Canning would be a better shot than the average cop. Also factoring into Thornton's calculations, 90 percent of handgun wounds aren't lethal if the blood loss is controlled; even 70 percent of head wounds from handguns are survivable. The Amphibian rated among the world's most sophisticated and versatile firearms, but it fired relatively minuscule twenty-two-caliber rounds. In this case, its bullets were made of just thirty-eight grains of soft lead. Or, as Canning had revealed over the phone, *two and a half grams of lead.*

Completely defying Thornton's calculations, Canning allowed the cell phone to hit his jaw. His eyes remained locked on Thornton, even as the phone fell to the driveway. Then Canning fired the Amphibian, its integrally suppressed report no louder than a finger snap.

The simultaneous motions of Thornton pivoting, aiming the Beretta, and pulling its trigger shifted his torso to his right by six inches. So the twenty-two-caliber bullet that would have nailed his sternum instead struck him in the left clavicle—the break of bone was audible even over the roar of his Beretta. The "minuscule" soft lead round felt like a railroad spike pounded into him by Jack Armstrong. It knocked him off his feet, the motion causing his own blood to stripe the station wagon's hood. Gravity exacerbated the flaring pain as he hit the driveway, his spine and then his skull. The fender smacked the Beretta out of his hand.

Rolling after the gun, he saw Canning rise, the disposable cell phone in hand, his index finger settling on the center key. The 5, Thornton figured, to speed-dial the phone that would trigger the E-bomb.

As Canning pressed the key, he fell to the driveway, landing on his side and lying completely still. Thornton noticed the dark cavity where Canning's left temple had been; he was down permanently. Not that it made any difference: The E-bomb would have the same effect, momentarily. On Thornton, too. And everyone else in the vicinity of Washington.

Thornton flung himself toward Canning, landing beside him and snatching the phone from his lifeless hand. The LED read, DIALING—the wireless network was still in the process of routing the signal to the bomb.

Thornton stabbed the END button. DIALING faded, replaced by CALL TERMINATED. He lay still on the dirt, holding his breath and praying that the signal hadn't touched its recipient despite the message on the LED. A connection lasting just a fraction of a second could be enough to initiate detonation. He heard only choppy gusts off the bay and a wave sizzling onto the rocky shore. Which didn't necessarily rule out detonation.

He staggered up and into the house to get Mallery. Tripping on the threshold, he grabbed at a curtain to

regain his balance, but only tore fabric, loosing the
metal tension rod. One of its fleur-de-lis finials sliced
his forehead. Just a scratch in the scheme of things;
it felt as if the bullet were exploding inside him. Hot
blood poured over his brow, stinging his eyes, blind-
ing him. He used the tension rod to prop himself up.
He was hurrying in the direction of the broom closet
when everything went white.

56

Thornton awoke to the blips of an electrocardio-graph, opening his eyes to a fluorescent haze that gradually subsided to reveal fresh flowers. A galaxy of them, wall to wall, floor to ceiling, packed into temporary shelving units that must have been brought into the hospital room for that reason. The sweet scent took him back to Barbados, until motion to the right of his hospital bed drew his focus. The boxy man in a rumpled gray business suit was Special Agent Jim Musseridge of the FBI.

Thornton raised his head from the pillow, sending fiery pain the length of his spine. But the pain was nothing compared to the fear that he'd dreamed the events leading to his being shot—and that he'd dreamed Beryl—all while lying here in Staten Island

University Hospital. He looked to his patient identification wristband. Gone.

He asked, in a croak, "What happened—?"

"Hoagland wasn't telling us shit, but the LoJack in his car showed us where to find you," Musseridge said. "Ms. Mallery managed to get out enough about the E-bomb that we made it to South Atlantic before anyone could detonate—"

Thornton cut in. "I meant, what happened to her?"

"Got you." Musseridge lowered himself into an armchair.

Thornton felt a prickly foreboding.

"I take it you noticed all of these flowers?" Musseridge pointed a thumb.

"I did." Thornton braced himself.

"She keeps ordering them for you from her room upstairs—these are just today's. Other than that, she's okay."

Thornton sat up, intent on getting out of bed and taking the elevator up to see her. Nausea flooded him, however. The room tilted.

The FBI man restrained him. "Don't go just yet, bud."

Thornton grasped the metal side rail. "Am I under arrest?"

"No." Musseridge appeared puzzled. "But I figured you'd want the exclusive on why Washington is still standing—"

"Good." Thornton tried to prop himself up, but

bandages practically mummified his torso, causing him to topple forward. Blood jumped from the vein as the IV detached. He fell to the floor, landing face-first. It felt like he'd been shot all over again.

It was the best day in a long time, he thought, scrambling up and stumbling out of the room.

Epilogue

When news broke of the corrupt Department of Commerce officer's plot to bomb Washington, D.C., blogger Russ Thornton and Senator-elect Beryl Mallery had no comment. They were aboard a small yacht in the Caribbean, unreachable by phone, e-mail, or text.

Acknowledgments

This book would still be a bloated Microsoft Word document if not for extraordinary editing by Phyllis Grann, and that Word doc would have had humongous gaps if not for information generously and patiently provided by Bill Abelson, Elizabeth Bancroft, Kyra Tirana Barry, Tim Borella, Fred Burton, Keith Eure, Christian Floerkemeier, Emily Giglierano, Mark Greaney, Kam Kuwata, Steve LeVine, Jane Mayer, Steve Nelson, Gary Noesner, Bob Noll, Elizabeth Pyeatt, Fred Rustmann, and one other source who wisely wants his name kept out of this. Thanks to all of the above, as well as to Richard Abate, Grant Bergland, Rachel Clevenger, Michele Crawford, John Felleman, Chuck Hogan, Melissa Kahn, Edward Kastenmeier, Jennifer Marshall, Barbara Peters, John Pitts, Nora Reichard,

Jake Reiss, Roy Sekoff, Liz Sullivan, Karen Shepard, Southside Ball, Adrienne Sparks, Henry Steadman, Bill Thomas, Angie Venezia, Holley Wesley, Adam White, and anyone else who has read this book to this point.

Please send any questions or comments to
kqthomson@gmail.com.

ALSO BY KEITH THOMSON

ONCE A SPY

When Charlie Clark takes a break from his latest losing streak at the track to bring home his Alzheimer's-addled father, Drummond, they're attacked by two mysterious shooters. At first, Charlie thinks his Russian "creditors" are employing aggressive collection tactics. But once Drummond effortlessly hot-wires a car, Charlie discovers that his unassuming father was actually a deep cover CIA agent . . . and there is extremely sensitive information rattling around in his troubled mind. Now the CIA wants to "contain" him, so the two embark on a wild chase through the labyrinthine world of national security that will force them to confront unspeakable danger, dark conspiracies, and what it means to be a father and son.

Fiction/Thriller

TWICE A SPY

Twice the speed, twice the trouble, twice the fun, Charlie and Drummond Clark return in *Twice a Spy*. Charlie and Drummond are on the lam, hiding out in Switzerland near a clinic that is testing revolutionary treatments for Alzheimer's on Drummond. With them is NSA operative Alice Rutherford, who has been working to exonerate them—but before she can make any headway, she is kidnapped by a terrorist group. To get her back, Charlie and Drummond are forced to plumb Drummond's damaged memory for the location of a secret cache of weapons, then turn over the most lethal of the lot. At the same time, they must find a way to thwart the terrorists before they can use the weapon for unspeakable destruction.

Fiction/Thriller